THE FIRST CENTURY CHRISTIAN SAGA

BOOK ONE

SIMON OF CYRENE

SIMON OF CYRENE

A Catholic Christian Novel by
JOSEPH L. CAVILLA

With the exception of historical events and personages, all the characters and events in this book are fictitious, and any resemblance they might have to actual persons, living or dead, is purely coincidental.

ISBN 978-1-5056663-9-7

Second Edition
August 2015

For Marion

ACKNOWLEDGEMENTS

I wish to thank my son Paul for the suggestion that I write this book, and for encouraging me once I had embarked on the project. My further thanks to him for putting aside with filial dedication, his own writing for a while, so as to perform the intricate task of publishing the book on my behalf.

Thanks also to my brother Charles for his understanding, sincere comments, and enthusiasm as he read through the book and spurred me on.

Finally, my sincere thanks and appreciation to Susan Sakal to whom I owe a debt of gratitude for her dedication and professionalism in the editing of this book. Her knowledgeable and encouraging comments, gave this 'rookie' author some badly needed confidence.

FOREWORD

The history of the early Christian Church is the subject of much speculation. There is very little information with respect to the first century C.E. The amount of reliable information is confined almost exclusively to that given to us by the Bible's New Testament, including the Acts of the Apostles. The contribution of the contemporary historian Josephus is notable but not extensive.

Simon of Cyrene's claim to authenticity is his historical role in the Passion of Jesus Christ, during which he assisted Jesus (Yeshua) in the carrying of the cross. He is described by the evangelists as having two sons named Rufus and Alexander. Nothing further is mentioned with regard to this man; he simply disappears into the nebulous pages of history.

It is my humble opinion that anyone who came into contact with Jesus in a meaningful and interactive way, would hardly walk away unaffected by such an awesome encounter. The story that follows is an attempt to give a fictitious identity to the historic Simon of Cyrene, giving the reader some insight into the power and effects of Divine Grace as a gift of faith in Christ, of which Simon would have been the recipient.

The fictitious world of Simon is therefore interwoven with Holy Scripture in such a way that it relates to, and is absorbed by, scriptural truths to which I have scrupulously adhered. The uncertain nature of the early liturgy in its infant state allows once again for much speculation. In a world where communication was difficult and slow, unorthodoxy prevailed, and a separation from Jewish roots took time to realize.

A conscientious attempt has been made to keep the developing liturgy within the parameters of Biblical constraints. Several of the fictitious characters who influence Simon's world come into contact with real Biblical personalities. These personalities are absorbed into the narrative as well, allowing both fictitious and historical characters to play active roles in the story of the growth of the early Christian Church, as I would have imagined it.

I also attempt to provide an insight into one of the many scenarios that the developing Christian communities may have witnessed as they watched their Church expand during the course of that uncertain first century. I try also to mentally transport my reader back to that time, and acquaint him or her with the intense hardships that were endured as a part of everyday life.

Travel both by land and sea were painfully slow and extremely dangerous in those days. Passenger ships were unheard of, and seafarers often struggled to survive the open decks of cargo boats, where even their basic needs were unmet.

On land, the wayfarer was similarly plagued with a lack of proper accommodation. Their nights would often be spent out in the open, under the stars, and during the day they would often be exposed to attacks from the many bandits who preyed on defenceless travellers. For safety's sake, wayfarers would be obliged to travel in groups, which slowed up their progress considerably. The main roads were patrolled by the Roman Legions, but this still left much to be desired in the way of adequate security.

CAST OF CHARACTERS

Yeshua — Jesus
Simon — Simon of Cyrene
Ruth — Simon's wife
Alexander — Simon's older son
Rufus — Simon's younger son
Rachel — Simon's elder daughter
Lucila — Simon's younger daughter

Marcus Tricius — Merchant
Julia — Marcus' wife
Letitia — Marcus' daughter
Damian — Marcus' servant and manager
Zaphira — Marcus' slave and Letitia's tutor
Silia — Marcus' slave and cook
Tecuno — Marcus's slave, gardener and gate keeper
Marius — Captain of the *Stella Maris*
Jason — Mate of the *Stella Maris*
Lucius — Helmsman of the *Stella Maris*
Silas — Captain of the *Pretoria*
Bashir — Captain of the *Mermaid*
Aula — Wife of Bashir
Cratius — Captain of the *Neptune*

Jechonias — Sanhedrin spy
Judith — Sister of Jechonias

Simon the Tanner — Tanner in Joppa (biblical)
Hannah — Simon the tanner's daughter
Drucila — Rufus' landlady in Rome
Erasmus — Rufus' employer in Rome
Gaia — Erasmus' wife
Vibia — Erasmus' daughter
Publius — Erasmus' clerk
Servi — Erasmus' messenger boy

Claudius Tricius — Marcus Tricius' brother in Rome

Lucia — Claudius Tricius' wife
Lavinia - Claudius Tricius' daughter
Livia — Claudius Tricius' elder daughter
Naomi — Joseph of Arimathea's wife
Miriam — Joseph of Arimathea's maid
Jerobaum — Naomi's uncle

Cassius — Merchant in Tarraco

David — Simon's assistant and neighbour
Tobias — David's father
Esther — David's mother

Ahmed — Caravan Master
Sicmis — Ahmed's wife
Kimi — Ahmed's son
Isha — Ahmed's daughter

Naomi — Joseph of Arimathea's wife
Miriam — Joseph of Arimathea's maid
Jerobaum — Naomi's uncle

Cassius — Merchant in Tarraco

David — Simon's assistant and neighbour
Tobias — David's father
Esther — David's mother

Ahmed — Caravan Master
Sicmis — Ahmed's wife
Kimi — Ahmed's son
Isha — Ahmed's daughter

Manius — Farmer
Tita — Manius' wife
Sarah — Hannah's neighbour in Joppa

BIBLICAL CHARACTERS

Joseph of Arimathea — Councillor in Sanhedrin
Nicodemus — Councillor in Sanhedrin
Gamaliel — Councillor in Sanhedrin
Peter — Apostle
James — Apostle
John Mark — Evangelist
Mary — Mother of Yeshua
Mary — Magdalene
John — Apostle
James — John's brother (apostle)
Judas Barsabas — Disciple (minister)
Rhode — Door-keeper
Cornelius — Centurion in Caesarea
Paul — Paul of Tarsus (Evangelist)

DAYS OF THE JUDEAN WEEK

Dies Solis — Sunday
Dies Lunae — Monday
Dies Martis — Tuesday
Dies Mercuri — Wednesday
Dies Joves — Thursday
Dies Veneris — Friday
Dies Saturni — Saturday (Sabbath)

ROMAN TERMS

Palla — Shawl
Stolla — Outer garment
Cena — Supper
Peristyle - An open colonnaded courtyard decorated with plants
and flowers, and covered by a surrounding inward sloping roof all
around. A pool which was actually a cistern, called an 'impluvium'
for storing rainwater was normally located at its centre. It was the
preferred living space of the house, all bedrooms and kitchen
opened into it, and it was located at the rear end of the house.

Atrium - A courtyard similar to the peristyle, situated near the
entrance to the house and decorated more formally.
Visitors and business personnel were received and entertained
there. It had a small opening in the ceiling, a sloping roof all
around, and an impluvium much smaller in size than that in the
peristyle.

MAP GLOSSARY

Genua — Genoa
Nicea — Nice
Arelate — Arles
Narbo — Narbonne
Tarraco — Tarragona
Sagantum — Sagunto
Carthago Nova — Cartagena
Pillars of Hercules — Calpe — Gibraltar
Tingis — Tangiers

SIMON OF CYRENE

CHAPTER ONE

YESHUA

It was a bright morning and promised to turn into a hot day in Jerusalem. The people were out in numbers even though it was still very early in the morning; making it quite difficult for a group to walk and stay together at the same time. The scene was a colourful and animated one as befitted Passover.

Everyone who could afford to be in Jerusalem was there, milling around the bazaars and shops taking advantage of what that beautiful city had to offer.

"Try to stay together," said Simon to his two sons and two daughters. "If we lose sight of each other it will take us all day to get together again."

They continued walking, letting the flowing mass of humanity carry them in their wake. Suddenly, there seemed to be some sort of blockage up ahead, and some in the crowd which had confronted this, were turning back. Simon stopped his small group, and cautioned them to stay where they were until he returned. He squirmed his way through the crowd and approached the blockage. Being a big man, he could see over the heads of those standing in front of him and became aware that people were lining both sides of the road that was crossing his path. It seemed as if they were waiting for some pageant or procession to pass.

He turned to a woman that stood beside and asked:

"What is this all about?"

"They are going to crucify the young rabbi who has been preaching all around," replied the woman.

Simon seemed to recollect someone commenting on a young preacher who was going around the Sea of Galilee preaching new things to the people.

'What could he have done to merit being sentenced to death?' thought Simon. 'He probably lost his head and insulted Caesar. Poor fellow. These preachers do get carried away sometimes.'

He made his way back to his little group accompanied by his thoughts. The boys were still there but the girls were nowhere to be seen.

'Ha!' thought Simon. 'They're in the bazaar, where else?'

"Well Father?" asked the twenty one year old Alexander as he arrived. "What is happening up there?"

"There's going to be a crucifixion and the people are lining the route to see it."

"Oh great, that sounds real cheerful!" cut in nineteen year old Rufus with a smirk on his face; betraying the fact that he had come to Jerusalem for a good time.

"I think," said the father, "that I'm going to stay and see this Rabbi they're going to crucify. I'm just curious. You can all go around on your own and do as you wish. Just keep a close watch on your sisters, especially Lucila, or she'll disappear into the shops and you'll go mad trying to find her. I have things to do, make sure that you are all back at your uncle's farm by dusk. I'll get back on my own.

Simon began to walk away. Then he stopped, turned around and shouted back to his sons. "Don't let the girls spend good money on nonsense."

'What a bunch,' thought Simon, shaking his head as he navigated his way back to the blockage. 'All they ever want to do is have fun. That's because their mother spoils them. Mmm... I must get her something before I go back to Mordecai's farm, seeing as she couldn't come with us today. That back of her's keeps giving her trouble every now and then, especially when she travels."

His thoughts kept running. 'Those boys do what they want with her, so I have to be twice as severe with them. They're a little crazy, especially the young one. That Rufus is a clown, one never knows what he's going to do next. They're good carpenters though, just like me, and they get their work done with enthusiasm. I really can't complain.'

'As for the girls? well, what man doesn't have a weak spot for his daughters especially when they are so beautiful.'

Then, something else got into his train of thought.

'Oh yes, now I remember. It was Aaron the baker who was telling a customer about the young Galilean preacher....Ah yes! from Nazareth he comes and a carpenter too. Aaron thought his name was Yeshua, and he was going all over Judea curing many sick people and claiming to be the Messiah. That is probably what got him into trouble.'

He reached the blockage once again. The mob by the road was tightly knit, and it was with some effort that Simon worked his way as near to the front as he could. There were a couple of women just in front of him, and he stayed behind them. He could see clearly from his position standing on the crest of an incline in the road.

The morning was well on its way by now. The sun was beginning to be felt, and the shadows on the road cast by the people lining up were defining the route with severity. It was almost the fifth hour, and now at last slowly moving shadows could be seen near the bottom of the road.

These shadows soon translated into the substantial figures of people, actually Roman soldiers, dressed in their ochre coloured tunics and red capes. Some carried lances; their helmets glistened in the morning sun.

As the soldiers approached, Simon's angle of vision widened. A solitary figure could be clearly perceived, moving very slowly, doubled over with much uncertainty under the weight of a beam which he carried and struggling to keep his balance.

Simon instinctively knew that the man was going to fall; he clearly could not cope with the situation. The advancing soldiers were now in front of Simon, obstructing his view.

"There!" shouted one of the soldiers angrily. "Down he goes."

"Make him get up!" shouted another with hatred in his voice.

The lash was applied again and again, until finally the prisoner caught hold of the rough beam he had been groping for amidst the rain of lashes. With great difficulty he stood it up on end, and letting it fall carefully onto his right shoulder, succeeded in holding it there. Slowly, very slowly, he managed to get back on his feet, the beam nicely balanced at last, and the trudging forward began again.

The procession continued its slow progress amid jeers and insults from the crowd, until all at once, as if by some mysterious spell, a silence fell over them.

A handsome, middle-aged woman of great dignity and bearing though in simple attire, and accompanied by a young man, appeared at the front of the crowd to the right of the prisoner. One of her hands was clasping at her heart whilst the other was nervously clutching the young man's wrist. Her habitual good looks were masked by the flood of tears which flowed from her eyes and ran down her face.

"That's the prisoner's mother," someone whispered.

Mother and son looked at each other with fixed gazes through mutually tearful eyes. But only briefly; each comprehending the enormity of the tragedy they were sharing. Then, the son turning, moved on once again. The crowd resumed its jeering with an element of disappointment in their tone.

It took a while for the condemned rabbi and his cruel escort to reach Simon's location at the crest of the incline. The prisoner was struggling to keep the cross beam balanced whilst he himself became progressively more unbalanced.

Just then, the soldier who had been obstructing Simon's view, stepped forward, and shouted, "If you fall again, you're in for it, Jew."

However, despite the threats and occasional lashings, the prisoner still swayed precariously as if suffering from dizziness which was giving him great trouble in maintaining his balance. As the party drew closer, Simon, attentive to the rabbi's plight, awaited the inevitable fall.

Suddenly, Simon felt two strong rough hands clamp onto his arms, and he was pulled rudely past the women in front of him. The poor women found themselves on the ground with a frightened and bewildered look on their faces.

"You'll do just great," shouted one of the soldiers in Simon's ear.

"Just great for what?" shouted back Simon,

"To carry his beam, that's what."

"I will not, you have no right to force me to do that," protested an indignant Simon.

"No right, Jew?" retorted the soldier, slowly pulling out his sword.

That was enough for Simon. He knew that the Romans could with impunity, commit any act they wanted, and the Jewish nation was impotent against them.

Slowly and grudgingly he approached Yeshua. The victim's head which had somehow escaped Simon's earlier scrutinies was crowned with thorns much to his horror. The preacher's eyes gazed down under blood stained eyelids as if in a trance, appearing to disregard what was going on around him. His face was bloody and swollen from having been beaten, and an ugly looking black eye appeared to block his vision completely.

Simon leant over, and gently taking the beam from him, shouldered it himself with ease. He walked forward slowly, glancing back to make sure that Yeshua was following. The crack of a whip sounded again followed by a muffled groan.

"You'll never get him to that cross if you keep lashing him like that."

The words were out before Simon realized what he was saying. He was fortunate that the whip was not turned on him. The lashings did stop however, as the boorish soldier realized the truth of the remark.

Simon now fell behind the struggling victim, who continued to make very slow progress despite his having been relieved of the beam. As they continued on, it became obvious to the Cyrenean that the preacher was uncertain on his feet even without a load to carry, and judging by the amount of blood seeping through on to the back of his heavier outer garment, he must have sustained many lashes prior to his having been given the beam to carry. His back wounds were surely still bleeding, and it was the loss of blood that was draining all his strength and upsetting his balance.

A stray, protesting, egotistic thought suddenly came to Simon. 'What has all this got to do with me? I was enjoying my holiday with the family; my first in twenty years, and then I get caught up in this. Why?...It is upsetting my whole apple cart. Still, in an hour's time all will be over. I can then return to my brother-in-law's house and continue to celebrate the remaining days of the Passover.'

This sombre cloud of selfish thoughts completely covered the landscape of Simon's soul, threatening to shut out any ray of charitable light which may have infiltrated so far.

He was suddenly aroused from his self-serving reverie. A woman had just run out of the crowd, and approached Yeshua with a look of great pity on her face. She removed her white veil and handed it to him. He smiled at her, took the veil, wiped his blood spattered, sweat covered face and gave it back to her. This earned him another lash from the soldier's whip. The woman returned to her place in the crowd, madly waving the open veil.

As the group moved on again, the unsteady trudge of the sentenced man resumed, but in a worsening state, and presently, he fell again. He tried to get up but could only manage to achieve a seated position. Simon quickly took one of his outstretched hands and pulled him back on his feet with comparative ease still balancing the beam on his other shoulder. He had performed the whole feat so quickly and with such dexterity, that the soldiers had had no chance to use their whips.

At this point, the crowd had somewhat thinned out on that portion of the route, as if some other distraction had temporarily captured their interest and enticed them away. There remained however a fairly large group of women up ahead, some with children. All were waiting and crying.

Simon and the group slowly approached them. The preacher, straying to their side spoke for the first time.

"Weep not for me, but for yourselves and for your children," he said, followed by some other words that Simon could not make out.

But what he did hear stunned him. What ominous words, and spoken with such authority. It made his hair stand on end.

'This,' thought Simon, 'is no ordinary preacher. 'He, surely, is some sort of prophet.'

The rabbi was looking as if he could not take another step, though by now the hill and crosses were in sight. Three in all, with two already occupied; leaving the centre upright stark and threatening, awaiting its cross beam to make it the ultimate instrument of torture. These were however, still at some distance.

True to Simon's expectations, down went " the prophet." Stretched out prostrate his face turned towards Simon.

'If he dies now,' thought Simon, 'he'll save himself from the horrors to follow. Would that Yahweh were merciful, and remove him from this cruel world which has so unjustly condemned him.'

Balancing the beam on his right shoulder, he bent down and stretched out his left arm saying:

"Take hold of my arm, and try to pull yourself up."

There was no answer. But as Simon looked into the eyes of Yeshua, a unique feeling came over him. A feeling of indescribable peace, a yearning to be of help, a need to sacrifice one's self. He had experienced this feeling once in much milder form whilst tending to his wife Ruth during one of her illnesses, but the intensity of this feeling was overwhelming. Simon did not know it then, but this wordless exchange with Yeshua was to change his whole life.

Slowly and painfully the "prophet" pulled himself up using his brother carpenter's arm as a rope. He hung on to Simon's left shoulder, whilst the latter put an arm around his waist. They set off together once again towards the gruesome destination.

It was getting close to the sixth hour as they reached the summit of Calvary. Such was the name of that hill which stands just outside the city gate, and which was to be known forever as the place of infamy.

Two soldiers pulled Yeshua away from Simon who went over to the waiting upright and dumped the complimentary crossbeam at its feet. As he did so, he was suddenly aware of a stab of pain on the calf of his right leg and realized that one of the soldiers was 'thanking' him with the end of a horse whip. He looked over at Yeshua once more. The latter was undergoing great pain as the soldiers ripped off his inner garments which had stuck to his wounds. Nonetheless, he still managed a slight nod with a loving gleam in his unencumbered eye.

'Now that!... was a thank you.'

'Well, that's it,' thought Simon to himself. 'Now I'm off.'

But he could not get his feet to follow the instructions his brain was giving them; they simply would not move. He was not tired physically, but mentally?... That was another matter. Well, he would stay a little longer. There was plenty of time left, and he needed very badly to learn more about his brave and suffering "prophet," as he had come to see Yeshua.

He got out of the reach of the soldiers, and stood there contemplating in genuine horror the mass of bleeding wounds that covered the rabbi's back. They roughly dropped the prisoner onto the crossbeam, his thorn-crowned head hanging loose whilst they stretched his arms and drove a nail through each wrist.

Simon went over and joined a group of people who were looking on with horror and great sadness on their faces. They watched the soldiers tying the prisoner's arms to the crossbeam for extra support, and raising him up using "Y' ended branches under each end of the beam. One of them on the top of a ladder, directed the tenon of the crossbeam into the mortise of the upright, and used wood wedges to secure a tight fit.

The worst and most horribly torturous part it seemed to Simon, came at the end. The centurion, who had been supporting Yeshua's legs together in a bent position during the elevation of the body, placed one of the prisoner's feet over the other and held them there. A soldier then put a very long nail through both the feet, binding them together in an excruciatingly painful way. Simon looking away, fully expected a loud distressing yell, but all he heard was a deep groan.

The bulk of the crowd, now having used up all their jeers and insults began to disperse, except for some of the officials and Pharisees whose hatred kept them there. No doubt they were much pleased with themselves, and determined not to leave until the Galilean was pronounced dead.

The soldiers having finished their gruesome work for the day, retired well out of the way behind the crosses, and got down to the business of playing dice. The rabbi's clothes were their prizes.

Those remaining were Yeshua's mother and followers, who spent their time in prayer and sorrow, as their beloved one endured the endless cramps, and continuous excruciating pain which comprise the horrors of a crucifixion.

Simon reviewed the group as he walked over to join them. There was a woman of early middle age with a beautiful profile and dressed in dark clothes who stood rigidly looking up at the cross as if in a trance, tears running down her cheeks, her lips occasionally moving though no sound was to be heard. Simon remembered her as Yeshua's mother, and whose name he later learnt was Mary.

Another younger woman sat on the ground beside Mary also contemplating the figure on the cross endlessly with wet and adoring eyes. This, as Simon also later learnt was Mary of Magdala, or as she was commonly known,...Mary Magdalene.

There were two other women sitting a little further back, as were four men. One of them was John; the young man who had accompanied Yeshua's mother all day long.

"I suppose you must be his disciples," Simon began.

Three of them nodded in the affirmative.

"I helped him with his cross beam, and I wish to know more about him," continued Simon. "I don't know what he could have been convicted of. He seems such a mild and kind man. There is something very, very special about him, of that I have no doubt."

"They have crucified him because he claims to be the Messiah and the Son of God," replied young John with great bitterness.

"I have heard that he has worked many miracles and cured many people. But living in Cyrene which is where I come from, I hear very little of what goes on in Judea, my being so far away. My name is Simon, and I am a carpenter just like him. I came to Jerusalem to celebrate the Passover with my family who live in the country close to the city."

"We greet you in his name," said another whose name was Joseph, and turning his head towards the cross explained. "His Holy Name is Yeshua, the Anointed One. He is dying on that cross in atonement for all our sins whether we be Jew or Gentile."

"I experienced something truly astounding when our eyes met at his last fall. I felt it was something truly awesome, but I knew very little of him then," owned Simon looking up at Yeshua, and nodding with reverence.

"I am James," said the third man, "and he is my younger brother." He pointed at young John who could not have been more than sixteen.

"And I am Nicodemus," volunteered the fourth and last man, his face partly covered by his shawl. "Peace be with you." Turning to Joseph who also kept his face partially hidden, he said. "And this is Joseph of Arimathea. We are both members of the

Sanhedrin, but we secretly follow our Lord Yeshua the Son of God."

At that moment the sound of voices was heard coming from the crosses on which hung two thieves.

"If you are Christ, save yourself and us," said one of the thieves.

The other thief rebuked his companion.

"Do you not even fear God, seeing that you are under the same sentence? And we indeed justly, for we are receiving what our deeds deserved; but this man has done nothing wrong."

And he said to Yeshua.

"Lord, remember me when you come into your kingdom."

Then amid the great silence that followed was heard but very faintly, words that stunned all who were listening around the crosses.

"Amen I say to you, this day you shall be with me in paradise."

Simon was awestruck.

'What words were these? Carrying such power even though so faintly uttered? This man must truly be the Messiah, the Son of God.'

The day progressively grew darker and darker. What had been a beautiful sunny morning, now threatened rain. The sun had completely disappeared, the sky was of a deep metallic grey hue, and there was an eerie feeling in the air that penetrated to the very marrow.

The thought of his family anxiously awaiting him came to Simon, and once again he felt he should go. But he could not move away from the cross just then. Even if he could go, the four remaining disciples would be hard pressed to get the body down from the cross, and any help from the soldiers would be out of the question.

'No!' he continued to say to himself. 'I cannot leave Yeshua whilst he is alive. I must stay here like the others and keep him company. Once I explain these things to the family I know they will understand. Especially my Ruth, whose soft heart will probably keep her sleepless all night, thinking of the young Rabbi and his mother.'

There was something magnetic about the cross. It held him captive with that peaceful, satisfying feeling, that was so totally new to him.

As time continued to pass, grunts and groans of deep suffering came from that centre cross, as the young body it held in its mortal grip became drained of all its energy. The end beginning to appear.

"Woman behold your son," came the feeble command. John embraced Mary.

"Behold your mother."

Then silence again. More silence, and still, the silence reigned; but for the sobbing of the women. Once again the stillness was broken as the ever weaker voice was heard.

"Father, forgive them, for they do not know what they are doing."

Then as the ninth hour arrived, the bystanders once more heard the faint tone.

"I thirst!"

One of the soldiers got up, and going to the foot of the cross where stood a small clay vessel holding vinegar, took a sponge which was wrapped around a stick standing in the vessel, and held it up to Yeshua's parched lips. He took some, and said, "*It is consummated*," and died.

Just then a great bolt of lightning fell near the cross, followed immediately by a deafening clap of thunder. The earth shook violently, and a mighty gust of wind exploded, whipping up the dust into a thick choking cloud, and sending a wave of fear into all those around.

The centurion, whose horse reared up in panic, almost throwing him out of his saddle, was heard to exclaim:

"Truly this was a just man."

When the sudden violence in the atmosphere had calmed down, Joseph informed them all that he was going off to ask Pilate, the Roman Governor, for permission to take the body down and entomb it.

He explained to Simon that he owned an unused tomb which had been hewn out of the rock, and after a hasty embalming, the body of Yeshua would be entombed there, as the Sabbath was approaching.

Once again, the thought of leaving began to disturb Simon's mind. But at that very moment, Nicodemus turned to him and asked his assistance in getting the body down.

Just then, one of the soldiers shouted that the thieves had not yet expired. They took hold of two heavy sticks and proceeded with great brutality to break their legs. The shock silencing the pair forever.

At this point the women clustered around their master's cross as to dissuade the soldiers from breaking his legs also. Instead, the centurion approached the cross on horseback, and using one of the soldiers' lances, pierced Yeshua's side. Blood, followed by water, gushed out. He had to make sure that the man was dead. There was a sad and regretful look on his face, as he looked down at the small group of mourners who looked back at him with dread.

With Yeshua now having expired, Joseph knew that he could go to Pilate. He left immediately, giving Mary a nod of assurance.

It was a silent group that eagerly awaited Joseph's return.

Everyone else had now gone, excluding the gloating Pharisees and members of the Sanhedrin who would not leave before they had heard Yeshua pronounced dead. The centurion, whom they now interrogated, assured them that the condemned man had indeed expired, and they all left.

At last, after what seemed to all to be an interminable wait, Joseph returned leading a donkey loaded with a couple of sacks, and tying the beast to a nearby tree, rejoined the group.

The plan for the descent from the cross was quickly discussed. The unanimous decision was taken that the body should come down exactly in reverse of the way it went up. The ladder was still lying nearby as were the needed tools, and the work promptly got under way; the nails in his wrists being left till last when the body was finally on the ground. Once again, a rock of adequate size was used to keep the pry bar from damaging the hands.

All went according to plan, and Simon was very content that he had been there to help. They removed the crown of thorns and placed the body in the arms of his devastated mother who sat on the ground waiting to receive him. What a truly pathetic picture they made. One that would never be forgotten, and would inspire artists throughout the ages to follow.

Now at last Simon took his leave. Approaching Mary the mother, he took her hand and gently pressed it. She, amidst her tears looked up into his eyes and said. "Thank you for being there."

A tearful Simon now deeply shaken, walked away; his head bowed and trying to digest as best he could all that had happened that memorable day.

As he walked down the hill he became aware of something sticking to his ankle. It felt and looked like a piece of parchment. He was about to shake it loose, when he noticed that there was an inscription on it, and bending down he picked it up for a better look.

"Oh, me!" he exclaimed. "It's the proclamation which was nailed to the tenon on top of the cross. That powerful gust of wind that hit us must have blown it down since it has clearly been ripped off the nail that secured it." It read:

"Yeshua of Nazareth the King of the Jews," written in three languages, Hebrew, Greek, and Latin.

'I'll keep it,' declared Simon to himself. 'Who else would want it?'

And so doubling it up, he put it into his tunic and hurried back into the city to find a gift for Ruth, before returning to his brother-in-law Mordecai's farmhouse.

The streets were much clearer than they had been earlier that day as most people were at home getting ready for their second day of Passover meal. He was just in time to dash into an Arab bazaar; since all the Jewish ones were closed. He quickly purchased a very pretty amulet, and tucked it into his tunic.

* * * * * *

It was a very tired and confused Simon, who finally arrived in the dark at Mordecai's farmhouse just a few miles from Jerusalem. The family was gathered in the carpeted living room sitting on their cushions, chatting noisily, and anxiously awaiting his much anticipated arrival. He was sadly conscious of the difference between this and the place he had just come from.

All looked up. Their faces showed relief and joy at his return, but only his wife got up, and with a loving smile embraced him tightly.

He tried to look cheerful but failed. They in turn knew that he had something of importance to tell them but would wait patiently until he was ready.

Mordecai, was the first to speak.

"Welcome back brother. We thank God for your safe return."

"Sit, and make yourself comfortable," interposed Martha his sister-in-law with her habitually pleasant smile.

Sarah, one of his nieces got up, and brought him a cup of wine along with a big smile, but said not a word.

Simon sat down beside Ruth. He looked at all those familiar faces which he loved. They bore the same look of eager expectancy; each pair of eyes resting on him. The food was in front of them now, and hunger took precedence over mystery, especially among the younger ones.

Prayers were said but perhaps a little hastily (who could tell), and for a while only unintelligible noises of appreciation could be heard. Finally, one thundering belch tore the silence of the room. The culprit, Mordecai, attested by the miniature volcanic eruption to the excellence of the meal, bringing a smile of satisfaction to the two sisters who had slaved over the spit all that day.

"And now!" announced Rufus. "My wayward father is going to tell us a story which we are all dying to hear."

"At least, he came back to you mother," teased Lucila with a mischievous smile that her father loved so much.

It came to Simon in a flash that he had not given Ruth her the trinket, and reaching into his tunic, he pulled out the amulet and handed it to her, accompanied a big hug and a warm kiss.

"Aha!" cried Rachel, his eldest daughter. "A guilty conscience."

Ruth gave her husband a thankful smile. The whole party clapped their hands in joy at the touching scene. Another cup of wine was passed around, and more food was placed on the trays as the feast continued with enthusiasm.

Simon sat in a morose mood. He could not join in on the frivolous conversation around him. His unusual mood was particularly apparent to his wife, and son, Alexander.

The latter, who by virtue of his quiet nature had not as yet offered any comment, took a gulp from his wine cup, and addressed his father in a sober tone.

"Father, it's obvious to us all I am sure, that you have had a very disturbing day, which you may or may not want to share with us."

Simon pulled out of the dream-like trance that had absorbed him for the last while.

"What was that?" he looked around the room and realised that it was Alexander who had spoken.

A great silence fell upon the party. All eyes were on Simon. Alexander had broken a spell, pregnant with contrived merriment and abandon, which if the truth were told, did not reflect the present feelings of that family. Concern for Simon's aloofness and secrecy, was being felt around the room.

The son repeated what he had just said; feeling very strongly that his father had been contemplating something which greatly troubled him despite his attempts to hide it. Simon looked around the room, and detected an eagerness in all their faces which led him finally to start on his sad but unique story.

"God has put me through my paces today," he began in his customary rough way. "He has made a new man of me. In what way? I can't yet say, but my whole life as a human being has been turned upside down."

Everyone was enthralled with these words which made no sense. Simon was known as a man of strong character and sure of himself. What could possibly have caused such a disruption in his being?

They were all awaiting with unabashed eagerness the continuation of his adventure. Simon reached over for the wine jug, poured himself a full cup, and taking a sip, continued to relate his story with which you, my reader, are well acquainted.

It took a good while for the story to be told, and a good number of sips from the wine cup before our hero's narration came to an end.

Simon surveyed his audience. His eyes had been cast down during the greater part of his narration, and it was only by observing their individual faces that he could assess the effect that his story had had on them.

The women's faces were wet with tears. Alexander was also tearful. Only Rufus and Mordecai displayed dry eyes, though they were both much moved nonetheless. Ruth leant over, and put her head on her husband's shoulder, her eyes swimming with tears.

Simon's words proved prophetic as Ruth uttered, "Poor young Rabbi, and poor mother."

The unique story was discussed all that evening and well into the night. It was the type of occurrence which could not easily be passed over.

Mordecai and his daughters (for he had only daughters, three of them in fact), related to Simon and his family a number of Yeshua's parables which they had heard about from Galileans whom they knew, and who came to Jerusalem fairly often on business. They told how the Pharisees hated the young Rabbi because he was constantly exposing their hypocritical ways, and it was Mordecai's opinion that this had been the cause of Yeshua having been put to death.

Mordecai had further learnt that the preacher had performed many miracles. Some of which he explained to Simon and family; including his calming of the Sea of Galilee; his walking on the water; and even the raising of a man called Lazarus from the dead, which had occurred only a few days back and had taken Jerusalem by storm.

Simon and his family were now in a much more knowledgeable position than hitherto concerning the life of Yeshua.

Finally, a week after Passover, Simon's family began to make ready for their long journey back to Cyrene, which is a seaport in North Africa between Carthage and Alexandria. (As you my dear readers will surely know.)

Their return journey could have been made by land again, but it had proved to be a strenuous ordeal. Especially for Ruth, whose back had given her much discomfort during the thirty days it took to get to Jerusalem from their native Cyrene. They opted therefore, to return by sea which even though hazardous from the point of view of the weather, could possibly get them home within twelve days.

The following day, Simon's family took loving leave of Mordecai's family, thanking them with all their hearts for the hospitality that had been shown them for well over three months. The girls obtained promises from their cousins for a reciprocating visit to Cyrene where they would enjoy bathing in the blue Mediterranean Sea.

Mordecai accompanied them to the caravan assembly point in Jerusalem from where they would start for Caesarea on the first leg of their journey. There, they would board a vessel for the second and final leg.

As Simon looked back at that unique city which was the heart and centre of Jewish faith and culture, he had an eerie feeling that he could not describe even to himself. Jerusalem seemed to beckon him back.

He dismissed the feeling, and turning back to his wife said:

"Now my dear, let's get back home, and to the normality of our lives."

'Peace be with you Jerusalem,' prayed Simon to himself, as each member of the family mounted their camels. Looking back in unison, they waved farewell to Mordecai who returned their salute with moistened eyes.

CHAPTER TWO

THE STELLA MARIS

At last Caesarea came into sight, its high encompassing walls and imposing turrets, giving notice of its impregnability to the outside world. The caravan plodded on as it had done for days, having carried its members in relative security along its guarded route through towns and deserts alike.

The smell of the sea began to tantalize their nostrils as they approached the city gates, where there were soldiers on guard, inspecting and questioning each person prior to allowing the caravan into the city.

"That's the first leg done with and not soon enough," protested Ruth, whose back had been giving her some discomfort during that long camel trip.

"Yes dear, you will have a comfortable bed to sleep in tonight, and you will feel much better in the morning," said Simon reassuringly.

"I can hardly wait to see the bazaars," cut in Lucila with her usual enthusiasm for shopping.

"Seeing that we shall be here for another three days, we will have a chance to visit the amphitheater and see a performance," said Rachel.

"And what mischief have you two in mind?" asked the father, addressing his two boys. "I hear they've hidden all the girls to keep them away from strange boys coming into town."

"Father, you do us an injustice," protested Rufus with a wink at his older brother. "You know very well that girls don't interest us in the least."

"That greatly worries me," cut in the mother humorously. "I am petrified at the thought of having you both around my apron strings for the rest of my life."

The inspection by the guards once completed, the camels were led towards the part of the city where the majority of the inns were located. The travellers followed on foot.

Caesarea was a very modern city. Herod had recently built it as a showpiece for all Judea, and the world. Its man made harbour was spectacular in that it was semicircular. Its high walls with their imposing, intermittent turrets, provided more than adequate protection for vessels sheltered there.

The entrance to the harbour, flanked by beautiful statues, imparted a look of grandeur; confirming the prosperity of the city as they welcomed visiting mariners and their passengers.

Simon and family reached the inn which had been assigned to them, and proceeded to make themselves comfortable in their new surroundings. Since they had arrived in mid afternoon, there was still a good part of the day left in which they could all get to do some of the things they wanted.

After resting for an hour or so, and having enjoyed a good meal, they all scattered to do as they had planned.

Simon, Ruth, and the girls, visited the monumental new forum where they met fellow travellers, and refreshed themselves with exotic fruit drinks which had become a hallmark of Caesarea. The girls had joined their parents in the expectancy that they would later accompany them in their assault on the bazaars.

Alexander and Rufus longing for a swim, made their way to one of the well kept beaches which was situated near the Amphitheater. There, they could have a good swim, and at the same time try to find some pretty girls to befriend.

Their stay day in Caesarea was spent very enjoyably. The third day found the family boarding ship for the last leg of their journey home.

March had just gone, and hopefully with it, its rough seas, which formed a typical behaviour pattern in the Mediterranean each year. The journey home was expected to be a tolerable one for them and their fellow passengers. They would be accommodated on deck, where they would make do for the next twelve days using awnings and mats rented from the captain. Whatever food they needed for their journey they carried themselves, so it was important that they had correctly assessed their needs to see them through the first leg of the journey.

The ship's captain, had informed them the day prior to their sailing, that they would be stopping after six days or so, at a village situated in a bay, on their route, where they would replenish their food and water supplies. This meant that they would have to take enough food to last them six or seven days.

Despite their pretended Spartan outlook, feelings of apprehension were being felt by the family, even if only mildly, as the little "corbita" vessel glided out of the imposing semi-circular harbour, and headed out to the open sea; westbound under full sail.

The day was warm and sunny with small flaky clouds that seemed brushed on to the bright blue sky. If the weather held, the sturdy Roman cargo boat with its load of wine amphorae and cork, would have the coast in view constantly. The captain, who strove to make his passengers as happy as he could, would have the opportunity to point out, and acquaint them with all the significant landmarks on the route.

The passengers were at the moment being very pleasantly entertained by a school of dolphins which accompanied the ship on both sides, and were performing various antics to the delight of the people.

Simon left the rail on which he was leaning, enjoying the dolphins' aquatic performance, and got down to the business of finding a spot which promised good protection against the wind and the spray. He suspected the mildness of the weather might not continue, and the family should be as well sheltered as possible in those exposed conditions.

He found a suitable spot at the stern; immediately behind the captain's cabin which stood on deck. He motioned to Ruth to join him. She, having been following him with her eyes, went to him.

"This looks like the only sheltered spot on the whole deck," she declared. "But shan't we be in the captain's way?"

"We can always ask him," said Simon seeing the man approach.

"Welcome on board!" greeted the captain with a smile to match the phrase.

"Thank you!" replied husband and wife simultaneously.

"Would we be in your way, if my family, all six of us were to settle in this spot behind your cabin?"

"Oh no! it is the most sheltered part of the ship, and you were alert enough to find it." replied the captain approvingly. He reminded them once again, that the ship would stop six days later, to replenish food and water supplies at a village in a bay on their route. Then wishing them a pleasant voyage, walked away to talk to some of the other passengers.

Having for the moment had their fill of the dolphins' antics, the boys and girls came over and joined their parents who were busy planning their temporary living arrangements.

The other passengers, numbering eight in all, were moving around looking for spots in which to settle. Simon was pleased that he had had the foresight not to have let the dolphins' act distract him from his quest. He now asked the two boys to go and bring back a large awning and six mats giving them some money to pay for them.

The next chore, was to re-assess the amount of food that they had brought with them, and which was to last them for the estimated six days.

They opened their large food basket which was made of sturdy woven reeds, and took stock of the items: Three dozen loaves of flat bread, three dozen dried fishes, a whole cheese, a bag of dates, another of almonds, another of dried figs, a large container of olive oil, two dozen fresh oranges, and a bag of fresh figs.

Wine had not been included because it made up most of the ship's cargo, and could be purchased no doubt, quite cheaply from the captain.

"This should see us through the trip," commented Simon.

"I expect so, but with four young mouths to feed as well as ours, I am still wondering," responded his wife, not realising that wind conditions could also determine the duration of their trip.

The remainder of their possessions were all around them, and they hastened to organize the space before their children returned with the tent and mats.

"Here we are," announced Alexander, as he and his brother appeared loaded with the needed items.

"Let's set these out and see just how they are going to fit back here," said Rachel who immediately began to arrange the mats on the deck.

"Mother, you and we girls will be right behind the cabin. father, and the boys, can lie down directly opposite, like this." She placed the mats where she proposed.

"That looks pretty good," asserted Simon, admiring his daughter's practical sense.

"Now, the boys can set up the tent," chirped in Lucila who had been unusually quiet.

"Back in a moment," said Simon, "I am off to find some nails and a hammer." He disappeared around the cabin as he spoke.

"I think I know what he is going to do," said Alexander, who was already trying to solve the manner in which the makeshift tent would be installed.

After a brief interval, Simon returned. Not only with the nails and a hammer, but also with a goodly length of heavy rope.

"Now, we can get busy," he said in a cheerful tone as he threw the coil of rope at Rufus who caught it in mid-air. The rope uncoiled around him; much to the amusement of his sisters.

Whilst our heroes toil over their unique tent, I invite my good reader to survey with me the activity absorbing the remainder of the passengers and crew.

Following the instructions of the captain, and assisted by a sailor, the male passengers were busy installing smaller tents for themselves and their families.

Captain Marius, with his ample sea going experience and having had to contend with the needs and safety of his passengers for many years, had prepared a series of pseudo tents which he simply called shelters. These, could easily be hitched onto the railing of the ship and hooked down onto the deck where a series of small metal rings had been installed.

As was the case with every ship of the day, there was no shelter for the passengers anywhere. The Stella Maris, as the captain had named his little ship, was no exception. The little tents that he provided his passengers with, provided the only means of shelter available against inclement weather, or the heat of the sun…(Provided that the occupant sat, or lay down.) The tents were made of a thick cotton, lightly covered with a coat or two of tree sap, which as intended, made the material reasonably impervious to water. With their low profile, these tents when installed, were no higher than the ship's railing, and so were somewhat sheltered from the wind.

The captain, now having seen that all the installations were complete, advised the passengers to keep the tents rolled up and hung on the inside of the rail when not needed. The deck, he instructed, should be kept as clear as possible for walking around, and for the crew to manage the rigging as needed.

The little ship sailed along at a fair pace with a very favourable wind at its back. Good progress was being made to everyone's satisfaction.

Seeing that much was happening at the ship's stern, Marius left his passengers; having promised to sell them wine, and providing a free daily allowance of water. He, with some curiosity, now made his way over to where Simon and family were hard at work on their unique tent.

"Great Caesar be honoured!" exclaimed the captain in amazement. "What type of house are you building here?"

"Just making some use of an otherwise wasted space which will aid my family greatly," answered Simon with a smile.

"Are you a tent maker by trade?"

"No, but we are a family of carpenters," said Rufus proudly, throwing his arm around his older brother's shoulder.

"I wondered what you were going to do with the ropes and nails. But since one is always learning new things I controlled my curiosity till now."

"I can see what you mean by wasted space," continued Marius, suddenly realising that this new innovation might allow him to sell the sheltered space with the new covering at a premium on future voyages.

Simon was entertaining other thoughts regarding the tent, but he kept silent in the presence of the captain until he had had a chance of discussing the matter with the boys. They were now experienced enough carpenters to contribute to the development of his ideas.

Captain Marius offered them free water and good Hispanic wine at a very attractive price, and Simon, now ready for a period of rest after his labours, got the boys to follow the captain and obtain a skin of wine and one of water.

Some of the other passengers were also in need of water and or wine. They too, headed for the captain's cabin which was a virtual store room, as with the hold full of cargo there was no other storage space on deck. The captain and his small crew slept on the open deck in good weather, and in inclement weather, on top of coils of rope which were stored in his cabin.

The girls had been sitting with their mother near the tent builders, watching and waiting for them to complete their labour of love, not to mention necessity. They now got up and crossed the deck to make the acquaintance of a girl their age who stood by the railing presumably with her parents, talking among themselves. Lucila, who was sixteen, and a counterpart of her brother Rufus in her vivacious nature and outgoing ways, took the initiative. She managed the introductions on behalf of herself and her sister with great ease and charm. Once invited to sit with them, the girls proceeded to make their acquaintance with that family.

Simon and Ruth sat on their mats in the tent, relaxing in their new "home," awaiting the boys' return.

The sun was setting, and the beautiful day that had started them on their voyage so pleasantly began to ebb away. A cool soothing breeze, strongly flavoured by the characteristic odour of iodized brine, now carried them smoothly and elegantly over the glassy blue-green sea.

"Here's the wine!" chirped Rufus, and in a lowered tone. "And, the water too."

 His mother pulled out three metal cups from which they drank in turns. Ruth had brought only three so as to cut down on weight

"When we return home," began Simon, "we're going to make a nice bit of money. I have just had a great idea, but I didn't want to say anything in front of the captain. I noticed a twinkle in his eye when he praised our work on this tent.

"You see," he continued, " this is fine as a temporary shelter which is what the captain was thinking. But I am thinking that a permanent shelter would be much more advantageous, and bring in better revenue for this captain, and all the captains in the merchant fleet."

"Do you boys follow me?"

"Yes!" was the unanimous answer.

"Now," continued the shipboard genius. "This cabin, built of wood as an extension of the captain's cabin, but separate to it as indeed this is, would add very comfortable and secure quarters for two people. So, when we get back, we're going to go down to the harbour and get us some contracts to build such quarters on any boat we can fit them into."

"What a wonderful idea," broke in Ruth. The boys enthusiastically nodded their heads in approval.

"You are a genius father," declared Alexander laughingly; but in truth he was already designing the cabin in his head. There were many features which had to be built into such a tiny space, and as every designer knows, tight spaces with many requirements make for the biggest challenges. He was looking forward to it all just the same.

"Where are the girls?" asked Simon, not being able to see them from where he sat.

"They have been away for a while," answered Ruth.

"Rufus! Go find them please, and bring them back. They have not had a cup of water all day. We are now ready to eat before it gets too dark to see inside the baskets."

Rufus got up, and went around the cabin. From there, he could then see his sisters across the deck sitting and talking with a girl and a middle aged couple; presumably her parents. On approaching the group, he stopped in his tracks, stunned, as his young eyes beheld what seemed to him the most beautiful girl he had ever seen, and he had looked at a lot of them. In fact, sometimes it seemed that that is all he ever did. Or at least, that is the way his sister Rachel would have put it.

It seemed that the girl in question had caught Rufus at that unguarded moment when he became aware that the normal pink of his cheeks had suddenly turned into a heated red and in no condition for public exposure. However, not being aware of having been scrutinized by the girl's keen feminine perception, he proceeded forward with some of his usual bravado reduced to, let us say,... a lower grade of personal confidence.

At that moment his sister Lucila turned around following the gaze of her new friend, and seeing her brother, blurted out:

"Rufus, we were just talking about you!"

"So that is why my ears were burning," he said jokingly, but somewhat defensively.

"This is Rufus, the younger of my two brothers," volunteered Rachel, "no doubt he has been sent out to take us back to our parents."

"A good evening to you all," said Rufus with a pleasant smile, looking at the parents rather than at the girl.

He then turned to the girl with an even brighter smile on his face, and nodded appreciatively at her; his cheeks, having now recovered their normal colour.

"I am Marcus Tricius. This is my wife Julia, and this is my daughter Letitia," smiled the girl's father, as he extended a hand to the young intruder, who taking it and smiling once again at all of them said:

"I am Rufus, younger son of Simon of Cyrene, and I'm honoured to meet you, and your charming family."

"We are very taken with your sisters young man, and judging by the look on her face, my daughter is greatly enjoying their company. Will you not join us?"

"I am afraid I have come to take my sisters back for now. My mother is anxious, since they have neither drank or eaten anything all day, and she wishes them to come back with me before it gets dark."

He gently motioned to his sisters who immediately got up, took their leave, and all three walked across the deck, to their place behind the captain's cabin.

"Nice young man, commented Marcus." His wife and daughter enthusiastically assented.

"And now let us all sit down, to eat and drink, before it gets any later," he said reaching for their food basket.

The sun slowly extinguished itself amidst a panorama of ever changing soft, wispy, diffused colours. The hitherto blue of the sky intensified and blackened little by little, to provide a perfect backdrop for those incomparable celestial jewels, the stars.

The ship plodded on under a crescent moon, as its passengers prepared for a night's rest. The captain and a crewman after having finished their walk around the deck ensuring that all the passengers were reasonably comfortable, retired to the side of the cabin and tried to get some rest. The ship was left in the capable hands of the helmsman, who from his elevated post on top of the captain's cabin, steered the vessel with confident hands; being well acquainted with the waters on which he navigated.

By now it will have become obvious to my perceptive reader, that the gallant crew of the endearing *Stella Maris* consisted of three very able Roman seamen: the captain, the helmsman, and the mate. All of whom took their fourteen trusting passengers' welfare very much to heart.

Life on board the corbita became habit forming. Much as would have occurred on land, given the circumstance that a group of people had to live with one another under similarly restricted conditions, such as were being experienced on board this vessel. People grew to know one another, to like or dislike one another, approve or disapprove of each other, as their varying natures tended to dictate.

In reality, their differences were not disparaging in the main. But there was one individual who differed markedly from the rest of the passengers and whose aloofness was causing some suspicion among his fellow travellers. The middle aged man in question was not guilty of anything but what seemed eccentrically unsociable behaviour and unusual personal independence, which was interpreted as disdain by those around him. The man was of medium build, but well on the stout side. His age might be guessed at around forty three or forty four, and from his physiognomy, one could with reasonable certainty, label him as Jewish. His eyes, very dark and withdrawn, were divided by a sharp ridged nose with compacted nostrils, which contrasted unnaturally with the plumpness of his face and the thickness of his lips. His mouth which drooped somewhat at the sides, was surrounded by a thick moustache and full beard, giving his face a stern expression. These, echoed by his bushy eyebrows contributed markedly to the cynical aspect of his eyes.

One would have supposed him to have found friends in Simon and family who happened to be the only other Jews on board. But this was not the case. He coldly reacted to Simon's greetings, and expressed his desire to remain aloof when invited by our intrepid hero to meet his family.

The three girls continued to spend time together, and grew to become quite good friends. Their respective parents also conversed with one another and became better acquainted as the days passed; the fair weather persisting.

Marius, who was discovered to be a very good story teller, entertained his little bunch of passengers every evening with exciting stories of the sea. Giving them all something worth looking forward to every day.

It was not until the tenth day, on the second leg of their journey, that the weather began to show signs of change. By the sixth hour of that day the sky which had been showing rain clouds earlier that morning, began to darken, and before long, the rain started.

Because of the captain's earlier warning, everyone had prepared their tents in readiness for the downpour which was soon to commence. They took cover accordingly.

Simon and family had nothing to do. Their tent had been open on a permanent basis, and only the side flaps had to be dropped and anchored to the metal rings the captain had given them to nail into the deck.

The rain soon accosted the little vessel, and as it increased, the sea began to swell. The boat followed its motion, progressively intensifying, and causing sea sickness among some of the passengers.

This seemingly unforeseen storm gathered strength as the day progressed. The oscillating movement of the ship became more pronounced as the waves increased in size.

The main sail had been partly furled, and the artemon sail deployed. It being low over the bow, would help lighten it, and keep it from dipping too harshly into the oncoming waves. The wind increased, and the sea grew rougher. The constant dipping of the bow into the waves threw up huge volumes of water at every plunge. The captain went around with great difficulty tied to a long rope, giving everyone lengths of rope with which to tie themselves to the railing. The sea threatened to pull them overboard.

Simon made sure that Ruth and the girls were tied to the cabin with ropes that they had used as support for the tent, which was now in tatters, having been hammered every time the ship slid and exposed its side to the wind.

The girls were crying in fear. The boys who had tied themselves to the rail as had Simon, were obliged to keep ducking

SIMON OF CYRENE

every time the swell of water that was scooped up by the bow's dipping, reached them at the stern. It smashed into them with great force, at times knocking the wind out of them. Simon was greatly relieved that the women were protected by the cabin. Ruth and Lucila were continuously sea sick. Rachel seemed to be holding her own even though she was crying and very much afraid.

The other passengers were faring even worse, some of their little shelters had been ripped off by the wind, and those remaining were flapping around dangerously as the metal hooks threatened to cut whoever got in their path.

Letitia and her parents were huddled together on the deck just hanging on to the railing to which their ropes were secured as they were mercilessly accosted by the heavy winds and spray.

Unbeknown to the passengers, Marius had set a course out to sea when he realized that the storm would eventually catch up with them. He ensured that at least they would not end up on the rocks. A real danger when following a coastal route. Now that the passengers were finally tied down, and with luck no one would be lost, he began to be very concerned with the cargo shifting despite his precautions.

The amphorae had been carefully shelved so as to resist pitching as much as possible. The cork cargo which was in slab form, had been used to pack the amphorae tightly, so that if shifting did start, it would be cushioned to a large degree by the cork. Since the condition of the cargo could not be checked until the storm abated, Marius had to content himself, as did his passengers, with the hope of the storm spending itself soon.

It was early afternoon, though it looked more like dusk.

Simon's mind wandered as he was accosted by the ever stronger incoming blasts of water. He thought back on his incredible day with Yeshua, and how John had told him that they believed him to be the son of God. That look that Yeshua had given him at his third fall with the incredible feeling that followed, preyed on Simon's worried mind. Quite significantly he remembered how Joseph of Arimathea had told him, as they spoke of things Yeshua had done, that He had once walked on the sea and even calmed it by command; just as Mordecai too had heard. His eyes, were constantly checking his family, but his thoughts were now with Yeshua. He remembered the proclamation, and with

49

great difficulty he put his hand into his soaked tunic. 'Yes!' It was still there. Leaving his hand on it, and subconsciously using it as a link with Yeshua, he cried out, though the wind muffled his voice.

"Yeshua! Yeshua! I believe you to be the son of God. Please calm this angry sea, and save these people."

He really did not expect to be heard, being the practical, and unworthy man that he was. However, the next lashing of water seemed less forceful than the previous one. Then came the next, still milder. In quick succession, the force of the water decreased. All of a sudden there was an opening in the clouds, and some diffused afternoon light shone through. The storm abated, the sea became calmer, and very soon the wind dropped to a more normal strength. The clouds parted, and the vessel settled peacefully on a tranquil sea.

The helmsman untied himself, and slumped over the 'clavus' or helm lever, quite exhausted, as the response of the ship improved. The crew rushed to the rigging and began to unfurl the main sail which instantly caught the now milder wind. The *Stella Maris* was once more thankfully underway, and on course once again.

Suddenly in the midst of this new activity, a feminine scream was heard from midships. All eyes turned in that direction.

A girl was leaning over the rail, hysterically pointing at something overboard. Rufus, once free from his security rope, made a dash to midships, realising that the woman screaming for help was no other than the lovely Letitia, whom he had been observing during the storm. He had helplessly watched her and her family, as they struggled to keep themselves secure just like everyone else on board.

Reaching her side, he peered over the rail. He perceived the figure of a man, partially wrapped up in a sail, and entangled with what looked like a small mast and some rigging. The man was dangling on the security rope that held him against the side of the ship just beyond reach.

"My father! my father!" cried the girl. Her mother struggled to get on her feet.

Rufus tried to pull the man up, but quickly found that he could not do so by himself.

"Alexander!" he shouted looking back, trying to secure his brother's attention.

The latter having just finished untying his sisters, heard him, and came quickly followed by the captain and his mate. They all got a hold of the rope and pulled together. The mast appeared to have snagged on something on the ship's side, and fearing they would hurt the man, they slackened their hold till they could assess the situation better.

By this time, Simon and the rest of the family had crossed the wet and littered deck, and were assisting Letitia and her mother. They gently pulled them away so as to allow the would-be rescuers more room to work.

Rufus asked Captain Marius for a longer length of rope than those that were at hand, and the latter made haste to procure it from his cabin. Soon, he reappeared, also carrying a grappling hook that he felt might come in useful. In the meantime, Alexander, who had been trying to establish verbal contact with the entangled man to no avail, noticed as the body swayed to and fro' on the rope which held him, that his eyes were open. Turning to the man's daughter and wife, he reported what he had seen as a hopeful sign that he was alive.

Rufus took the rope from the captain, and tying it around his waist and handrail, climbed over the side. His brother and the captain lowered him down to where Marcus was dangling. Reaching the man, he tried to unwind the rigging from the body, but soon found that it would have to be cut away since it was horribly entangled all around. He yelled for a knife.

As he waited, he kept his feet against the ship's side to avoid being continually bumped against the hull, as had been happening to Marcus for quite a while before the storm subsided. It was a wonder that the man was still alive. The knife was lowered in a small basket, and Rufus immediately began to cut away the rigging in an effort to free the entrapped man. But presently,...he stopped.

The mixture of rigging, sail and mast, had become one homogenous mass. The wet sail formed a tight cocoon around the body making the use of the knife a perilous operation. Carefully surveying the situation, he decided to cut around the mast instead of the body. He soon discovered however, that the mast which had broken as it snapped from the bowsprit that had held it, was snagging under a wide board that ran along the ship's side ending up near the helm where it acted as its major support. He now had another plan.

If he could dislodge the mast from its entrapment, the people on deck could pull the whole thing up as they had tried to do before. Passing over the body to the other side where the mast was snagged, he could see that a large piece of it was secured under the protruding board.

He braced himself, and pulled with all his might; the mast held tight. He tried again. This time standing on the free part of the mast very carefully to avoid stepping on Marcus. He proceeded to perform a series of jumps, and finally after many tries, the hold on the mast having been loosening more and more each time, finally gave way. Rufus received quite a jolt as his inevitable fall was arrested abruptly by the rope around him.

"Ahoy up there!" he shouted after recovering his breath," pull up slowly."

Momentarily the whole configuration began to rise until it was lifted over the rail and carefully deposited on the deck by many helping hands. Marius, knife in hand, began the cutting in earnest, now favoured by more amenable surroundings than Rufus had encountered.

The young hero was then pulled up, and promptly found himself enveloped in his mother's embrace the moment his feet touched the deck.

All attention was on the entrapped Marcus who was now being slowly, and carefully, extricated from his deadly cocoon. Once free of his entrapment, he was left to his wife and daughter who were anxiously but very gently, trying to revive him. His eyes were open but expressionless. He could not speak. He lay there on the wet deck in shock, and totally exhausted.

The captain came over once more. He gave the man's wife a cup of water, and told her to try and give it to him very slowly in small sips. He also gave her one of his tunics which had been hanging in his cabin and was quite dry. Marcus' wife Julia, with Letitia's help, managed to pull off his wet clothes and wrap him up in the dry tunic. His wet clothes were tied around the rigging to dry in the afternoon sun, which by its welcomed reappearance, acted as a soothing balm on those unfortunate people who had been so savagely accosted by the sudden gale.

As the ship altered course, and once again drew closer to the coast, a fair amount of debris could be seen floating on the water as they passed. A sign that some other ship had not been as fortunate as the *Stella Maris*. Marius stood at midships scanning with a seaman's eye, the water on the port side of the ship. The same was being done on the starboard side by Jason his mate. Presently there came a shout from the mate… "Men in the water off starboard."

The captain crossed the deck and confirmed the sighting of two persons in the water hanging on to a large piece of timber. Quickly, with great agility, he and his crewman made for the rigging and began to furl the main sail to slow down the ship. The captain, shouted to the helmsman:

"Hard to port, and hold. There are two men in the water."

The ship circled using the momentum it carried, until it once again came close to where the men were waiting and hanging on to the floating piece of timber.

"Tie the ropes around yourselves," shouted the captain in Latin, throwing down two long ropes.

They must have understood since they each tied a rope around their waists, and were then pulled up. The two grateful mariners were immediately given water to quench their thirst followed by some wine to warm them up. They sat leaning against the rail, quite exhausted.

"We thank you for saving our lives," said the older one.

"March is gone! where did that confounded gale come from?" enquired the younger one. "It's a good thing we had no passengers this trip, otherwise we would surely have lost them."

"What ship were you sailing?" asked Jason.

"A smaller corbita than this, to be sure," answered the older sailor.

"We are going to Cyrene," said Marius. "Where are you from?"

"Alexandria," answered the younger one.

As the sailors continued to talk among themselves, the little group that comprised the Simon and Marcus' families were sitting around the latter, feeling rather miserable in their dripping wet clothes. Unfortunately, the sea had washed off all their luggage along with everyone else's on board. No food or clothes were to be found, and still two days remained before they would reach Cyrene.

A meeting was convened by Marius, who proposed a stop in one of the bays along the coast so that some food might be purchased, including some fresh fruit for which every soul on board was yearning. After some discussion, it was agreed that the captain's plan be adopted. Once more, under full sail, the helmsman was instructed to change course.

By late afternoon, the *Stella Maris* had anchored in a small well-protected bay. A couple of boats rowed up to greet them, anticipating the reason for their unscheduled visit, and bringing with them much needed victuals.

A basket was lowered on a rope time and time again, with food and money moving in inverse direction. Soon, the little corbita was exiting the bay adequately victualed, including a fresh supply of water.

The two shipwrecked newcomers were looked after by the benevolence of all on board since they possessed nothing. Similarly, it could be said, that none of the passengers had anything either in the way of possessions; except for the clothes on their backs and their money belts; which being the custom, they had prudently strapped to their midriffs.

The remainder of the journey proceeded uneventfully, save for the fact that a friendship had been struck by the Simon and Marcus families, as could well be supposed after Rufus' valiant efforts in saving Marcus' life.

The 'independent member' of the ship's complement remained as suspiciously aloof as ever having taken no part in the rescuing of Marcus, or anything else for that matter. The latter had recovered sufficiently by the time Cyrene was finally sighted, as to be able to stand and walk with a limp from a very badly bruised left leg. His thoughts it seemed, were very muddled, and he uttered not a word.

It was to be hoped, his wife Julia had said. That with a little time to rest in the comfort of his own home, he would get back to his normal self.

Soon after the *Stella Maris* had safely docked, a gang plank was passed up from the quay and the deboarding of the passengers commenced.

The 'independent man,' (as I have chosen to label him for the time being, my esteemed reader, who will return later to take a part in our story,) was the first to disembark. He, taking leave of the captain with uncalled for formality, ignored all the others around him.

The other passengers followed. They consisted of two middle aged couples, who had managed for themselves during the voyage. They took leave of Marius, and thanked him for having brought them through safely. They now leave us, and melt unobtrusively into the pages of history, having no further role to play in our little saga. The two shipwrecked sailors remained on board, awaiting further developments.

Rufus and Alexander, after having helped their sisters down the rickety gang plank, returned to the deck to bring down Marcus, and then again for Letitia and her mother, who was gripped by a great fear of the plank which appeared very unsafe to her.

Simon and Ruth were the last to leave. They delayed, so as to converse with Captain Marius. Simon made arrangements to start early the next morning on the repairs that required to be done on the ship.

Letitia, anxious to get her father home, called over a little beggar boy who was nearby watching her with admiring eyes. She promised him some money if he would run to her father's house and have one of the servants come down with their donkey cart to collect them at the quay.

Rufus walked over to her and offered to keep her company until the cart arrived. She, feeling much more at ease now that she was on 'terra firma,' smiled at him sweetly, and throwing a guarded glance in her mother's direction gave his arm a loving squeeze, thanking him for the offer. Simon, and the rest of the family now approached them and took their leave. The girls promised Letitia to get together again very soon. Lucila gave Rufus a pinch in concert with a mischievous smile as they walked off and left him with his new found love.

Walking a little way, Simon and his family found a horse and cart for hire that looked reasonably clean. They hired it for the night. The girls sat in the cart with Ruth at the reins, and their baggage at the back. Father and son walked alongside. They knew that the hill would be too much of a challenge for a single horse, as they started on their way home.

"Rufus knows his way," said Simon in answer to Ruth's anxious enquiry regarding her younger son. "I hope he won't be too late getting back. We have work to do tomorrow," he added.

After what seemed to Letitia an interminable wait, she caught sight of the beggar boy followed by the donkey cart driven by one of the servants.

The boy ran up to her with a beaming smile on his dirty little face, hand outstretched in expectancy of his reward. His benefactress smiled back at him, thanked him, and gave him a farthing. The urchin received it with a gasp of joy, and offering copious thanks, quickly disappeared from view.

"Welcome home m…master, and, and you m…my ladies," cried the servant with a look of genuine joy in his face and his customary stutter. "It is t…truly wonderful to have you home again. The g…gods be praised."

"Good to see you too Damian," retorted mother and daughter simultaneously.

"The master is quite ill, he has had a nasty accident, and is still suffering its effects," continued Julia.

"O dear, that is t…terrible, let me get him in the cart and m…make him comfortable on those cushions which I brought for all of you, and," continued Damian, "with your perm…m…mission my lady, I shall go and get the doctor as soon as we get the master home."

"Let me help you," volunteered Rufus taking a hold of Marcus' arm and gently leading him to the back of the cart.

He sat him on the edge, whilst Damian, climbing into the cart, arranged some of the cushions to receive his master. He then caught Marcus under the arms, as Rufus climbing up, lifted him by the legs, and together they laid him down gently. Letitia and her mother got up on the back of the cart and settled down gracefully among the many cushions.

The cart moved on at a walking pace, allowing Rufus to converse with the ladies as he walked alongside.

Their house was not far, but situated on its own. It was surrounded by a high wall and closed off by a heavy double leafed wooden gate with an iron grated opening on each leaf. It was opened as they approached by another excited servant who bowed, smiled, and enthusiastically proffered his greetings as the cart passed.

Rufus, was taken by surprise at the size and beauty of the house with its brightly painted stucco facade: colonnaded entrance, ornamental iron gate, high windows, and striking red tiled roof. It was set well back from the gated entrance. The gardens fronting it were meticulously kept, and displayed a great variety of plants and flowers. A pool, with a beautifully carved life size statue of Venus at its centre, formed the heart of the garden. It reflected, on its calm glassy surface, the surrounding manicured trees and exotic shrubs to great effect, creating in the golden light of the evening, a delightful feeling of peace and tranquility.

The little cart came to rest at the front door where two women servants stood anxiously awaiting the family's arrival. They both bowed reverently, came forward with joyful exuberance and busied themselves helping their two mistresses out of the donkey cart. The gatekeeper, whose name was Tecuno, ran back, and with Damian's help, proceeded with great care to extricate their beloved master from the cart.

"I shall take my leave now, seeing that you are all in such good hands," said Rufus, addressing himself mainly to Julia, who stopping at the threshold, turned, and with a tired look on her face but still managing a smile, once again offered her thanks to the young man. She expressed her wish that he, and his family should visit them again soon.

Letitia watched her parents and servants disappear into the house. Looking tenderly at Rufus, she walked away from the door, crossed the stone path, and followed by him, approached the pool where the statue of Venus reposed in all her feminine glory.

"Tomorrow, I must pick the most beautiful flowers I can find in the garden, and bring them to the goddess," she said, looking at the statue. "I have her to thank for many things."

The many things that Letitia was contemplating in her young mind included most ardently, apart from the survival of her dear father whom she worshipped; her opportune meeting with the now beloved Rufus. He, standing by her side, with the biased eyes of love, compared her more than favourably with the statue that she so revered.

If the statue of Venus had had carnal eyes, she would have beheld reflected in the shallow water of that lovely tranquil pool, the images of the two young lovers who as yet had not declared their love for one another; though it burned with the force of a raging fire within their bosoms. The circumstances that had brought them together, had as yet kept them apart. But tomorrow would be another day.

Letitia could feel Rufus' eyes moving softly, and lovingly around her face. She slowly turned to face him; heat rising to her cheeks, and yet, with a fluttering teardrop in her eye. Her entranced lover looked into her eyes, took her hands in his and with a slight tremble in his voice said:

"How beautiful you are.... And I love you."

The fluttering tears on her beautiful eyes suddenly lost their hold and ran down her hot cheeks. Her whole body stirred with an excitement that thrilled her by the very newness of its nature.

Her delicately sculpted full red lips parted alluringly, as if heralding precious words that were to follow. Then, of a sudden, they closed together again; as a rose bud might close in fear of the night's dew. A servant's unexpected presence shattered the magic aura that surrounded the lovers, sending them back into the world of cold reality and leaving Rufus in total distress.

"Your mother wishes you to come in directly my lady."

"I shall say goodnight then," whispered Rufus, from the depth of his distress. Yet happily aware that a whole new world had opened to receive him, at whose centre was his darling Letitia.

"Good night to you too," she whispered, and may Venus reward you with sweet dreams."

He lovingly pressed her hands; the pressure being returned in equal measure much to the enjoyment of the servant who still stood by. Rufus made his way slowly down the path to the gate, where Tecuno the well-built Nubian, wearing a slave's band around his muscular upper arm, was back at his post and ready to open it for him.

"May you have a good night young master," said the man in a Latin somewhat adulterated by the intrusion of phonetics inherent of his own mother tongue.

Rufus returned the compliment and started happily on his way home with one singular thought absorbing his whole mind.

'When shall I see her again?'

CHAPTER THREE

HOME AT LAST

The clatter of a horse's hooves brought Lucila to her feet, as she and the family were in the middle of their evening meal. She approached the open window. A horse had just come to a stop outside, allowing one of its two riders to alight.

"Here's Rufus!" she announced with great excitement. Her inherent sense of curiosity had accompanied her all that evening anticipating the return of her brother.

'He may, if he is in the mood,' she thought, "reveal to us all, the details of his little adventure earlier that evening.'

Jaunty footsteps could be heard, as she drew away from the window and rushed to the door to greet her brother whom she adored in spite of their constant teasing of one another. To her surprise, she found herself embracing David.

"Mmmmm," laughed the visitor looking back at Rufus. "I really am popular tonight. I wonder what I have done to deserve this loving hug," he joked, his pleasant young face beaming with pleasure.

"Oh! you brute," she quipped with cheeks as red as ripe apples. Betraying the fact that she had a more than usual regard for this young man, who happened to be a neighbour three years her senior.

Rufus, who followed on his friend's heels, did not miss out on his sister's enthusiastic hug which was given him not only out of love, but would she hoped, prove efficacious in paving the way later, when the divulging of his evening's mysteries would finally satisfy her feminine curiosity.

"Come and join us," bellowed Simon with his mouth half full. The young neighbour walked in, saluted everyone, went over to Ruth, and gave her a fond kiss on the cheek.

"Ah, David, what a lovely surprise. We've missed you, you know."

"I am so happy that you are all back safe and sound," said David, giving Lucila a passing glance so as not to alarm her, and resisting the temptation of teasing her once again.

"I'm starving," announced Rufus, using one of his habitual phrases, which immediately propelled his mother in the direction of the kitchen. She, with knowing anticipation had hidden away a good chunk of meat which thankfully, was big enough to placate the voracious appetite of two young men.

"Have you eaten David?" she asked, poking her head out the kitchen doorway.

David was reticent to answer. He did not know if she had enough food prepared to take care of another stomach.

"I saved enough for the two of you," came her own answer as she disappeared back into the kitchen. The hungry pair went off to their ablutions.

They soon returned, and sat down in readiness for their meal. Alexander, who had as usual sat quietly listening to all the small talk earlier, asked David how his family had been coping with Simon's two horses and donkey. David's father had offered to look after the animals, and make use of them whilst they were abroad.

"They have been well enough behaved," answered David.

"The donkey has a mind of its own," said Alexander with a knowing smile. "And as you have probably found out can be just as stubborn as a mule when he wants to."

"Poor thing!" quipped Rachel suddenly coming to life after having been nursing her thoughts for the past while.

"Incidentally Rufus," she continued, "how did you bump into David?" She tried to open the subject she knew her sister was anxious to discuss.

Of course, this did not mean that she had no interest in it herself; after all it was pure feminine curiosity, and even her mother would love to know.

"Oh," he answered, "I was just walking away from Letitia's house as David happened to be riding by."

"How did you get along at Letitia's house?" asked Ruth, walking into the room with a tray of sliced meat, vegetables, and bread. She put them on a low table between the two boys, and looked at her son, expectantly.

"Oh, keep quiet, and let them eat in peace," interjected Simon clumsily. Inadvertently squelching the delicate subject that the women had laboured so hard to spawn.

"Now," continued Simon, feeling it was time that some practical topic be discussed. "Tomorrow morning, Alexander, you and I will get all our tools onto the rented cart, and go down to Apollonia quay where Captain Marius will be on board the *Stella* waiting. We can quickly assess the damage which as you know is mostly to do with the artemon mast."

"Which almost killed poor Marcus," interjected Ruth.

"Once we fix that, and make a new mast," explained Simon, ignoring his wife's remark. "We'll be in a better position to sell Marius on the idea of the cabin extension. If we play our cards right it'll bring in a fair business in the future."

"Now! Rufus," continued Simon, turning to his younger son. "In the morning whilst we're gone, go to David's place and bring back the two horses and the donkey. Feed them, put Topo into the stable, take the donkey to the pasture, hitch "Pepper" (who was a spirited black horse; Rufus' favourite) to the cart, and come find us in Apollonia. By the time you get down there it'll surely be close to midday, and after we eat the lunch that you will bring us,, you can either join us in the work, or go buy wood and other supplies that we'll need."

"When they are all gone," said Ruth addressing the girls, "we have to get this house cleaned and everything in order. Then I shall prepare their lunches for Rufus to take down.

The girls got up and began clearing the tables, leaving Rufus and David who had finished eating, admiring a dagger that the latter had bought.

Alexander got up, walked to the door, and with a backward glance, announced that he was going out for a short walk to enjoy the night air as it was a beautiful night out.

"Can I come?"

He turned around to find Rachel, tidying her long, curly, raven black hair, that floated softly around her perfectly oval face. The artist in him awoke as he studied her exceptional even though familiar face. Her straight black eyebrows, curving down gracefully at the ends, set off her alluring almond shaped green eyes like two amethysts reflecting the light of the oil lamp that hung on the wall by the door.

"Yes, of course!" replied Alexander, snapping out of his momentary reverie and letting his beautiful sister pass; smoothening her stolla as she went.

"Rachel!" called out her mother who hurried after her, carrying a palla. "You must not go out without this. Here! put it on."

Rachel placed the shawl over her head, and off she went with her brother, whom she looked up to; he being twenty one, just a year older than herself. Alexander's quiet nature and even temperament (an attribute from their mother) mimicked hers perfectly, making them very good friends.

"Full moon out tonight, sister," commented Alexander as his eyes swept the evening sky.

"Yes, and I am very pleased to be watching it with my feet firmly on my own soil, and not in the middle of the sea," responded Rachel, with a sigh of relief.

"I agree my dear. We all had a pretty tough time of it."

"I don't think I shall willingly set foot on another ship again," she assured him.

"Only time will tell," said Alexander in his usual thoughtful way as they walked down the hill passing by houses and shops on their right, and open country on their left. The road culminated at the sea four miles away.

The sea glittered like a deep blue sequin spattered mantel in the moonlight, peeking through blackened trees and hedge-groves; some, familiarly on their own property.

Their house, now behind them, was of a plain clay brick under a stucco facade, showing little signs of elegance, much to the regret of Alexander in particular, who had a keen architectural perception, and imagined a few ways in which he could improve its aesthetic integrity.

The homestead stood on a large piece of ground about four hundred feet above sea level, and formed part of the continuous terracing ascent, which ended up the long hill in Cyrene at two thousand feet above sea level, and six meandering miles from the house.

At the bottom of this winding hill, and at sea level, stood the town of Apollonia. It acted as sea port for Cyrene, and where my good reader will recall, stood that beautiful house hastily described earlier, belonging to Marcus, who was a very wealthy merchant, and a prominent member of the council in Cyrene.

As the pair continued their walk in silence, absorbed by the beauty and tranquility of the night, their private musings were suddenly disturbed by the approach of a galloping horse emerging from the darkness. It appeared before them as the gallop they heard became a trot, which in turn became a walk. The rider, assuming the form of David, cheerfully bade them both good night and continued on his way, resuming first the trot and then the gallop.

"I think we had better turn back now," suggested Rachel, slipping her arm under her brother's.

"How do you think David views Lucila?" asked Rachel tentatively.

"I think he is very fond of her, but at present he certainly doesn't take her seriously. She still has much of the girl in her, though the woman peaks through ever more often."

"She is quite taken with him I know and could easily get hurt," commented Rachel, with a gentle nod.

They continued their uphill walk in silence for a few moments, and then Rachel again addressed her brother with some concern in her voice. "What do you make of Rufus' infatuation with Letitia?"

"He is I believe, head over heels in love with her, and by what I see and feel, she may very well be just as much in love with him."

"We may find out more tomorrow," suggested Rachel," if we can get him to tell us what he experienced earlier this evening when he accompanied her and her family home."

"Oh, I am so glad to be back home and on solid ground," she suddenly sang, as she stretched her arms out in a devil-may-care manner, and pirouetting gracefully, acted out her joyful feeling. He chuckled at her uncharacteristic gay abandon.

They had now arrived at their house, which following the rhythm of the night, held the household in its peaceful embrace; not a sound was heard as they tip-toed through the door.

Alexander took down the oil lamp which hung on the wall by the door, and guided his sister to her room, where she would undress by moonlight. He then returned, locked the door, put the lamp back in its place, and found his own way to his room which he shared with Rufus. The latter was asleep.

So ended a day of joy for this happy family after their terrifying ordeal with the sea, which if not for Yeshua's intervention, would have spelt tragedy for them all.

"Why did life have to be so tough." As Simon always remarked whenever he faced adversity."

Daylight had broken but one hour when Ruth woke up and gently shook her husband.

"Wake up Simon, it's time to get up."

"But I had just fallen asleep," complained a tired Simon.

"Yes, and I am the Queen of Sheba," answered Ruth in her humorous way. She knew he had slept like a log.

"Up you get! I'm off to wake the children." And away she went.

Soon, the whole family was in motion. The men went off to a small room that stood apart from the house in the back garden. There, they kept water for their ablutions in a large earthenware jar which held ten buckets. From this great jar they filled their individual basins. These were lined up on three separate wooden shelves of Simon's making; finally positioned at an equal height following many adjustments over the years.

The women had a small closet adjoining the girls' room, also with similar provisions. They had however, a larger mirror than the men. It too, was actually a polished piece of brass which served as a mirror, and catered to their feminine vanity with particular attention to the dressing of their hair,... the crowning glory of all three. They, too, were seeing to their toilette with as much urgency as their male counterparts, as they hastened to go and prepare the family breakfast.

With the women in the kitchen, and the men hastily dressing after having returned from their ablutions, the day could now be confirmed as on its way. Simon went around opening the window shutters, allowing the early morning sun to bathe with its still soft feathery light, the room where most of the family activities were carried out, and which also served as a dining room.

The room, large enough to accommodate two good sized Persian rugs, was decorated with textile wall hangings and illuminated by six oil lamps. These, sitting high on wall brackets provided the necessary lighting. One wall, which accommodated the back door to the garden, was covered by a colourful painting depicting musicians and dancers in varying postures, performing their dances with the ocean and a rocky coast at their backs. The adjoining wall showed signs of continuation of the mural, but in a state of expectancy. The artist, no other than our worthy young friend Alexander, had yet much more work to complete. The ceiling, white-washed, as were the remaining walls, displayed exposed beams supporting a flat roof accessible by an outdoor staircase which served as a terrace looking out onto a not too distant sea.

This terrace, with its many well tendered colourful potted plants and reed furniture, provided a comfortable and picturesque exterior living space, which the family enjoyed throughout most of the year.

To add to the charm and practicality of this rooftop terrace, Alexander had constructed a pergola style lightweight structure, supporting a cane covering by means of slender posts. This in turn provided a most welcome shade to a section of the terrace which in the day though scantily used, gave relief from the scorching sun. In the evenings, blessed with a constant and balmy sea breeze, it made a most pleasant place for the family to sojourn, particularly during the summer months.

Simon now having finished his round of shutter openings, sat down with the two boys on one of the many comfortable, colourful, cushions that contributed so markedly to the transient aesthetics of the room.

"All is ready! settle down," announced Ruth, as she and the girls entered the room carrying the morning's repast between them.

The men could not restrain a look of pleasure and admiration, as the three women gracefully floated in; their enchanting fresh perfume fanned by their dresses tantalised the men nostrils, as they busied themselves serving the tables.

"My, don't we all look beautiful today!" exclaimed Rufus who was an incurable flatterer.

"He must be after something," quipped Lucila. "We too, are after something," she jested, looking pleadingly at her brother.

"For instance," she challenged, "what have you got to tell us about your little adventure accompanying Letitia and family home?"

There! She had finally taken the 'bull by the horns,' as that crude expression goes. She cast one of her most bewitching smiles at her brother, and prepared herself for the consequences.

Rufus, could sense that the whole family suspected that by his silence hitherto, something of interest, if not of importance had occurred the previous evening. After a couple of bites of his food, he proceeded to relate the evening's adventure; cunningly leaving out any reference to his romantic episode by the *Venus pool.*

"And so it is," he continued between bites and gulps, "I believe Marcus is a very rich man; a merchant I think, though I am not entirely sure as yet. But he has a beautiful house." He went on to describe the house to his family who eagerly listened.

"Oh, what a beautiful house Letitia has," sighed Rachel visualising it from her brother's description.

"And they have at least one servant and three slaves," confirmed Ruth with a touch of envy. "One could hardly tell from the way they were dressed on board the ship that they were so well off."

"What did Letitia have to say to you? asked Rachel, trying to assist her sister in her investigation. "Surely, you must have had a chance to talk to her alone?"

Rufus, was taken aback by Rachel's question. Noticing that his mother and father were looking at him with prying eyes, he replied with a certain clumsiness (inherited from his father no doubt), that his conversation with Letitia had been cut short just as it had started. She had been summoned back into the house by a servant who interrupted their conversation in the garden just as it had started.

"How terribly untimely," blurted out the 'chief investigator,' sarcastically, once again. She had maintained her silence up to then. Quite an achievement for the bubbling sixteen year old.

"Yes it was," confirmed the culprit who having finished his meal, got up from the table, went over to his unconvinced mother, bent down, gave her a kiss and a hug, and waiving his hand to all, proceeded with unwarranted haste out the door with David's house as his destination.

"Well!" exclaimed Simon getting up from his cushion, "we're off now, and we'll leave the solving of the mystery to you ladies who'll probably take all day doing it. But we have work to do," he continued, displaying a typical masculine attitude by mentally disparaging the women with regard to the lightness of their chores as compared to his heavy, manly, work.

Ruth, of course, knew what he meant. Years of experience coupled with her inherent good nature, allowed her to take such masculine sorties into the sanctity of her challenging domestic responsibilities, with patience and forbearance, as befitted a loving wife. She went over to him and Alexander, gave them a hug apiece, and with tongue in cheek admonished them not to work too hard.

Alexander went to the stable, and brought out the hired horse. He hitched it to the cart, and took it to the front of the shop which stood as an extension to the house. The shop, elongated the frontal facade of the house, and had a large opening with a double leaf door. It was always kept open when any of them were working there. A well stocked woodshed, adjoining the stables, and concealed from street view, answered to most of their professional needs.

"Help me with these tools," cried Simon, taking an armful of those he had selected.

Alexander picked up another armful, and loaded them into a long wooden box they had placed in the cart.

This being completed, they shut the shop doors, and climbing into the cart, proceeded down the hill to Apollonia where the redoubtable *Stella Maris* was berthed.

CHAPTER FOUR

SHIP SHAPE

Ships' masts were clearly discernible, above the roofline of the surrounding buildings, as the cart levelled out on reaching the bottom of the hill. Arriving at the quay where the *Stella* was berthed, they were cognisant of much activity occurring in its vicinity. Drawing closer, and judging by the number of mule-drawn carts in line, and the constant stream of men laden with amphorae descending from the ship, it became obvious to them that the cargo was being unloaded.

"This is most unexpected," remarked Simon, realising what a blunder he had made by not having foreseen the necessity of unloading the cargo prior to any repairs to the ship.

'But then,' he said to himself. 'I'm no expert on mercantile marine procedures, and Marius didn't mention any of this to me.'

"We are never going to get any work done today," protested Alexander.

"Well, at least we can survey the damage carefully and assess the materials we'll need to make the repairs."

"And," cut in Alexander, with sudden enthusiasm, remembering the new cabin, "we can measure the space available for the cabin extension so that I can complete my drawings for it."

"In any event, I'll go up and see what Marius will permit us to do," muttered Simon. "But first, help me up with the tool box. Then you can go and return the cart whilst I talk to the captain."

Together, father and son struggled with the long, heavy box, and using the handles at each end, precariously made their way up one of the two gang planks. The unloading proceeded with great efficiency.

Once on deck, they deposited their load behind the captain's cabin; where they knew it would be out of everyone's way.

Alexander prepared to leave his father as Marius approached them with a broad smile, and bid them good morning.

"I have two thousand wine amphorae to unload," said the captain. "It will take the whole day and most of the night. I cannot spend much time with you today. However, there is much you can do by yourselves, as long as you don't get in the way of these people." He pointed at the busy scene behind him. "Later," he continued, putting a hand on Simon's shoulder, "when I have an opportunity, you can acquaint me with your list of materials, and give me a price for the whole job. If I find your price fair, I shall then authorize you to proceed.

"Very well. It'll be as you say," answered Simon, heading in the direction of his toolbox. He took out a smoothened piece of wood which would serve as a writing tablet, a charcoal stick, a measuring stick, and made ready to begin his inspection.

Presently, having returned the cart, Alexander joined his father on deck. They took to the starboard side, staying clear of the unloading, and made their way to the bowsprit, to begin their inspection.

Surprisingly, there was no visible damage. The artemon mast had been ripped off quite cleanly, by the force of the water during its many dips under the waves.

"Good," remarked Simon. "We need to make a new mast complete with iron rings and hooks to take the rigging. The captain will have to help us there, unless we find another similar ship in the harbour from which we can copy the position of those rings etc. When we finish our assessment here, we can wander around the quays and see."

They continued with their inspection. Minor damages became apparent here and there, and they noted them down on their wooden tablet. Finally, the captain's cabin was measured, its exact position relative to the stern noted, and the space available for the projected cabin extension recorded.

The hive of activity continued at a brisk pace. The foremen shouted their orders, keeping the men moving relentlessly; yet allowing a group to rest and refresh themselves as another group took their place. Thus, good order and industry prevailed.

Rufus, having arrived with the family cart, called out to his father and brother. They promptly joined him, and all three rode off eating the midday meal that Rufus had brought, as they searched for a ship with a similar artemon mast to that of the *Stella*.

They visually examined a good variety of vessels before they came across another corbita which happened to be identical to the *Stella Maris*. They stopped in front of the ship's bow, and Alexander made a quick and accurate sketch of the rigging and mast; the length of which he had to guess. They were now in a position to ride over to a nearby blacksmith shop, and get a price on the ironwork.

"You'll have to bring me the mast so that I can get a tight fit on the rings," said the swarthy blacksmith, whose very flat nose told of a rough past, and a stormy temperament.

"What's your price?" asked Simon.

"Four denarii for the lot," replied the blacksmith, with a confident look on his face.

"Sounds like a lot," said Simon; suspicious of the speed with which the man had priced the work.

"It's a lot of work, with all those accompanying rings and hooks, but I shall do an excellent job for you," said the man with an intense look in his eyes.

"Very well then," conceded Simon. And with that said, he and his sons left the blacksmith shop, and made their way back to the ship.

As the cart pulled up at a little distance from the gangplank so as not to obstruct the stevedores, Rufus called out to Simon.

"Father, that man over there, supervising the unloading," he pointed to Damian, "is one of Marcus' servants whom I met yesterday at his house."

"Which one?" asked Alexander, with some uncharacteristic curiosity.

"That one," said Rufus, pointing to Damian again.

"This cargo must then belong to Marcus," conjectured Simon.

"We had a cargo of cork too," remarked Alexander, "I wonder if that was also his?"

"The captain will know for certain. We shall ask him when we go back on board now," assured Simon. They tied their horse to a ring on the wall of a building opposite the ship, and made their way up the gang plank onto the deck.

Marius, who saw them coming back on board, approached them immediately.

"Ah! you're back," he said looking at all three in turn. "I have a few moments to spare. We can now discuss your assessment of the damages. I need it for the people that have insured my ship, and who will I hope, pay for them."

"We are ready now, so let's sit over there by your cabin where we'll be out of the way, and finalise things," suggested Simon pointing to the cabin.

"If I can get your approval," said Simon with a smile, "we can start the work tomorrow."

They talked and bargained for a while until Marius' approval was given. Then Simon presented his idea concerning the cabin extension; stressing accommodation of passengers in 'luxurious style.' The Captain was very impressed, even excited, as he listened to Alexander, who being the designer of the family sketched his proposal on the back of the wooden board, explaining as he went along.

Once Alexander had completed his presentation of the plans, Marius conceded with obvious pleasure. "I love the idea! but I shall have to bear the cost myself since this does not concern the insurance people."

"Yes, but think of the profit you'll make," remarked Simon. "How much do you think you can charge?"

"Well, let me see....Possibly three denarii per day. That would be about forty five denarii for a passage from here to Caesarea."

"By Jupiter! said Simon. That would almost pay for my work in a single trip."

"Why almost?" asked the captain with an astute grin on his face.

Simon gave him a deep and searching look, and said. "What if I agree to leave it at forty five denarii, provided you promise to show it to other captains whom you know, and encourage them to let us put one on their ship for say fifty denarii. I'll give you five denarii for every ship I work on."

"Mmm... Interesting idea... Mmm... Very well... Done!" conceded Marius. And they all shook hands on it.

As the captain was about to leave them to return to the supervision of the cargo, Rufus addressed him.

"Captain, may I be permitted to ask you what may be a delicate question?"

"Ask, by all means."

"Can you tell us if the cargo belongs to our friend Marcus?"

"Well, I normally keep my clients' names to myself. Not that I am bound to, but it is simply good business to keep their names from competitors' ears. When you are older young man you will understand," he replied putting a firm friendly hand on Rufus' shoulder.

"But in your case, considering the little adventure that we have all been a part of, " he turned to look into each of their faces with a smile, and continued. "I shall confess to you that Marcus was indeed the man who owned the wine, which comprised the major part of the cargo. However, the cork which has served me so well in making his amphorae secure, was unloaded earlier this morning, and belongs to another client whose warehouse is up in Cyrene."

Rufus then explained to the captain how he had recognized Damian from the previous evening, when the latter had brought the donkey cart to pick up the Marcus family.

Fully satisfied with the day's progress despite his pessimistic attitude that morning, Simon settled with Marius the last item on his list. The type of wood to be used on the project; which was to be Lebanon cedar. Father and sons, then departed on their quest for the materials needed to enable them to start the work next morning; leaving the captain to his thoughts.

Marius found himself with time to think whilst he kept an eye on the unloading of the cargo which seemed endless.

'A nice family,' he thought, as his eyes followed the carpenters down the gang plank. 'It is a fortunate man who can depend on two strong sons and have such a beautiful wife and daughters. The gods have favoured him well. I do envy him that. But I cannot help liking the man for his openness, and perhaps even honesty. Still, he is a Jew, and as such, a shrewd business man. I shall have to watch him for a while till I am convinced of his sincerity.'

Marius was in his mid forties. A bachelor; gentle in nature, self confident as bachelors tend to be, somewhat suspicious in his assessment of people, but willing to give the benefit of the doubt whenever his feelings warranted it. He was a tall man; distinguishable when not wearing a hat by a crop of unruly curly light brown hair, which seemed to be parted by a greying band running uninterruptedly from the centre of his forehead to the back of his head. There it intermingled with thick curls that covered his neck. He was firmly built, and rugged in appearance as attested by the weather-worn condition of his skin. His eyes were blue and had a lively and engaging aspect about them. His large, but well formed Roman nose, was the most prominent of his facial features, and drew, by the straightness of its lines, attention to his thin lipped mouth that, when laughing, displayed a set of reasonably healthy teeth.

He had had a hard life in his earlier years as he endeavoured to rise through the marine ranks which ultimately gave him the command of ships. By frugal and sober living, clever dealings and dedicated work, he managed at last to own his beloved *Stella Maris.* Having acquired it only three years earlier as the result of a good bargain.

'I hope this new cabin will allow me to pay off my loan, and then she will be completely mine,' he thought. Not out of avarice, but as a sense of pride and achievement.

'But for who's benefit? I have no one to leave my money to when I am gone. I cannot stand the thought of getting married and being pinned down on land. The sea is my land, and its salt, the elixir of my life. Still,' he continued to muse, ' what would happen to me if through sickness or accident I were unable to work? I am no longer a youngster.'

"You over there! be more careful," he yelled, as he was rudely pulled out of his daydream by one of the workers, who almost dropped an amphora.

He adjusted his hat, took some dates from his tunic, put one in his mouth, and chewed away contentedly continuing to muse.

'Well then, if illness forces me to sell my ship, I shall at least have money to purchase a little house by the sea. And if I am lucky, find myself a good woman to look after me.'

Evening came, and still the unloading continued. The fast pace of the work slowed down somewhat as the men tired despite Damian's efforts to the contrary. Even so, the uninterrupted unloading continued. Each cart once loaded with amphorae was driven to a nearby warehouse, emptied, and driven away as another arrived. It would have been obvious to any bystander, that this well oiled operation had been performed many times before and would account for its impressive efficiency; reflecting good managerial skills.

It was dusk once again as father and sons made their way home. They had on second thought retrieved their box of tools, since they had the wood for the mast in the cart, and knew that they could best work on it in their shop. There, with its work tables, clamps, and other necessary tools, they would work in comfort, shaping and smoothening the mast in readiness for the ironwork.

Letitia had been uneasy and fidgety all day. The best part of the morning had been spent in the garden, picking flowers for the crowning of Venus in thanksgiving for her father's life, and praying to her for his speedy recovery.

Tecuno had obediently waded into the pool, and set the fresh, fragrant flowers on the venerated statue's head. Time after time she had fought the temptation of walking to the gate, even though she knew that Rufus would be working, and the likelihood of his coming during the day was small. She did not want to arouse suspicion in either her mother, or the women servants. As a result, she had spent the afternoon with her father, singing to him softly, and accompanying herself on the lyre, which she played with ease and great feeling; thinking all the while of her lover.

Marcus, who was showing no improvement thus far, and was confined to his bed following the physician's advice, listened to his daughter's voice with moistened eyes but devoid of any other form of expression on his catatonic face.

"Letitia!" called her mother from the peristyle. "Please get ready for your cena. I shall be there presently to stay with your father."

Mother and daughter passed each other as they traversed the elegantly landscaped peristyle. Letitia, made her way to the daily dining room, and Julia, to her bedroom to be with her husband.

"Silia has cooked an excellent mullet stew with garum and shrimp for our cena," said Julia, as she passed her daughter. "I shall have some later." And so saying she stepped over the solitary step that divided the peristyle from the floor of the house, and disappeared into her bedroom where her husband lay.

The multi-colonnaded peristyle, with its many potted plants, manicured trees, and central impluvium, (pool and water cistern) presented a habitual feast for the eyes, and was the preferred living space of the house. Especially in the evening, as was the case in many Roman homes. The more formal atrium being used for the entertainment of guests, and business functions.

The little dining room that Letitia walked into, was the room that the family used daily when they dined alone. It was an exceptionally well appointed room with profusely decorated walls, depicting a seascape with boats, and fishermen, in vivid colours running all around the room. This colourful mural was separated from the floor by a continuous wainscot of "faux" black and red marble, giving a realistic impression of solidity to the walls. Both wainscot, and mural, were interrupted at each corner of the room by painted double black marble columns with composite capitals and corresponding bases. They extended from floor to underside of a continuous faux architrave which they seemed to support.

The ceiling was painted to imitate a blue sky animated by feathery clouds seen through faux trellising. From this trellising hung realistically rendered bunches of grapes intermingling with their leaves and coming alive with their dominant deep blues and vivid greens. Finally, the whole room, devoid of windows, was lit by a large brass lamp hanging directly over the table, and though a trifle large for the room, somehow melted into its surroundings; its eight flames endowing the little room with a fantastic atmosphere. Two doors, which cut through the mural were framed by faux black marble moulding in keeping with the columns. The floor, of polished black marble with a red marble border circumscribing the room, beautifully complemented the colourful murals.

Into this world of fantasy entered Letitia in a most familiar manner, oblivious of her beauty's contribution to the aesthetics of that little room. She sat on a chair that Silia had pulled back for her; one of the six backless chairs that surrounded a highly glazed cedar wood table dramatically lit by the lamp which gave the room its magical ambience.

Her cena was promptly served by the slave. She brought her mistress that delectable dish that her mother had promised as they passed each other in the peristyle, and which was unquestionably Letitia's favourite.

"We were very fortunate to find some of this wonderful mackerel garum my lady," said the Egyptian slave with a triumphant tone in her voice.

"I brought home the very last jar."

Her young mistress tasted the fish, smiled, and nodded approvingly.

"Lovely!" she said; sending a wave of satisfaction through the cook's diminutive frame. "You are a great cook Silia."

"Have some wine with it my lady," suggested Silia dismissing the complement. She picked up a small silver jug from the sideboard behind her, and approached the table.

"Well, perhaps just a little. Did you put some water in it?"

"Yes, of course my lady. I know how you dislike strong wine."

"The figs are as ripe and sweet as can be," coaxed Silia. "You really must try them. You know how good they are for your complexion."

"I shall try one, but I am really not very hungry," conceded the young mistress.

"You may go now," concluded Letitia of a sudden with girlish impertinence. She wanted to be left in peace, her mind suddenly carrying her back to Rufus. She wondered once more if she would see him that evening. It would soon be dusk, and then she would go down to the gate and wait for him for a while. Tecuno would be there, but he would not betray her, of that she was certain.

'Silia was right, the figs were excellent,' mused Letitia, taking two, and walking away into the atrium.

She finished eating the one she had in her hand, and took the other one with her out to the garden, eating it as she made her way to the gate.

'Oh!' she thought as she walked, 'suppose he does not come?'

"I refuse to think about his not coming," she said impetuously to herself. "I shall go and pray to Venus." Turning around, she headed for the pool.

Letitia, being an only child of wealthy parents, who had indulged her in every way, and being the fair haired beauty that she was, had never had a problem in obtaining her wishes. Despite her having laudable qualities and virtues, her one fault if one could call it that, was her impatience. One, however, would wonder if boredom was not the real cause of that impatience. She spent most of her days alone. Her best friend Saturnia, had gone to Hispania with her family; her father being a high official had been posted there for a term of at least three years. Her other friends from her younger days were all in Rome. So really, she had no close friends her age. That, made her keen to see Rufus again not only for his own sake, for she was very much in love with him, but to continue her friendship with his sisters as well.

Having finished her prayers to Venus, Letitia once more headed for the gate which appeared to be deserted. No one was there as yet it seemed, not even Tecuno. As she reached it however, she spotted him pulling up some weeds from a flowerbed hidden behind some small trees that stood nearby.

"Good evening my lady," said the Nubian. " A beautiful evening, is it not?"

"It is, and we shall have a full moon tonight," she answered, anxiously looking out through one of the two grates that allowed some visibility through the massive wooden gate.

She pressed her head against the bars straining to get a view around the corner of the street in the direction from which her lover would be coming. A deep blue shawl or 'palla' hung back on her head, emphasizing the tuft of golden hair which had escaped its hold and hung gracefully over her brow drawing attention to her soft blue eyes. Eyes which were at the moment racked by uncertainty, as was readily apparent by the complementing pout of her full red lips involuntarily betraying her concern.

Tecuno noticed the look of anxiety on his mistress's face and drawing nearer her, said in an encouraging low voice:

"Your young friend is surely delayed, but he will come."

Letitia, who had not realized the length of time that she had lingered at the gate lost in her thoughts, turned abruptly, faced the slave with a guilty expression on her face, and recovering herself, quickly started to move away in the direction of the house. She had not taken four steps, however, when the sound of a horse's hooves reached her expectant ears, and turning around precipitously went back to the gate.

The black slave melted quickly into the dusk and made his way to the house. On entering, he was accosted by Silia, who enquired as to her mistress' whereabouts.

"She is at the gate," he answered.

Her large black Egyptian eyes gave him an enquiring look.

"Be sure to look all around the garden first before you find her," he continued, giving her a wink as he walked past her and into the house.

Letitia's heart leapt within her as the phantom horse and rider materialized outside the gate before her eyes. The rider, no other than our hero Rufus, dismounted and went swiftly to her. Two pairs of young hands clutched each other through the grating, and two sets of lips bonded in joyful triumph their faces pressing against the iron bars.

"I thought you would never come," sighed Letitia with another of her bewitching pouts, which this time produced the desired effect as Rufus' guilty face attested.

"I am so sorry my love," murmured Rufus. "I was delayed at my 'arms drill,' which dragged on tonight and has made me so late. See! I still have my weapon with me," he continued, pointing at the short Roman gladius in the scabbard that hung from his belt.

"Oh, you are bleeding!" she exclaimed; a small wound in his arm catching her attention.

"Ah, that's nothing," he said, and pulling out a small piece of cloth from his tunic he pressed it against the wound, and quickly put it away again.

"Come, give me your arm," she said with a slight nervousness in her voice, and taking out a small perfumed handkerchief from her stolla. She tenderly placed it over the superficial wound and tied it around his arm.

"Be sure to bathe it as soon as you get home," she admonished with a hint of desperation in her voice..

"Will you come tomorrow?"

"I certainly want to, but I'm not sure. We have a lot of work to do on the ship. The captain wants to leave as soon as possible."

"Incidentally, I saw Damian directing the unloading of the wine amphorae. I did not know the cargo belonged to your father."

"Yes, that is..."

"My lady!"

The voice of Silia interrupted Letitia's words in mid delivery.

"My apologies to you both, but my lady your mother, is likely to appear any time as I have already taken some time finding you," continued the slave, looking at her mistress with a look of urgency and waiting for her to follow.

"Good night Rufus! it was so good of you to come," said Letitia in a formal tone. She meaningfully pressed his hand, and turned to follow Silia into the house.

"Good night to you both," answered Rufus, watching with adoring eyes the departing object of his love.

One last time she turned and waved to him as he mounted Pepper and trotted off.

CHAPTER FIVE

AN INSISTENT FEELING

Rufus returned directly home after his rendezvous with Letitia. The family had already finished their supper. Ruth, anxiously awaiting his return, and suspecting the reason for his tardiness, quickly returned to the kitchen as he walked in the door. He greeted his sisters who were engrossed in a conversation, no doubt regarding his activities.

"Welcome, family soldier," teased Lucila, noticing the sword hanging from his side. "What battle have you come from?"

Her brother smiled tolerantly. His handsome face and intelligent brown eyes glaring suspiciously. Lucila, contemplated him with marked curiosity in her lively and similar but more thickly eye-lashed eyes.

Just then, Ruth appeared. She crossed the room, and giving Lucila a forbidding look, kissed her son, and said. "Go do your ablutions whilst I finish heating up your supper." With that, she walked back into the kitchen; Lucila following.

Rufus took his belt off, and as did, the sword and scabbard fell on the floor. He stooped, picked it up, put it on a table close to where Rachel was quietly sitting, and walked off to the ablutions. He took a lighted lamp from the wall bracket beside the back door as he passed.

Rachel, who had been following her brother's movements with admiring eyes, noticed that something had fallen from his tunic as he left the room, and she hastened to pick it up. It was a piece of cloth, which on closer scrutiny as she drew nearer to one of the lamps, was actually a handkerchief and appeared to be blood stained.

Alarmed at the sight of the blood, she ran to the kitchen and gave it to her mother. She, after examining it and confirming Rachel's suspicion, was surprised by the perfume it exuded.

Lucila, having also smelt it gave it back to Rachel saying:

"I'm pretty certain that this is Letitia's perfume."

At this point the women became more alarmed by the presence of the blood stains which appeared to be fresh, than they were about the source of the perfume. Lucila's eyes lost their joviality and took on a more sober look.

Rachel looked at her mother as if asking:

'What do we do now?'

They all awaited Rufus' return to see his wound, which they naturally imagined worse than it actually turned out to be. As the 'family soldier' walked back into the room, all three women converged on him simultaneously asking what had occurred and demanding to see his wound.

Rufus was taken aback by this eager confrontation, and realised when he saw Letitia's kerchief in Rachel's hand, that the 'cat was out of the bag.'

"I'm fine," he began, taking a seat beside one of the tables. "It is only a scratch that I got at sword practice. See here!"

He showed them his arm, which had finally stopped bleeding. Relief showed on all three female faces.

"I'll get you your food," said Ruth going once more into the kitchen.

She returned immediately with a steaming earthenware casserole and a big chunk of bread, which she placed in front of him.

"Get your brother some wine," said Ruth addressing Lucila, whose eyes were once again signalling that jovial mood.

The two sisters playfully slumped down on the floor hemming their apprehensive brother in, and impishly staring straight into his face. Ruth burst out laughing as she beheld the picture.

"Where are father and Alexander?" asked Rufus as if crying for help. He picked up his cup and gulped down some of the wine his sister had just placed in front of him.

Unfortunately, for Rufus, no help was about to materialise, and he had to explain things as best he thought.

His amorous involvement once confessed came as no surprise to the women of the house. His sisters hugged, and kissed him with sincerity and a little playfulness. Ruth, however, though she smiled lovingly at her young son, felt a certain discomfort at the tidings. She tried to appease her uneasiness by questioning him with regard to Marcus' state of health. She then retired to the kitchen, leaving the young ones to entertain themselves.

The evening spent itself pleasantly for the family. Simon and Alexander had the story of Rufus' adventures related to them with enthusiasm by Lucila, who was beside herself with excitement. Soon, the time for all to retire for the night arrived, and the house once again took on its habitual peaceful state.

Ruth, felt perturbed. An hour after having got to bed she awoke, and turned to cuddle up to her husband for moral support. To her great surprise, he was not there. She got up, stepped into her slippers, pulled down a long shawl from the hook on the wall near the bed, wrapped it around herself, and with a light step proceeded to check all the rooms.

"Simon! Simon!" she whispered.

He was nowhere to be found. She began to feel a little anxious.

'Perhaps,' she thought, 'he is in the toilet.'

She took the lamp which burnt all night by the back door and stepped out into the garden, gently closing the door behind her. There was no light coming from the toilet at the back of the garden.

'There's a full moon tonight," she said to herself. "He probably did not need any.'

She heard a cough, coming from the terrace it seemed. Lamp in hand, she climbed the stairs. There he was; standing at the terrace wall looking wistfully out to sea.

"Simon, what is the matter?" she asked. "Are you not feeling well?"

"Hello my love," he replied, turning to her. "I'm sorry to have disturbed you."

She had left the lamp on the post at the top of the stairs, but by the light of the moon she could see the gleam of tears in his eyes, and her heart fell.

'Simon is a tough man,' she thought. 'Strong in every way, and even obstinate at times."

His strong features breathed of confidence and manliness. A determined chin hid under his square jaw and was covered by a short dark brown beard. As he turned and looked again out to sea, Ruth silently admired his familiar profile. His nose, somewhere between Roman and Jewish, sat over a well cropped moustache and his beard framed his large, thin lipped mouth, complementing his face and giving it strength.

He faced her once more. His dark honest eyes, which she knew were incapable of hiding his emotions from her, expressed deep sadness. Now, as she looked at him in the moonlight, his eyes moistened and gleamed, and she knew that something was very far wrong.

'It must concern the family, for only then does his tough nature melt like butter...Yes, it must be Rufus' predicament that has upset him.'

"Is it to do with Rufus and Letitia?" she asked.

"No my dear, it has nothing to do with them. Though there could be some problems there a little down the road."

"What is it then, that has upset you so?"

He turned towards her, took her still beautiful face in his large hands, and with more tears in his eyes which completely unnerved her, he said:

"I have to leave you for a while, I must go back to Judea. Back to Jerusalem. I'm experiencing the same feeling as when Yeshua looked at me during his third fall, and now beckons me there."

She crumbled into his arms as a faintness gripped her. Here she was, barely forty years old, and most happily married to this wonderful man since she was Rufus' age. Now, in the prime of their lives with their darling children at an age when they needed their father more than ever, he was going to risk another two sea trips, and God knows what troubles in between, because he had been 'bewitched' (what other word could she use) by a dead man who no longer existed.

"Oh, Simon! Simon!" she cried through her tears. "Must you go?"

"Yes, my love! If I do not go, I shall never be able to live with myself. Remember what I told you at Mordecai's house. Yeshua claimed to be the son of God, the son of our beloved Yahweh, and the Messiah. How can I ignore this, and not try to find out more about his life?"

Ruth's sensational eyes searched those of her husband. Hers' were the eyes that Rachel had inherited along with the black hair and most other features. Simon who was her senior by just one year, was entertaining similar regrets as he looked at his wife in the moonlight. His stomach cramped at the thought of leaving her even temporarily. He had every intention of returning home within a couple of months at most.

"Let's to bed," he said putting his arm around her, gently leading her towards the stairs and retrieving the burning lamp as they passed on their way down.

Ruth and Simon lay in bed in a loving embrace; their bodies at peace, whilst their minds were in turmoil amidst a storm of thoughts that gave them no mental rest.

"Darling," whispered Simon, caressing her hair.

"Yes, Simon," she answered, lost in her own dreams.

"I want you to think back to the gale that accosted us onboard ship."

"I would rather not think of it," she replied as she cleared her mind and listened to her husband.

"Do you remember how suddenly the storm abated?"

"It lasted long enough for me…but…yes, since you mention it, I remember it did stop rather abruptly, thank God."

"I'll tell you something which I have kept even from you my love, as it would appear incredible to anyone. Do you remember the parchment I showed you and asked that you keep it a secret from everyone?"

"Yes."

"You know, Ruth, that I'd never lie to you. Keep some things from you at times? Yes, but I have never, and will never, really lie to you my very dearest."

"I know full well," she assured him.

He then recounted the calming of the storm, and pointed out that no one had heard his cry for help.

They lay in silence for a short while. Ruth's mind absorbed and digested what her husband had told her, and understood with great awe, that there had been a singular and divine intervention with the power to change lives.

"Now I understand," she said.

There was a touch of reverence in her voice as she cuddled up to Simon and kissed his cheek tenderly.

Morning broke to find this loving couple asleep at last in each other's arms after a long and restless night. As the early morning's rays beamed softly through the cracks in the shutters, Ruth, gently and silently drew away from her husband. She stepped into her red Arabian slippers and made her way through the house as was her habit, waking up her girls first, and then the boys.

"Where is father?" asked Alexander, as he threw a towel over his shoulder.

His naked, muscular torso caught his sisters' attention as they made for their toilette. Ruth, joined them, and as she passed, told the boys that Simon would be with them presently at the ablutions.

Simon however, was still asleep. Ruth re-entered the bedroom and approached the bed. She gently shook him, woke him up, and told him that the children were all back from their ablutions and were having their breakfast.

"Why did you let me sleep in woman?" he roared, jumping out of bed, and hurriedly beginning to dress.

"You needed that little extra sleep," she said as their eyes met.

"I have a lot of work to do today," he said with exasperation, and vanishing from her sight, ran through the family room ignoring everyone and disappeared out the back door.

"We shall have to watch our step today," warned Rufus as his father slammed the door.

The usual morning chatter was markedly absent from the room as the children exchanged looks and enquired of each other in hushed tones, the cause of their father's behaviour. Ruth, who was now to be found in the kitchen awaiting Simon's return, wondered what explanation she could give the girls in particular for their father's unusual mood. On reconsidering, and knowing her husband would hardly keep quiet, she opted to say nothing. 'Let him disentangle the web of intrigue that he had spun,' she thought, smiling to herself.

"Your mother decided to give me a holiday!" He blurted out sarcastically, on re-entering the room where they were all finishing their breakfast.

"With all the work awaiting us today she let me sleep in. Can you imagine?"

Ruth floated quietly into the room avoiding his accusing look. She placed his food and drink on the table in front of him, turned, and without saying a word, made her way back to the kitchen.

"You two go, open the shop, and start work on the planks for the cabin!" snapped the irate father at his boys. "I'll start on the mast as soon as I'm finished here."

As their brothers left, the girls rose and began clearing the tables around their unhappy father, who sat eating his meal in a precipitous manner. Not a sound emanated from the kitchen as the girls kept their mother company; all three women sharing a sympathetic visual conversation. Soon, the sound of the door firmly closing announced that Simon had left.

"So what was that all about?" asked Lucila as Rachel's lovely eyes also sought her mother's with a questioning expression.

"Nothing really," answered Ruth. "Your father was unhappy because I let him sleep in as he had had a very disturbed night. But he will have got over his little temper display by lunch time I am sure."

"Father is so touchy at times," stated Rachel with a tone of regret in her raspy voice.

"Later on, I shall go and cheer him up," declared Lucila. "It never takes him long to come around."

A look of certainty evident in her vivacious brown eyes displayed womanly confidence in her remark, rather than her usual girlish coquettishness.

By midday the mast was ready. Simon took out the old brown horse who bore the rather insipid name of Topo, hitched him to the cart, and putting some tools in the long box, left the boys to work on the cabin, and started down towards Apollonia.

Late afternoon, found the tired carpenter urging Topo back up the hill on his way home.

'Well! That gets the mast, and all the little repairs out of the way,' he mused to himself. 'Marius seemed quite satisfied with the blacksmith's work...And mine. His sailors will be kept busy for a while with the rigging of that new mast, but that's their problem. I'm surprised though at his enthusiasm regarding the new cabin; he's like boy anticipating his birthday.'

He dismounted and walked beside the old horse. The animal was having trouble pulling the cart up the hill with him in it.

'Alexander and Rufus, will have made good progress today I'm sure. For the next two days whilst the ship is being loaded with all that grain, we'll work from home. The job should be job finished in three days at the most. The sooner the *Stella* sails, the sooner I'll get to Jerusalem and back.'

Simon continued with his thoughts as Topo, continued laboriously, to climb the hill that he knew so well.

'Mordecai is going to be very surprised to see me again so soon. Hmm... I wonder if I should tell him why I'm really returning to Jerusalem until I'm certain myself. In fact, maybe I shouldn't even let him know when I'm there.'

His thoughts ran on.

'I must make it up to Ruth for my being so cutting this morning. She only did it for my sake, so that my head would have a little more rest after last night. What an unselfish person she is. She probably got less sleep than I did, and then had to contend with my bad temper. Poor soul, I'm really going to miss her.'

Simon's impulsive nature presented his actions in a bad light on many occasions. His quick reaction to disagreeable situations got him into trouble which he very quickly regretted. If angered, violence would hardly be an automatic response. He was mild tempered, but with a strong sense of personal justice (not always justified) which when violated in any way would produce a quick reaction, and verbal condemnation. Sincere apologies for his hasty behaviour, usually followed by word or deed. Those who knew him would simply wait; restitution would soon follow.

By now the house was in sight, and as soon as Simon walked in the door, the women came to greet him; Ruth, leading the bunch. She embraced her husband with a knowing smile, as he, with a look of repentance in his eyes reciprocated. He gave her a kiss as well, for good measure.

The two boys appeared, and taking their father by the arm, led him to the shop to get his approval on their day's work.

* * * * * *

The following two days passed without incident. The woodwork progressed at a good pace until all came to a standstill the evening of the third day, as the family celebrated the beginning of the Sabbath.

As was their custom, they attended the local synagogue, which was within walking distance of their house, and half way down the hill to Apollonia. It was after the morning service, as the family made their way home, that Rachel told them that she had seen the stout man who had travelled with them on the *Stella Maris,* and who had kept to himself all through the passage.

"Did he see you?" asked Simon.

"I am sure he did, but bade me no salutation," she answered.

"Strange man," said Ruth. "I don't like him."

Nothing further was said with regard to the so called stout man, whom as you my dear reader will remember, was known to us as the 'independent' man, and who was briefly described as he disembarked from the *Stella Maris*. He now captures our attention once again, as he, leaning against a tree just outside the synagogue, followed Simon and family with a cold and deliberate gaze.

Having now confirmed that Simon was a practicing Jew, (for his interest lay solely in Simon), he walked back into the synagogue to find out more about him from the local rabbi. He found the rabbi sitting on a stone bench in the shaded part of a pretty little garden adjoining the building; his prayer shawl over his shoulders, and contemplating a serene little pool surrounded by a colourful array of potted flowers.

"Good morning to you Rabbi," he said forcing a smile.

The holy man looked up and saluted him with true cordiality.

"Good morning and blessings to you my friend. How can I be of service?"

"I would merely like to know more about a man who attended your morning service."

"Can you describe the man?" asked the rabbi innocently, with a willingness to be of help.

"He is taller than average, well built, with a short beard and a cropped moustache. He has a wife, two sons and two daughters. His occupation I do not know."

"Your description fits Simon the carpenter. His sons are also carpenters. They have done quite a bit of work here in the synagogue over the years. He is a very fine man, and has a lovely family, quite the pride of the neighbourhood," confirmed the old rabbi with enthusiasm, stroking his long white beard and thinking of his friend.

"May I be permitted to learn the reason for your enquiry?"

"I was merely curious," answered the stranger. "He, and his family, were fellow passengers on a sea voyage recently, but we never spoke to one another. I thank you sincerely for your information. Enjoy the day/"

He turned and walked away. The rabbi was not happy with the answer he had got, nor was he impressed by the person who had asked the questions. He made a mental note to mention to Simon his meeting with the stranger who had not even given his name.

The stranger's name was Jechonias; a Pharisee from Jerusalem. He had been employed by the Sanhedrin to persecute the disciples of Yeshua. He had decided to follow Simon, whom he had seen mingling with Yeshua's followers after the crucifixion, and even helping them with the dismounting of the body from the cross.

Jechonias was actually one of the group that accompanied the soldiers to the Garden of Gethsemane when they arrested Yeshua. Like most Pharisees he had hated Yeshua, whom he had once tried to trick, and had been thoroughly humiliated by the young rabbi's answer in front of a crowd of people. Now his hatred was transferred to Yeshua's disciples and followers, particularly Simon. The Sanhedrin meant to keep watch on all the Galilean's followers, considering them to be trouble makers. Jechonias however, had developed a phobic hatred for Simon in particular, for no logical reason stemming back to the crucifixion of Yeshua, and the fact that Simon had helped with the carrying of the cross.

'I shall keep an eye on this fellow. He will not escape me,' Jechonias promised himself. 'If he starts his preaching here, I shall be back with help, and we will put an end to him before he can spread his poison to these local Jews who have not as yet heard of the Galilean. I was a bit of a fool asking that old rabbi for information; I had no idea he was a friend of his. I shall have to keep away from that synagogue in the future. The synagogue up at Cyrene will have to be my place of worship.'

The Sabbath day passed peacefully, and prayerfully at Simon's house. Rufus was the only one who impatiently awaited the morrow. He could not take out Pepper on the Sabbath, as Letitia's house was beyond the permissible Sabbath travel distance.

The following morning, which opened a new week, found Simon's family involved in their usual routine. The men were in the shop working to get their project completed and installed on the *Stella*.

"How are things coming along, Alexander?" asked Simon.

"Most of the cutting is now completed, as per the templates," answered his son. "If you are free to give us a hand Father, we can start assembling and numbering them."

"You mean that we are going to build the cabin here?" asked Rufus incredulously.

"Only in sections," replied his brother with a confident tone.

They all busied themselves once again, and the work continued all day till dusk when Rachel came to fetch them for supper.

"One more day, and we are done here," assured Alexander as they walked into the house to prepare for their meal.

* * * * * *

In the meantime on board the *Stella*, Marius sat on deck with his two mariners also having their 'cena.' They had brought it in from a shop near the quay where they obtained their meals every day.

"Tomorrow, hopefully, we shall see the end of the loading since they refused to continue tonight," said the captain. "These people are not as well organized as those of Marcus."

"If those carpenters finish this week we shall be in good shape," said Lucius the helmsman, with his mouth full.

"This time we are bound for Joppa," remarked Marius. "The trip will be shorter by at least three days if the weather remains good and the winds favour us."

"Jason," said the captain addressing his mate. "You will have to supervise the loading tomorrow morning, as I shall be going up to Simon's house to see how they are progressing."

"Very well Captain," answered the sailor with a touch of pride.

The following morning Marius paid a surprise visit to Simon. He had been given a future invitation by the carpenter; specifically when the work was installed. But he could not wait. He simply had to see how the work for the cabin was progressing.

He was received with great cordiality and shown the work; some of which had been assembled. It pleased him greatly, which made everyone happy. And even happier when Ruth served them all a delicious lunch upstairs on the terrace under the cool shade of the reed canopy. It was agreed that the following day the assembling of the work would start on board ship, and away went Marius; more pleased than anyone had a right to be in this cruel and problematic world.

"Stella Maris bound for Joppa, will sail very soon."

So read the sign that was hanging on the side of the ship. It was written in Latin and Greek. Marius, on approaching it as he returned, smiled and thought how possibly by 'Dies Joves'(or the fifth day of the week, and Simon would have called it) he could include the actual day of departure. He was itching to get out to sea again.

He suddenly had the sensation that he was being watched. Turning quickly, he managed to catch sight of someone's shadow, its owner disappearing behind the building opposite the ship.

"Ah!" blurted out Marius. "Why would anyone be spying on me?"

He mounted the gang plank, joining the flow of labourers which were carrying their heavy grain bags into the ship's hold.

'I must put something on that sign that tells people that I have this new facility,' he pondered as his mind flashed back to the departure sign. 'What shall I call it ?'

He removed his cap and scratched his head as he mused.

'Passenger cabin perhaps might do… Hmm…'

'Two-bed passenger cabin' would be better. It entices a couple, maybe even a newlywed couple by ensuring them some privacy.'

He laughed to himself.

'Would that not be fancy? The *Stella Maris*, a honeymoon ship.' Ha! Ha! Ha!"

This time he laughed aloud. Lucius, the short, powerfully built helmsman looked straight at him and was instantly infected by Marius' joviality.

"What's so funny?" he asked as the captain put a hand on his shoulder and gave it a squeeze.

"This is going to be a honeymoon ship," said the latter quite taken by the thought.

Merry tears ran down his face as he laughed.

"A what?"

"A honeymoon ship! A honeymoon ship!" repeated the captain doubling over with laughter.

"Are you getting married, chief?"

"Certainly not!" came the quick and defensive reply.

"Then?"

"Come," he said, "I need a drink!"

And throwing his arm around his mate's broad shoulders he led him towards his cabin.

"Ahoy there!" called a voice from the wharf. "Ahoy there!"

Marius, wine cup in hand, left Lucius in a reverie regarding the new cabin, and went across the deck to the port side in response to the yelled enquiry.

"When will you sail?" asked a boy from below.

"Will you be sailing with us?" asked the captain.

"No, but my parents might," answered the boy, lying.

Jechonias, who had sent him, anxiously watched from his hidden vantage point.

"I cannot tell you as yet, but come back in five days, and I shall be in a better position to tell you then."

The boy, possibly twelve years of age and dressed very shabbily at that, made Marius somewhat suspicious.

'Why would his father not have come? And he made no enquiry regarding the cost of the passage as is more usual…'

Dismissing the whole episode, the captain took another sip of his wine and returned to continue his unfinished story in the cabin where Lucius eagerly awaited him.

The cargo had been loaded at last, and the new day had just begun. Simon, Alexander and Rufus, arrived at the ship; their cart laden with all the new cabin's components ready for assembly. Marius and Lucius, were there to greet the carpenters.

"Ah! The big day finally arrives!" cheered Marius as the three stepped on deck.

The two excited sailors helped Simon and the boys unload their cart, and got out of their way so as not to hinder the carpenters' progress.

"I have to see about some money," announced the captain to Lucius, his helmsman. "I shall return by lunch time. I'll bring you, and Jason some lunch."

So saying, Marius departed, leaving the carpenters to do their work in peace. By the time he returned, the four walls of the cabin were up, secured to the deck, and the roof was half finished.

"We've spent a good bit of time securing it and applying the pitch all around," said Simon. "We will soon test its efficiency with regard to water proofing."

As he spoke, he continued to fan the fire under the iron pot, where the pitch was being melted for the water-proofing of the joints.

"After what we went through on our last trip, we will make very sure that the water is kept out of this cabin," assured Simon.

As the day progressed, the shutter was fitted onto the small window, and the cleverly designed door was hung to fit over a palm-high threshold. It opened to the outside on large iron hinges. The exterior face of the door opened against the wind coming from the bow of the ship and acted as a shield. An iron latch installed on the inside of the door ensured a tight fit, as it compressed a rope that was fitted all around the inside edge to keep the water out.

With the shell of the cabin completed, the pitching began in earnest. Father, sons, and even Jason, who had enjoyed watching the work progress, applied the hot pitch to the exposed joints, with particular attention to those on the roof.

Once more, the horses pulled the cart up the familiar route. The two boys walked alongside to lighten the load, as their father sat in the cart, reins in his hands, allowing his back a needed rest.

An unobtrusive and sinister figure watched from a distance in the dusk of the evening, as the three carpenters began their ascent homewards.

* * * * * *

As had been her habit since her last *tête-à-tête* with her lover, Letitia stood at the gate in the hope that he would come. She had many questions to ask him. The abruptness of their last meeting however, had precluded her extending him her invitation to his sisters, whom she was most eager to see and spend time with.

Tecuno had kept her company during her daily visits to the gate, having done his best to cheer her up. That evening, as she stood there, he tried once again to reassure her that Rufus' absence that day had simply been due to his religious customs.

"He's a Jew," he said plainly. "The laws of the Sabbath don't permit him to travel outside a stipulated distance. Your house is probably too far away."

The mentioning of the Sabbath brought an unpleasant thought into Letitia's head. The sudden realization that Rufus was a Jew entered intrepidly into her consciousness.

'But I knew this all along,' she said to herself. 'Why do I suddenly feel this discomfort? He certainly does not look Jewish… His beautiful face, with such perfect features; the nose that could well be a Roman nose; that sensitive thin lipped mouth devoid of moustache; that short light brown beard; that wonderful untamed mop of curly hair… And those incredible eyes full of merriment and love."

She continued with her attempts to persuade herself.

'Why does this disturb me? He even resembled a Roman soldier with that sword hanging from his belt, and what a physique he has. So tall and strong.'

She was lost in these thoughts as she walked slowly away from the gate, and resigned herself once more to her solitude. Tecuno watched her with a touch of sadness in his heart, for he adored his amiable young mistress. If he could find the time, he would go to the wharf the following day and see if he could find Rufus, for whom he had taken a liking.

'Damian said that he had seen him and his father and brother surveying the ship's damages," he told himself. "Chances are they are involved in repairs to the ship.'

Supper had been served and eaten at the house of Simon. The girls, after having helped their mother to clear up for the night, were enjoying themselves playing a game of beads with her and Alexander. Simon sat nearby in the corner of the room resting on a bunch of cushions; his eyes closed, soberly entertaining his own thoughts.

"I am off to David's," announced Rufus as he made for the door.

A short spell later, the clatter of a horse's hooves were heard, and slowly died away in the night.

'It's too late to go down there tonight,' thought Rufus as he rode Pepper to David's house.

'But wait a moment… Tecuno will probably be at the gate. He spends a lot of time there. Maybe David will accompany me if he does not mind harnessing his horse.'

And so our young enamoured hero arrived at his friend's house, and acquainted him with his intentions. After a little coaxing, David (who had harnessed his horse on two previous occasions that day) finally acceded to his friend's request.

"I shall do the same for you some day," assured Rufus with a bargaining tone.

Off went the pair down the hill and soon rounded the final corner which hid Letitia's gate. Tecuno, as luck would have it, still sat near the gate. He stood up quickly as the two horses arrived. His face, pressed against the iron gate, beamed with a cordial smile, and a sigh of relief escaped him as he greeted Rufus, who dismounting, approached leading his horse.

"Greetings Tecuno," began Rufus casting a warm smile at the slave.

"My greetings to you and your friend," answered Tecuno.

"I would like you to give my humble apologies to your young mistress, and tell her that it has been impossible for me to see her these last two days. I have been working on the *Stella Maris*, which is the ship she and I travelled on recently. We are carrying out an extensive renovation and damage repair. My father has been in need of my help constantly," he explained.

"Is there any improvement in her father's health?"

"No young master, I am sorry to say."

"Please tell her that unless something unforeseen occurs, I shall come to see her tomorrow. We have almost completed the work, and it is possible that I may be able to get away in the afternoon instead of at dusk."

"She will be very relieved and happy when I give her your message," assured the slave.

Goodnight wishes were then exchanged, and Rufus remounting Pepper once more, rode off into the night with his friend. The Nubian directed his steps towards the house to secretly deliver his message.

The house was deserted. The *cena* had long been concluded, and it was immediately apparent to Tecuno that the family had retired to their chambers for the night. Low voices could be heard in the direction of the kitchen, as he passed through the atrium, and onto the peristyle. He decided to join them and await developments as the evening progressed.

"Sailing soon, probably by the end of the week."

The voice of Damian sounded in Tecuno's ears as he entered the room.

"Tomorrow I shall have to take the money for the cargo passage to the captain," he announced with an air of responsibility that impressed his colleagues.

Damian was a small man, fifty two years of age though looking younger. He was a Roman, and as such, a free man. He had rather small but vivacious eyes, a pudgy nose, and a pleasant full lipped mouth with some missing teeth. Being aware of the condition of his teeth, he rarely laughed openly, but sustained a smile which kept pace with others' laughter with convincing effect. He had a habit of stuttering in the presence of his superiors, but never when he spoke to his equals or inferiors. He had been with the Tricius family since his youth and had been educated by the benevolence of Marcus' father. Being considered one of the family, he became Marcus' right hand man, running the latter's business on a daily basis with commendable efficiency.

Now that Marcus was incapacitated, everything rested on Damian's shoulders, and he dispatched his new responsibilities with pride and determination. His counterpart on the staff was Zaphira, a highly educated Greek slave from a noble family, who had been enslaved by the Romans. Marcus' father had bought her at a slave market in Rome when she was in her late teens.

She was above average in height, had a good figure, and moved gracefully. Her face, which just fell short of her being classified as a beauty, enjoyed a certain refinement of features. A straight classical Hellenic nose-brow combination crowned by heavy but well tended eyebrows, bore evidence to this. Scanty eyelashes however, somewhat deadened the aspect of her intelligent dark green eyes. A delicately delineated mouth which held an incongruent relationship with her rather pointed chin completed the picture. She wore her hair in the Hellenic style, attractive in its light brown coloration, and carefully arranged to partially cover two slightly over-sized but well shaped ears.

Her performance in the role of governess and tutor, had endeared herself to the family. She had earned the love and respect of her talented young ward, despite her menial situation.

As often occurs when the fluidity of a casual conversation is interrupted, the participants are reminded of more urgent matters and disperse to deal with them.

Damian, got up and departed to his room in the atrium, to prepare the money for the following day's disbursement, and to record the transaction. Zaphira, made her way across the moonlit peristyle to her mistress' chamber to make sure that nothing else was required of the staff that evening. Silia and Tecuno found themselves alone at the kitchen table.

"I have a message for the young mistress from her young man," he quickly confided. "It would be good if she could get it tonight."

"I must await the opportunity," answered Silia.

"Tell me, and I shall do my best to get it to her," she promised, cautiously looking around.

He made haste to tell her. The sound of Zaphira's footsteps returning could now be heard, and the conversation quickly changed to a more mundane topic.

"The mistress wants a cup of pomegranate juice," ordered Zaphira on entering the kitchen.

"I shall take it right away," volunteered Silia, welcoming the opportunity and leaving a satisfied Tecuno to converse with Zaphira.

Letitia was with her parents in their bedroom. Her mother was immersed in a number of parchments perusing some accounts that Damian had brought for her to examine and approve. Julia, whose keen intelligence was awakened by the incapacity of her husband to attend to the business, had moved quickly to acquaint herself with all aspects of the family's mercantile affairs.

A look of concern spread over her attractive face, as she examined with intense interest the documents before her. Her golden hair, falling lazily around her well formed fleshy white shoulders, partially covered her face and obliged her every now and then, to part it clear as she read. Her downturned eyes, whose shape and colour Letitia had inherited were a steely blue, imparting an almost unobtrusive glint of hardness, which was however absent in those of her daughter's. A straight and well proportioned nose, and a slightly open full lipped mouth, completed the momentary portrait, as she continued to survey her work without lifting her head to acknowledge Silia's presence. The latter, took advantage of her mistress' inattentiveness to signal Letitia with widening eyes and a nod of the head, that her attention was required in her room. Marcus, sat like a non-entity literally staring at the blank wall.

"Silia, where did you put my rose stolla?" asked Letitia, in support of the wordless charade that the slave had begun.

"I'm fairly sure that it is in your closet my lady."

"I'm sure it's not," insisted Letitia, with feigned impertinence. "Let's go see."

And off they went, with Julia unsuspecting the pair's little collaborative scheme. No sooner were they in Letitia's room, than Silia relayed the gate-keeper's message. The young mistress' eyes lit up at the news, giving her new hope for the coming day. She returned to her parent's room, kissed them both and retired to her room for the night, to dream of her lover. The slave hastened to report her success to Tecuno. This she did, as soon as Zaphira had retired for the night.

The following morning found Simon and the boys putting the finishing touches to the new cabin with an excited Marius by their side, impatiently awaiting its completion. When the two built-in beds were finally completed, the captain could not contain his enthusiasm, and threw himself on one of them testing their comfort.

"This is wonderful!" he exclaimed. "I wish I had a bed like this in my own cabin."

"If you give us one more day," said Simon, "we can put one in for you."

"Could you really?" asked the captain incredulously.

"Certainly," affirmed Alexander who was much animated by the captain's exuberance. "We cannot put in a fold-down table for you though, as there isn't enough room to open it. Your bed, must be raised so as to allow as much storage room under it as possible, but I am sure you can climb up to it quite easily. All those coils of rope you carry," he continued, "can fit under it."

"Go ahead," said Marius. "We may as well do things right."

It was past noon as their work for the day on board came to an end. Simon, the boys and Marius, sat on the beds and enjoyed their lunch on the new table.

"So you will come tomorrow with my bed?" asked the captain.

"In the afternoon," replied Rufus, "as we have to obtain the materials first. We can do that now as we leave, including buying the mattress. Then, we can work on the bed in the morning and install it here in the afternoon."

Simon and his sons had just got up to leave the ship, when Damian stuck his head in the door. He greeted the group with a hearty smile, and announced that he had business to complete with the captain. The carpenters hastily took their leave. They picked up their tool box, found their way to their waiting cart and went off to purchase the materials. Rufus, who was thinking of the promised visit to Letitia's house, obtained permission from his father and directed his footsteps accordingly.

"Here you are captain," said Damian as soon as he and Marius found themselves alone.

He handed over a bag containing the money previously agreed upon by them for the delivery of the cargo.

"Thank you, my friend," returned Marius. "And thanks to your master. I trust the gods will make him well soon."

"So be it," agreed Damian.

"Will you be able to bring us a load of olive oil from Caesarea on your return trip?"

"I think so," said the captain. "I am bound for Joppa this trip, but I will go to Caesarea after unloading this cargo and meet with your agent."

"When will you be sailing?"

"Within two days or so. As soon as I have some passengers."

"I bid you a safe and speedy passage," said Damian, and shaking hands with Marius left the ship.

* * * * * *

Rufus arrived at Letitia's gate. It was early afternoon, and he eagerly awaited her appearance. Tecuno was not there. His duties kept him in the vegetable garden at the back of the house where he spent many of his daytime hours.

The gate not being discernible from the house, Letitia had been going outside on a few occasions to keep watch for Rufus' arrival. Julia, who was awaiting Damian's return from the *Stella Maris*, noticed her daughter's many sorties into the garden, and wondered at them.

"Zaphira," she said addressing her slave. "Why is your mistress spending so much time in the garden? Go and see. I would like her to be with her father since I cannot be with him at this time."

The slave attended to her mistress' request with promptness, and finding the daughter, informed her of her mother's wishes. Letitia, who was approaching the gate as Zaphira found her, and having seen Rufus' face peering through the grating awaiting her, became indignant. She instructed the slave with exasperation in her voice, that she would be in presently as she had something to attend to first.

The slave returned to her mistress with her daughter's answer as her young mistress hurried to the gate to welcome her lover.

In the twinkling of an eye, two pairs of eager hands joined each other through the iron grate, and enamoured eyes met in delicious frenzy as the lovers greeted each other.

"I prayed you would come today," she said, her eyes sparkling with excitement.

"I am so sorry for not having come before my beautiful one, but I simply could not get away," he said apologetically.

"I have missed you so much," she declared with a frown.

"And I have hated every moment away from you my love… How is your father?"

"No better, I am afraid," she lamented with a shake of her head. "We are so concerned about him,"

"These ailments take time. Keep your hopes up. He will be better soon."

"I would like it very much if you could bring your sisters to visit me. I did so enjoy their company on the voyage, and it would be so nice if I could spend some time with them."

"I am sure they would love to come and see you, " he assured her with a smile. "I shall ask them."

"Has your wound recovered now?" she enquired anxiously, looking at his arm.

"Oh, that was only a scratch."

He shook his head and smiled.

"When your sisters come, make sure to accompany them."

"I certainly will," he assured her with confidence.

"Good day, Rufus."

The greeting, was as unwelcome, as it was unexpected. Turning around, Letitia found herself face to face with her mother.

"Good day to you," replied Rufus with a warm smile, though a trifle shaken."

"Rufus has come to enquire about father's health," explained Letitia.

"That is very kind of you," remarked Julia, accurately suspecting that the young man had an additional motive for his visit.

"As Letitia has probably told you, there has been no change in his condition as yet, and we are very concerned."

"From what I have heard these maladies take time," said Rufus with an affirmative nod of the head. "I feel sure that he will regain his health soon."

Julia gave a polite smile of thanks.

"Please give my regards to your parents," she said. "Hopefully we can meet with them again soon when my husband recovers. And now, I shall bid you farewell, and thank you for your concern. Come Letitia! Here's Damian. I have business to see to with him. You must go and keep your father company."

Damian approached the gate at that same moment, pushed it open as Rufus stepped back, and walked into the garden towards the house. Julia, accompanying him, cast a look back beckoning her daughter to follow.

"Goodbye," said a dejected Letitia.

"Goodbye," answered Rufus with a sinking heart.

Simon was in his workshop as usual early in the morning. He and the boys worked solidly till noon on the extra bed for Marius' cabin. After a hearty lunch prepared by Ruth and served by the girls, Simon and his sons having packed their cart, headed once more for the *Stella* to finish their work.

Marius was on deck awaiting their arrival. He had the money ready for them now that Damian had paid him.

"Have you passengers for the new cabin?" asked Simon, nodding a 'thank you' as he received the bag of money from the captain's hand .

"Not yet," replied the latter, "but as soon as I have, we will sail."

The bed was soon installed. It was a truly delighted Marius who thanked the three carpenters for their excellent work. Simon asked his sons to take the tool box back to the cart and await him. As soon as they were gone he turned to the captain.

"My friend. Keep me informed as to your sailing date. You know where to find me. I will sail back with you to Judea, but please keep it a secret. Send Jason to let me know when you are ready, and I will join you without delay."

"You can count on it," replied Marius greatly surprised, as they parted.

Hardly had Simon gone, than a man in his fifties, rather short, and with a pronounced wobble in his walk, went on board asking for the captain. Lucius, who happened to be on deck at the time, crossed over to Marius' cabin, and poking his head in the door, announced the presence of the newcomer to the captain, who was trying out his new bed. The latter, jumped up and quickly appearing on deck, greeted the visitor with a polite smile.

"I hear you have a cabin on your ship," said the prospective passenger on seeing Marius. "I would like to book it for the voyage to Joppa,"

"Are you travelling alone?"

"No, my wife will be with me. What is the cost?"

"Forty five denarii."

"May I see the cabin?

The captain led him to the newly finished cabin. He waited outside till the man had inspected it. A few moments later he emerged, and placing the required money in Marius' hand, said:

"I was not aware that a ship would have such good accommodation."

"It's a new feature, and you will be the first to use it," asserted the captain with a certain disappointment, which did not manifest itself in his voice, but which was felt in his heart.

'So much for my honeymoon cabin,' he said to himself with regret.

Simon, riding in the cart with Alexander at his side, caught up with Rufus who was walking up the hill.

"Where have you been, son?" asked Simon.

"I have been at Marcus' house," answered his youngest with a melancholy look.

"How is the man?" asked Alexander.

"Still in the same condition," replied Rufus, keeping pace with the cart.

"I suppose you did not see his beautiful daughter," asked Simon jokingly.

"Now you are teasing me."

"Just a little," returned his father. "But seriously son, bear in mind that she's not a Jew but a Roman, and as I hear, much wealthier than you."

Rufus made no answer. The three travelled in silence until they reached their home moments later, to the usual warm welcome from their women folk.

Supper had been served and eaten with great gusto. Simon, raising his hands, called for their attention to something important that he wanted to share with them. The mood of the room quickly changed from light hearted merriment to concern, as they waited for the head of the family to divulge his intentions.

Simon looked at Ruth who knew what he was going to say as he began to address his beloved children.

"I'm going back to Judea for a while. It's not on business. Though, if any one enquires you must say that business is my reason for going. It's very important to me that I go. Your mother knows why, and understands. However, you have to trust me in what I'm about to do. When I return, I'll tell you all about it. Or, if your mother wishes she has my permission to tell you after I leave. Know that my love for you all will never waver, and I'll think and pray for you all the time that I'm away."

He looked at their concerned faces, and continued.

"You boys, are well able to carry on the family business, and I trust you to see that your mother and sisters are looked after in the same way that I've have always looked after them. You'll be building many new cabins on ships, and that'll guarantee a good and constant income. You both have to go and sell the idea to the captains who dock in Apollonia. In any event you'll also have the normal work load that'll continue to come in."

Once again he paused, and turning to look at his two teary-eyed girls, said:

"Look after your mother. She'll miss me as much as I'll miss her."

He then looked lovingly at his wife, whose eyes were wet with tears.

"I'll be sailing on the *Stella Maris* with Captain Marius. I hope to be away no more than two months. The moment the captain is ready to sail, he'll send one of his mates to let me know. I could be leaving as early as tomorrow or the following day, so I'll pack tonight and be ready."

The following morning, Jason came for Simon, and the whole family went with him in the cart to the quay to see him off. The family's farewell was a doleful one, leaving them with heavy hearts and enquiring minds. Ruth was tearful as usual, as were both the girls. The two boys, put up a courageous front, but they knew that they would miss their father inordinately. Marius, who welcomed him on board, had now fifteen passengers, including the couple that had booked the new cabin. The *Stella Maris*, with its passengers waving back to those on the wharf, pulled away silently, and was soon out of the harbour under full sail, on its way to Judea on a beautiful spring day.

CHAPTER SIX

A PROBLEM ARISES

The beautiful spring weather greeted those on board the *Stella Maris*, as the little ship plodded on through the Mediterranean Sea on its journey with the port of Joppa as its destination. Back in Apollonia, however, a frustrated Jechonias was staring at the water as he stood on the quay where the *Stella Maris* had been berthed the day before.

Despite his resolution to watch Simon on a daily basis, he had been lax lately. He knew that the carpenter whom he had been sent to watch, was working on the *Stella Maris,* and would most probably be there for another five days or so. The ship's departure sign had been vague and confusing, and he had badly underestimated the duration of the work. Great was his surprise, however, when he came to the quay two days later and found neither ship nor carpenter.

He immediately made his way up the hill to Simon's house where he began his watch from a concealed vantage point; standing there for hours. He could see Alexander and Rufus at work in the shop, but to his annoyance, Simon was not with them. He looked all around the town for him. He asked as many people as he could as to his whereabouts, but could obtain no answers.

'Now,' he wondered, 'where, do I find this man?'

Jechonias was not aware that the carpenter whom he so earnestly sought was actually on board the *Stella Maris,* and therefore continued to look for him on land. He could not risk asking the members of Simon's family, as they would remember him from the voyage. He wandered around the streets of Apollonia for a number of days, in the hope of encountering him by chance, but to no avail.

'Where has the rascal got to,' he thought. 'I wonder if he has taken work out of town, and that is why I cannot find him. His family are all at the house. I think I shall follow his women, and see where they shop. The shop keepers who probably know them, may have been told where he is.'

Jechonias, his head well covered with his shawl, hid behind a tree near Simon's house, and waited patiently for the women of the family to come out on their way to the shops and bazaars. The morning progressed. A little after the sixth hour he saw Alexander leave, riding Pepper down the hill in the direction of Apollonia. From where he stood he could see Rufus busily working in the shop. He took out a piece of bread and some cheese which he had brought, and sat behind the tree eating his makeshift mid-day meal. Every now and then, he nervously peered around the tree, at the house.

The day passed without any of the women leaving the house. As dusk began to set in, the sound of Pepper's hooves made him take cover. Alexander rode past the tree, and arriving at the shop, dismounted, and disappeared behind the house, leading his horse and followed by his brother.

A little later the spy saw the brothers once more. They closed the shop doors, and made their way into the house.

'That was a waste of a day,' said Jechonias to himself, greatly irritated with the whole situation. He made his weary way to his lodgings in Apollonia, sulking and tired.

As the villain of our story walked away, very disheartened at the uselessness of his day, Alexander and Rufus, were at their ablutions in readiness for their supper.

"Well?" asked Ruth, once they had all sat down, and commenced their meal. "How did you get on Alexander?"

"Not badly at all mother," he answered. "I may have a contract for a cabin on another ship. I shall not know however, until tomorrow. The captain had to check with the owner of the vessel who was not there today; but will be there tomorrow morning. I shan't go until the afternoon. That way, they will have had time to think about it, and will be able to give me a definite answer."

"We have all the patterns ready," remarked Rufus.

"The beds and table will always be the same, but the size of the cabin is going to vary with each ship," answered his brother thoughtfully. "Some may not have enough room with the 'swan's head' in the way."

"Father had a great idea when he thought of this cabin thing," interjected Lucila.

"Can you imagine how proud of you both he will be if you can have a few of them built by the time he gets back?" pointed out Ruth, with a touch of pride.

"Letitia has invited you both to her house," announced Rufus, changing the subject.

"Oh! how wonderful," chanted Lucila.

"That will be great," agreed Rachel. "When do we go?"

"The first day of any week would probably be a good time to go," suggested Ruth. "Your brothers could take you there in the morning on their way to work and bring you back before dusk."

"With a little luck, we will have a contract," concluded Alexander, hoping to secure it the following day.

The family continued to talk of their hopes, and expectations, as they entertained themselves all that evening. Coincidentally, their father, stood on the deck of the *Stella Maris,* contemplating a reasonably calm evening sea, and thinking of them back home.

'What strange things happen in life,' mused Simon, with a puzzled frown on his face. 'Here I am because of one extraordinary incident that happened in what seems like a flash. The things I thought I had full control of, now elude me to the point that everything in my life is an uncertainty. I feel like a rudderless ship at sea. What's going to happen? What am I going to do?'

These thoughts tormented Simon nightly. He seemed to forget who he was, and what he was doing there in the middle of the sea, when he should be at home enjoying his life as he had hitherto been accustomed.

'What am I looking for, and what am I going to find?'

He looked intently at the dark night sea. His gaze attempted to penetrate its sparkling silver mantel which spread before him. It seemed to cover with its deep blue intensity, the secret solution that Simon so urgently longed to find. Instead, it enchanted him with its deceptive and silent tableau. Every moonbeam was reflected back in a mysterious dance of lights, animating each ripple, and acting out its brief performance on the surface of the magical moon-lit sea. To his detriment however, this tranquilizing scene contributed nothing to the calming of his thoughts, which churned away relentlessly in his beleaguered head.

"Lovely evening," came a voice from behind him. Turning, he saw Captain Marius approaching.

"The sea is so very beautiful when it's calm," remarked Simon.

"Yes, but we do not want it too calm or we will never get to where we are going. I would welcome a little more wind my good friend."

"Quite true."

"I do not mean to invade your privacy, but you seem to have many thoughts to consider. You are a far different man this trip than you were on your last. Can I help allay your concerns in any way?" enquired the captain, feeling sympathy for the man whom he could now truly call his friend, and who appeared to be deeply troubled.

"No my friend, the thoughts that fill my mind day and night, are of such a nature, or should I say, so unnatural, that I can find no answers to them."

"Has it anything to do with your work?" asked Marius with a look of surprise. Simon shook his head in denial, and the captain continued.

"I trust all is well with the family?"

"God be praised....Yes!"

"Well then, be of good cheer. Surely nothing else can warrant your concern," said Marius gesticulating. His arms in the air and an expression of finality on his face.

"You are not a Jew my good captain. Your gods do not impact your life as my God does mine. They demand little more than worship from you, and perhaps a celebration each year. My God being a living God, has laid down laws which have been obeyed and lived by for thousands of years. They have governed our lives and become a part of our very nature."

"Yes, I have heard of your God, and there is much jealousy concerning him. It has caused your people much anguish over the years. But Caesar lays no restrictions on you at present. Other than the special tax which he imposes on you, even though you are a Roman citizen as well as a Jew."

"All you say is true Marius, but my concerns are occasioned by a newness that has entered my religion, putting some very grave doubts on my faith, and weigh heavily on my conservative mind."

"I begin to understand," affirmed the other.

"You may have heard of the Messiah whose coming, we Jews have awaited for centuries."

"I have, yes."

"Well, the Messiah, when he eventually comes, is expected to set us free from... at the present time... and no offence meant to you personally.... Roman rule, and establish our own kingdom in all of Israel.

"Go on!"

"Very recently, a young rabbi from Nazareth in Judea, appeared among the people. He preached to them a new way of living our lives in keeping with what we already believed. Yet, giving a new interpretation to our beliefs."

"So, if his ideas did not violate your belief in your God, why the concern?"

"Ah! but he claimed to be the Son of our God and also, the Messiah. However, he was not the military leader the people expected from the Scriptures they had traditionally learnt. This man spoke of love for every one, regardless of race or creed. He cured many people of their illnesses and even brought dead people back to life."

Simon paused and smiled, as he perceived how attentively, the captain was listening to his words, and continued:

"The Jews in authority in Jerusalem, seeing that he was gaining a large following, tried to silence him, but they couldn't. 'I have come as your Messiah,' he would tell them. 'To liberate you from your sins. My Father, whom you call your God has sent Me, and I am here to do His will.' Then they crucified him. So you see," concluded Simon .

"That is certainly new to me, I have never heard such a thing. And you are now struggling in your mind as to whether to accept this man's teaching or not. But why are you fighting this battle in the middle of the sea, instead of in your house with those you love?"

"Marius, the sea has given you a depth similar to its own," answered Simon putting his hand on his mariner friend's shoulder. "You see my good and trustworthy friend, as you correctly suspect there is more than that to my story. Much more…"

"I shall enquire no further. I see how personal it is," concluded Marius; searching Simon's eyes in the moonlight, and perceiving the struggle they reflected.

"Good night, and may sleep calm your mind," he said, and walked off to his cabin and his new bed, leaving Simon leaning on the rail wrestling with his perturbing thoughts.

A few moments later, Simon made his way to the stern of the ship beside the new cabin. He lay down on his mat, and after some further mental wrestling, fell asleep; his shawl around him, his head resting on one of his bags.

* * * * * *

At the break of the new day; in actual fact the Sabbath day, or as Letitia would call it, 'Dies Saturni,' Simon's family found their habitual way once more, to the morning service in their synagogue. They were carefully scrutinized by a hidden pair of sinister eyes, belonging to the ever present Jechonias, the Pharisee.

'I shall attend a later service in Cyrene as soon as these people are back in their house,' he promised himself and followed them all the way to their synagogue.

Unbeknownst to Jechonias, who chose not to enter the synagogue, the old rabbi asked Ruth and the family to remain behind after the service as he desired to talk to them.

The interview with the rabbi was short. The holy man informed his friends of his meeting in the garden with the Pharisee. Learning of Simon's absence, he warned them with regard to the man.

Their meeting with the rabbi was the subject of speculation and conversation in Simon's house for the remainder of the Sabbath day; being interrupted every now and then by prayer. They tried to picture their father's day on board the *Stella* with Marius, and included some additional prayers for good sailing weather for them.

* * * * * *

The picture in the Tricius household differed somewhat on that "Dies Saturni," from that in Simon's. The family sat in the shade on an array of colourful cushions under the colonnaded peristyle, keeping Marcus company as he reclined on his couch. Zaphira played her harp in harmony with Letitia's lyre; both women singing in concert, as Julia listened in a dreamy haze.

This enjoyable musical performance continued for some time to everyone's delight, including it would seem, Marcus, on whose staring eyes hung a single tear. It gave credence to the fact that a modicum of awareness lingered in that otherwise petrified face.

As the music stopped, Damian joined the group. He carried a few parchment scrolls, and approaching Julia, sat by her side on a vacant cushion.

"I brought these for you to examine m…my lady," he stuttered.

"I have asked Marius to try and b…bring back a c…cargo of olive oil from Caesarea on his return trip," began Damian solemnly.

"I have at his request also authorized him to include a c…cargo of c…cork."

"Cork? enquired his mistress, surprise showing on her handsome face.

"Yes… Marius assures me that in this last voyage the c…cargo of c…cork that he was carrying for another merchant from Cyrene, and which he arranged very c…carefully to protect the wine amphorae from damage, did an excellent j…job, and brought the wine unharmed through that gale."

"Really?…well, we are to be grateful to the captain for his foresight. Permit him to secure the cargo as he wishes. Can we find a market for the cork?"

"U…undoubtedly m…my lady," assured Damian, bringing a contented smile to Julia's face..

Letitia, noticing that her mother was seemingly in a good mood, now ventured to inform her that she had invited Rufus' sisters over to the house, and they were waiting for an actual date to be given them for their visit.

Julia, still contemplating the business of the cork, looked up sharply on hearing her daughter's words.

"You invited the girls over?"

"Yes mother," was the tentative answer.

"I do not remember you asking my permission."

"I didn't think you would refuse. I am very bored. I need some company of my own age. Rachel and Lucila were so nice on board. I thought you also, would be glad to see them again," said Letitia with some confidence.

"I am not sure that they are the right company for you to keep," admonished her mother to Letitia's amazement.

"Mother! they are such nice girls, you said so yourself. Why have you changed your mind? And after Rufus saving father's life, how can you refuse to let them come and visit with me?"

"Please leave us," said Julia, nodding to Zaphira and Damian. They got up and made their way, one to the kitchen, and the other, to the office in the atrium.

"Now listen to me Letitia," began her mother, moving her cushion closer to her daughter's, and taking her hand. "I have nothing against the girls, or the family for that matter. It is just that they are of a different class and also Jews. That boy Rufus, has taken a liking to you, and he must under no circumstances be encouraged."

Her mother's words were tearing at Letitia's heart. Tears streamed down her beautiful face. She pulled her hand away with a feeling of betrayal, occasioning a profound and unpleasant shudder through her body.

"You are so cruel!" she wailed in utter desperation, her world falling apart. "How can you do this to me?"

"You cannot see it now, but it is for your own good. If your father were well he would agree with me. We have made great plans for your welfare, and your relationship with those friends would only get in the way.... Please sit!" she ordered, as Letitia tried to get up to leave.

"I have not finished!" continued Julia in a very sober tone.

"You know that you have been promised to Linus Septavius.

It was arranged as you know when you were both children, and so it must be. I received word from his mother a month ago, where she expressed the wish for her son to come and stay with us for a spell prior to the wedding. Linus will surely be a senator when his father dies. Maybe even before," said Julia, with a degree of certainty born of fanciful expectancy.

Letitia felt ill. Her pretty head was swimming with emotion, and a cold sweat began to oppress her whole body. Presently, she fainted; her head hitting the marble floor with a dull thud.

"Zaphira!...Zaphira!" screamed Julia, raising her daughter from the floor and placing her head softly on her lap.

"Bring me some water and a towel.... Quickly!"

The slave hurried away to the kitchen, and reappeared a few moments later carrying a jug of water and a towel. Followed closely by Silia.

"Shall I run for the doctor my lady?" asked Silia, seeing her dear young mistress lying there unconscious with her face covered in her own tears.

Julia began to sponge her daughter's brow and face with the water. A look of grave concern on her face was apparent, as she glanced with wishful eyes at her unconcerned husband who lay on his couch oblivious to all that was occurring around him.

"If only you could see and hear us," she muttered, with a tremor in her voice; a tear gently falling down her delicate cheek.

Presently Letitia opened her eyes, still filled with sadness, as she looked at her mother's face. Tears began to flood her eyes again.

"I love him! I love him!" she repeated over and over in a pitiful voice which had both Silia and Zaphira in tears.

"You had better get her to bed," said Julia.

The two slaves lovingly picked up their young mistress and assisted her to her bed.

A distraught Julia, walked slowly around the peristyle pondering how she could mend her daughter's condition from the damage already caused by her relationship with Rufus. She acknowledged that the family was indebted to the young and amiable Jewish boy for having saved her husband's life. But to sacrifice her daughter's future on the merits of that one act for which no one, least of all Letitia was to blame, was simply too much for Julia to accept. Her husband's incapacity to advise or assist her, was another great handicap which she would have to overcome. Her mother's intuition told her that as long as the situation remained unaltered, it would simply become more serious as the days passed, and soon there would be nothing that she could do to mend the problem.

'It is quite obvious that they love each other,' admitted Julia to herself. 'At that age it poses a big problem. They could try anything to have their way. I better have a word with Damian. He has a good head for problem solving.'

She walked to the little office close by in the atrium where Damian sat amidst his parchments.

"Did you hear what was going on just now?" She asked.

"Yes, I th...think so my lady, but I f...felt it was more of a woman's affair, and I thought it best not to interfere."

"It's not exactly a woman's affair. It would have concerned Marcus also, except we cannot count on him now. It has now become clear that my daughter and that young Jewish boy Rufus are in love. As you know, she has been promised to Linus Septavius since they were children, that is what Marcus and I always wanted for her. Now we are looking instead at a disastrous situation which can only bring problems in more ways than one." She paced the little room nervously, then turned abruptly, her eyes meeting Damian's with apparent determination. "I am thinking of sending her to my brother-in-law in Rome. He will see that she meets young Linus before the marriage takes place. It will give them a chance to get used to each other."

"What do you think, Damian?"

A few moments of silence followed. Damian rising from his cushion, slowly walked around the office, as he pondered his reply. Thoughtfully scratching his head, and meeting Julia's expectant gaze, he answered:

"As a mother with the responsibility of ensuring the b...best for her daughter, it is p...probably the only way to act. However, it will be a huge heartbreak for them b...both and could have health, and other repercussions."

"You are right, of course, but I shall have to chance it. Letitia is strong in mind and body, and will get over this in time. She is only sixteen and very bored here. When she is with other young people of her own age and rank, she will forget this boy."

"When do you think the *Stella Maris* will return?" she asked.

"With luck it should be b...back in a m...month, my lady."

"Do we have any business with Rome?"

"Why ye...yes my lady, we occasionally send them grain, usually b...barley."

"Good, then make sure that a cargo of barley is ready for loading as soon as the ship docks," directed Julia with authority.

"The *Stella* now has a very c...comfortable c...cabin with two beds which Simon built for Marius following his eldest son's design. It is a new thing that so far no other sh...ship has, and will provide comfortable accommodation for the young m...mistress, and whoever a...c...companies her."

"It will be Zaphira," stated Julia without hesitation.

"Good, then this matter is all settled. Thank you Damian for your help." And with that she withdrew in search of Letitia who was still in her bed, overcome with grief.

"My dear she said, approaching her daughter's bed. I have been thinking that you may go ahead and set a day for the girls coming to visit. Rufus can drop his sisters off in the morning and pick them up in the evening. You shall have a whole day with them. Does that please you my dear?"

Letitia looked at her mother with suspicion on hearing those words. She shifted uncomfortably on her bed. Her mind tried to guess her mother's intentions. Such condescension could only mean that a bigger plan had been hatched by her clever mother and soon enough it would be made known to her. She would have no option but to obey. Whatever the plan, it would not be immediate; all plans took time to fulfill. She would have time to tell Rufus what had been arranged for her, and how they might act as a consequence.

Letitia made an effort to get up and shake off her melancholia. With Zaphira's help she rose, washed her face, and allowed her slave to comb her long silky golden hair. It was now dusk. Silia and Tecuno busied themselves lighting the many lamps required to illuminate that large house. The peristyle took its nightly bland grey aspect, giving every plant and object the same grey discolouration, dissolving each individual outline and awaiting the appearance of the moon to accentuate them once again with its silvery magic.

In contrast to the greyness of the peristyle, the rooms that surrounded it were glowing with the golden light of the oil lamps. The family prepared for their cena and evening's activities, which would inevitably be of a tense, and melancholic nature as occasioned by their recent concerns.

.

CHAPTER SEVEN

CIRCUMSTANCE DICTATES

As Alexander had promised the family, he left the house after lunch on the cart with Pepper in harness. They started slowly down the hill towards the harbour in Apollonia. There, he was to meet with his prospective clients and find out if they would give him the order to proceed with the new cabin.

He gave no second thought to a figure who seemed to be busy tying some branches together by a tree at the side of the road. 'Pretending' to tie, would have more accurately described the action of the mysterious spy, who had been watching the house all morning in the hope that the women of the house would decide to go shopping.

'Don't these people ever run out of things?' he asked himself in disgust.

Jechonias could see Rufus in his shop moving things around, as if making space for something that he was preparing to start on. The door of the house then opened, and two young women came out, each with a basket on her arm. Both stopped to talk to their brother. The spy, quickly left his hiding place and started down the hill at a good pace. He would try to stay ahead of the girls, showing them only his back.

'They will never suspect any one following them if he keeps in front of them,' he thought. Pleased with his own cunning.

He could hear them talking and laughing with each other as they went down the hill passing a number of shops. People were now coming and going into the various establishments. With all kinds of noises intermingling, Jechonias lost track of the women. He halted for a moment and cautiously looked around. They were no longer in sight, lost in the crowd for the time being.

He carefully retraced his steps shielding his face with his shawl, inspecting each shop as he passed. Suddenly, he recognized their voices again. They came out of a bazaar right behind him. He barely had time to bend down, and pretend to adjust his sandal strap.

When they had passed him, he made a mental note of the bazaar they had visited and began following them again, now from a distance. Soon, he saw them go into the baker's shop. He mixed with the crowd waiting for them to come out.

After a good while they appeared again and kept descending the hill, leaving the shops and bazaars behind. All of a sudden, they disappeared through a small gate.

'Could be a private house,' he thought. He waited, and waited, but the girls remained inside.

Jechonias was not to know that the gate the girls had entered was that of David's house. They had gone to visit David's mother and sister as was their custom. He grew impatient, and decided to forget the girls.

'I shall go talk to the baker,' he said to himself, 'maybe he can give me some information as to the rascal's whereabouts.'

He walked quickly back up the hill and into the well attended baker's shop. Aaron the owner and his wife, were busy serving people. The frustrated spy, impatiently awaited his turn. He constantly peered at the door, hoping the girls would not return before he could get away. Finally, the baker asked him what he needed, and whilst buying a loaf of bread he asked:

"I have been looking for Simon the carpenter, but I hear he's not in town. Where could he have gone?"

"His daughters were just here," said Aaron. "I think I heard them say something to my wife," and turning to her, he asked. "Where did Lucila say her father had gone?"

"He has gone on business to Judea," she said.

Jechonias was stunned at the news. He paid for the bread, thanked the baker and hurried out of the shop, not caring any longer who recognized him.

'A curse on him,' he hissed to himself as he sped to his abode as fast as his legs could carry his cumbersome body....'That confounded rascal must have sailed on the *Stella Maris*. Stupid me, why did I not see that? but then,... how could I?'

He reached the door of his lodgings, but did not go in. Instead, with the loaf of bread still in his hand, he made his way down to the docks. Finding the Registry Office, where the records of all ships that came and went from the harbour were kept, he walked in with determination stamped on his shawl covered head. There was a man in his fifties behind the desk, fumbling around with some scrolls. He looked up at Jechonias with a bland look as he entered.

"How can I help you?"

"I would like to know if you keep records of passengers arriving and departing, as well as the ship that they come and go on."

"We keep a record of the ships and the number of passengers, but we do not keep names."

'Oh,' muttered the dejected spy, to himself, 'everything is problematic.'

"Can you tell me when the next ship bound for Judea leaves?"

"Yes! Give me a moment or two, and I shall tell you," answered the man, reaching for a scroll from under the desk.

"Here we are....The *Pretoria* leaves seven days from now if they can get some work completed by then."

"What type of ship is it?" asked Jechonias

"It's a corbita. *The Pretoria,*" he repeated.

"Thank you, I shall make arrangements with the captain."

Away went the Pharisee; relieved at last that he had tracked down Simon, and could now start to chase him on his own turf in Jerusalem. There, he thought, he would doubtlessly have all the help he needed from the local authorities to apprehend him.

'He will not be at liberty long enough to cause any trouble,' he swore with malicious intent. 'And he will never ever get back here.'

On leaving the Registry office, he spotted Alexander further down the quay, walking down the *Pretoria's* gang plank.

'What business could the son have on board that ship? he wondered. I must find out.' He made his way to the ship, which to his amazement turned out to be the *Pretoria.* He quickly boarded it, and asked a crew member for the captain.

"Hello," shouted a gruff voice from the other end of the deck.

The spy encountered a man of medium but solid stature, with a somewhat small head poised solidly on a thick neck. His face, characterised by a large bulbous red nose, small beady but mirthful eyes, and raised bushy eyebrows had a quizzical look about it. A thin lipped mouth that was too large for his relatively small face gave the impression when he smiled, that his chin was being abandoned by the remainder of his countenance. He came across the deck, his whole body swaying from side to side as if oscillating to the rhythm of imaginary waves.

"Hello," returned the Pharisee.

"Are you looking for a passage?" asked the captain.

"Yes, to Judea, as your sign says."

"We will not be sailing till next 'Dies Veneris' (sixth day of the week)," announced the captain, who went by the name of Silas.

"You see, we are having a new cabin put in, and it will take three or four days to finalise. And," he added proudly, "we shall be only the second ship to offer two of our better paying passengers a proper shelter from the weather."

As he stated this, his merry eyes sparkled, and his near lipless mouth dissected his happy face.

Jechonias, a man of few words when the conversation did not produce any gains for him, paid the captain his fare, and having informed him that he would be boarding at the very last moment as he too, had work to accomplish before the ship sailed, walked away.

'At last, I can rest for a while,' he told himself. 'I do not have to follow these people around anymore. I shall just go where I will not be recognized, and make sure that I do not bump into those two sons of his at the last moment.'

As the spy trotted off to his lodgings in a more pleasant mood (in as much as the word pleasant could be applied to that evil, maniacal creature's character), Alexander, riding the cart with both Pepper and Topo pulling, was just arriving home bearing good news, and the materials for their new project.

On hearing the sound of hooves approaching, Rufus, who as he worked had been keeping a look out for his brother's return, rushed out of the shop to welcome him. Alexander waived a scrolled parchment over his head as the cart came to a standstill.

"You got it!" shouted Rufus with glee.

"He got it!" echoed in the house, as Rachel, who had been at the window, drew her beautiful head back in, and relayed the message loudly enough for all to hear.

A wave of hair, clothing and perfume rushed through the front door as the women of the family shot past the younger son and engulfed the happy older newcomer with hugs and kisses. A mild touch of jealousy pervaded Rufus' heart. He, having been forgotten in the excitement. He looked at Pepper dejectedly. The horse in turn, nodded his great head, as if in sympathy with his master's temporary plight.

Before long, and having finished their supper, the family settled down for the evening in their customary way. Tonight, however, there was an air of celebration. Rachel who was a gifted musician, took her lyre and began to play. The music enticed her sister to sing. Alexander and Rufus, both having had a little too much wine, lent their baritone voices with enthusiasm. Ruth sat humming as she nostalgically thought of Simon.

The following day at lunch time, Rufus was once more riding down to Letitia's house. He munched on some bread and cheese as he rode, knowing that he had to be back at the shop within the hour to continue work with his brother on the new cabin.

Rufus reached the gate and peering in, caught sight of Letitia as she and Tecuno were busy with their gardening. He cried out to her, but she could not hear him, since he tried not to shout too loudly fearing her mother would hear. He picked up a stone that was lying nearby and proceeded to rattle it across the iron bars of the grate. Finally, the Nubian, looking over, approached to investigate the sound.

"Good afternoon Tecuno," cried Rufus with a sigh of relief.

"And to you, young master."

"Please ask your young lady to come. I need to talk to her for a few moments."

The amiable slave nodding in assent went back to inform his mistress. She was already on her way to greet her lover with a frail and wounded heart, that belied the strength with which her young legs carried her to him. A loving smile spread her lips as they gave evidence of her immediate emotions. Yet, her eyes overflowed with tears of sadness, presenting a puzzle for him, as he, with extended welcoming hands, reached through the grating.

"Oh Rufus, they are going to take me away from you, I can feel it," she blurted out with a girlish spontaneity which spoke of candidness, honesty, and belonging solely in the realm of youth.

"Who is?" asked Rufus, his eyes widening, his eyebrows dipping, alarm written all over his face.

"My mother and her friends in Rome," she replied, tears flooding her sad blue eyes.

A tight, wrenching feeling, gripped the young man's stomach. He squeezed her hands lovingly in total sympathy with her emotions.

"She has not told me yet, but I strongly suspect it," she affirmed with woman's intuition.

Rufus was devastated by the news. His father's words of warning though given in a half serious mood now came tragically to mind. He, realising the very real threat that this news posed to their happiness, swallowed hard, as he attempted to hold back the tears that were struggling for release.

'If she is sent to Rome, how can I follow? As yet I have no money. And besides, how would I even find her in that big city among all those rich and influential friends?... But I will find her no matter how long it takes! Soon I shall have money. The business is coming on well, and I shall save every denarii I get. I will not give up,' he heroically said to himself.

The distressed young lover looked deep into those heavenly blue eyes of his beloved, and attempted to reassure her of his eternal love and determination to follow and marry her against all odds. But there was still some of the boy left in him. She, as is common in the female species at that age, was the more mature of two. She realized that in spite of her hopes and his heroic intentions, there was very little that he could do to help her out of the huge catastrophe which had engulfed them so mercilessly.

As he calmed down after the initial shock, she, still in need of more sympathy asked him to bring his sisters on Dies Solis, or the first day of the week in his calendar. This coincided with what his mother would prefer, and he assented with a mild nod of his head, which as he raised again, caught sight of Julia coming down the garden towards them.

"Good afternoon Rufus," she said with a smile.

Rufus returned the greeting with a forced smile that was readily apparent to Julia, as her daughter stood by with a pout on her pretty face.

'Why is she here?' Letitia wondered. 'Is the scheme going to be unfolded now… Here?'

She watched Rufus' face as her mother proceeded to make known her intentions.

"Please ask your mother to come with your sisters when they visit us," said Julia with a smile.

And turning to her daughter she asked.

"What day have you given Rufus for the visit?"

"We have agreed on Dies Solis of the following week in the morning," replied Letitia dryly.

"That will suit me fine if it is acceptable to your mother," said Julia smiling at Rufus.   Then, taking leave of him, she made her way back to the house, leaving the young lovers unmolested for the moment.

The distressed pair, talked of different things for a little while, trying to allow their pent-up feelings to dissolve; their young minds still contemplating their unhappy situation.

"I have something more to tell you which is going to cause you as much grief as it does me," she said.

The look of alarm invaded Rufus' face once again, wondering what other horrors could be tormenting her mind. He took her hands in his, and looking into her tear laden eyes, encouraged her to tell him what she was finding so difficult to relate.

"I have been promised in marriage to a friend of the family whom I have not seen since we were very small children. The commitment was made then at that time. His mother and my mother are childhood friends. She recently wrote to my mother suggesting that her son come for a visit here to meet me. But now that she has discovered that you and I love each other, she wants me to go to Rome instead. I am sure, though she has not as yet told me."

She stopped for a moment. He looked at her dumbfounded. She continued:

"My uncle; my father's brother that is, lives in Rome, and is very friendly with the boy's family, so they can spin a very tight web around me. I shall be nothing more than their prisoner till they marry me off."

She burst again into tears, and was inconsolable, despite Rufus' attempts to calm her down.

"I shall always love you, no matter what happens, or to whom they marry me," she sobbed. Pulling away from him, she broke into a run, and soon disappeared around the side of the house and into her little arbour, that the ever devoted Tecuno had made for her out of carefully tended branches. These were now entwined by clusters of lavender coloured wisteria in full bloom; their intoxicating perfume happily producing a calming effect on her excited nerves.

Rufus was reluctant to leave considering her abrupt, despairing departure. After waiting a little longer however, he remembered that Alexander needed him back in the shop, and he was already late.

Pepper had stood still all this time, his only movement being the swishing of his long black tail, fending off those pesky flies that insisted on pestering him.

It is difficult for man to know just how much an animal understands, but there is an intelligence in some animals that surpasses that with which they are credited. There was a certain sadness detectable in those large, dark, long-lashed eyes of Pepper's which an observer could not but conclude with amazement, that this noble animal was completely in sympathy with his master's sad situation.

Rufus, realised that he had let the reins fall from his hands a while back, yet Pepper had not moved. He turned, and lovingly stroked his horse's nose. The noble beast, still without moving, bowed his head in recognition of his master's grateful gesture.

Rufus mounted his equestrian friend, and made his way home at a brisk trot.

"Well, it's about time you returned," bellowed Alexander as his younger brother passed by to put the horse in the stable behind the shop.

"Don't talk to me!" shouted back Rufus.

The older brother felt a pang of remorse at his own sarcasm. It was not like his brother to snap back at him like that. Normally, he would have given some ridiculous excuse, half serious, and half in fun, and got on with his work.

Alexander walked around to the stable where a very sad Rufus was leaning on his sympathetic horse with tears running down his face.

"I'm sorry I snapped at you. What has happened to make you so unhappy?"

No answer came.

"You did see Letitia, did you not?"

Still there was no answer, as Rufus was busy drying his eyes with the sleeve of his tunic.

"Please tell me," insisted Alexander. "Father being away, I am the only man you can come to, and besides, I feel responsible for you."

With that said, he approached his brother, and tried to embrace him. The latter pulled away.

"I'm alright now. Let's get back to work. I shall tell you all about it later," mumbled Rufus.

Going back into the shop, they busied themselves with the work on the cabin. They continued without a break or word till dusk, when their younger sister came to fetch them for supper.

Lucila, her face brimming with enthusiasm as usual, burst into the shop announcing supper. Suddenly, flinging her arms around her younger brother's neck, she asked him what day had been set for their visit to Letitia's house.

Rufus, having recovered somewhat from his ordeal, squeezed her waist, gave her a kiss, and told her what she wanted to know. Alexander also got a kiss from her, and leaving all the tools out, the brothers locked up shop, and went by way of the garden into the house.

Supper was eaten amidst much chatter among the two sisters. Both were naturally excited about the upcoming visit, and eager to spend the day with their beautiful young friend who so admired and loved their brother.

The boys kept to themselves, discussing their present work, and their business plans for the immediate future. Ruth sat silently by herself, nodding and smiling, as the girls turned to her every so often during their animated conversation. She was troubled. What seemed a late invitation to herself from Julia had to have some pathos behind it. It was only a feeling, but she was Jewish after all, and her race had become accustomed to being treated inconsiderately by just about everybody throughout history, not just the Romans.

'Julia would not treat me harshly. God knows she has her husband's life to thank my son for. No, no, that could not be it. There is no logical reason why we were not invited with the best of intentions; even perhaps, as thanks again to Rufus. She must also be lonely, and sad over her husband's illness which seems to have got no better. We shall have to wait and see,' she concluded in her generous way, observing Rufus, who had hardly looked her way all night.

"You are very quiet tonight my boy, does something ail you?" she asked.

"No mother," he lied, with a forced smile.

Alexander then came to his rescue, suggesting they take a walk down to David's house to see if he would go out with them for a while, or do something together. Ruth had Rachel play something quiet and romantic on her lyre. All three sang softly with their beautiful voices, enjoying as usual, each other's company until bedtime. Alexander, of course, had not the slightest intention of visiting David. As soon as they were out of sight of the house, the acting head of the family turned to his brother.

"Are you more of a mind to tell me what happened at Letitia's house?"

They walked a little further down the hill, and Rufus, taking a deep breath, opened his young heart to his brother, relating in his own way all that had occurred.

"Good grief!" exclaimed Alexander, little wonder you are so upset.

"That is a terrible break for you both. But she must have known that she was promised to that other boy."

"I suppose she must have known, but since no one talked about it with any regularity, and the fact that he has always lived in Rome, she probably did not even think of it. They knew each other when they were around five years old, just babies."

"I don't see any solution Rufus. It is just a horrible situation for you both. My dear brother you just cannot win. They outclass us, and a normal friendship between our families is the most that we can expect. And that, in any case is because of your having saved Marcus' life."

"Should we tell mother and the girls, or should we let them learn it all from Letitia's mother when they visit?"

"I'm thinking about that," said Alexander soberly.

They continued to walk in silence, and leaving the road, started across one of their neighbour's fields just for a change. The sea, best visible from there, presented a tranquilizing sight aptly suited to their mood.

They found a large rock to sit on and made themselves comfortable. Each looked for some miraculous solution to the sudden tragedy that had befallen them. In a loving family such as theirs, what affected one, affected all.

After quietly sitting and contemplating the moonlit sea, which gave them as little help with their problem as it had done with their father's on board the *Stella,* Alexander spoke up. He suggested not telling the girls, so as not to spoil the day they had so longed for.

"But mother... We shall have to tell her," continued Alexander. "She must be in a position to acquit herself if Julia makes any accusations against you; which I very much doubt since she holds you in high esteem regardless."

"Do you agree?"

"Yes. She is already suspicious of my behaviour, as I noticed earlier," replied Rufus.

By now, they supposed, the women of the family would have gone to bed, and so the brothers made their way home. Rufus felt somewhat more comfortable with his predicament after having shared it with his brother. They tiptoed into the house. They were silently traversing the family room towards their bedroom when they heard a whisper... Both froze, and turning slowly, they could just make out their mother. The lamp by the back door betrayed her presence in a 'chiaroscuro' scenario.

She got up, and taking the lamp from the wall bracket by the back door, went out, waving for them to follow. All three made their way up to the terrace. Ruth walked towards the pergola, found a stool and sat down. The boys sat on the floor at her feet. They looked up at her beautiful face which now wordlessly addressed the pair with an expectant stare, her lips pressed together with a tight pout, awaiting her sons' explanations.

"Mother, as you obviously suspect, all is not well with Rufus and Letitia's family, or should I say, mother; since her husband doesn't come into the picture. Rufus has just explained everything to me, and we decided that we would tell you alone as soon as the chance presented itself. The girls are not going to be told just yet, unless you think otherwise. They are so looking forward to that visit, that it would be a pity to spoil it for them."

Ruth looked at the two impatiently. She needed to say no more. By the lamp light they could read her thoughts, and Alexander continued as Rufus held his peace.

"It so happens, that when Letitia was yet a child, her parents promised her in marriage to a little boy of her own age whose mother has been a close childhood friend of Julia's. They all lived in Rome then. The boy's father is a Senator, and the boy now Rufus' age, is expected to become one also in time."

The older son continued with the story as his brother had related it to him, and which he finished without a single interruption. There was a long silence, as the boys waited for their mother to give her opinion on what should be done.

Ruth got off her chair, sat down beside her younger son, and holding him in a maternal embrace, kissed him warmly, and said:

"Son, my heart breaks for you. I know what you are feeling. Especially at your age when expectations are unlimited, particularly when it comes to love. You must bear in mind that we mothers want the very best for our children whom we dearly love. For this reason we cannot fault Julia for having arranged a marriage for her daughter which would guarantee her the brightest possible future. I would do the same for your sisters, or for either of you.

"However, life presents circumstances which we humans cannot prevent, or even deal with to our satisfaction. Such circumstances have now affected your life and that of Letitia. They offer no solution whatsoever as things stand at the moment. Perhaps, God willing, time may bring a solution. But that is in the future. Now, is when we have to either solve, or accept the circumstances as they exist.

"If you both must part, then you have to accept it as God's will, and hope that he will open some door for you both later in your lives. Apart from all this, you have to realise my son that there exists a great gap between us socially, and the fact that we are Jews does not help. A close friendship would hardly be possible, even though I feel that her father, if he were able to reason, would accept us as repaying a debt which they feel they owe to you, Rufus. Not that Julia does not feel obliged as well, which is the reason why she is inviting us over. Besides, her daughter is in need of friends her own age, and it seems she has none at hand."

"So, do we tell the girls?" asked Alexander.

"I am not sure,... if only your father were here."

"Is it not strange," remarked Rufus at last, "that both fathers are absent, each in their own way. But absent nonetheless, when they are so badly needed?"

"Another instance of circumstance interfering in people's lives," she wisely answered.

"Say nothing to the girls for now. I need to sleep on this."

And so saying she rose, and all went back down to the house for the night.

Ruth did not get much sleep. Her only companions were her tears. Her heart ached for her son, and for the girl too. As the Romans would say, they had both been smitten by Cupid's mischievous arrows.

'Poor children, love has no respect for anyone. What a beautiful couple they make. Why could life not be easier? Why so much suffering? Life is causing havoc in my family. Why are you not here Simon?' she pleaded, touching his side of the bed, though she knew there would be no answer.

She got up, and walking to the window opened the shutters and gazed up at the moon. In her fevered mind she felt she could connect with her beloved husband if he too were looking at that full moon. After a little while she felt cold, and closing the shutters softly went back to bed.

'The girls must not be told,' she decided. 'Either we refuse the invitation and break with Letitia's family forever, or we go and let the girls talk among themselves. Let's see how things develop. It would go easier for Rufus if we went along with things for the moment. Julia will probably have them watched, but will not stop them meeting at the gate. On the other hand, if we break all relationships, they will keep her in the house until she is sent to Rome, and poor Rufus will not be allowed to see her at all.'

She kept tossing her own arguments around until she was so exhausted that she finally fell asleep in the early hours of the morning. Being the Sabbath, she allowed herself to sleep in a little, easing her mental ordeal.

For the next three days following that same Sabbath, the boys worked to finish the new cabin, and on the fourth day they were on their way to install it on board the *Pretoria*. They worked from early morning till the light failed them at dusk as was their custom; managing to put up the four walls of the structure, and water-proofing where the cabin walls met the deck. The fifth day saw them install the roof, the beds, door, and window shutter. On the morning of the sixth and final day, Dies Veneris, and as scheduled, they installed the new bed in the captain's cabin. In the afternoon, they finalised the water-proofing, bringing their work to an end just two hours before sunset. They got home with their money, and very pleased with themselves, a little over an hour before the Sabbath broke.

No sooner had the happy duo climbed into their cart, and started off on their way home, than the sinister figure of Jechonias, who had been watching the brothers hurrying to complete their task before the Sabbath began, quickly crossed the quay where he had been hiding, and climbed up the gangplank with his luggage on his shoulder. The captain, busy with the couple who had booked the cabin, gave him a welcoming nod as he joined the other passengers on deck.

Having now boarded its passengers, sixteen in all; fourteen on the open deck, and two in the new cabin, the ship was now ready to sail before the light gave out. The gang plank was taken down, and the securing ropes released. Captain Silas commanded the sails unfurled, and the wind filling them, pulled the ship gracefully out of the harbour and on to the open sea. Destination... Caesarea. Hopefully, in twelve days.

CHAPTER EIGHT

JERUSALEM ONCE MORE

'You called me back and here I am,' said Simon to himself, as he beheld Jerusalem once again.

His journey on the *Stella Maris* had gone well this time. The weather had been favourable, and he had spent many enjoyable hours with his friend Marius; cementing a friendship which had been promising from the very start; both men's personalities and temperament being quite simpatico with one another.

Simon's journey from Joppa to Jerusalem had been a pleasant one, having ridden all the way on a camel. He was sitting on the animal now, as he contemplated the city with both admiration, and resentment.

"You. Oh queen of Judah," he sighed. "So beautiful and yet so cruel. You have killed many prophets throughout history, and now, you have killed the Son of God. You have been punished by God many times before, but what punishment awaits you now?"

"Gidup!" He shouted to the camel. It started once again, its long languid steps heading for the city gate along with the rest of the caravan.

Once rid of his mount, Simon made his way to the temple carrying his few belongings on his broad shoulders. There, he meant to enquire as to the residence of Joseph of Arimathea. After much debate with himself, he had decided not to let Mordecai know that he had returned, until he had had an opportunity to find out exactly what disturbed him so inexplicably, and insistently.

It was the seventh hour of the day, Jerusalem was bustling with people. The bazaar vendors surrounded by their colourful wares, worked hard to attend to the many customers who accosted them.

Roman soldiers in full garb could be seen mingling with the crowd as they kept watch for thieves and pick-pockets, always in abundance. Women leaning out of windows lowered their empty baskets to vendors below, who continued to shout out their wares even as they served their customers. Handcarts were everywhere; loaded with water and wine skins, fish, meat, vegetables, fruit, and many other commodities essential to the daily lives of the people of that great city.

Simon followed the same route that he had previously done on the day of the crucifixion. He entered by the Joppa gate which being a reasonably direct route to the temple, saved him from having to fight his way through the many narrow and stepped streets that characterized most of the city.

He was conscious of the imposing Hasmonean Palace on his right as he turned left and entered the temple's outer court. It too was buzzing with activity as vendors of all descriptions busily disposed of their merchandise: live stock, sheep, goats, pigeons, doves, or clothing such as prayer shawls, tunics, sandals, and many other items.

Donkeys and mules were tied to the pillars close to their owner's stalls, patiently waiting; their large drowsy eyes accosted incessantly by flies, keeping them shaking their heads, and swishing their tales. Both Pharisees, and Sadducees, dressed in resplendent garments, could be seen among the crowd strutting around like peacocks. Money changers boldly called out to passersby as they carried on a brisk business from their tables, shaded by awnings on wooden posts. Simon approached one such stall, and tentatively enquired where he could find Joseph of Arimathea, who, being a member of the Sanhedrin, would surely be well known within the confines of the temple.

"Yes, everybody knows Joseph; an excellent man," replied the fat vendor, as he wiped incessant sweat from his huge round brow with a large beige cloth, that was so wet that Simon wondered what good it was doing him.

"Where can I find him?"

"At this time of day he is usually in the temple. But in another hour or so, he will probably show up, as he seldom stays there past the ninth hour."

Simon thanked the man, and made his way into the temple to pray for a little while, and to thank God for his safe passage.

He was soon back out however, fearing that he might miss seeing Joseph. Feeling the pangs of hunger, he decided to eat whilst he waited.

A few stalls away there was a vendor selling food. He went over to see what he could buy. The stall was well stocked with many appetizing items, and it took him a while to decide what he wanted to eat.

"I'll have a slice of that mutton," said Simon pointing to a leg of mutton that had already been sliced; the vendor having just uncovered it to show another customer, and from which he now took two slices. He gave one to Simon, and one to the other man, placing each on a large fig leaf. He quickly covered the mutton again due to the insistence of the flies.

"And what else would you like?" asked the man as the other moved away.

"Give me a loaf of bread as well please."

Simon took the bread, paid the man, returned his smile, and walked away in search of some shade.

'I need something to drink too,' said Simon to himself. But since both his hands were full at the time, he opted to eat first and drink later. It would be better that way as he had a while to wait, and felt like some wine. He would drink it slowly and while away the time, in a shady spot by the temple wall from where he could see Joseph when he would eventually appear.

Having enjoyed his bread and lamb, he purchased a small skin of wine, and retiring to the same spot, sat down to enjoy it whilst he waited for his friend to pass.

The wait was entertaining, since many things were happening as is natural when crowds of people interact. He watched those who were buying, those who were selling, those who were there to mix and meet with people, those who hurried into the temple, stayed a while, then came out squinting at the afternoon sun; the expression on their faces unchanged. As they passed him he wondered what they were really like? What concerns they had? Was their family life satisfying? Apart from the time they may have spent in the temple did they often think of God, and how he influenced their lives?

He thought of Ruth and the children, how very fortunate he was, and thanked God for his munificence. Then his present uncertainties came to mind again and captured his attention completely. Staring vaguely at the crowd, he noticed the fat money changer pointing at him as a well dressed man stood there, his back to Simon..

'That's Joseph!' exclaimed Simon to himself. The man, who was indeed Joseph, turning around, approached, and recognizing him, made haste to embrace him.

"Ah! my friend," said Simon his eyes sparkling, his lips spreading in a sincere smile.

"My friend from Cyrene!" exclaimed Joseph, "I rejoice to see you again."

"Where have you been? We spoke of you to Peter and the other disciples, and they all wish to meet you," he continued with great enthusiasm before Simon could answer.

"I went back home to Cyrene with my family after the Passover. But here I am again with a great weight in my heart."

"Once having met Yeshua we knew you could not forget him," replied Joseph with a tender look in his knowing dark brown eyes and a slight pout on his handsome full lipped mouth, giving his middle aged sallow face a glow of wisdom.

"Would you take me to meet his chief disciples?" asked the intrepid carpenter; his big dark eyes brimming with enthusiasm.

"Immediately if you like. I would advise against it however, as they would prefer us going to them by night when darkness will hide our identity. They fear the Sanhedrin's spies who are keeping a close watch on all Yeshua's disciples. You best come along to my place since you are not suspect, and later tonight I shall take you to meet Peter and the others."

Simon thanked him warmly, and both walked out of the outer temple bound for Joseph's house which was reasonably close by. After walking through two winding streets, they came to a little garden. At its end, another narrow, stepped street, could be seen. Joseph led the newcomer in that direction.

Half way up, there was a small landing which interrupted the steps for two or three paces before continuing. On this little landing were two doors, one on each side. Joseph knocked on the one to the left, and presently it was opened. An old man appeared and saluted them both from a stooped position with a warm toothless smile. His wrinkled, pock-marked face animated by two vivacious eyes, and a long white beard, bore witness to his more than eighty years. He wore a red skull cap; tired, white hair peeking out thinly all around it.

"Good day Joseph, and to you his friend!" he said, shifting his gaze to Simon.

"Jeroboam, is Naomi home?" asked Joseph. And without waiting for an answer he introduced the old man to his guest, as a widower uncle of his wife who lived with them.

"She is upstairs," he answered at length, taking Joseph's shawl and hanging it up for him.

"Naomi!" called out her husband, "I have a friend with me whom I would like you to meet."

"Come!" said the host taking Simon by the arm, and leading him into an enchanting courtyard enclosed on all sides.

A second floor balcony composed of brick arches joined by iron railings encompassed its perimeter. Potted plants and flowers were everywhere; the sun bringing out their colours with stunning vividness in sharp contrast to those in the shaded side of this beautiful internal garden. The focal point of this delightful open air space was a square sided well, its stone walls carved in bas relief with figures of maidens dancing gracefully, hands joined, hair and dresses blowing in an imaginary breeze. On its stone sill sat an earthenware jug and a silver cup. A wooden well bucket hung from an overhead arched iron support, completing the design of the well.

Joseph approached it, and taking the jug, filled the silver cup with water and handed it to his friend. The coolness and quality of the water pleasantly surprised Simon. He gratefully thanked him, and asked for a second cup of the refreshing elixir which he again quickly drained. His host, taking back the cup, poured himself a draught and said:

"I am very fortunate to have water such as this. The water in Jerusalem is generally of inferior quality as I have often found. I suppose it all depends on the ground under the well. Fortune happened to favour me in this."

They both walked towards the shaded side of the atrium, and sat down on two stone benches facing each other, and flanked by a wall covered with light purple wisteria. Presently, the musical click of sandal heels was heard, heralding the woman of the house, and Naomi made her appearance.

A woman of medium stature met Simon's gaze, and approached to welcome him. It was immediately apparent that she had been a beauty in her younger days. Not that she had lost those features, for fine features do not easily change, but a certain fullness had surely altered her otherwise fine elegant figure to some degree. It seemed, however, to add a pleasant homeliness to her manner, which Simon was quick to notice, and approve. Her face, rounder now than it had been in her youth, still displayed a distinctive well shaped nose with the slightest downturn tendency, as one's gaze followed it down to a thin lipped, delicate mouth with pale rose lips. Her hair was pulled tightly back, and clasped to form a horse tail which fell over her left shoulder, and lay elegantly over her breast.

As she smiled, her almond shaped light brown eyes seemed to be somehow oppressed by a certain sadness, even as she attempted at joviality. Simon bowed his head in greeting her, and turning to Joseph complimented him on having such a beautiful wife, which brought a smile of satisfaction to the amiable couple.

All three, sat and talked for some time, amidst the delicate, insistent perfume of the wisteria, acquainting each other with regard to their families, and their ways of life.   Presently Naomi left them, deducing with natural feminine instinct during the course of their conversation, that the two men were eager to discuss things between themselves, and her presence could perhaps make her guest uncomfortable

"You know," said Simon when his hostess had gone. "I noticed a sadness in her eyes. The reason, being clear to me now that I have learnt of the tragic death of your two beloved little daughters, that most certainly broke her heart."

"It was the worst thing that ever happened in our otherwise happy lives. To lose both one's darling daughters in only a few days and be left childless..." protested Joseph, tears suddenly appearing in his soft eyes. "It happened four years before I knew our Divine Master, or else he would have saved them for me. Of that I am sure," lamented the distraught father.

Simon, at a loss for words, simply gave his friend a sympathetic gentle shake of the head.

"Tell me about Yeshua," urged the carpenter.

Joseph then proceeded to give his Cyrenean friend as complete an account of Yeshua's life as he himself knew and could remember; including the Lord's glorious resurrection. It was a long story, and the atrium where they were sitting began to grow dark.

A young woman of pleasant countenance, and about twenty years of age, appeared. She carried an oil lamp which she then place on a wall bracket close to where the men were sitting, and announced with a bright toothy smile, that supper was ready.

Joseph and Simon performed the required ablutions in a well appointed little room at one end of the courtyard right beside the kitchen, by the light of a lamp that the young woman had lit. She, as Simon learnt later, was the cook, and as he could also perceive, the lamp lighter.

Naomi was waiting in the dining room as they entered. The food was all laid out in colourful abundance on a handsome table. The menorah was lit by Joseph who then recited a short prayer of thanks, and supper began. Simon was surprised that old Jeroboam was not at supper.

"Why?" he tentatively enquired of Joseph when his wife had temporarily stepped out of the room.

"Oh no," replied Joseph candidly, "he never comes to supper when we have guests. He stays in his room, and the women attend to his needs. Most of the time he sups there alone, as he spends his days in prayer, and with his own thoughts."

"He is not a follower of Yeshua then?"

"No, he is strictly old school. At his age what can one expect. He never did meet our Lord."

Naomi related with pride, that she had met Yeshua on one occasion, and how he had given her consolation merely by his gaze. She was sure that he had understood her sadness, and now, strengthened by his grace she found new hope and purpose in her life.

"We have yet to be baptised, but Peter promised to do it as soon as the Holy Spirit comes, and instructs them as to how they should proceed," commented Joseph looking at his friend.

"They are also giving much thought and prayers as to how best to perform the changing of the bread into his body, and the wine into his blood, as Yeshua asked, and empowered them to do in commemoration of his great sacrifice on the cross."

"Oh my," said Simon, "did he really do that?"

"Yes," cut in the wife. "And from what Joseph tells me the body still tastes like bread and the blood like wine."

"Why would he do that, and how do you know it is true?" asked the bewildered visitor.

"He did it so that he could be materially present with us always, after he went to his Father. And as far as being true? Yeshua being the Son of God, would never lie, just as he would never sin. As you already know, he gave his life to 'free' us from sin. This was done so that he may be always with us in visible and palpable form; to constantly nourish and strengthen us in our battle against sin, and so by his grace, gain us our eventual salvation."

"But!" interjected Simon ablaze with interest, "did he not save us already by his death on the cross?"

"Absolutely!" responded Joseph. "He saved us by opening the gates of heaven to us through his resurrection. But that does not mean that we can, as a result of that, live a life of abandon and sinfulness. In the end, we will only be saved if we live a life that follows his divine example and teachings. Remember that one cannot enter the kingdom he has promised with the stain of sin on our souls."

"I understand," said Simon, "and I believe it."

"We shall all three of us be baptised soon now," promised Joseph, thinking also of Miriam, his servant.

By the time the enjoyable supper had come to an end, the three were solidly entrenched in friendship, and looking forward with joyful anticipation to the beginning of the new era which the coming of the Holy Spirit would launch. It was dark outside, and had been for quite some time. At Joseph's suggestion, they prepared for their visit to the apostles, and taking leave of Naomi, they started on their way.

"Is it far?" asked Simon, as they crossed the little garden again.

"It is a bit of a walk. They are further south in the pool of Siloam area more or less."

"It's a pleasant night for a stroll in any event," said Simon contentedly.

"You will stay with us for the time being," assured his councillor friend, "as they are somewhat restricted where they are lodged now, and are in danger of the Sanhedrin finding out their whereabouts."

"That is very good of you, but I shall be an imposition on your family life."

"Nonsense. Naomi and I greatly enjoy your company."

"And speaking of family," continued Joseph, " did you not tell me at the crucifixion that you were staying with family?"

"You have a good memory," replied the carpenter.

"My brother-in-law and his family. They have a farm in the country, just outside Jerusalem. But I do not want them to know that I have returned until I find out what is happening to me. And now, if we are being persecuted I certainly do not want to implicate them."

"I think you have acted wisely; at least for the moment," stated Joseph as they walked. At length, having reached their destination, the councillor pulled Simon back by the arm into a dark archway. Both waited to see if anyone was prowling around spying on the house.

"Cover your face with your shawl," instructed Joseph following his own advice.

Seeing nothing suspicious, they crossed the street and knocked on the door three times, waited and knocked once again, as was the arranged signal. The door was opened by a young woman servant of the house in her early twenties with what appeared to be a pleasant vivacious face, or so it seemed, for the light was very poor, and she kept the lamp hidden behind the door as she spoke.

"Good evening Rhode. Is Peter in tonight?" whispered Joseph.

In answer to his question, the young woman nodded her head in the affirmative, and motioned for the two new arrivals to follow her. She led, lighting their way with her lamp held high.

Nothing caught their attention as they climbed a set of wooden stairs which took them to an upper chamber. On reaching the top landing however, and at the parting of a heavy curtain, a very large room opened up before them. It exposed a large group of people seated on cushions, many with their backs resting on the walls and all chatting in muffled tones. The room was poorly lit, and the windows were heavily curtained so that the light from the lamps would not be seen from the street below; part of the cautious, apprehensive feeling which the room exuded.

Just as they were reaching the far wall, a man jumped up, locked Joseph in a brotherly embrace, and turning to Simon asked:

"Who have we here?"

"This fine man," said Joseph, "is the man we have talked about occasionally....Simon of Cyrene."

The words were hardly out of Joseph's mouth, than Simon found himself in another tight embrace with a man nearly his own size. This was Peter, impulsive and warm-hearted as was his habitual manner. His vivacious eyes sparkled as they were caught in the light of the lamp near him. His full lipped mouth surrounded by hair, spread itself happily over his rugged congenial face, and with nostrils dilating slightly as he caught his breath, said:

"You are most heartily welcome in the name of Yeshua our Lord and Saviour."

"I am honoured to meet you," said Simon with a touch of reverence, as it occurred to him that this seemingly gruff man had been so intimate with the Son of God Himself.

"Honoured? I am a simple fisherman, a man who works with his hands. If there is any honour in me, it is only because I am by his divine grace, an apostle of Yeshua. Of myself, I am nothing," assured Peter humbly.

"Come let us sit down, and become acquainted, "invited the apostle.

"Tomorrow when hopefully you visit again, I shall introduce you to the other apostles, and some disciples," he promised with a smile.

The three sat down. Peter, resumed his place with his back to the wall. Joseph and Simon sat opposite him.

"Is Yeshua's mother Mary here too?" asked the Cyrenean, his eyes trying to penetrate the dimness of the room.

"Yes," answered the fisherman. "She is with that group of women over there," he replied, pointing across the room at some women, who appeared as visions in a fog, reposing on their couches, and talking quietly among themselves.

"From what Joseph has told me," said Peter, "you were made to carry the Master's cross when his weakness would no longer allow him to do so. But it seems you were happy to help him in the end."

"Yes, I really felt sorry for him, and when I looked into his eyes at his third fall, I felt something that I had never felt before. Since then, even though the feeling fills me with a wonderful tranquility, I cannot rest my mind. I have to find out what has happened to me. I am hoping you can help me."

Peter looked at him intently for a few moments and said.

"The answer is very simple my new friend. Yeshua wants you to follow him, just as he asked of us."

"When you say follow him, what exactly do you think he wants me to do?" asked Simon in complete wonderment, and with some reticence.

"Again, a very simple answer. He wants you to become a 'fisher of men.'"

"A fisher of men?" gasped our incredulous carpenter, as the word, 'fisher' presented a new, and unwelcome occupation to his muddled mind.

"In other words, he wants you to go and convince people to accept him as their God, and Messiah," smiled Peter, seeing the bewilderment in Simon's eyes.

A sigh of relief escaped the carpenter as he heard the apostle explain.

"Did you tell him, Joseph, how our blessed Lord rose from the dead after three days, and appeared to us all right here a number of times. And how he ate in front of us, and after a while ascended into heaven to his Father Yahweh, taking us all along to see him go?"

"Oh my," said Simon regretfully. "Yes, he told me, and I am so sorry I missed it all."

Once again, Peter recounted to the enthusiastic newcomer as Joseph had already done, ...the 'Breaking of the Bread, ' and its meaning and purpose.

"Soon," he said, "when the Holy Spirit arrives, he will instruct us in many things."

Our amiable Cyrenean was very excited, and listened very attentively to all that the holy fisherman related to him. They sat and talked till late into the night.

As Simon listened to Peter, his mind occasionally wandered back to his family, and recalling the comforts of his normal life at home, considered how uncomfortable it must be for so many people, (for there must have been close to twenty five persons, whom he was told actually lived there), to be imprisoned in this room for so many days, away from their homes. However, unbeknown to our hero, there were a number of rooms downstairs, this being a public house, with a large kitchen, store rooms, ablutions and toilets, to adequately meet the needs of that unique group.

He also observed the room itself, and the people who were occupying it. The few women present were reclining on couches, whilst most of the men, many of them visitors like himself, sat on cushions on the floor. Low tables were scattered all over the room, being used as needed. Wall decorations were vaguely discernible as in a haze, consisting mostly of wall hangings in woven fabric of varying designs, their colours muted by the dimness of the room, which though having an abundance of lamps, relied on the light of just a few.

The coming of the Holy Spirit was the central expectation of their lives. The room was thick with expectancy, excitement, curiosity, even a touch of fear for the unknown could be detected in some of them. For the majority, there was joy in their expectancy. Yeshua had promised them instruction and direction from the Holy Spirit, and that, they very badly needed. They spent their days and nights in fear of the authorities and uncertain as to how to proceed now that their beloved Master was no longer there to direct them.

Joseph and Simon finally took their leave. Peter accompanied them across the room as far as the landing. They once again made their way downstairs to the light of young Rhode's lamp. She, seemingly having appeared from nowhere.

Covering their faces as much as possible, they both made their way hurriedly to Joseph's house as morning was breaking. Naomi and Miriam, were both asleep. Jeroboam, hearing their knock, came to the door and let them in. He wore a different skullcap on this occasion; one that perhaps he favoured for lying down. An interested observer would have noticed that by his alertness at such an hour of the morning, he was a very light sleeper and used to little sleep. He was also quite accustomed to receiving Joseph at that unusual hour, and actually knew where he was coming from. Nodding his head to the pair, he disappeared from their sight.

The master of the house took one of two lamps that were burning near the door, and gave the other to his guest motioning him to follow.

They went up the stairs, and on reaching the upper gallery, a door stood open. Joseph motioned Simon to go in.

"Sleep well!" my friend.

"Thank you, and you too," replied the sleepy Cyrenean.

The tired, but contented carpenter extinguished the lamp which really was no longer needed. The soft morning light flooded in through the window of that upper storey, unveiling a well furnished room which welcomed the guest, and promised to provide amply for his comfort. A few moments later, Simon collapsed onto a most comfortable bed, and quickly fell asleep.

It was well past midday when the high pitched chanting of a pedlar immediately under his window, brought our adventurous Cyrenean out of his slumbers. Barely awake, his eyes floated aimlessly around the room noting every detail, and realising how thoughtfully and tastefully, Naomi had equipped this room for his comfort.

The bed was superb its mattress filled with what…? He was unable to guess. There was a tall table on which rested a good-size basin with a large glazed jug full of water, a towel hung on a hook attached to its side. A glass mirror was positioned at face height on the wall above the jug.

Against the other wall of the room stood a wooden trunk for the storage of clothes, and beside it a stool with very prettily carved legs covered with a red and gold cushion. Behind the door there were some small iron hooks for the hanging of tunics and other clothing. A beautifully woven piece of fabric ornamented with vibrant colours, hung on an iron bar, and covered the wall behind the bed.

The floor, made from smoothened wooden planks, was partially covered by two soft and colourful woven mats, one on each side of the bed. There was also a small low table by the bed and under it sat the familiar glazed earthenware pot with a handle. The window commanded a good view of the city and beyond, since the house stood half way up a hill. It was a delightful room with some appointments that unfortunately lacked in his own home. He made a mental note of them all, so that he might tell Alexander, and the family about them on his return.

Simon made use of the basin, jug, and towel. He dressed himself, and went downstairs to the courtyard to meet whoever might be there. Naomi heard him descending the stairs, and went to meet him.

"Good afternoon to you Simon. Did you sleep well?" She asked nodding her head as she spoke

"Oh yes, I slept wonderfully well, thank you. That's a delightful room you have there, and the view is most enjoyable," replied Simon.

"We want you to be comfortable whilst you are here with us. God knows how you are going to be living when you go to spread the good news with all the other disciples....Do you have any means of sending news to your family?"

"I really hadn't thought of that just yet," replied the guest, "but now that you bring up the question, I think I have. I know the captain of a vessel that sails regularly from Caesarea or Joppa, and if I can send a message to either of these places in his name, he would be glad to deliver it to my house in Cyrene."

"There is no problem sending a scroll to Caesarea from here or anywhere in Judea, so your family will hear from you occasionally at least," asserted Naomi.

"Good day!" greeted Joseph as he joined them, and smiling at his wife, he said. "I am as hungry as a bear dear wife. What are we having for breakfast?"

"Breakfast?" laughed his wife. "It is closer to supper I think."

"Ha! Ha!" laughed Simon, "if we'd slept any longer we'd have missed that too."

"You are not going to miss anything. Come into the dining room and I shall have something nice for you both." So saying, she led the way.

Once the meal was over, they sat and talked for a long time in their favourite nook by the wisteria till supper time. Then, after another enjoyable meal, the pair took their leave of Naomi, and made their way back to the house where the apostles were hiding.

They took the same precautions as per the previous evening and knocked at the door. Young Rhode was there once again to allow them entry and light their way. No sooner had they stepped into the room, than Peter, detaching himself from the little group he was talking with, approached them with open arms.

"Good to see you both again. Now come Simon, I want you to meet everyone."

Smiling at Joseph, he said.

"You know them all."

Joseph went over to the women and saluted them, whilst Simon was introduced to the other apostles, and some of the disciples who were present.

"Well," said Peter as they finished, "now I want you to meet a countryman of yours." He called over a man somewhat younger than Simon, and introduced him as John Mark of Cyrene.

The two Cyreneans, embraced with enthusiasm. John Mark was soon eagerly asking Simon questions about their hometown, he, having been away for many years. Peter left them to themselves. But as he walked away, he felt that they would be a good pair to send off together on missions when the time came.

The next fifteen days passed without any extraordinary incident. Simon continued to enjoy his home away from home. Naomi and Joseph dedicated their time most unselfishly to making their friend's stay a most pleasant one.

Simon had to tread cautiously through the ensuing Sabbath days, as Mordecai and family attended the temple also on those days as was natural. He made sure that he was one of the last going in, and the first to come out, and hid behind a column whilst he was inside.

Late one morning on the first day of the week, as Joseph and Simon approached the temple during one of their walks together, they saw a great crowd of people gathered around some men who were standing on the temple steps talking to them in loud voices. As they drew nearer, they recognized Peter and the apostles dispersed at some distance around him. They were all preaching with great exuberance to different crowds of people that must have numbered in the hundreds or even thousands.

'What has occurred?' wondered Simon, 'and why am I hearing Peter in my own language? I didn't know that he spoke my native tongue.'

He turned to a man on his right and asked:

"Where are you from?"

The man answered:

"Greece."

"How can you understand him? he is speaking in my Cyrenean tongue."

"No." said the man, "he is talking Greek."

"Moses be praised!" said Joseph. "I can hear him in my native tongue too, and I know that they only speak Aramaic and Greek, being Galileans. The Holy Spirit must have come," concluded Joseph quite bewildered.

"Oh dear me!" lamented Simon, "I missed another great event."

Seeing that people were being baptised, Simon felt a sudden need for the sacrament also. He informed his friend, that he was going to try to reach James, who was nearer than the other apostles, and he began to squirm his way through the crowd, and little by little, reached him.

James recognized him instantly, and asked him to bow his head. Simon reverently did so, and James with the words, "I baptise you in the name of the Father, the Son, and the Holy Spirit," poured some water over his head at the same time.

"There!" he said. "Now you are one of us," and smiled.

Simon thanked him, and was about to walk away, when James caught him by the arm and said.

"Take that other jug," and he pointed to one that was at the far end of the ablution trough from which he was baptising. "Help me baptise," he said.

Simon was much surprised, but listened carefully to James' words as he poured the water. A few moments later, our intrepid Cyrenean, was busy baptising all who came to him.

When Joseph saw his friend involved in the Baptismal service he walked away into the temple. He guessed that Simon would be busy for a few hours, judging by the number of people that had gathered there. As he walked into the temple he was accosted by two colleagues of the Sanhedrin.

"What do you think of the mess out there?" asked one of them, with disgust showing angrily in his wrinkled old face.

"They seem to have attracted an awful lot of people," said Joseph trying to play down the matter.

"They are actually baptising people on the temple grounds. That is going to cost them," hissed the other one with a malicious look in his puffed eyes. "If there weren't so many we would have sent out the guard by now, but the crowd could get nasty, and we would be in a fix," he asserted.

"Yes," agreed Joseph, "it would be foolish to interfere," and walked away from the irate pair.

'Dear Lord,' prayed Joseph, ' please keep increasing the number of disciples daily, for their strength is in their numbers,'

He continued walking until he reached a chamber which was used as the temple library, and there, he met Nicodemus. They sat down to talk about the arrival of the Holy Spirit, making arrangements to visit the apostles later that night.

It was dark by the time the crowds had dispersed, and the apostles made their way happily but wearily to their house to eat and rest.

Joseph and Nicodemus, having then joined Simon and James, were joyfully invited by the exhausted but happy apostle, to join the other apostles for their supper of celebration. The enthusiastic trio accepted with great pleasure, and much curiosity regarding the arrival of the Holy Spirit.

Yeshua's mother Mary stood by the curtain at the room entrance greeting each of the apostles as they returned, which crowned their success. In the eyes of all those who had lived with her inspiring and exemplary presence, Mary as the mother of the Son of God had now earned their homage and deepest respect, and a smile from her beautiful lips was worth a king's ransom to them. Their faces were jubilant, but showed fatigue after such a gruelling day. Peter raised his arms, and offered a joyous prayer of thanksgiving to Yeshua and the Holy Spirit for the huge success of the day. All joined in the acclamation, after which the holy company attacked their supper with voracious appetites.

Suddenly, half way through the meal, Peter, arms raised, signalled all to hush, and taking a small loaf of bread, offered thanks to God, broke it in two halves, and said: *TAKE AND EAT.*

THIS IS MY BODY." He then passed each half around in opposite directions keeping a piece himself. Those at the table took a small piece each as the half reached them, and passed it on, till everyone had a piece, and then in unison, they reverently ate it.

After a few moments of private silent prayer, they all resumed their supper and joyful talk filled the room; now quite resplendent with every lamp burning. All the fear of earlier days was gone, as the inspired group felt with exuberance the power of God's presence.

Simon was ecstatic. The moment the sacred piece of bread touched his mouth the feeling of tranquility overcame him again, only this time more powerfully than ever before, and he entered into a deep trance. He felt himself to be in a long tunnel of light, at the end of which, and covering the whole opening, appeared the face of Yeshua with the same agonized expression that he had seen on that third fall, and it brought tears of compassion to Simon's eyes.

Just as supper ended, James now, raised his hands. Once he had the attention of all, he took a chalice that was on the table for that explicit, and sacred purpose, and filling it with wine held it out and said:

"ALL OF YOU DRINK OF THIS; FOR THIS IS MY BLOOD OF THE NEW COVENANT, WHICH IS BEING SHED FOR MANY UNTO THE FORGIVENESS OF SINS."

And with those words said, he passed the chalice around for all to drink; finishing it himself when it returned to him.

Again, Simon had the same experience, and James glancing at him from the opposite side of the table, realised that his new friend was in the grip of the Lord.

After the chalice had been carefully rinsed, drank again and dried by James, it was put away, and each filled their own cups with the ordinary table wine mixed with water as they began again to talk over the things of the day.

Peter, the rock, as he had been called by his Master, having finally eaten, sat with a very satisfied look on his face surrounded by his brother Andrew and friends. They reviewed the day's work, and the immense power of the Holy Spirit who had so powerfully ruled over that auspicious event.

Joseph and Simon who were eagerly awaiting news of all they had missed, finally approached Peter, and the councillor asked him to relate what happened when the Holy Spirit arrived.

Peter, seeing how keenly they enquired, leaned back against the wall and began his awesome story.

"There was a mighty rush of wind through the room, and of a sudden tongues of fire sat on our heads. We were filled with the power of the Holy Spirit, and we all began to talk in different tongues as we were prompted each of us to speak. Then we were filled with great strength and confidence, all fear dissipated in the face of this powerful force. We all rushed out into the city, reached the temple, and began to preach the risen Lord Yeshua to all nations. The fear has never returned."

"God be praised," answered all in unison.

The councillor was suddenly aware of Peter's gaze, and returned it with an enquiring look.

"Joseph, my good friend. As was evident at the breaking of the bread, and drinking of the sacramental wine, when you and Nicodemus wisely withdrew from the table, neither of you have as yet been baptised as I recall."

The amiable Pharisee looked at Peter with regret in his eyes, and admitted that he was right.

"I know that it is better for you to continue being one of us in secret. You can help us more that way at least for the present. The same applies to our good friend Nicodemus. But to be truly one of us, you must both be baptised… Shall I do it now?"

Joseph nodded in assent, and kneeling in front of Peter he bowed his thickly haired head, and waited. Peter, having called for a jug of water, a basin, and a towel, baptised him as he knelt. Nicodemus also, came over to Peter, and he too was baptised.

A smile of approval showed on every face around the newly baptised pair. Peter, after embracing them, let them and Simon go, as it would soon be light. Nicodemus walked with his two friends part of the way.

It was a happy pair that knocked on the Arimathean's door waiting for Jeroboam to open. As they walked lamp in hand upstairs to their room in silent exhilaration, they both knew that from that day on their lives would dance to a new rhythm.

The following day in the afternoon, when they sat in the cool shade, enjoying the enchantment of the sunny courtyard, resplendent once again with colour, Joseph recounted the marvellous events of the previous day. Upon hearing the extraordinary news, both Naomi, and Miriam, asked to be baptised as soon as possible.

"We can do it right here, right now," asserted Joseph with a determined smile, looking at Simon. "And we have just the person to do it since he is well practiced after yesterday's performance."

"Surely," he added, catching Simon's gaze, "you must have done it a few hundred times at least."

Simon did not know what to say, but Joseph lost no time asking Miriam to fetch a jug of water, basin, and towels.

"And now my disciple friend, please do us the honour."

To refuse would have been hurtful to them. So he willing acceded to their request, much to their joy and satisfaction.

Naomi was first. Then, Miriam followed her mistress' example. Simon, having performed the Sacrament with great reverence and love, pondered as to when he would be able to do the same for his own family.

A great meal followed, to celebrate the momentous occasion, after which, Joseph and Simon, went out to observe the people's reaction to the previous day's extraordinary occurrences.
Once again, there was excitement throughout the city, as the apostles were at their posts without the least temerity, continuing their work of conversion and baptism.

CHAPTER NINE

PERSECUTION

The followers of Yeshua were aghast at the news that young Steven, one of the newly appointed deacons had been stoned to death by the Sanhedrin. The traumatic effect of the event spawned fear into the followers and disciples of Yeshua in Jerusalem. The fear was well justified, as before that day had spent itself, the Sanhedrin guard, and other volunteers were dragging the faithful from their homes, beating them, imprisoning them, and even killing some of them.

The apostles remained undisturbed by the authorities due to of their popularity. Their large following would rebel against the Sanhedrin. However the ordinary new converts who, in their joy, had been declaring their new faith openly without reservation and had come to the notice of the guard, were now being persecuted mercilessly.

Much was being done by the apostles and disciples to hide and evacuate those in need. New converts were advised not to make known their faith voluntarily and openly.

Public preaching by the apostles continued, but all missionary work was now performed underground, so as not to expose, and incriminate the new faithful.

A few days after the persecutions began, Mary, Yeshua's mother, along with the women who had been with her in Jerusalem, were escorted back to Galilee by John and some other disciples. The apostles were still living at the house of Mary, the mother of John Mark. The latter, had now been sent by Peter to Antioch, with Barnabas and some others.

Apostles and disciples were leaving on a daily basis on missionary work all over Judea, Syria, Samaria, Galilee, and many other destinations. Peter would leave for Samaria with John, as soon as the latter returned from Galilee. They intended to visit Philip the deacon, who was said to be doing good work there, and the apostles wished Peter to go and see for himself.

Simon was still in Jerusalem, and consequently in danger of being apprehended; especially as he had doubtlessly been seen baptising with James.

Joseph had advised him to go out only during the day, when he would be in the crowd so to speak. That would make it more difficult for his would-be captors to apprehend him in broad daylight, in full view of all.

Simon heeded Joseph's advice in timing his daily walks, which he took unaccompanied, and became well acquainted with the city; in particular, the area surrounding the latter's house. The two friends never walked together, as the councillor had also to tread very carefully during those dangerous days.

* * * * * *

"I know he is in Jerusalem. I can feel it in my bones."

So, spoke Jechonias to his sister, thinking of Simon; the object of his malicious infatuation. The speaker, had now been in Jerusalem for almost a week, and had scoured the city for his unsuspecting victim, with little success.

'Now, the climate is just right for putting him away for good,' he said to himself.

'When I walk, I must take a couple of guards with me so that he cannot elude us. When I have him, he will tell us who, and where, others are. We simply must exterminate the lot before they get to be too many.'

These ugly thoughts filled that man's warped mind. His religious zeal had nothing but hatred as its foundation. His, was a personal vendetta against a man who no longer lived. The hate that he had nursed with devilish dedication, for Yeshua, he transferred to the apostles and disciples, particularly Simon.

His widowed older sister whose name was Judith, watched him as he paced the room like a caged animal. Though she loved her brother whom she lived with and looked after, at times such as these, she could detect a touch of insanity in him, which frightened her.

There he stood; his nose accosted by a nervous twitch; his chin stuck out; his eyes staring in anger; his thick eyebrows defining a furrowed frown; and his unruly hair falling over his brow as if reaching for his eyebrows.

"Why do you get so upset Jechonias? Is this man you so hate, a murderer?"

"Worse than a murderer," he cried. "He follows a man who tried to murder our faith. He claimed to be the Son of God. Ha! ...and the Messiah. Can you imagine that? as if Yahweh had a son. And what kind of Messiah was he? The Romans are still here oppressing us day after day."

"Oh, you mean that young preacher whom they called Yeshua."

"Yes! that was the one; with all his talk of love and virtuous living. All he was trying to do was to attack our traditional faith with new tactics. Well! we fixed him. Now all that remains is to sweep all his supporters into oblivion, and our faith will no longer be threatened and imperilled."

"I think you are being too hard on these followers of his. They are not keeping us from our worship, and if we choose not to listen to them, how can they harm us? They think the Messiah has come, and they are wrong. They think that Yahweh has sent a son down to us, so we don't believe them, and that's that. Why do you wear yourself out letting this thing take over your life? Think of all the enjoyable times we could have if you just let go of this. God will sort the whole thing out as he knows best. Soon, they will have a place of their own to worship in, and they won't interfere with your life anymore."

"Woman! you don't know what you are talking about. They want to change our religion, can't you see that? They want to destroy my life, and that of every honest Jew who lives by the law."

With that, he pushed his hair back from his brow, strutted into the hallway, and pulling his shawl off a hook by the door went out in a rage, slamming the door behind him.

His poor sister collapsed onto the plump cushion which lay at her feet and pondered over what she had just heard. She was a reasonably handsome middle-aged woman with a kindly face; her skin, still soft and smooth, greatly enhanced her regular features. Her curly hair was almost black and hung pleasantly around her shoulders; a golden band keeping it away from her face. Her eyes spoke of mildness, and though similar in shape, were the antithesis of her brother's in feeling. Her nose somewhat thick on the bridge lent solidity to her sensitively curved pale lips and slightly recessed chin.

'I have to get used to these outbursts all over again, after almost two months of peace and quiet,' she said to herself, and felt that he was never going to change.

'Even when he was little,' she mused, 'how easy it was for him to become obsessed with anything that displeased him, instead of dismissing it, and moving on to something more pleasant. How he acquired this insanity? Surely not from my mother or father.'

And so, we leave her musing to herself, dear reader. We now follow her tenacious and tempestuous brother, as he paced hurriedly down the street in search of a couple of guards who would accompany him on his walk. It took him a good while before he encountered them.

"I am with the Sanhedrin, and I am going to apprehend a man," he said, as he approached the first pair he met. "Will you walk behind me please, so that you can apprehend him when I alert you?"

"Can you see the man?" asked one of the guards with a questioning look.

"No. But as soon as I spot him I shall signal you."

"Sorry," said the other guard. "We have our route to follow, and unless we see a disturbance, or an offender, we cannot deter from our route."

"Then, I shall walk behind you as you follow your route, and if I spot him, at least you will be somewhere close by," said Jechonias, falling in behind them.

He had walked for a while, and was beginning to feel tired and frustrated again, when all of a sudden a man walked past him, and as he passed he recognized Simon.

"Hey!" he shouted at the guards. Simon turned, and recognizing him, stopped; thinking himself rudely addressed by Jechonias.

"This, is our man!" he shouted, taking a firm hold of Simon's arm.

Our hero attempted to free himself. But the guards were upon him very quickly, and he was held tight. His captors headed him in the direction of the temple.

"I got you, you scum! let's see if your Messiah will come to help you now," teased the Pharisee, gloating with satisfaction.

'Now I see why he was so unfriendly onboard the ship,' thought Simon. 'And to think that he has been trying to find, and apprehend me all this time.'

'Lord Yeshua,' prayed Simon, with a pleading look to heaven. 'I haven't had a chance to do your work yet, and I'm in danger of death already. They know I'm a disciple of yours, and I'll not deny it. My life is in your hands. Please save me. I want to do your work in my town with the people I know and love, and bring them all to you. Help me Yeshua!'

This time he could not touch the proclamation parchment in his tunic, but he felt Yeshua would hear him. He would keep very alert, and if the opportunity presented itself, he would pull free.

The group continued to walk, and soon they reached the market place. It was so crowded that they were having difficulty making progress four abreast. A handcart suddenly crossed in front of them. All four stumbled over it. Jechonias crashed into one of the guards, someone having pushed him from behind. The guard, fell over the cart with the Pharisee on top of him. Simon, recovering first, ripped himself away from the guard that was still holding him, and running ahead, lost himself in the crowd. He glanced back. They were about ten paces behind.

The spy jumped up and down, trying to see over the heads of the crowd. The guards pushed roughly past all who got in their way. Simon ducked in between two stalls, and disappeared into a bazaar that sold women's clothes, and where five or six women were browsing. He crawled under one of three skirted tables; the fabric reaching the ground. Two of the women saw him, and distracted the vendor who did not see him enter and hide.

"Have you seen a man running past here?" asked one of the guards, on reaching the bazaar.

"I was too busy to notice said the vendor," quite truthfully.

"Let me take a look in your bazaar," insisted the man.

"Certainly," consented the proprietor, " but walk carefully. I have many delicate fabrics that can easily be damaged." He pointed at the merchandise, with trepidation.

The guard went in. His companion waited outside, while the Pharisee searched another bazaar across the way. The man worked his way along the sides, feeling around the line of hanging garments. Finding nothing, he approached the first table, lifted up the fabric skirting and looked under it.

He then approached the second table and on bending down to look, one of the women purposely bumped into him as the other also drew close to him.

"You clumsy man!" screamed the woman who had bumped into him. "You move around like a bull. You pushed me into my friend here and see... I have hurt my sore leg." She complained with a slight lifting of her dress, a tantalising pout on her lips, and a pained frown.

"She stepped on me, because of you," said her friend with feigned annoyance, and eyes glaring at the man; both women taking care to stand in front of the third table.

The man was taken aback, and feeling somewhat embarrassed, apologized to the women, and walked out of the bazaar joining the other two. The would be captors, resumed their walk in the direction of the temple; looking here, there, and everywhere.

Once the danger had passed, one of the women made her purchase to distract the vendor's attention, whilst the other cautiously lifting the table's fabric skirt, motioned to Simon with her hand, that it was safe to leave. He crawled out quickly, and taking her hand, kissed it thankfully, gave her a smile which was enthusiastically returned, and gingerly made his way out. He quickly mixed with the crowd and proceeded in the opposite direction of the temple.

He soon lost himself in winding alleyways, and up stepped streets, until he came out into the street where Joseph's house was;

though a little further up the hill. He would have to take a chance on them not having chosen that particular street to look for him.

Saying a short prayer of thanks to Yeshua, he stepped boldly down the street and knocked on Joseph's door. A sigh of relief escaped his lips when Miriam opened the door and welcomed him in.

* * * * * *

Jechonias arrived home in a surly, defeated mood.

"You are back soon. Supper is not ready yet, but I can give you something in the meantime if you are hungry," offered his sister.

"I'm not in the least hungry. I have had a very upsetting experience," he said with childish contempt.

Judith, knowing that he was working himself up to one of his moods, did her best to calm him, and try to distract his mind.

"I am sorry to hear that dear. Would you like me to play my lyre for a little while? It's still early for supper."

She suggested this, knowing that music usually calmed him down.

"No. I don't feel like listening to music. I'm too upset."

"You know it always makes you feel bet…"

"I said, no!" he exploded impetuously.

"That d….d vermin got away from me, when I had already captured him. What rotten luck. Now he is aware that I am after him, and he will keep a lookout for me, making my life more difficult. Or, he may try to run…. God knows!"

"Did you apprehend him yourself?" enquired Judith.

"I held him till the guards that were with me came and got him."

"How then did he escape?"

"Some fool pushing a hand cart cut across our path in the market, and the guards tripped over it. I got pushed by people walking behind us. He pulled loose, ran into the crowd, and we lost him."

"Oh my! That was a piece of bad luck," she said with a soothing intonation in her voice.

"I'll get him though. Even if it takes me the rest of my life to do it. I'll get him." With that, he walked off to his room to hatch up some new malicious scheme.

* * * * * *

Simon made his way to the courtyard as soon as Miriam let him in. He went directly to the well, and pouring himself a glass of water, took it over to the bench to drink amidst the perfume of the wisteria which he delighted in.

Miriam informed him that Naomi had gone to the bazaars with a friend. But would be home shortly as she had been away for quite a while already.

"May I get you something to eat, sir?" She asked.

"No thank you Miriam. I only needed to drink."

"The figs are really fresh, please let me get you some," she smiled.

"Yes, that would be lovely thank you. But just a couple."

"Incidentally," burst out Simon. "How is Jerobaum? I never see him around the house. I suspect my presence disturbs him."

"Oh no sir! As you see," she said, turning around and pointing a finger. "The door to his room is always closed, and remains that way every day, even if you were not here. My lady and I go in regularly and take him his food. He rarely comes out. I don't know how he can stand it. Except, he prays continuously, and sometimes reads."

The maid was soon back, with a small reed platter in her hand. Three black figs lay familiarly on a large fig leaf, most enticing in its presentation. Simon, thanked the woman, and leant his attention to the delightful fruit. She, glided elegantly back into the kitchen, bringing to mind his beloved Ruth and daughters, whose similar grace of movement had always won his admiration.

The lingering sweetness of the figs, and the ever intoxicating aromatic perfume of the wisteria, transported Simon, mind and soul to his beloved Cyrene. He sat daydreaming about his hopefully worthwhile new life on his return home. His eyes, which had been closed as he entertained himself with all those thoughts, suddenly opened at the sound of Joseph's deep voice.

"Your thoughts must be quite beautiful since you are smiling in your reverie."

"A…ah! my dear friend! you surprise me. I did not expect you to come so early. I'm indeed very pleased to see you."

"I came away early from the assembly. The topic was most uninteresting, and since it did not require a vote, I decided to call it a day," he explained in a matter-of-fact way.

"And how was your day?"

"I had a very exciting, but rather frightful day," explained Simon.

"Oh dear, please tell me all about it," requested Joseph taking a seat opposite Simon. The latter, picking up the remaining fig, offered it to his host, who refused it with a shake of the head. He then began to peel it, and proceeded to relate his adventure.

"I was rudely apprehended just after noon by a Pharisee and two Sanhedrin guards during my daily walk."

Joseph's face became very disturbed on hearing the opening of his friend's story. He continued to listen most attentively to the remainder, with which you, my esteemed reader are already acquainted.

As with all good listeners, the councillor kept his peace until his friend's narration was over. Then, pertinent questions were asked and sincere answers given.

"God be praised for your deliverance!" exclaimed Joseph.

"There is no doubt in my mind that the charity of those two women was heavenly directed, as you have no doubt realised."

"I would like Peter, or James, to give me some ministry to fill, before I depart from Jerusalem," said Simon. "It is now very clear to me that I must go. This man will continue to follow me, of that I feel sure. From now on my life will be in danger."

The concerned Cyrenean, got up and approached the well. He poured some water into the silver cup, and turned to address his host.

"I am considering going to Joppa and preaching there, if I can get permission from the apostles to do so. But this will entail the 'Laying of Hands,' and I dare not be seen on the streets, especially on the way to their house."

"I can be your contact with the apostles," offered Joseph, pointing to himself. "Tonight I shall visit them and find out what they plan to have you do.

Genuine gratitude showed in Simon's eyes, as he lifted the cup to his lips.

"Thank you, I am further indebted to you my good friend," he said and drank the water.

"If you have to leave the city," continued Joseph, "we will have to plan everything very carefully since there are now three people who can recognise you instead of one, and they are probably watching the gates."

The two friends began their planning with sad hearts. They knew that their time together was about to run out, and there was a very good chance that they might never meet again. Naomi was informed of Simon's impending departure during the course of their evening meal. She was instantly overtaken by the sadness which pervaded her husband and her guest.

"Tomorrow, when I return to the Sanhedrin I must find out who this man who accosted you is, and who has given him the task of spying on you. " Joseph leant forward, blew out the menorah flames, and in his next breath said. "Also, if he is connected or working with a man by the name of Saul of Tarsus, who is very active in the persecution of the disciples. Perhaps our friend Nicodemus can help us in this matter. I believe he knows Saul, but he must be very discreet in his enquiries."

"Peter was so right, when he suggested that you keep secret your brotherhood with the disciples," pointed out Simon. "You are in such a central position that your assistance is crucial to the disciples' security, and the progress of the community."

"It is my way of serving Yeshua," smiled the councillor with a tilt of the head.

"I used to go to him by night, and now I continue to serve secretly. That appears to be his divine will for me and also for Nicodemus."

"We shall all serve him the best way we can," piped in Naomi with determination, looking at Miriam for concurrence.

When supper was ended, the three friends sat in the courtyard enjoying the summer night by the light of a half moon and a few lamps that were placed with strategic acumen around that little outdoor paradise.

"What am I doing here?" burst out Joseph, suddenly jumping to his feet.

"I must go to Peter right away now that it is dark, and acquaint him with your predicament."

"I wish I could come with you, but I dare not. The incident is too fresh in their minds, and they may have a patrol out looking for me," sighed Simon.

"No, no, we cannot risk that. In fact, do not leave the house for the moment. There is no need to expose yourself until the time for your departure comes."

"Oh dear," sighed Naomi. "We are going to miss you so much. We have become accustomed to your being with us. You have entertained us so enjoyably with your adventures, and stories of your family in Cyrene. I would love to visit your family, but you are all so far away, and the sea voyage so dangerous," lamented the woman of the house.

"I'm sure that you and Ruth would greatly enjoy each other's company, and the children would give you and Joseph much joy, as they are of a very congenial nature." Simon smiled as he said this; remembering his children especially Lucila, who thrived on enthusiasm.

"As far as the sea voyage goes," explained Simon. "If you remember, I told you of the new cabin that we built on the *Stella Maris*. It's reservation can be previously arranged, and it would serve you very well. The captain, who is a good friend of mine, puts in at Joppa often, and he would look after you like family during the trip. So who knows? we might have much time to spend together yet. The Lord willing."

"I'm on my way!" announced Joseph. He went to his wife, and gave her a kiss. She, returned it with a warm smile.

"Don't be too late my love," admonished Naomi.

Her husband pressed Simon's shoulder, and made his way out covering his head with his shawl as he swept past Miriam, who with a big smile on her pretty face, held the door open for him.

Hostess and guest continued to chat for a while, and then retired for the night; both anticipating with great expectancy what the new day would bring.

Joseph arrived at the house of Mary; John Mark's mother. It was, devoid of women save herself and Rhoda, who opened the door for him with the customary warm greetings.

"Good evening Rhode!"

"Good evening Councillor!" replied the young woman, lighting the way for him as they climbed the familiar stairs once again.

There were a number of vacant spots along the wall, which bore witness to the effects of the ongoing persecutions, and of the missionaries who had left on their evangelical journeys. As usual, Peter came across the room to meet and embrace Joseph, in whom he had much confidence.

"What news have you for us tonight?" enquired Peter. "Come, let us sit down and share a cup of wine."

They sat leaning against the wall. Peter, poured some watered wine into two cups that were on a table beside him.

"Now!" He roared in a jovial tone. But suddenly becoming aware of Joseph's sober expression, his smile left him, and his countenance sobered instantly. "Not good news I take it?"

"I regret to say," answered the councillor, slowly shaking his head.

"Please continue," said Peter with an expectant look in his concerned eyes.

Joseph narrated his story with accuracy, and even colour, as he became absorbed in the excitement of Simon's little adventure.

"Now," he concluded. "What is to be done?"

Peter, thought for a few moments, and looking up, asked James who sat nearby to join them. The latter, after embracing Joseph, sat down. Peter in turn repeated what had been related to him, and they began to discuss Simon's predicament.

"He told me," continued Joseph, "that he had a mind to head for Joppa. He has a good friend who captain's of his own ship and could get him back to Cyrene, whenever he needed to return. He also said that he was keen to preach there if you would approve, and honour him with the 'Laying of Hands.'"

"His going to Joppa is a good idea and should be made possible. But the 'Laying of Hands.' That, would present a difficulty since he cannot leave the house, and unfortunately we cannot be seen entering. It would put you Joseph, and your family at risk," explained James as he met Peter's approving eyes.

"As to the procedure, or disguise, or whatever arrangements need to be done," said Peter. "We shall leave it up to you and Simon. You are probably better versed in that sort of thing than we are."

"However," continued Peter, raising his hands. "Once he makes it to Joppa. Have him enquire for one, Simon the tanner, who has a place near the harbour and will give him refuge. It is also very probable that I myself visit them there some time soon, since Joppa will be on my route. Then, I shall be able to ordain him."

Having taken his leave from the two apostles, Joseph started back to his house with a lighter frame of mind. He entertained himself as he walked home, with the designing of an escape plan for Simon.

CHAPTER TEN

THE PLAN

The day of the much anticipated visit to Letitia's house had finally arrived. Rachel and Lucila were preparing to leave accompanied by their mother. The chitter chatter, and gay demeanour of the girls brought smiles to their brothers' faces as they assisted them into a clean and cushioned cart. The boys had transformed it from its habitual dirty, work oriented condition, into its now clean, comfortable, and presentable state. The whole family piled in. Rufus took the reins, and off they went down the hill, both horses pulling.

Ruth, sitting in the centre with an excited girl on each side, was lost in thought; wondering what the end of the day would be like for her daughters. Her thoughts then strayed to her husband, and how ignorant he was of Rufus' unhappy plight. She wished with all her heart that he were home.

'God alone knows what he is going through. He has not sent us a single word, and he has now been away for almost two months. Please God, keep him safe,' she prayed; a tear in her eye.

The cart turned the last corner and stopped at the large wooden gate. Rufus alighted and looked through the grated opening. Tecuno was there, sitting to one side. He jumped up when he saw Rufus.

"Good morning young master," he said, and with his usual sunny smile, made haste to open.

"This is my family," said Rufus, waiving his hand in concert.

Tecuno bowed, and wished them all good morning, as the cart rolled through and towards the house. On approaching the main door, Letitia, her mother and Zaphira, were waiting with smiles on their faces.

"Welcome to you all," said Julia as the cart stopped. Alexander and Rufus, hastened to help the women down. They watched with satisfaction, as their mother and sisters became locked in embraces with the mother and daughter of the house.

The boys took the outstretched hands of Julia and Letitia, informing them that they would be leaving; having come only to bring their womenfolk.

To Rufus' amazement, Julia would not hear of the boys departing so soon. She insisted they come in to have some refreshment and spend a little time with them before leaving.

Letitia, throwing a loving glance at Rufus, led the way into the house accompanied by the girls, and followed by Julia, Ruth and the boys. They walked through a narrow hallway with an arched ceiling and tastefully decorated walls which opened up into a sumptuous atrium, with great effect. The visitors were awe struck by the design and furnishings of that magnificent room. A number of rooms opened into that very formal space, and between their doors there were either niches housing marble busts or couches which were set up around the room away from its centre, which featured an opening in the ceiling over the impluvium allowing the rain to fall into the room and be collected by the central pool. The beautiful mosaic floor depicting various colourful designs, sloped slightly towards the impluvium, so as to direct the water into it.

Passing through another arched hallway, somewhat wider but shorter than the entrance hallway, the party entered the peristyle, which was the preferred living space of the family.

This cheerful area was larger and much more open, and was virtually an indoor garden. It too, was surrounded by a number of rooms that opened into it. Again the design of the space was similar to the atrium but much less formal. It had a stone floor instead of mosaics. The roof surrounding the space sloped inwards to an opening over a larger, centrally located impluvium, and was supported by marble columns with Ionic capitals.

The women settled down in this admirable space on a myriad of beautiful cushions that were grouped together under the colonnade.

"Oh what a beautiful house," escaped at least three people simultaneously. One of them being Alexander, whose eye swept the peristyle, taking in with great delight and artistic acumen, the architectural characteristics of that section of the house.

The vivid colouring of the flowers, intermingling with the cool greens of the plants; the reds of the many clay pots; the shadows cast by the colonnade; the inward sloping slate roof sparkling in the morning sun; and finally, the array of beautiful women sitting amidst the explosion of colour occasioned by their clothes, and the cushions they sat on. The beauty of it all, rendered him breathless for a moment.

Julia noticing his appreciative look, invited him and Ruth, to see a little daily dining room which was her favourite room, leaving Rufus and the girls to their own devices.

"Can I see Marcus?" asked Alexander.

"Yes, of course, but he will not be responsive," she warned, leading them to her husband's room where they found Tecuno seated by his master.

"There, you see. He has not looked at anyone, or said a single word for months. Ever since the accident on board the ship."

Ruth went over, took his hand, and looked at his catatonic face. There was no movement whatsoever in his eyes which stared aimlessly directly in front of him. She looked at Julia with sympathy in her lovely eyes, and gently shook her head.

"Come, young man," said Julia taking Alexander by the hand, and leading him towards the beautiful family dining room. "I know you will appreciate this room which I want you to see."

They crossed the peristyle, and on arriving at the room the lovely hostess purposely stepped aside, motioning for Alexander to enter first. She and Ruth traded smiles, as they gave him time to become absorbed by the aura of the room.

"Well," said Julia as she and Ruth joined him, " what is your verdict?"

"I am speechless... It is superb. What a wonder; it is a place of its own, an enchanted world... So beautifully designed, so well executed... Every element in perfect relation to the other. A little gem. I congratulate you. Who designed it, may I ask?"

Ruth, too, was mesmerised by the feeling which the little room imparted. Indeed, she was mesmerised by the whole house. It presented to her humble eyes, the huge social gap that existed between them. Pondering over these things, she had a feeling of inadequacy, as she listened for Julia's response.

"It is a favourite place of mine and Letitia's," explained Julia smiling at Ruth.

"We use it for almost every meal when we are alone; which is most of the time. The designer is Faustino. We were very fortunate to have him. He was only visiting Cyrene for a month," she continued, "and Marcus who knew him, enticed him to come and stay with us for a week. Once he had completed the design, we got an excellent artist from Alexandria, who worked here in Apollonia for three or four years, to follow with the artwork."

"I do this work also, and execute my own artwork, though I am only just starting," said the young designer, turning to look at Julia.

"You would do well to have a few designs ready to show," she advised. "People have no idea what they want most of the time, and must be shown something that takes their fancy. When you have a design to show, let me know. We have friends who want such decorations and are willing to pay well for them."

"He does very nice sculptures too," added Ruth, but that is such a messy sort of work, that it needs a proper workplace.

"Oh," said Julia. "But sculptures are so very beautiful. Later, I shall show you our goddess Venus whom Letitia has a lot of faith in. It's a beautiful piece. You will like it, I am sure."

They returned to the peristyle where they found themselves alone. The others had gone off to the garden it seemed.

Julia clapped her hands, and Zaphira appeared with a tray full of fruit, a jug of wine mixed with cool water and a number of silver cups, which she set it in front of them on a low table.

Alexander had a quick drink, took a fig, and announced his departure. He had an appointment with a captain for a cabin on his ship, and he and Rufus were to be at the meeting for which they were already late. After taking leave of Julia, and kissing his mother, he went into the garden to look for Rufus whom he soon found with Letitia and the girls.

"Sorry brother to have to pull you away, but our client awaits. We can delay no longer."

The girls protested vigorously, but to no avail. Rufus knew that his brother wanted him at this meeting, and it was with a sad heart that he rode away with him, promising to return later as agreed.

The two mothers now found themselves alone under the colonnade, and Julia thought it an opportune time to have the matter of the two lovers cleared before they all got back.

"I am glad that we have these few moments together to talk frankly about the problem that we both share with regard to my daughter and your son."

"Yes," agreed Ruth, "it is a problem, which no matter what the solution, will hurt them both."

"I want you to understand Ruth, that it is something that cannot be changed. We are committed to this arrangement that was agreed on many years ago when Letitia and Linus were mere children. Perhaps in future times it may change, but in our present time such agreements are binding in every respect."

"I understand," nodded the doleful visitor.

"Also, as a mother you will agree that we want what is best for our children. The future that awaits my daughter in this arranged marriage is a brilliant one. I could not have hoped for anything better for her. Linus' father is a very wealthy man, and Letitia would lack nothing. Surely, if such an opportunity would come to any one of your daughters you would not wish it to be missed."

Julia waited, giving her friend a chance to digest what she had just said, and having received a nod of concurrence, continued:

"I have as yet not told her of my decision, which has been a very difficult one without my husband's advice, which as you saw for yourself is impossible to obtain. What I have decided to do, and I would not be surprised if she has already guessed it, is to send her off to my brother-in-law in Rome. He and his wife, would arrange for the two young people to meet, and get to know each other before the marriage takes place."

"It will break their young hearts," replied Ruth with tears in her eyes.

"Yes, that is the part that upsets me too, but I have to be strong for her sake. Though she is almost a woman, she still has some of the child left in her. Much like Lucila I would imagine, for they are the same age. Rufus is what nineteen?"

Again, the visitor nodded but said nothing as she wiped her eyes.

"I completely sympathize with your feelings my dear friend. You too, are alone to deal with the hurt that your son is suffering, and to whom we owe my husband's life. I will be most happy to assist you and your family in any way. I want us go be good friends. But in this matter, I must act in Letitia's best interest. I hope you will forgive me if my decision is disagreeable to you."

And getting up, Julia, now with tears in her eyes, sat down close to Ruth and gave her a hug, which was returned, but with great sadness.

The girls, arriving as the mothers separated from their embrace, became conscious of the fact that something serious had been discussed by them. They all looked at the older pair as if expecting an explanation, but sadly for them, none was forthcoming.

"I suppose Letitia has shown you every corner of the garden?" asked Julia addressing the girls, who by the look on their faces betrayed the fact that they had some knowledge of the young lovers' plight.

The girls went on to explain to Ruth the wonders of the garden, and soon they were all out again, admiring the pool, statue, flowers and all its colourful attributes. Upon their return, a long musical interlude ensued, culminating in a sumptuous supper. Shortly after, the two boys returned, and at Julia's insistence, stayed for a belated repast. It was late that night when the Simon family finally returned home; all sharing the same somber mood.

* * * * * *

As the days passed, it became a ritual for Rufus to stand at that fateful gate every evening after work, and talk to his beloved Letitia through the grate, with Tecuno and Zaphira as chaperones.

Finally, the sails of the *Stella Maris* drifted into the harbour and with it, the apparent end of the love affair that had given the two families so many hours of mental anguish, as the inevitable began to be unfold.

Rufus promised Letitia, that as soon so he could put some money together he would go to Rome, abduct her from her uncle's house, and lose themselves where they would not be found. She, in turn, promised to delay the wedding as much as she could to give him time to come to her.

Young love; the most romantic of all the loves. For young lovers there are no insurmountable challenges; waiting is not measured in years, but in weeks, even though they may finally translate into years. The world's opinion is of little consequence to them, and their expectancy can reach the very skies. The perils they may face are all imaginary, and will never materialise.

Promises had been made, and eternal love sworn, as the *Stella Maris* with its cargo of barley, and its cabin at the disposal of Letitia and Zaphira, finally sailed out of Apollonia harbour. Both families waved God speed to the two women of the house of Marcus, as they commenced their inevitable journey to Rome.

* * * * * *

Simon waited with child-like anticipation for the news which his host would bring him from Peter. He sat impatiently on the stone bench in the courtyard awaiting his friend's appearance. He had got up early that morning after a good night's sleep. Joseph however, had been very late coming in and was sleeping late as a consequence.

Naomi, who had been tending to her household duties, now joined her guest. Sensing his impatience, she distracted him. She talked of many things, especially things which involved his family.

"When you are in Joppa," she said, continuing to entertain him. "It will be easy for you to meet that captain friend of yours and send news home. He may even be there to take you home once Peter has ordained you. Perhaps, you may be the first one to carry the good news to your country." She rose, walked over to the well, and poured herself a cup of water.

"That might be too much to hope for, but, one can dream," replied Simon. Praying that her words would be prove prophetic.

"We'll know as soon as Joseph joins us," he asserted with great anticipation.

She retuned to her seat opposite him.

They sat for a while longer discussing plans for sneaking out of Jerusalem. A number of options were considered, including shaving his beard and trying to pass for a Roman. As they bandied about ideas, the sound of footsteps on the stairs brought their eager chatter to a sudden halt. Joseph made his much anticipated appearance with a jovial smile on his pleasant face.

"Good day to you both!"

"Here you are at last. We have been patiently waiting for you, knowing you bring us news from Peter," said his wife with a touch of eagerness in her voice.

"First you must eat," suggested Simon. "A man can't talk on an empty stomach."

"Let's go into the dining room, and we shall keep you company whilst you eat.... Miriam!" called out Naomi.

"Bring in my husband's food, and some figs for us please."

Joseph, sitting down, soon acquainted the eager pair with what had been said at the meeting with Peter and James, and their subsequent approval of Simon going to Joppa.

Simon, who was particularly pleased to learn that Peter had every intention of stopping at Joppa on his forthcoming tour of the coastal towns, made a mental note of Simon the tanner with whom he would be staying once he got there.

Joseph's meal arrived, and he attacked it hungrily, saying not a word till he was finished. Naomi and Simon, for their part did justice to the figs whilst they waited.

"Now we must devise an escape plan for you Simon," he began. "And it must be a good one." He wiped his mouth with a little cloth that lay near him.

"We were discussing that earlier," stated Simon, smiling at Naomi. "We really came up with some tentative, if somewhat amusing efforts."

"Ha! Ha! Ha!" laughed the hostess, as she thought of one disguise in particular.

"Let us start suggesting possible strategies," urged Joseph, with a more sober bent.

All became silent; losing themselves in their own thoughts.

Simon broke the silence.

"We know," he said. "Or, at least we believe, that the gates will be watched. That, will make a disguise essential."

"We also know that you cannot leave on foot," further remarked the councillor.

"If you leave the city alone, you will be questioned directly, which will give them a better chance of recognising you," added Naomi motioning with her hand.

"So there now. We have already made some decisions," stated Joseph emphatically.

"One, that you need a disguise; two, that you must ride a horse or camel; three, that you must be in the company of one or more persons. Let us continue," said Joseph with a shrewd smile, and twisting his moustache as he spoke.

"You could make your escape by night," added Naomi raising her eyebrows quizzically.

"I don't know about that!" interjected Simon. "The caravans never leave at night. If I were to join a caravan here in the city that would be bound for say, Caesarea, just to put them off the scent. It would leave in the early morning would it not?"

"Assuredly so," replied the host, still fumbling with his moustache.

"That is no good. The caravans are the most prone to an identity check," stated Naomi.

"Mind you," said the guest, "I shall have to catch up with it after they have travelled for almost a day."

The planning went on till supper time, and still they had not come up with a workable plan. After supper, the trio retired to the enchanting courtyard where by the light of a full moon, the golden light of the oil lamps, and the aroma of the wisteria, they were lulled into a semi stupor after the fullness of the meal. The three friends sat in silence, entertaining drowsy, vapoury, flitting thoughts.

"Aha! I have something."

The sudden exclamation from Joseph, shocked the other two out of their lethargy, and brought them back to rude reality.

"Do tell!" chorused the pair simultaneously.

The man of the house, then alluded to his ingenious plan:

"First, I have to talk to Nicodemus tomorrow. I shall ask him to find this man by the description you have given me. Then he tries to meet him accidentally on purpose, if you follow my meaning. He then prompts him for information as to how he is dealing with this follower of Yeshua, and does he think that he can catch him. The idea is to find out whether the gates are being watched or worse still, controlled. If Nicodemus can get us that intelligence, then I can formulate the plan that I have in mind.

"I shall not disclose it to you yet until I have the information I need from Nicodemus. He, I feel sure, will be a part of our escape act."

"Now, let us to bed. Tomorrow will be a busy day for me, and a long one for you Simon," declared his host leading the way upstairs.

Joseph was up early, and after breakfast, left hurriedly for the temple in search of his friend and secret disciple, Nicodemus. They usually found each other in the library room, but this morning Nicodemus was not there as yet. Joseph pulled out a couple of scrolls to read, and sat down. Whilst he was browsing the parchment, someone walked into the room. He looked up, expecting to see Nicodemus, but found Gamaliel instead.

This man Gamaliel was a good friend of his, and the most respected man in the Sanhedrin. He was a large man, possibly in his late fifties, or early sixties, and taller than average. He had an intelligent moonlike face with well proportioned features and bright enquiring eyes, giving notice of constant awareness. By the way he wore his prayer shawl, that draped over his great wrinkled brow and delineated the contour of his head, it would have surprised no one to discover that he was bald. His moustache and long beard streaked with grey, adequately made up for the barrenness under his covered head. Seeing his friend sitting there, he went over and greeted him warmly; a twinkle in his eye.

"Good morning Joseph. What commands your curiosity today?" he asked, glancing at the parchment that his colleague was reading.

"Just passing the time... Nothing special."

"Were you at the meeting last week, when the committee proposed that the disciples of that man Yeshua, who was crucified, should all be apprehended and thrown in prison?"

"Yes, I was there," replied Joseph. "And you wisely suggested that they wait to see whether it was man, or God who was directing them in their preaching and baptising."

"They are too impatient and could rake up a lot of trouble, upsetting people and getting the Romans involved. Individuals like

Saul of Tarsus, who at one time was a student of mine, and this man Jechonias, are stirring up the pot, and it could boil over in any direction to our detriment of course," explained Gamaliel with visible concern.

"Of Saul, I have heard. But who is this Jechonias?" asked Joseph in a seemingly disinterested way.

"You have seen him before. He is a plumpish man in his mid forties, with a perpetually sour look on his face and seldom speaks to anyone. He is a loner and works for our security people as some sort of free agent. Strange man,... a bachelor I believe."

"Come to think of it, I have seen him. You are right my friend, I just did not remember. He has never captured my attention to any great extent," asserted Joseph with a nod.

Nicodemus, middle aged, tall and thin, a congenial smile lighting up his long bony face, appeared in the room at this point in his colleagues' conversation, warmly greeting them both.

Taking a seat beside his disciple friend, he removed his white shawl. A good head of hair streaked with the occasional strand of grey caught Gamaliel's eye, and a touch of envy registered on it, as the conversation continued on general lines. Gamaliel, although a friend and colleague of Joseph's, was however, not one of his confidants. He had to wait till the former had left before he could talk with Nicodemus in private.

"Let us go for a walk," suggested Joseph, once Gamaliel had made his exit.

"In fact, why don't we walk over to my house," he added, thinking that Simon would like to see Nicodemus again.

"Have you some time at your disposal?"

"Oh yes. Your invitation is most welcome. I have not seen Naomi since the last time you visited us."

The two friends discussed a few things on their way, but were careful not to mention Simon's name or particulars. Miriam was there to open the door for them on their arrival. They went directly to the courtyard, suspecting that both Naomi and Simon would be there. They were not mistaken. Naomi left her seat by the wisteria, approached Nicodemus and warmly embraced him.

"Welcome my friend, and how is Susannah and the children?" she asked with fondness in her lovely eyes.

"They are all well thank you, the Lord be praised," he answered with a big smile, which momentarily puffed up his bony cheeks, and lit up his soft green eyes. Simon came forward and embraced him warmly, then all three settled down in that favourite perfumed alcove by the wisteria.

Naomi left to arrange for refreshments; calling back, asking them to await her return before uncovering any news. Presently she returned, assisted by Miriam who was carrying a little table which she set in front of them and on which the hostess placed a number of delicacies. The maid returned to the kitchen to fetch some wine and cups.

The congenial host poured the wine for them, and cup in hand began by uncovering the identity and activities of Jechonias. Nicodemus agreed to extract intelligence from the delinquent brother Pharisee, and depending on what he could learn, the plan which his host uncovered, would or would not, be adopted.

Nicodemus and Joseph did not stay long. They were eager to go after the man, since everything depended on the information they could get from him. If all went as they hoped, the plan which was now in place would see Simon safely on his way to Joppa.

For two days Nicodemus looked in vain for an opportunity to contact Jechonias in what would look like a 'by chance' and disinterested encounter. Not until the third day, did the occasion present itself. He spotted the spy by himself, leaning against the wall of the Damascus gate and peering out at the countryside. Nicodemus walked over to him and saluted him.

"Good day to you, friend!"

The other simply nodded in acknowledgement.

"Are you waiting for the caravan from Damascus?"

"No."

"Oh, I thought you were, pardon me."

"That's all right."

"Your face is familiar," persisted Nicodemus with a smile. "You are often at the temple are you not?"

"Yes, I work there."

"I thought so," continued Nicodemus. "I am a councillor and member of the Sanhedrin. My name is Nicodemus."

The spy's attitude changed abruptly.

"Yes, I think I have seen you around the temple too."

"You are not a councillor though, as I have not seen you in chambers."

"No, no, my name is Jechonias, and I am engaged by the security office of the Sanhedrin. Not every councillor knows of my work."

"That's very interesting. Am I permitted to learn what your work is?" continued Nicodemus feigning great interest.

"I am engaged in tracking down and apprehending the disciples, one in particular, of that imposter from Nazareth who was crucified a little while back and claimed to be not only the Messiah, but also the son of God."

"Oh, I see," nodded Nicodemus. "And have you been able to track him down?"

"Once I had him, but he slipped out of my hands just as I was marching him off to the temple prison... What rotten luck."

Nicodemus asked him about Simon's escape, which the spy explained in detail.

"And now how are you going to find him again? Jerusalem has many places for a man to hide."

"That is the problem. Only myself and two others who are not under my jurisdiction, can identify him. I am concerned that he may have already left the city, and if not, he will try to in any event."

"I see your problem," concurred Nicodemus. "There are seven gates out of Jerusalem, how do you intend to guard them all?"

"I simply cannot. It is impossible. But I shall continue to keep watch," assured Jechonias with hatred in his eyes.

"Have you alerted the customs people who check all traders at the gate. Might they be able to help you?"

"There is no point asking them. They are busy with their own work, and besides, they do not know what he looks like. There are at least a thousand men in Jerusalem that answer to his description."

"I see you are favouring the Damascus gate, you feel he is likely to go to Damascus?"

"No, not as far as that. But it would get him to Samaria where I am told that many of them have gone."

"Oh! I see," said the shrewd and amiable Pharisee feigning innocence once again.

"He could also be thinking of going to Caesarea or even Joppa. Being from Cyrene, I suspect he plans to go home, so the other gate I must watch is the Joppa gate which puts him in the right direction."

"Seems to me that you have condensed the problem down very nicely."

And with this, Nicodemus, not wanting to lie in wishing him luck, took his leave by nodding and saying that he would see him around.

Jechonias lingered at the gate after his interrogator had left, becoming increasingly frustrated. The satisfied councillor made straight for Joseph's house, where for the rest of the evening they planned their strategy based on all that he had learnt.

"We have just one more thing to ascertain," said Joseph as he accompanied his friend to the door. "It must happen on a caravan day, so that Simon can catch up with it before nightfall. I shall make enquiries myself tomorrow and let you know."

"Have a good night," smiled Nicodemus.

"You also," replied Joseph closing the door after his friend.

CHAPTER ELEVEN

ESCAPE

It was about the third hour on a beautiful spring day. Three horsemen slowly and cautiously approached the Essene Gate. One of the riders scrutinized the solitary Sanhedrin guard who stood talking to two Roman soldiers also on duty at the gate. Content with his findings, he nodded to his companion riders, one of whom moved on in front of him, and the other took up the rear as they rode past the guards.

"Hello there!" shouted one of the Romans.

All three horses stopped. The guard approached the leading horseman. No other than Nicodemus.

"Good morning!" greeted the rider.

"Good morning to you too!" replied the soldier. "Are you all together?" he asked, pointing at the other two horsemen.

"Yes, we are friends."

"Where are you going?"

"We are going for a ride around the city to enjoy the beautiful day."

"Very well. When you return come back by this gate, and check in with me," ordered the Roman.

The three horsemen rode out the gate, and once out of view of the guards, closed ranks and conferred together with regard to the unexpected obstacle in their plan.

"He'll be looking for three horsemen to come back through his gate. What are we going to do?" asked Simon.

"It is going to prevent your escape for today," answered Joseph.

"Let's just think for a little while as we trot along," suggested Nicodemus.

"We must keep well away from the Joppa and Damascus gates whilst we are riding around," said Joseph with a note of caution.

"Suppose we let Simon go," suggested Nicodemus, "and we come back through this same gate, telling the guard that his horse became lame, and he had to go back in through another gate. Say, the Eastern gate."

"Mmm… You may be onto something there," agreed Joseph.

"Suppose the soldier reports it tomorrow, or even tonight. The guard at that other gate, will deny my entry," said Simon. "I shall be gone, but you would both be in trouble."

"I doubt that. But it is possible," admitted Nicodemus.

"What if we go back in, and leave again by another gate?" suggested the Arimathean.

"I think we better get back in and call it a day… But just one moment!" said Nicodemus thinking aloud. "We need one more rider to make our little plot a success, so it cannot be today in any event."

The three were forced to return. The next time they would be better prepared, they promised themselves.

They made their way back to the gate, and just as they were about to enter, Simon spotted one of the guards who had detained him. He must have been in the customs hut, on their way out. Simon jumped off his horse, and had just enough time to let Joseph know why he had dismounted, and that he should say that his friend's horse had hurt its leg and was being walked. Joseph informed Nicodemus, and they entered the gate with the Cyrenean walking on the far side of the guard his horse shielding him partially from view. The Roman guard walked over, and asked Nicodemus if they had enjoyed the ride.

"Yes!" he answered with a smile, "But my friend's horse hurt his leg, and even though it it isn't limping, we thought we had better walk it back."

The soldier glanced in Simon's direction but Joseph urged his horse forward and obstructed his view, at the same time wishing him a good day. All three moved on ahead slowly.

"Just a moment!" someone called out.

Nicodemus looked back, and realised that it was the Jewish guard who was calling to them. Simon and Joseph kept going as if they had not heard the man call.

"You called?" asked the councillor.

"You are a councillor of the Sanhedrin are you not?" enquired the soldier, recognising Nicodemus from sight.

"Yes," he answered, assuming a more sober attitude.

"Are you perchance going back to the temple?"

"No, I took the day off."

"Very well then. Pardon my having troubled you," said the soldier uncertainly, and with a somewhat disappointed look returned to his post.

The councillor breathed a sigh of relief.

'I wonder what he wanted me to do for him?' he thought to himself, hastening to catch up with his friends.

Simon was still in danger of bumping unexpectedly into Jechonias, so he continued to walk his horse. It was an effective way of shielding himself from view.

The horses were returned to the stables where they had been hired, and all made their way to Joseph's house without any further incident. The fugitive would stay there once more until the next caravan day, when the revised plan would again be put into action, hopefully with better luck.

The third hour of the morning three days later, confirmed a rider of approximately Simon's build, on a black horse, trotting through the Joppa gate allegedly on his way to Caesarea, as the guard was informed on interrogating the rider..

A half hour after the third hour, once more, out of the Essene gate rode the same three horsemen as on the previous occasion. The Roman guard; a different soldier that day, was given the exact same story. The Sanhedrin guards were both different also, and posed no danger to Simon who in any event did his best to obscure his face. As was expected, they were waved on with the proviso that they should return by the same gate. This seemed to Joseph a normal procedure, and he made a mental note of it.

After an hour's ride, the trio met up with the rider on the black horse that had left through the Joppa gate earlier on. The man who was also a disciple, and a good friend of Nicodemus, exchanged clothes and provisioned horse with Simon. He gave him the address of the place in Joppa, where the rented horse was to be returned at the end of his journey.

Simon, greatly moved by the cordial assistance of Joseph and Nicodemus, gave both men an appreciative hug, expressing his gratitude, especially to Joseph whom he had grown very fond of, and wondered whether he would ever see them again.

A prayer for the welfare of all was said there on the spot, after which Simon holding Joseph's arms, and with great feeling, addressed him.

"My friend or should I call you, my brother, for you and Naomi are like family to me now. I can never thank you enough for your wonderful hospitality. May the Lord Yeshua continue to bless and protect you both for many years to come. I shall never forget you. You will always be in my prayers."

Joseph, with sadness in his eyes, wished his brother disciple, health, and success in his missionary work, and a safe journey home. Adding, that he or any member of his family would always be welcome in his house.

The parting having been completed, Simon rode off with a heavy heart, to catch up with the caravan for Joppa which had left by the Joppa gate two hours earlier. It had been thoroughly inspected by Jechonias himself,... to no avail.

Three hours after the departure from his friends, our adventurous hero caught up with the caravan plodding along at its normal pace. Simon asked permission to join them, which was presently given. He rode near the head of the column as it approached the mountainous country which would challenge them for the next few days.

The sun set over the mountain directly in front of them. They had just started the climb, and Simon wondered how much further the caravan master would continue before he stopped for the night. The terrain was wild, and the path narrow. It seemed to offer no suitable location for camping. The caravan master whose name was Ahmed, was an Egyptian, about thirty years old. He urged the caravan; consisting of eight camels, four horses (including Simon's horse,) and two donkeys, to increase their speed.

It was getting quite dark. Suddenly, the path opened up into a rough terrace-like   promontory, fronting two caves. One, with a very large opening. Once on the terrace, a general dismounting ensued, and great haste was made to start a fire in the open between the mouths of the caves.

Torches were quickly lit, and the guards who accompanied the caravan, entered each cave in turn with swords at the ready, to ensure that no wild animal was hiding inside. A wild cat dashed out of the large cave, growled angrily and quickly lost itself in the night. The animals were taken into the larger cave. All were relieved of their saddles, and given some water and grain that the donkeys had been carrying, along with firewood.

The people who made up the caravan began to sit around the fire. Simon approached the master, and after a little haggling, settled on a fee for partaking in the benefits the caravan had to offer; such as protection provided by the guards, and other small things that might cause inconvenience. Supplies, he did not need, since the man who had left him the horse, had also left enough provisions, (including a skin of water and one of wine) to last him and the horse for four days.

Soon they were all engrossed in consuming their meagre rations, which each person carried for their own sustenance; some being cooked over the fire whilst others eaten cold.

The travellers comprised a mixed group of men and women. Four of them knew each other intimately, and kept to themselves on one side of the fire. The two guardsmen also sat together, desiring to keep a certain aloofness from their charges. Simon chatted with the four remaining members and Ahmed, who seemed an amiable enough fellow, and knowing the route, explained the harshness and steepness of the terrain that they would be travelling over the coming day. This was not news to Simon, who was aquatinted with the route. This time however, he was travelling on horseback instead of camel.

"We shall be out for three nights," explained Ahmed to the group. "The distance is not much, but the steepness of the climb, and ruggedness of the terrain, makes our path dance around so much that it is greatly increased."

The caravan master often gesticulated with his hands as he spoke; his large vivacious dark eyes glistening by the light of the fire lending credence to their every movement.

"It will be slow going until we reach the upper paths," remarked the man sitting to Simon's left, looking past him at

Ahmed. A wheeze accompanied his statement, as he pulled up his shawl which had slipped down around his narrow shoulders.

"Are we likely to be accosted by robbers?" enquired a woman whose short brow catching the light of the fire exhibited wrinkles of concern as she appealed to the caravan master for an answer.

"I have not yet had any experience of that kind on this particular route. Perhaps the fact that caravans have their own guards, and that these roads are patrolled by the Romans, poses too much of a risk for the bandits," concluded the Egyptian, with a consoling look at the aging woman.

The campfire talk did not continue for long. The caravan was to resume its journey shortly after dawn, and supper had been over for the best part of an hour. They all retired into the smaller cave, which was illuminated by two torches stuck into holes in the wall. They used their mats, saddles, and bags, making themselves as comfortable as the rocky cave floor would allow.

Ahmed, and one of the guards remained by the fire. The caravan master as was his habit wrapped himself in his blanket, and leaning against the rock face, quickly fell into a light sleep. The guard on duty, following his example, drew a blanket around himself, and with his sword lying beside him, prepared to remain vigilant for his three hour watch. He would then be relieved by the other guardsman, who would sleep during the first watch.

Simon's eyes scanned the cave amidst a cacophony of snores that collectively made the cave sound like a beehive. He tried to imagine the need of some of these people undertaking an uncomfortable journey such as this. His mind naturally found its way back to his family.

'How are they?' he wondered. 'How well are the boys coping in my absence? Have they been able to install more cabins on those corbitas? How is Rufus progressing with his love affair? I must see Marius as soon as the *Stella Maris* makes it to port in Joppa. Hopefully soon. Ruth had to be told of my whereabouts, my state of health, and my plans.'

His thoughts ran on. He now wondered what sort of person Simon the tanner would be, and if he would be as welcome in his house as he had been at Joseph's. With those thoughts, he fell asleep.

The piercing voice of Ahmed jarred him into the reality of the morning. He briskly raised his head from the saddle on which it had been resting. He felt cold and stiff from the cool mountain night, and quickly made his way outside. There, after jumping around, and swinging his arms as some others were also doing, he began to warm up. The rays of the sun soon swept the mountain, bathing them with their warm glow.

A most welcome, and soothing herbal tea was boiled over a revitalized fire. Bread and cheese appeared to be the breakfast of choice as the little party prepared for the gruelling day ahead.

The camels, and horses, were brought out by the guards, who readied them for the people, and assisted some in mounting. Simon saddled his horse, hung his baggage on it, mounted, and assuming an easy stride, followed Ahmed's lead once more as the caravan began its climb again.

The day warmed up quickly, and soon the rigours imposed by the ever climbing route retarded their rate of progress, as had indeed been predicted by the caravan master. The latter took the matter with total unconcern. He smiled contentedly with nods of encouragement to those who needed his sympathy.

A short stop was made for lunch after four hours on the hoof, which was the absolute limit for many of the group, including Simon. The dismounting was immediately followed by a general dispersion among the boulders and bushes. Once reunited, a half hour rest period was proclaimed by the master. Jaws of varied shapes, sizes and colours, seemed to move in unison as the food was consumed with keen appetites; their owners reclining against the boulders bordering the trail. Soon the group was on the move again.

Simon, being no stranger to hill country, felt a certain comfort of spirit and admiration for the beauty of those Judean hills, with their abundant vegetation in varying shades of green and distant blues. The myriads of multi- coloured wild flowers, impressed themselves on his senses and held his appreciative attention as he rode.

From his lofty perch on that ever climbing, ever winding path, he could see the rugged arid desert that they had crossed the previous day, with Jerusalem twinkling in the afternoon sun in the far purple distance.

Awakened from his deliberations by the distinct, and musical sound of water, Simon's attention was now captured by a short wooden bridge, which Ahmed's camel was now traversing. The heavy clomping of the camel's feet drowned momentarily the pleasant sound. Simon followed, his eyes curiously searching for the water. It appeared in the form of a small mountain stream merrily tumbling and dancing over the rocks immediately below him. As he left the sturdy little bridge, he was confronted once again with a truly amazing sight. There, ahead of him, carved out of the rock, was a trough filled with sparkling clear water. As it overflowed, it was redirected by a similarly carved long gutter, sending it back into the tumbling spring.

The trough itself was filled by another smaller trough positioned directly above and overflowing into it. That smaller trough was fed by a natural spring flowing gently from a cleavage in the rock face. This ingeniously designed mechanism captured the attention of man and beast. Their tongues and mouths yearned for the taste of that clear, sparkling water.

The path widened considerably once the bridge had been passed. Ahmed called for a halt. All dismounted quickly, and headed cup in hand, for the upper trough which beckoned them with its cheerful little waterfall. The nectar of the Gods could hardly have vied with the taste of that tingling, inebriating mountain water, which gave flight to the spirit as it refreshed the body.

The animals, contemplating this spectacle, pawed at the dirt impatiently. Giving notice it would seem, that they too, were the work of the Creator, and having borne the burdens of the day's heat, were fully entitled to feast on that tantalising water. Their wish was granted of course. The moment the human thirst was quenched, they were lined up side by side three at a time, as the water in the large trough was eagerly ingested by those noble servants of man.

The animals were then tied to nearby trees, and the hour of rest was welcomed by all.

They chose their places around a clearing surrounded by boulders just ahead of where the fountain was located. Simon pulled down a bag of grain which his horse was carrying, and putting some into an old hat he had with his belongings, filled and held it, while the beautiful black animal ate.

He then returned to the group with his supper and wine skin in hand. A fire had been lit over the dregs of a previous fire that another caravan had made, and a few had already started eating. Others waited for their food to cook as several pots were suspended side by side on an iron rail resting on two legs, permanently set into the rock for the use of travellers.

Simon's meal consisted of dried fish, bread dipped in olive oil, some cheese, and dates. He then sat back and enjoyed a little of his wine.

"We shall be on our way as soon as we are finished here," announced Ahmed once again. "We have to reach our camp for the night, and it is still two hours away."

Just then the sound of many voices were heard, and presently another caravan headed in the opposite direction arrived. Greetings ensued, as the masters embraced, and the travellers began to dismount. Simon decided to keep a low profile just in case these people were interrogated by the ever prying Jechonias on their arrival in Jerusalem. He did not feel threatened, but from now on he would have to try to curb his natural inclination at being so openly friendly with strangers, and become more reserved.

'What a terrible nuisance,' he thought to himself. 'That a man should have to change the way God has made him, simply because one evil and misguided person endangers his existence. And yet,' he continued to muse. 'Peter, perhaps the most threatened of all Yeshua's followers, was as friendly disposed as he, and yet did not fear anyone. But then, he was Peter, and had not the Lord called him Petrus? …Yes, a rock indeed.'

He was all absorbed in his thoughts, when he heard the caravan master call out for his group to mount. Making haste, head down, he made his way quickly to his horse, mounted, and began to move forward slowly so as to allow Ahmed to overtake him.

"You are in a hurry to get to night camp, yes? Are you not feeling well? You were very quiet at supper," said Ahmed, stringing his words so that Simon could not immediately reply.

"I have a headache," said the Cyrenean, trying to look dejected. "It'll pass soon I hope."

"This pure mountain air sometimes has that effect on city dwellers," was the master's reply.

Simon made no further comment, but rode on quietly for the next while; the caravan continuing the uphill climb. Ahmed, a little concerned about Simon, started up a conversation with him.

"Is your headache any better?"

The carpenter whose mind was again in Cyrene, shook himself free of his thoughts, and answered.

"Yes, thank you. It's almost gone."

The caravan master was relieved. The last thing he wanted was someone getting sick on the trip. Life was tough enough he thought, without more complications.

"I am truly glad to hear that," he asserted.

Simon was beginning to like the man, who seemed to have a touch of affection for the people under his charge. He now wondered whether the master of the caravan would not be a good candidate for conversion to Yeshua.

'Yes,' said Simon to himself. 'He certainly would be, but,... he's a gentile and I can't help him. But then did Yeshua not say that he was dying for all men? Now I'm really confused. I must ask Peter when I see him again in Joppa. Let's see what he says.'

"You are a good man Ahmed. You care about the people who have placed their trust in you," Simon assured him.

"Good of you to say so. You are a perceptive man. I do care very much, and I try to do what I have to, in the best way I can."

"To please who?"

"To please myself I suppose."

"Do you believe in an Afterlife?" asked Simon.

"My ancestors were very sure that there was one, and they made elaborate preparations for that life. Still I often wondered what happened to the poor people who could not afford to be mummified. Finally, I just gave up thinking about it. I must say though, that even the lowliest person is such an amazing creature, that it is hard for me to believe that we will disappear into nothingness."

"No, Ahmed. They, you, or I, won't disappear into nothingness. We're all created for a better life than this I can assure you."

The Egyptian's dark eyes widened with consummate interest.

"How would you know that?"

"If I confide in you, and tell you something of great interest, will you promise me that you won't tell anyone where you heard it?"

"I swear it," said Ahmed brimming with enthusiasm.

"Have you heard of a man named Yeshua, the Nazarene?"

"Who has not heard of him? He was crucified about three months ago... I heard him speak once. He was a good man, spoke only of love. Everyone expected him to defy the Romans, but he just told them to be better people, and be good to one another .... A beautiful message I thought. But what good did it do him? What chance did he have against those wolves?"

"Do you know that he rose from the dead?"

"No! how could he do that?"

"He did! ...He died on the sixth day of the week, which is the Dies Veneris of the Romans. They buried him in a tomb which had never been used. It was hewn out of the rock, and closed by a great round stone. I know the man who owns it. The stone had even been sealed by the Sanhedrin's guards who had been assigned to guard the tomb. On the morning of the third day, a few of the women who followed him, and looked after his needs went to the tomb with more spices to finish the embalming. They had not been able to complete it on the sixth day because the Sabbath hour was approaching.

The Egyptian's dark eyes were fixed on the Cyrenean's earnest face as the latter related his story.

"When the women reached the tomb at dawn, that morning, there was an earthquake, and the large stone that enclosed the tomb fell to the ground and an angel sat on it. The women were petrified with fear, and the guards were paralyzed.

Ahmed, looking down at Simon, shifted uncomfortably in his saddle.

"Go on," he said.

"The angel told them not to be afraid. That Yeshua was not there, but had risen to the Father."

"To the Father you say? ...his Father?"

"Yes, indeed, since he had claimed to be the Son of God and the Messiah."

"That would be the Jewish God, Yahweh."

"Yes," confirmed the carpenter. Happy that his new friend was well informed on such matters. "But here is the most impressive part," he continued looking up at Ahmed, whose eager eyes were reflecting the excitement that was stirring his soul. "He appeared to one of the women, and then to all his disciples. He ate in front of them, and touched them, to show he was alive."

The Egyptian just stared straight in front of him. Not a further word was said by either of them. They travelled in silence until another widening in the path appeared. The caravan master, jumping out of his reverie, lifted his hand and announced a stop for the night. This campsite, it appeared, was not as well suited to their needs as that of the previous night. There were no caves visible, and very few trees on which to tie their animals.

No one dismounted. All looked at Ahmed in the hope that he would uncover some mysterious shelter, but the latter seemed to offer no consolation for their concern.

"This," he announced. "is where we will spend the night. The animals can be tied to those hoops." He pointed to some that had been set into the rock, and which no one had yet noticed. "And now, please follow me," he ordered, disappearing behind a rock, and waiting for the others to follow.

The group followed, and as they turned the corner, they were pleasantly surprised by the entrance to a cave. It was rather low, but a cave is a cave they reasoned, and all were content. A fire was lit, and once again they grouped around it, preparing to have something to eat and drink prior to their retiring for the night.

Simon once again went to see to his horse. The two guards were there, feeding the other animals. Simon, not seeing any water around, asked them if they had a basin, or bucket which he could use to give his horse a drink. One of them pointed to a bucket lying by the side of the road that had escaped his notice. It was there he supposed for all caravans to use. He fed the horse, and shared the contents of his water with it. Tomorrow he remembered, they would pass by another spring and replenish their supply.

This being done, he walked off with the saddle and his meagre baggage, joining the others by the camp fire. After a quick repast, they all turned in for the night. Ahmed stayed outside as usual with the duty guard.

Once again, the following morning, the sun rising behind Jerusalem, greeted them with its warming rays, and motivated the travellers to start on their day's journey, which would soon have them descending.

Two hours into the morning, the caravan reached the summit of the mountain range. Once over, the other side of the path would descend in the same winding pattern as they had followed in their ascent. The caravan master looked pleased with himself as he led his little fold. Simon who had not talked to him since the night before, rode up beside the former's camel and proffered his morning greetings.

"Here you are my friend, I trust you slept well," greeted Simon, with a big smile.

"You seem to be in a very good mood this morning. Is it because we are riding the summit of the mountain, and soon we shall start descending?" asked Simon.

"That is a good reason to be happy, but I have a better reason," replied Ahmed with enthusiasm.

"Oh?"

"What you told me last night has given me much hope and cause for happiness," he affirmed with a big smile, and continued:

"If what you say is true, then you have proved to me that there is definitely another life after death. As you say, no one has ever come back to tell us, except this man Yeshua who has appeared to men and eaten with them."

"The thing is," said Simon with some excitement in his voice, "he told his disciples that he would, rise from the dead. And not just his disciples, but others too. The high priests and the Sanhedrin were also told, but did not believe him. To tell you the truth, even some of his disciples doubted that he would rise again. They seemed not to understand. It was such a fantastic thing."

"I must know more about Yeshua... Much more," insisted Ahmed, looking pleadingly at Simon.

"I am still learning myself," answered our hero. "I was one of the last to see him, but I shall be meeting his chief apostle soon, and then he will tell me everything about him."

"I envy you," confided Ahmed.

"We shall meet again, and then I shall tell you everything I learn about him and his followers; for he has new followers every day. The Sanhedrin in Jerusalem are very worried indeed. Why, I don't know. His disciples are peace-loving and harmless, but, that is the way it is at the moment. Remember my friend," continued Simon. "That you promised to keep everything I have told you secret. My life could be at stake if you mention me to anyone. Especially, as you go into Jerusalem where there is a man by name of Jechonias at the Joppa Gate who relentlessly pursues me, and all Yeshua's disciples."

"I shall never betray you my friend, and I look forward to meeting you again. You know where to find me. So please do not forget me. I simply must know more."

One of the guards drew up to talk to Ahmed, and Simon fell back a little to give the man room on the narrow path. Half an hour later they began their descent, to the cheers of the caravan who could now feel the journey's end nearing. Their speed increased as the haze around them dissipated, and by lunchtime, the fertile valley far below could be clearly discerned.

The sight was truly breath-taking. There, before them, lay a glorious patchwork of colour stretching as far as the eye could see, running parallel to the mountain range. Its striking verdure predominated in varying shades; occasioned by various elements such as trees bunched together into little copses, palm groves, and grassy fields in sun-filled vibrant greens. Cultivated land, resplendent in its variety of flowers and vegetables, celebrated its exuberance in the form of varied greens and yellows. This vivacious symphony of colour, contrasted sharply yet somehow harmonized with, the arid patches of rough ground and ploughed land which having yielded their crop, now lay a fallow brown. Little villages sparkled in the morning sun, and roads crossed the land in many directions. At the end of it all, enveloped in a light haze, lay the majestic blue Mediterranean Sea.

'What a memorable sight,' thought Simon to himself, as he admired the stunning view, which by the inclusion of the Mediterranean Sea reminded him of home.

Lunch followed soon after the disclosure of this picturesque view, enjoyed by everyone during their meal, and customary half hour rest, before resuming the journey downhill.

The day went by quicker than the previous two. After a couple of stops during the six hour run since lunch, they were ready once more to stop for supper as the day began to wane.

Another little bridge came into view as if a wish had been granted, giving everyone the opportunity of slaking their thirst, and that of the animals. The same design around the water trough was evident. The sound of the water falling with even more force on this occasion was most pleasing to the ear, and presented a very pretty sight as it gushed merrily down on its way to the valley below.

Another shelter was soon discovered. This time however, the cave-like tunnel was man-made by Roman engineers, since the location did not offer a natural shelter for either soldiers or caravans. A widening of the path had also been carried out, and hoops had been installed in the rock for the securing of the animals.

A repetition of the previous two nights was re-enacted. When morning arrived the brave little band headed by their able master, and carrying with it our hero, continued their downward journey with the great anticipation, that when night finally arrived, they would all be sleeping in their own much desired beds.

Supper was eaten that evening on the bank of a small narrow river, born of one or more of those pure streams that they drank from in the mountains. There was no shelter to speak of. They simply tied their animals to the trees, and sat on the grass. No fire was lit either, as what they ate did not require cooking. An air of abandon pervaded the camp.

The striking valley; rich in orange groves, date palms, olive trees, and brimming with cultivation, was duly crossed, and by dusk they entered the city of Joppa with great relief.

The caravan master was heartily thanked by all without exception. He, wishing them well, collected the camels with the aid of his guards and prepared to march them off to his stables. Simon, who waited until all had gone, walked over to his new friend and promised to seek him out again soon, when hopefully he would have much more to tell him.

Ahmed, gave him directions to his house, and invited him to visit any time he wished. A warm embrace followed, and away went

Simon to return the black horse, and search out Simon the tanner's house.

CHAPTER TWELVE

SIMON THE TANNER

Simon the tanner had closed his door for the night over an hour ago, but he was still busy scraping the hair off a deer skin which had been soaking for a couple of days in lime and could no longer be ignored. His daughter Hannah quietly approached her father, and putting her hands gently on his shoulders announced that supper was not only ready, but getting cold.

"You should have been eating two hours ago Father," she said in a coaxing mood, knowing that he was always late for supper, and she felt hungry.

Hannah was twenty years of age and an only child. Her mother had died giving her life. She loved her father dearly as he catered to her every whim. He saw her as the spitting image of her mother, who had been a very beautiful woman and had died when she was Hannah's present age. The daughter was somewhat reserved and formal in her demeanour. She was wise beyond her years, which came perhaps from living with her father, assuming the household responsibilities, and not unduly exposed to the love of frivolity common to most women. She had but few women friends.

Though the totality of her face would aptly be described as beautiful, the regularity of each individual feature was unremarkable in itself. Her nose was straight and light, the oval of her face was pleasantly delineated, presenting her other features with a certain grace. Her large brown eyes, profusely eyelashed, crowned by delicately arched eye brows, gave notice of deep understanding and sympathy apparent in her soft gaze. She had a sensuous, full-lipped mouth and very dark brown hair, some falling gracefully over her well proportioned brow. It was combed back tightly and plaided into a long tail embellished with a red ribbon, sometimes draping over her back, and other times over her shoulder. These attributes contributed to the total aspect of her face, which was further enhanced by her small tightly contained ears on whose delicate lobes hung two circular gold earrings. Her figure was of average height, slim and elegant. Her well cared for and shapely hands, graceful in movement, surprisingly did not betray the hard work that she was occasionally called to do.

Simon stopped his scraping, and turned around at his daughter's touch.

"My dear, you must be famished... I get involved in my work, my thoughts take flight, and I forget how quickly time passes."

"You certainly do. Now please come along and wash up, you have done more than enough for..."

Bang! Bang!

A knocking at the door interrupted Hannah.

"I wonder who it could be at this late hour, " remarked a surprised Simon. "I shall go myself."

He cautiously opened the door. There on the threshold, stood our hero.

"Are you Simon the tanner?"

"Yes!"

"My name is Simon also.... Simon of Cyrene. I am a carpenter. I am so very sorry to come at this late time of the evening. I have just arrived by caravan, I know no one in the city, and Peter said that you would allow me to stay with you for a little while till he comes."

"Peter?" asked the tanner abstractedly. "What Peter?"

"Peter the apostle of Yeshua. He is a good friend of yours I believe?"

"Oh. ...That Peter! ...of course."

"Come in please. You are most welcome."

"Thank you," said Simon as he followed the tanner into the house.

"Leave your things here for now, and if you join me in my ablutions we shall have supper immediately. My daughter has been trying to get me to the table for the last two hours."

As they went past the kitchen, Simon poked his head in the doorway and asked his daughter to set up another place for his guest.

Simon the tanner was fifty two years old, sturdily built, and gifted with a very pleasant personality, which came through very distinctly in his smile, and the twinkle in his eyes. He had heavy brown eyebrows with a touch of grey that gave his lively eyes a comical look. As the carpenter was quick to notice, masses of unruly hair covered the sides of the man's head, joining his large beard and moustache, and winding around the back of his head in clusters; the head itself was totally bald except for a solitary outcrop of hair high in the middle of his forehead. His ears tight to the head, and hidden by hair, were invisible from a frontal position. He was not a tall man but his large belly gave the impression of being shorter than he actually was.

They both came back refreshed from their ablutions and entered the dining room, which as in Simon's house in Cyrene was the largest room in the house, and consequently the hub of all activity in their daily lives. Hannah emerged from the kitchen on hearing their voices, and her father promptly introduced her to Simon.

"This, is my daughter; housekeeper, cook, assistant tanner, and delight of my life."

Simon bowed his head slightly, giving her an admiring smile.

"She reminds me of my eldest daughter who is also quite beautiful," he said with sincerity and a pleasant smile.

The two men sat down on cushions which lay on the floor surrounding a low table suitable for four persons. Hannah brought in the food and wine, sat down, looked at her father who said a prayer of thanks, and all three began their meal. The tanner was the first to speak.

"So you are a carpenter from Cyrene? You are a long way from home. I take it you are a disciple of Yeshua."

"I am now, and that's why I came back from Cyrene."

Simon told them of his first visit to Jerusalem. How he had helped Yeshua carry the cross, and had to come back to learn more.

Hannah asked him how long he had been away from home, and he told them all about Joseph, Naomi, and lastly, about his escape. Father and daughter listened with great interest to the visitor's story.

"You have had quite an adventure," said Hannah with a beautiful smile.

"We also are expecting to become disciples of Yeshua. As soon as Peter comes we shall be baptised," assured the father with enthusiasm, reaching for his wine cup.

"Did you meet Yeshua?" asked the Cyrenean.

"Yes," said the tanner, "we met him over a year ago when we went to Galilee to visit my sister. That is when we also met Peter, who told us all about our Lord."

"I baptised over two hundred people on Pentecost day," said Simon, with a feeling of self satisfaction. "James the apostle baptised me on the spot, and asked me to help him. There were so many people, that he could not cope by himself. I could baptise you, but I think you had better wait for Peter. It will be an honour for you to have 'him' do it.

"We are well informed with all that happens in Jerusalem," said the tanner. "People come and go all the time, and it is very probable that Peter might head this way soon."

The two Simons talked late into the night. Hannah had excused herself earlier and after making the guest room comfortable for her guest, had gone to bed. The two men finally parted for the night, and Simon found himself in a fairly large room with a bed prepared for him. He lost no time in undressing, and delighting in a comfortable bed once again, fell asleep almost immediately.

Awakened by the morning sun, Simon stood at the window of his room looking at the fishing boats as they came in from their night of fishing. They were being welcomed by a crowd of screeching, hungry sea gulls. The boats were being dragged ashore by many willing hands; being made to ride over wooden logs that were progressively placed under them and in that manner, sliding them up the beach. To his right, he could see the port with many ships berthed along its quays. He could not name most of the ships, but he quickly recognized three corbitas, and wondered whether the *Stella Maris* was one of them.

It was a beautiful morning. Fair weather had held out since he left Jerusalem, and now the morning sun was reigning once again over a glittering blue sea.

Simon stood there a little longer, not wishing to leave the soul-soothing spectacle. He listened between the screeching of the gulls to the gentle lapping of the sea as it licked the beach, imprinting on the sand constantly changing circular patterns deepening in colour, and accentuating it with shades of violet amidst the delicate white froth of the advancing surf.

He turned to survey the room which as yet had not captured his attention. This one was larger than the one he had inhabited in Joseph's house, and accommodated yet another bed. Though the tasteful decorations that Naomi's excellent taste had created were conspicuously absent, the table with basin, jug, and towel were there, the bed was comfortable and clean, and a trunk for his clothes was also evident. A mat and low table had been placed beside his bed, under which, as in Joseph's house, sat the usual and indispensable glazed pot with a handle.

The walls were devoid of any decoration whatsoever, giving the room a bland, empty feeling, but Simon said to himself. 'The view from the widow more than makes up for the blandness of the room. When in Joppa, one must look out, not in.'

He went about his business; washed, combed his hair, and trimmed his beard and moustache using a polished piece of brass as a mirror. It hung on the wall immediately above the basin, as in the women's room in his own house.

'Ruth would not approve of my going around with a scraggly beard as does my new friend Simon,' he mused, as he left the room.

"Good morning," he sang as he entered the living room. "Another beautiful day greets us this morning, and the view from my room is indeed a glorious one."

"Good morning to you too," chorused father and daughter as they sat eating their breakfast.

Hannah tried to get up, but the guest, with a quick halting gesture, bade her sit again and continue with her meal. He then sat near them with an appreciative smile on his handsome face, and continued the conversation.

The tanner smiled back at him as he struggled to ensure that his food did not get entangled on the scruffy profusion of hair which surrounded his mouth. His eyes seem to twinkle with a certain enthusiasm which though involuntary, gave his wild countenance a quality of friendliness and innocence; if that were possible in a man of his age and experience.

"You must go out for a walk and see the town," suggested Hannah. She, now having finished, got up to bring her guest's breakfast before her father left for his work.

"Yes," responded Simon. "I would like to walk around the port as I wish to find out if a particular ship is in the harbour."

"You are doubtlessly waiting for a passage home," observed the other Simon with a sympathetic expression.

"Ultimately, yes, but only if Peter approves. You see," he continued, "just as you and Hannah are waiting for Peter to baptise you, I am waiting for his 'Laying of Hands,' which will allow me to spread the good news in my country, and minister to my people."

Presently, breakfast being over, the two Simons got up and at the tanner's invitation, the carpenter followed him into his shop to be shown the workings of the tannery. The guest listened attentively to the tanner's explanations on the procedures, materials and tools of his trade, and he was fascinated by the wonders that could be wrought on raw hide by this very experienced master.

The visitor looked around, and wondered if there was any way that he could improve the working of the shop or fix anything that may be giving his host trouble. At the moment all this being very new to him, he limited himself to offering his services gratis, whether with carpentry, or assisting in whatever might be needed.

"I thank you my friend," replied the tanner with a smile. "For the moment, nothing is needed, but if in the coming days the hours of leisure prove too hard for you to bear, your strong arms will be most welcome."

Simon felt happy at the disinterested honesty of his fellow tradesman. Taking his leave, he stepped out of the house, and turned to note its exterior stone facade with its distinctive arched entrance, not having properly observed it in the dark the previous night. Having become acquainted with the unique facade, he started off for the harbour which was nearby.

As he passed by the many ships that were either berthed, or lying at anchor in the picturesque harbour, he eagerly searched out the corbitas that he had seen from his window. He realised that of all the larger and more imposing ships that he saw, the modest corbita alone held a special place in his heart.

There, reposed the first one. His eyes unconsciously searched for the cabin extension that had now become so important in his work. There was none. He did not bother to make any mental note of the ship's name. It was inconsequential. Any corbita regardless of name that entered the harbour at Apollonia, would be fair game for Alexander and Rufus, if he knew his sons.

He continued his walk a little further, hoping to see *Stella Maris* painted on the bow of the next ship. But again his hopes remained abstractions as he now scrutinized it for the cabin extension. No, this ship also lacked that new feature.

'Maybe third time lucky,' mused Simon, as he approached the third ship. '...No, not the *Stella* either... But, wait a moment... It has a cabin extension...' The *Pretoria*, was the name on its bow.

Simon's heart was filled with paternal pride as he studied his boys' work.

'Excellent... Excellent," he repeated. 'I am a lucky m—'

"You can come aboard if you want a better look at my new cabin," shouted a gruff voice from the deck, who as my esteemed reader knows was no other than Silas, the captain of the ship.

"Good morning!" said Simon with his habitually pleasant smile, as he reached the top of the gang plank.

"And to you," replied Silas with one of his unique face-splitting smiles which Simon was quick to notice with some amusement.

"Come have a closer look," invited the captain.

Our hero, who found his new host most congenial, thought he would indulge in a little fun, and said."I'll lay you a wager of one solitary denarius, that I can describe to you the inside of that cabin in detail."

"I'd would love to take your denarius my friend, so go ahead," said Silas with another face-splitting smile.

Simon, tightening his lips together, and turning their ends down, tried to give his face a look of importance. He closed his eyes in imitation of a trance and proceeded to describe everything that was to be found in the cabin, right down to the hooks for tunics on the wall immediately behind the door.

Silas' comical face, stared at the carpenter with open mouth; his beady eyes enlarging to an unprecedented size almost converting themselves into circles.

"How can you possibly know all that, when you have never set foot on my ship before?" he asked.

"I have special powers," said the other with a big humorous smile on his face, and putting out his hand for the waged denarius.

The captain accepted his defeat and was about to hand over the coin, when Simon put his arm around his victim's broad shoulders and proudly said.

"My two boys built this cabin for you, following the design of the one that we built on the *Stella Maris* in Cyrene."

"You're the father of Alexander and Rufus?" gasped Silas incredulously.

"The very one," answered the proud father.

"You're indeed a lucky man my friend. Those two boys of yours completed their work well and in good time, allowing me to set sail on schedule for Caesarea....Come inside, and see how well they did."

"Have you had occasion to meet up with the *Stella Maris*?" asked Simon with a hopeful look in his eyes, and stepping into the cabin.

"Well no, I haven't," answered the captain. "Though I heard a rumour that she had sailed to Rome with a cargo of grain, and some special person on board."

"Oh yes, now I remember... The owner's daughter."

''That's strange," said Simon. Marius the captain whom I know well, told me that he was going to keep to his normal run from Caesarea to Cyrene or Carthage, as the furthest destination of his route. I'm expecting to find him soon either here in Joppa, or Caesarea."

"If you check with the Registry office down the quay there, they may be able to give you more information than I can," advised Silas, pointing down the wharf.

Simon and Silas, parted with the promise from the captain that if he met Marius, he would ask him to seek out the boys on the next trip to Apollonia, and tell them that their father is well and will hopefully be home soon.

It was not until he was drawing near the Registry office, that what Silas had said about the owner's daughter going to Rome, dawned on Simon, and his heart fell. He was so disheartened that he almost forgot why he had come to the Registry office.

"Can I assist you?"

Simon came out of his troubled thoughts realising that he had walked into the office he was seeking, and that the attendant behind the desk was addressing him.

"Yes," he answered almost involuntarily.

"Can you tell me where the corbita by name of the *Stella Maris* is at present, or indeed anything you know of her?"

The attendant, seeing that Simon was disturbed by something pertinent to the ship, asked.

"Do you have family aboard it?"

"No, answered Simon but Captain Marius is a friend of mine, and I'm waiting for him to come to Joppa."

"As far as I know, he left Apollonia bound for Rome and had arrived there with a cargo of grain. I cannot tell you if he is on his way back here or Caesarea. If you check back in a few days, I may have some better information for you. I'll question the captains as they arrive."

"That's very kind of you," said Simon, and gave the man a denarius which he thankfully acknowledged.

Simon walked away in a sunken mood.

'They have sent young Letitia away,' he mused. 'It must have broken Rufus' heart. My poor boy. I wonder why Marcus would do that. There must be a good reason to be sure, but how am I to find out?' he asked himself. 'Why must life be so tough. Especially on the young, with all their crazy hopes and plans. Perhaps he was thought not good enough for her, she being so rich. Perhaps her father wanted her to have a good education which she couldn't have in Cyrene. No, that couldn't have been the case. There are some very good tutors in Cyrene for those who can afford them. Maybe the fact that we are Jews and they're Romans, has something to do with it... Yes, that seems to me the most reasonable explanation. Our ways aren't their ways. Yet who knows? The way Yeshua's teachings are changing everything, who can say what will happen tomorrow? Oh, if I were only there to console him.... But his mother and sisters can do that better than I can. All I can do now is pray to Yeshua and his Father, that he find consolation in his anguish.'

Those thoughts haunted our hero as he started on his way to the tanner's house.

'Oh, I must not go there now. They will be at lunch, and I am another mouth to feed', he told himself, and changing his mind, directed his heavy steps to the commercial part of the city with its bazaars, and bought himself lunch in one of the food shops.

It was not till mid afternoon that he arrived back at Simon the tanner's house. He was met by Hannah at the door, who enquired with concern in her lovely eyes if he had eaten lunch. She was relieved when he answered her in the affirmative.

Simon went into the shop and found the tanner working a piece of leather strung up on an odd type of frame, by beating it with what looked like a wooden paddle.

"Hello my friend," said the tanner as Simon walked in. "Did you find your ship?"

"I'm afraid not," answered Simon. "But I got some very disturbing news from the captain of another ship."

"Oh dear… Is your family alright?"

"They are fine, but my youngest son has had a very heartbreaking experience, and I feel very badly for his sake."

"Will you permit me to know what occurred?"

Simon told him all about Rufus and Letitia. The tanner did his best to console him. Simon, still sulking, asked for something to do so as to distract his mind for a while.

The tanner gave him the paddle, and showing him how to strike, left his friend to work out his frustration on the piece of leather. Simon kept striking it until the tanner came back, and having felt the leather to see if it was dry, stopped him.

"Now," he said. When we take this piece down from the frame, you will see how soft you've made it."

"Have I damaged it?" asked Simon with alarm.

"Ha! Ha! Ha! …no," said the other. It is supposed to be dry, and it will be nice and soft.

"Ha! Ha!" laughed the tanner.

Simon felt the hide, which was really soft to the touch, and marvelled at how a raw, stiff, piece of furry hide could end up to be such a wonderful piece of material."

"And now," said the host. "We shall shock my daughter by being on time for supper."

* * * * * *

Things had gone very badly for Jechonias. He had completely lost track of Simon, and felt he was wasting his time keeping watch at the gates. He had to think of something that would get him back on his quarry's track, and quickly, before he lost the scent completely. He felt quite sure that Simon had given him the slip. and left the city probably by some other gate. How, he did not even venture to guess. The only thing that mattered was that he was gone, and he, Jechonias, would have to solve the riddle as to where.

'In the meantime,' he said to himself. 'I shall not waste my time. I am sure I can apprehend a few of his kind, and who knows what one can learn when they are squeezed. Maybe one of them knows where he has gone,' he mused with malicious intent.

Jechonias was preparing for his persecution campaign, when he was informed that Peter and John, two of the chief followers of the Nazarene, had left Jerusalem on their way to Samaria.

'I shall follow them, and they will lead me to him and perhaps many others that I can tear away from the pack and bring back in chains.'

Peter had a day's journey in his favour, but Jechonias knew that the apostle had gone on foot. He made arrangements to hire a horse, enabling him to catch up with the pair within a few hours. He arrived at his house in mid morning, much to his sister's surprise.

"Back already?" queried Judith. "Are you ill?"

"No. I am leaving town for a while. I have work to do," he answered dryly.

"Where are you going in such a hurry?"she asked with a suspicious look, as he made for his room and began to pack.

"I am heading for Samaria for a start, but I don't know where I shall end up."

"Are you chasing after that man again?" exasperation apparent in her voice.

He did not answer her. He detected criticism in her tone, and continued to pack for the journey.

"Have you anything to eat?" he asked. "I might as well have lunch so I shan't lose any time on the road."

"Yes," replied Judith. "Go sit down and I shall bring you some things."

She went into the kitchen, and a few minutes later emerged with some chickpea flower pancakes, olives, two hard-boiled eggs, a couple of vegetables, and some figs, and placed them in front of him.

"Get me some wine please," he asked.

Judith brought him a small jug of wine and a cup. She sat across the table from him, took a fig which she began to peel, and looking into his eyes said with considerable wisdom.

"What you need is a woman who can take your mind off this obsession you have for that man. You could have such a nice job as an official of the Sanhedrin, enjoying life, and bringing up a family… Little ones running around, loving you, and me. Oh! how I pray that this may happen."

"Will you never stop woman!" he snapped impatiently.

"I have told you how important it is for me to catch this man before he makes trouble. I can feel it in my bones. He is going to spread his heresy all over the place before we can get a hold of him."

"But no one is going after the people above him. Why are you persisting on apprehending him? He is not one of the leaders."

"You have heard of a man called Saul, how he incarcerates many of them. We simply have to stop them. Soon we shall be after the leaders too. We are only waiting because at the moment they are popular, but that will not last, and then we shall put an end to all of them. This cannot be allowed to go on," he said with intolerant resentment.

He got up to go. His sister came over and gave him a dutiful hug.

"Now you be careful," she said.

Off he went, with a large bag over his shoulder.

* * * * * *

Dusk began to spread its grey mantle over the rustic landscape, as Jechonias walked his horse into a small village looking for a blacksmith and a place to eat and rest for the night. He had ridden the animal so hard that it had lost a shoe. Fortunately for him, there was a smithy in the village with whom he left it. He put some grain into a bag he carried, hung it around the horse's ears, and went in search of a place to stay for the night.

"Tobias takes people in," said a ragged local hunchback, of whom he had enquired, and who sat on the stone threshold of a house. The man pointed down the road.

Jechonias, suspecting that because of his deformity, the man spent much of his time sitting around as he was presently doing observing people as his main form of distraction, addressed him again with a disinterested intonation in his voice.

"Tell me friend, have you seen a couple of men go by; one middle aged, and the other, a young man of about seventeen or so?"

"That sounds like Peter and John," replied the man innocently. "They left four hours ago, with some others from the village who took them in their cart."

"Thank you," said the spy, giving the man a coin and continuing on his way to Tobias' house.

Having made arrangements for an overnight stay at the public house, he returned to the smithy's shop. There he got some water for his horse, paid the man, and walked the horse down the road to the stables that the house provided.

The young man who took charge of his horse was promptly given instructions to rub down the animal before stabling him for the night, and have it fed, watered, and ready by first light in the morning.

'I feel good this morning,' said Jechonias to himself as he rode out of the village, invigorated after a good night's rest, and with food and water replenished.

'I shall soon be upon them. The question is what am I going to do? Shall I just tail them? They would doubtlessly get suspicious, and find me out. That hunchback seemed to know them, and Tobias spoke well of them, so someone may already have ridden out and alerted them as to their being followed.'

Jechonias, realising that he was very much on his own, had to make the difficult decision of either keeping a safe distance, or travelling with them, and run the risk of being recognised from his constant watches at the Jerusalem gates. If he stayed aloof, it would mean keeping them half an hour ahead of him, till they neared a larger town when he could close in on them and get assistance if needed. He put his horse into a fast trot, and followed the recent marks of the cart wheels on the dirt road.

As he entered a rocky bend on the road after two hours of journeying over the mountainous country, he suddenly and unavoidably fell upon a group of people sitting by the road under the shade of a eucalyptus tree having a meal. On seeing a donkey cart, he quickly realised that he had walked right into the fox's den. The clever Pharisee, quick to react, implemented with astonishing rapidity, his optional plan of action.

"Good day to you all!" he said with a false smile as he slowed his horse's trot to a walk.

"Good day to you stranger," returned various voices together.

He was in a quandary still, as he stopped, looked at the group and waited for developments to occur.

"Will you not join us and rest for a while?"

The invitation came from a big man in his early forties, with a pleasant but weather-beaten face, who sat in the middle of the group and who the misguided spy, suspected to be Peter. Young John who sat beside him confirmed his suspicion.

"Where are you all bound for?" asked Jechonius dismounting, and before they could ask him his own destination.

"At the moment, we are bound for Sychar," answered Peter. "You are welcome to join us, though it be slower for you, but at least we can offer you company. These mountains though beautiful, tend to make one a little weary by one's self."

"Thank you," returned Jechonias as he tied his horse to a nearby tree, and sat on a rock nearby.

"Do you hail from Jerusalem?" asked John.

"Yes."

There was silence for a few moments and Peter spoke, taking a noticeably deep breath and addressing the whole group.

"There is something invigorating about this mountain air he announced, spreading his arms and eyes directed to heaven. It rivals even our beloved Sea of Galilee air."

"I prefer our sea air," replied another of the group, with a touch of thin patriotism.

"You better get used to it Jesse, because we may be around these mountains for quite a few days," admonished Peter with a big paternal smile.

Jechonias had been silently listening to all that was said, and realised that they were in no hurry, and seemed to have no real destination. He felt confused. What were they wandering around for? His answer came sooner than he expected, but not to his entire satisfaction.

"We shall visit Cleophas first," said Peter. "He asked that we should come and instruct him as to some questions that he could not answer and was afraid of misguiding the people."

"Let us not forget the villages that we pass," pointed out another of the group.

"We shall leave two of you wherever you are needed, to instruct them, and join us again later in Sychar. We can then go from there if we need to go farther," responded the chief apostle with an authority that impressed Jechonias, and served notice to him that this was a very organized group of people highly motivated and well directed.

'Heavens!' he said to himself. "No wonder they are spreading their ideas so quickly. They are going to be hard to stop. Now is probably a good time to find out what they are telling people, and why they are so effective in converting them.'

"What business are you all in?" questioned Jechonias with feigned interest in his eyes.

Peter looked at him for what seemed to the Pharisee the longest time, and it was with great difficulty that the spy held the apostle's gaze.

"We have the unique business of spreading the teachings of our beloved Master Yeshua, the anointed one."

"I have heard of you, and many are set against you as they allege that your preaching violates the scriptures, in that your master claimed to be the Son of God, and the Maschiach (Messiah)," instigated the Pharisee.

"As for violating the scriptures, nothing could be further from the truth. You are a Jew as we are, is that not so?" asked Peter, leaning forward and bracing for battle. Yet, as he did so, he remembered Yeshua, and stayed calm.

"Our Lord and Master Yeshua always maintained that he had not come to change the scriptures, for he was also a Jew like us, and respected the tradition of our fathers. However, he said he had come from God who we call Yahweh," and here Peter bowed his head, and so did all, "to fulfill the scriptures, not to denounce them."

"He also claimed to be the Maschiach," broke in Jechonias with some boldness, which Peter interpreted as aggressive, and realised very quickly that he had to be careful with his words.

"Yes, he definitely claimed that too," continued the apostle. "And it has been received with great antagonism by all who hold too closely to the law. We were all expecting a Maschiach, who would take up arms and liberate us from the grip of the Romans. Nowhere do the scriptures support this interpretation of his purpose as we had expected. Only because we are so oppressed by our conquerors did we wish for this to be so.

Peter folded his hands and leant forward, eye brows raised as if expecting concurrence.

"These are human concerns, which in the eyes of God are important." He continued, not receiving any such concurrence from the Pharisee.

"Our supernatural lives however, are more important to God, who sees things in a deeper way than we can understand. To him, the saving of our souls which will be for eternity, is worth much more than freeing us from the yoke of the Romans here on earth. How many times has God himself allowed our people to be enslaved to a much greater degree than what we are suffering at the hands of the Romans. They at least allow us a certain amount of freedom." He stopped again, to gauge Jechonias' reaction.

"No, my friend,...Yeshua taught that love of neighbour was next after love of God. That is what our Ten Commandments also tell us. His miracles alone, prove his claim to being the Son of God. Raising people from the dead; curing the sick, casting out devils, and yes!...even forgiving sin."

"That is too much I would think," responded Jechonias, doggedly maintaining his point of view, and trying not to betray the rage that burned in his soul.

"Why?" Asked Peter. "If he is the Son of God what could be easier. After all, he died to atone for everyone's sins."

Jechonias' eyebrows dipped and merged together, and his lips tightened as he glared at Peter.

"How can you be so sure of that?" he exploded.

"He said so himself," assured the apostle. "He also said he would rise again from the dead, and I, and many bear witness to this. His tomb was found empty the third day after he was buried, and he subsequently appeared to us a number of times. He even ate in front of us."

Jechonias was momentarily dumbfounded as he tried to formulate his next attack, however Peter pressed his point further.

"I shall tell you something which may surprise you, as it did me." Peter shifted a little closer to the man, as if to confide the story he was about to relate.

"The morning when I first met Yeshua, my brother Andrew and I had been out fishing all night; for we are fishermen; and had caught nothing. Suddenly, as our boat reached the shore of the Sea of Galilee he called out to us. He asked to be allowed into our boat as the people to whom he was preaching were pressing him at the shore. We motioned for him to come on board. He waded over, climbed in, and began to preach from there. When he had finished, and the crowd had dispersed, he instructed us to put out a little way and let down our nets. We protested, and told him that we had been fishing all night and caught nothing. There was something about his eyes that made us do as he asked. To our complete surprise, the net filled to breaking point, and we had to hail our comrades, to help us pull up the net; their boat being close by. Seeing such an extraordinary miracle, I said. 'Depart from me Lord, for I am a sinful man.' And do you know what he said?"

Peter, paused to look at Jechonias, with a benevolent smile on his face. The latter, stared back at him blandly.

"And looking at all of us," he said. '*Come follow me, and I will make you fishers of men.*' What my friend," finalised the apostle. "Do you say to that?"

"It is hard to believe," replied the Pharisee, after a long pause, and seething with hate.

"We will pray that you may believe. By the way, what is your name? You have not told us."

"Jechonias!" was the answer.

"We are all brothers Jechonias, and as such must do our best for each other. And now, we have rested enough. Let us continue on our journey," directed Peter, looking at the spy, and waving to all those with him. They had all been utterly enthralled with the conversation.

"I shall tarry a while longer and catch up with you shortly," said Jechonias, with a sad, frustrated look on his sulky face.

'They have their story so well composed,' he said to himself once the others had left.'It is easy to see how simpletons are converted over to their ways. It is this love business that does it. Everybody dreams of a perfect life governed by love. But where is love when someone offends or hurts us? An eye for an eye as tradition tells us; that is what governs us.

How can one love some rascal that rapes our wives or abducts and murders our children, or steals our property? The old laws must be upheld, and the offenders punished. How about defending one's self? That is a basic instinct born of self preservation. Even animals are subject to this; save perhaps, sheep. Where would our nation be if we did not constantly fight for our rights whether we win or lose?'

These thoughts kept churning around in Jechonias' head, as he sat there by the road, staring at, but not absorbing the beauty of the panorama in front of him.

'There is little point in following them now,' thought the dejected spy. 'Jerusalem is the only place where I get any support, and at the moment they are taking a complacent attitude. I must talk to this man Saul when I get back. He at least is doing his best to stop these dangerous, heretical, dreamers.'

With these thoughts, he turned back to Jerusalem. Prepared to fight again another day.

On arriving back at the city, he made directly for the Sanhedrin, where he enquired as to the whereabouts of Saul of Tarsus.

"He has gone to Damascus, bearing a special letter for the Synagogue there, to assist him in apprehending a large group of followers of the Galilean," said the official whom Jechonias approached.

"When did he leave?"

"He has been gone for over a week, and we have heard nothing of him yet," answered the man with a look of uncertainty.

"Thank you!" said the Pharisee, and left.

CHAPTER THIRTEEN

THREE SIMONS

Simon had settled down to a routine at the tanner's house, as the whole household awaited Peter's arrival. There were rumours that he was in Lydda, where he had cured a man, and the news had spread widely.

As yet, nothing had been heard of the whereabouts of the *Stella Maris*. The *Pretoria* which had sailed for Cyrene had not yet returned to Joppa, as it had, according to the Registry office information, been posted to Caesarea on its return.

The two Simons had become good friends. Simon the carpenter made himself very useful, helping the tanner in his hard task of 'working' the hides, which was a strenuous process. He also made some improvements on the contraptions that were required for the stretching of the hides, and squeezing the water from them after the dyeing process. This gave the carpenter great satisfaction as he was in a manner of speaking, earning his keep. It was not worth his while to work at his own trade. He had no tools, or place in which to work, coupled with the fact that he did not expect to stay for long.

One day, returning from the market, Hannah brought the news, that a very well respected altruistic woman, a citizen of Joppa named Dorcas, had died. Peter, the apostle of Yeshua, who was in Lydda at the time they said, would be travelling to Joppa to attend the funeral..

"Peter is coming!" she announced as she ran into the tanner's shop.

Her father and Simon stopped their work, and rejoiced at the news. At last the day they had been waiting for had arrived.

"We shall all go to Dorcas' house and meet him when he arrives," declared the tanner with bubbling enthusiasm.

They immediately left the shop and went into the house, to prepare themselves for the visit.

Dorcas' house, was situated in the middle of the city near the market. It was crowded with people, many of whom were standing in the street talking and awaiting the apostle's arrival. Most of them were disciples; as had been Dorcas. Peter's coming was of great importance to them and it generated much excitement.

"His prayers at the funeral will carry much weight and surely guarantee her a place in heaven," said one of those waiting, with certainty.

It was an enthusiastic but weary assembly of mourners who welcomed Peter when he finally made an unexpectedly late appearance as dusk fell.

"The peace of the Lord Yeshua be with you all."

The words were delivered in a clear loud voice, as by one used to addressing a large crowd.

"Where have you laid her?" asked Peter in a lower tone of voice, as an old woman approached and embraced him.

"Come," she said, leading him into the house; the people parting to let them through.

The two Simons, and Hannah, had little by little, over the course of the past four hours, managed to squirm their way into the house. They were however on the ground floor, and Peter had been taken upstairs where the body of the deceased woman lay.

For the first time that day there was utter silence in the house. The people; some in silent prayer, and some with their own thoughts, awaited the reappearance of the apostle.

"She lives!...She lives!" rang the startling news. A woman, her arms waving over her head in exultation at her own words, appeared at the top of the stairs, sending the occupants of the house into a joyous frenzy.

Praises to God were offered by the believers in a continuous chorus until Peter came out. He, standing at the top of the stairs, addressed them.

"By the power of the Holy Spirit, and in the Holy name of Yeshua,...Tabitha, who is known to you as Dorcas has been restored to us."

"Rejoice therefore, and thank God for his great love for mankind."

Peter then mingled with those present. Some of whom he knew. Presently, he encountered the two Simons, and embracing them warmly, asked the tanner to take him to his house where he might rest.

Hannah, on hearing the apostle's request, quickly found a friend to escort her home and made haste to prepare supper for the visitors.

On leaving, Peter asked that the men who had come with him be taken care of by local families, and announced that he would be staying at Simon the tanner's house.

The three Simons were soon at the tanner's house where they were greeted by Hannah, who assured them that supper would be ready shortly. She was about to walk away when Peter held her back gently by the arm saying.

"Before we sit down to supper there is something I must do."

She gave him an enquiring look with her beautiful eyes, opening her hands in unison.

"Please bring me a jug with some water. Do not overfill it. I shall also need a small basin and a towel."

The girl hastened to bring them.

"Now," said Peter addressing the father. "Please hold this basin under your daughter's head."

Simon did as he was bid. His daughter stooped, and bowed her head over the bowl.

"Young woman do you wish to be baptised?"

"Yes!" answered Hannah with a slight tremble in her voice.

"I baptise you in the name of the Father, and of the Son and of the Holy Spirit," pronounced the apostle as he poured a little water simultaneously over Hannah's head.

"Now Simon," he said to the carpenter, "Please hold the basin for Simon." Hannah was busy drying her hair.

The tanner bowed his head over the basin, and Peter repeated the ritual filling the recipient with joy.

"And now, Simon of Cyrene, from what Joseph of Arimathea tells me, you have learnt much of the teachings of our Lord, and with my further instruction whilst I am here, I feel certain that you will make a good pastor in your own country, where I want you to spread the good news of our Blessed Lord and Master. Come and stand here please."

Simon did as Peter bade him.

"Kneel please."

Again, Simon obeyed.

Peter spread his hands over Simon's head and said:

"Simon of Cyrene, receive the Holy Spirit. Go forth, and teach in the name of the Father, and of the son, and of the Holy Spirit. And receive the power to forgive sin."

Simon felt a big lump in his throat, and then suddenly, the feeling he had felt when Yeshua looked at him, enveloped his whole body. He rose, with tears in his eyes and thanked Peter for bestowing such an honour on him.

Hannah, had outdone herself with the preparation of the meal, much to the admiration of the three Simons. She now sat with them, attentively listening to the apostle's fascinating stories as they ate their supper. Peter explained to them what the " Breaking of the Bread" signified, and prayed with them a prayer of repentance for their sins. He then paused, and looked at the three, to ensure their further attention. Then, taking a small loaf of bread which Hannah had placed on the table at his earlier request, broke and said:

"Take and eat : This is my Body."

He took a piece himself, and handed the remainder over for his friends to share. He ate his with great reverence, and the others following his example, did likewise.

He then explained the origin of the mystery that he had just performed, and empowered Simon of Cyrene, only, to do the same in the future.

The supper continued, and when it was finished, he pushed his cup aside. He took a silver cup that she had placed there for him, poured some wine into it, and again, capturing their attention, said.

"All of you drink of this, for this is My blood of the new covenant which is being shed for many unto the forgiveness of sins."

And so saying, he passed the cup around for the three to drink. He, finishing the contents when it came back into his hands again.

"Do this always in Yeshua's memory as directed by him," he said looking at the Cyrenean. Remember that it is His actual Body and Blood that you are consecrating, as he carefully washed the silver cup with water, drank the contents, and left it there to dry by itself.

The evening came to an end soon after the supper was over; Peter feeling very tired after his gruelling day.

It came as a pleasant surprise to Simon to discover that Peter would be sleeping on the other bed in his room. He had not given the matter any thought.

'What better roommate could any man have,' he mused.

The apostle's stay at the tanner's house was now public knowledge, and there were people standing outside the house at all hours of the day waiting to catch a glimpse of the man of God who had brought Dorcas back to life.

* * * * * *

In Jerusalem, recent news of Saul's conversion to Yeshua on the way to Damascus shocked the Sanhedrin. They were at a loss as to what to do, to stop the apostles from increasing their ranks in the light of what had occurred. If the news was a shock to the Sanhedrin, it was a complete disaster for Jechonias, who held a strong admiration for Saul and his ruthless tactics against the disciples of Yeshua.

'How could this have happened?' he asked himself, incredulously. 'It just does not make sense....A traitor! he is just a rotten traitor. How could he do this?'

He was most distraught as he slowly walked home aimlessly, his thoughts precluding all his other senses. He spun around.

'What am I going home for? My sister will distract me. No! I must think. Maybe now is my chance to get the Sanhedrin to take me seriously and endow me with more power and put more men at my disposal so that I can make an arrest on the spot with assistance as I need it. By myself, I can do nothing outside of Jerusalem. And even here. Look what happened when I tried to arrest that creature from Cyrene.'

Slowly his thoughts became more organized. He grew calmer and more cunning.

'What I need is a smart plan that will convince the Sanhedrin to give me a team to control. But I must act quickly whilst they are all in shock about Saul and convince them that I am more capable than he ever was.'

He finally got home, having unconsciously turned around twice, on his way.

'It is dusk now, my sister will have my supper ready,' he reasoned as he walked in the door.

"Judith, where are you?" he called out.

There was no answer. He checked all the rooms, but she was not there.

'Where on earth could she be at this time of night?'

He peeked in the kitchen, and yes, she had cooked his supper. All that remained for her to do was to heat it. He went up to his room to wait for her, and washed in the meantime. He then sat at his writing table, and pulling out a piece of parchment began to write down his plan.

The sound of the door closing downstairs brought him to his feet, and leaving the parchment on the table he went to greet his sister.

"Here you are," he said. "Where have you been?"

"I was visiting a friend, and I lost track of the time," she replied.

"I see you have already cooked the supper, so it should not take you long to serve it."

"It will be ready in a few moments," she promised, heading for her ablution.

Jechonias went into the living room, took a jug of wine and a cup, sat down on his favourite cushion and pulled a table over. He was deep in thought as he sipped his wine, and waited for Judith to bring him his supper.

"Here you are," announced his sister placing his food in front of him, along with some bread and a little flask of olive oil. "The fish looked so fresh today, that I could not resist it. You will like the sauce. I tried something new," she coaxed.

Jechonias felt more relaxed, and commented favourably on the sauce, which pleased his sister, who now serving herself, sat down and joined him.

"You seem to be in a good mood tonight," she commented tentatively.

"I wasn't a while ago, but I am much more relaxed now that I have solved my problem."

"I'm glad to hear that," she replied with relief.

"Did you hear? ...no, you couldn't have heard. Saul of Tarsus has betrayed us and gone over to those people; those disciples of the Galilean. Can you imagine that?"

"Was he not the man who was dragging all sorts of families to prison?"

"Yes."

"That is quite incredible. I wonder what happened to make him change so suddenly."

"They got him all mixed up I suppose, like they tried to do to me in Samaria. But I could see through all their fancy talk. I thought he was cleverer than that. Or maybe they offered him a lot of money....No. I doubt that, they do not have much money."

"It's good for me though as things go. This mess is going to put me in a very good position for advancing my career in the Sanhedrin. If all goes well for me, I can end up with a pretty important position."

His sister listened with great interest and not a little disgust as she suspected what his ambitious scheme would amount to. She decided to make no comment however.

"I am going out. Don't wait up for me. I may be late getting back."

"Good night," she said, and went back into the kitchen as he made ready to go.

Jechonias went directly to the temple to talk to a councillor whom he knew felt the same way as he did about the threat that the disciples posed to the 'status quo.'

He found him in the library, and presented the proposal that he intended to place before the Council.

"I want them to put twenty men under my command, and be given a free hand to deploy them as I see fit." Said Jechonias addressing his friend. "And I want them to set up a budget to enable me to pay for costs incurred by my people on travel, meals, lodgings, horse or camel rentals... In short all expenses. I shall answer to a small committee set up by them for the purpose of seeing that I am doing my work well, and getting results. Lastly, give me a good salary and by way of bonus, a percentage of any property or goods that I confiscate. Do you approve? If so, do you think they will vote for my proposal?"

"I like your plan, though you may have to settle for a lesser salary increase for yourself. I think they will prefer you to keep more of the confiscated goods, since it will cost them nothing. But then again," said the councillor bowing his head, "I could be wrong."

"How soon can I get a hearing?"

"Possibly within three days."

"Thank you," said Jechonias, and took his leave.

* * * * * *

One day, Peter was up in the terrace of the tanner's house all alone, enjoying the wonderful view of the harbour. He was biding his time whilst Hannah was preparing his lunch. For some reason he was feeling unusually hungry.

Suddenly, he fell into a trance, and had a vision.

He saw heaven standing open, and a certain vessel coming down like a great sheet, let down by the four corners from heaven to the earth; and in it were all the four footed beasts and creeping things of the earth, and birds of the air. And there came a voice to him, "Arise, Peter, kill and eat." But Peter said, *"Far be it from me, Lord, for never did I eat anything common or unclean."*

And there came a voice a second time to him.

"What God has cleansed, do not thou call common."

Now this happened three times, and straightaway the vessel was taken up into heaven. As Peter came out of the trance, and was wondering what the vision meant, three men were outside the house, knocking on the door downstairs. And the Spirit said to him:

"Behold three men are looking for thee, arise therefore and go down and depart with them without hesitation, for I have sent them."

Peter went down opened the door, and right away told them that he was the man they were looking for. What did they want of him?

The men told him that they had come from Cornelius who was a centurion, and a God fearing man. An angel had directed the centurion to have someone come and fetch him, and take him, to that same centurion in Caesarea.

"Please come in," said Peter, and calling out to Hannah, he asked her to include the men in the lunch.

The two Simons hearing voices, came out of the shop, and were introduced to the visitors. Hannah, with her usual efficiency, creativity, and the help of Sarah, her neighbour, managed to provide for all. When lunch was over much talk ensued among the company.

Peter informed them all, that he proposed to leave early the following morning, which sent Hannah and her father scurrying off to disciple friends to find the visitors, lodgings for the night.

All was set then; after supper, the three would be taken to the other houses, and in the morning they would all come back to the tanner's house after breakfast, and leave for Caesarea from there.

Once again, Hannah had her friend Sarah come and help her prepare supper, as the company had grown so big, and naturally extra shopping had to be done. The men, however, were oblivious to this; they were too engrossed in the next day's journey and what its purpose might be.

The supper went well, but there was no 'Breaking of the Bread', as the visitors were Gentiles. The group tarried a while after supper, and then the three visitors left for the other houses where arrangements had been made to accommodate them for the night. The tanner and his daughter acted as their guides.

Peter and Simon retired to their room, and soon after, Peter asked Simon to go with him to Caesarea. Simon acceded to his request with some regret at having to leave his good friends, Simon and Hannah. It seemed every time he made friends, he had to give them up. 'It is the will of God,' he said to himself, getting into bed.

The following morning realised a larger group than expected, as four local men also wished to accompany Peter on his journey. Simon the carpenter took sad leave of his friend the tanner and his daughter, hoping to see them again sometime in the future. The party started out on its journey leaving behind a now very popular house, and two very sad occupants.

* * * * * *

Jechonias stood in front of the Sanhedrin council presenting his well rehearsed plan with considerable skill. On finishing, he was instructed to leave the chamber and wait outside, to be recalled when a decision had been reached.

'I think I was forceful enough without overdoing it,' he told himself. 'There were a good many faces that seemed receptive, but that means nothing. I must have a majority.'

He paced up and down for quite a while. Then he tired, sat down on a bench which was at hand and waited. He must have sat there for almost an hour before the doors opened and he was called in.

The plan had been hotly debated they said, and the decision had gone in his favour. However, they could not agree to the salary that he had proposed, but if he took a smaller salary increase, and instead accepted a bigger percentage of the confiscations, they would accede to his proposal exactly as it had been presented.

Jechonias was ecstatic, though he dare not show it. He accepted their proposal, and left the building in very high spirits indeed.

'Now it is entirely up to me,' he told himself. 'I have to perform, or they will kick me out faster than they put me in.'

Part of the agreement was that they would give him an office near the temple, from which he would operate, and where he could always have a staff member on duty.

Two days later, Jechonias called a meeting of all his people. He set up different teams consisting of two men each, to begin spying. Once they had proof of the suspects' involvement with the

Galilean, one was to remain on the scene, and the other was to contact the office for help. Some teams he assigned to Jerusalem, but others he sent out to Samaria, Damascus, Caesarea, and one team to Joppa with a special assignment. Since the tanner's house had been brought to his attention by the popularity of the apostle Peter in that town, he wondered if by chance Simon was there too. His favourite quarry would not know the new men, and this gave Jechonias a great advantage, provided of course, that they could identify the Cyrenean from the description he gave them.

* * * * * *

The house of Cornelius was bubbling with excitement. A boy had just arrived and breathlessly announced that Peter was now in Caesarea, and on his way to the house.

The centurion had a large house with a well designed, zealously tended garden, which provided many cool, shaded areas, with a number of stone benches arranged in small groups allowing for the intimate entertaining of guests during the summer months. Visitors to the house who had been moving freely between house and garden in joyful expectancy, were now assembling near the large iron gate which allowed a long view down the street. Cornelius chose to remain in the house with his family till the apostle was announced, desiring to meet him privately.

He gave instructions that all visitors should be kept in the garden until invited to join them in the house; with the exception of a few people that he wished to be present, including any that Peter may bring with him.

Presently, a slave came rushing in, and bowing in the centurion's presence announced the arrival of Peter, who entered close on the servant's heels. Cornelius who stood in the atrium, approached and threw himself at the feet of the apostle, who promptly raised him up saying:

"Get up I myself also am a man."

Cornelius then introduced his family, who were bustling around Peter, Simon, and his travelling companions.

There was much talking and celebrating in that house that day. Peter gave a long discourse, listened to with profound interest by both Jews and Gentiles, as in this significant occasion, the formers who were forbidden by their faith to mix with the latters, found themselves happily co-existing.

An extraordinary event took place much to everyone's surprise, including Peter's.

The Holy Spirit descended on the mixed gathering, and all, regardless of being Gentile or Jew, were prompted by the Spirit to speak in diverse tongues. Peter quickly understood the significance of the momentous occurrence, as he remembered his vision on the terrace. He immediately baptised all present without hesitation, and welcomed them all without exception to be followers of Yeshua,

Simon was overwhelmed with joy, realising that he could now baptise people like his friend Ahmed, who so badly wanted to be a disciple of the Lord.

Peter and Simon were invited to stay a few days at Cornelius' house. This gave the carpenter an opportunity to visit the harbour Registry Office, which he urgently needed to do. He left the house as soon as the occasion presented itself, and found his way to the harbour with which he was familiar from his earlier visit a few months earlier. He soon found the office, where he was told that the *Stella Maris* was expected to dock in Joppa within three days time.

'I shall have to get down to Joppa without losing any time,' he told himself as he walked back from the harbour towards the centurion's house. 'I'll leave with Peter's permission, as soon after supper tonight as I decently can.'

Just then he heard someone ask him:

"Are you Simon of Cyrene?"

"Yes, I am," he answered, turning around.

In an instant, he felt himself being held from behind.

"Who are you?" asked Simon helplessly, as he was bound fast by one of the men.

"We greet you in the name of Jechonias our chief," responded the other. "And now we are going to entertain you."

With that, they marched him off to the local synagogue which had a partially underground cellar where all sorts of things not in current use, were stored. They threw him in and bolted the door.

Simon began to work on the ropes that were pinning down his arms, and after many tries, he managed to slide them off; they had been put on hurriedly so as not to draw attention to his arrest. He looked around the cellar which was lit by a very small barred window, opening into a walled yard with a planted area that appeared to be a herbal garden.

'Maybe,' he thought, 'it's the herbal garden for the kitchen. When the cook ventures out to pick herbs for the rabbi's meals, I can call out to him for help.' But then he thought. 'They would not have used this room as a prison unless the rabbi had given them his permission.'

'Oh my! the *Stella* is on its way to Joppa, and I am stuck in here after months of waiting for it... Oh my, oh my,' lamented Simon.

He tried to pry the window bars, but there was no give to them. He tried to force the door, but no luck there either. He looked around the room to see if among all those odds and ends that were stored in there, he could find some useful implement that he could use to free himself. There were many old earthenware pots, old wooden shelves, all sorts of baskets, even some lengths of rope, but not a single piece of iron was to be found. He sat down on a big box and began to pray to Yeshua, as he was now in the habit of doing.

'Lord, here I am in trouble again. My ship awaits me, and I'm powerless to get out of here. How am I going to get home and begin my ministry if you don't help me? Please tell me what to do.'

He waited... Nothing happened. He then thought of the parchment from the cross. He dug into his tunic, placed his hand on it once again and raising his eyes to heaven, invoked Yeshua to help him... Still nothing.

'Well Lord, I've tried everything. I suppose it's your will that I spend time in here....So be it.'

With that, he began to think of home and his beautiful Ruth and his children all able thank God, to take care of themselves, so what if God wanted to take him? It could have been worse if this had happened before, when his family really needed him.

There are men who will fight tenaciously when they feel they are in an impossible situation. The futility of their human struggles wear them out, like caged animals doggedly pawing at the bars of their cage. Men of faith are different.

Why beat one's head against a stone wall when there is a higher power that can help them if only they have the patience that faith brings. God acts in his own good time, and where man can do little or nothing to change his destiny, the almighty can play with destiny as a child plays with a toy, shaping it in whatever way he wishes, if asked with humility and resignation.

Simon was a fighter, but he also knew when to let God do his will. He resigned himself to wait for Yeshua to make his move.

The hours passed very slowly for him as he prayed or thought of home and patiently waited. Suddenly, his alert ears caught the sound of voices. He got up and went to the door. He pressed his ear against the cracks and listened. There was a heated argument going on upstairs, with one voice predominating.

"Bring him up right now, or I shall have my men tear the place down over your ears."

The sound of hurried footsteps was heard. Simon backed away from the door, as with a loud crack of the bolt the door flew open, and two men with an oil lamp, called out for Simon of Cyrene to come out.

As he reached the top of the stairs and into the light, he recognised the two men as those who had arrested him, and became aware of three Roman soldiers standing there waiting for him to be brought up to them.

Simon was overjoyed, realising that this must be Cornelius' doing, and thanked Yeshua for his delivery.

As six soldiers escorted Simon out of the synagogue, they left behind them Jechonias' men leering at him; vengeance glowing maliciously in their eyes.

Peter was greatly relieved at seeing Simon again, and thanked Cornelius for his kind assistance. The centurion in turn asked Simon, if he could be of further help.

"They had no right arresting you. You are a Roman citizen," he told Simon.

"How did you know where I was and what had happened?" asked the carpenter.

"I have a little slave boy," said Cornelius, "who sees everything. He followed you in the hope that he could beg a coin off you. He witnessed your arrest, and came back and told me. Peter was also uneasy about your tardiness."

Simon sincerely thanked the centurion for having delivered him from the hands of the Sanhedrin, and asked him for the loan of a horse so that he could quickly get to Joppa. He promised to return the horse at the Roman military barracks there.

"You may have an escort if you wish," offered the centurion with brotherly concern.

"Thank you, no," answered Simon. "It would only draw attention to me, and I have to keep a very low profile till I am aboard ship. I am sure that the house of my good friend Simon the tanner is being carefully watched, and I must avoid going there at all costs since it could incriminate them. I must hide in the harbour area, at another friend's house, until I can board my ship without being observed."

In the course of the day, the little slave boy was brought to Simon at his request, and was duly rewarded with two denarii, which made the little fellow very very happy. His master observed him with kindness in his eyes, and lovingly patted him on the head.

Our hero left Cornelius' house early next morning, dressed as a Roman soldier, and set out for Joppa. As he rode, his thoughts went back to Naomi, and her suggestion of his masquerading as a Roman soldier when they were planning his escape from Jerusalem. How amused she would be if she saw him now. He enjoyed a good laugh all to himself.

On his arrival in Joppa in the afternoon, he felt confident that with his beard cut closely to his face, his moustache similarly trimmed, and dressed in Roman uniform, he would avoid detection whilst finding his way to Ahmed's house.

He dismounted at the caravan master's door and knocked. An attractive woman in her early thirties opened the door. She was shocked at seeing a Roman soldier confronting her.

"Yes?" she asked with noticeable panic in her voice. "What can I do for you?"

"Don't be afraid! is Ahmed at home?"

"Not at the moment," she lied, "but he should be in later."

"Would you tell him that his friend Simon of Cyrene wishes to see him. I shall be back in a short while."

Suddenly, Ahmed's face appeared in the doorway. Seeing the Roman soldier, he was taken aback, and a look of utter confusion appeared on his face.

"Ha! ha!" laughed Simon, " do I look so much like a Roman soldier?"

"My goodness, you could pass for one any time," replied Ahmed, as relief clearly showed on his pleasant dark face.

"This my dear, is the Simon whom I talked to you about," said Ahmed, addressing his wife. Looking at Simon, he said. "Come on in, let me take your horse."

"No! but here, take my bags. I am going to return it to the Roman barracks, and I shall be with you in a little while. By the way, where are the barracks?"

"These Romans can't even find their way back to their own place," said Ahmed with a mocking laugh, and leaving Simon's bags with his wife, led the way for Simon to follow.

The barracks were not far, and soon Simon found himself saluting a sergeant of the guard and handing him the scroll that Cornelius had given him. The soldier took the scroll, and asked Simon to wait. He returned after a short while, took the horse, thanked Simon, saluted, and walked it away.

"Now," said Simon. "You're are about to entertain a Roman soldier for a few days if you be so kind."

"You're more than welcome," Ahmed assured him.

On arrival at Ahmed's house, his wife Sicmis quickly prepared something for Simon to eat, and the amiable couple sat down to talk and entertain their guest.

Sicmis was also Egyptian like her husband but lighter in colour. Her hair which she wore quite loose over her shapely shoulders was black, very wavy, and fell halfway down her back. She was small in stature, but the slenderness of her body made her seem taller than she was. She was a good listener and let the men do most of the talking. They had much to say to each other. Simon ate, as husband and wife sipped watered wine and kept him company.

"Before I tell you of my recent adventures, let me tell you something that's going to make you very happy," began Simon, looking at Ahmed with a meaningful smile.

"I am listening," said the other, his eyes brightening with anticipation.

"I can baptise you now."

There was a momentary pregnant pause, and Ahmed exploded.

"Wonderful! Wonderful! tell me, tell me more… Please."

Simon then recounted the story of his latest adventures, enthralling his two eager listeners. Sicmis gave her husband a loving hug as a congratulatory gesture for his impending baptism, or perhaps for no particular reason. Simply out of excitement.

"So you have had an exciting time my friend," said the caravan master as Simon finished. "Now what happens? When does the ship that is to take you home arrive?

"Two days from now," said the carpenter. "On the tenth day of the month, and it will be here for possibly four or five days, depending on whether it has to load or unload cargo, or just take on passengers. At most until the fifteenth."

"Mm… I have to leave on the fourteenth, and I won't be back from Jerusalem till the twentieth. I may not be here to help you if the ship's departure is delayed for any reason. Though the plan can still work, if I can get your baggage on board a couple of days before it sails. My friends the fishermen will get you on board, even if I am away." said Ahmed. "Hopefully it will all work out with Yeshua's help."

"Here's my plan if it suits you," began Simon. "And it must all happen as close as possible to the night before the *Stella Maris* sails. You go on board with my luggage, which you hide in a large bag as if you were selling something to the captain, and you leave it on board. The captain is a very good friend of mine. You explain to him that the ship is being watched day and night, and I have to get on board somehow. Now, I've been thinking. If I can get a boat to drop me off on the starboard side of the ship, and if Marius, that is the captain's name, leaves a rope ladder hanging over the side behind the cabins. Then I can climb up in the middle of the night without being seen from the quay."

"That is a good plan, but what would a rowboat be doing there at night?" asked Ahmed. " If it is not seen, it will surely be heard. The oars will splash in the silence of the night,"

"I get your point," conceded Simon." So how do we solve that?"

There was silence for a few moments, and then Sicmis spoke.

"Could not your fishermen friends help you there? They told me that sometimes, on a calm night, they go fishing inside the harbour, and they light a lamp to attract the fish."

"Yes, maybe they can hide Simon in the boat under a canvas and deliver him that way. As they become visible on passing the ship to whoever is spying on shore, they can move out a little, light their lamp and spend some time fishing," explained the caravan master.

"That would work well if you can get your friends to do it. I shall be willing to pay them for their trouble," said Simon.

"Yes, you will have to; those fellows like money," said Ahmed.

"There's one final thing. That's, getting rid of this uniform, helmet, and sword," pointed out Simon.

"They can dump them in the sea as they fish," suggested Ahmed matter-of-factly.

"The helmet, sword and scabbard will sink, but the clothes I will burn here," broke in Sicmis.

"I shall talk to Aram and Manasses tomorrow and see if they will do it. And now let us all to bed," smiled Ahmed, his hands gesturing finality.

"Give me a few moments to prepare a bed for you for tonight, right here, and tomorrow I shall organize things better," said Sicmis, addressing Simon with a big smile and vanished.

She returned shortly with a stack of cushions with which she formed a bed. The couple then left Simon to himself. He changed into his normal clothes, and soon fell asleep on the cushions.

The following morning Simon's day started with a bang. Two little children, a boy and a girl, burst into his room chasing one another. They tripped over his unexpected body and tumbled headlong over him onto some cushions that lay around. All three looked at each other for a moment. Simon, up on his elbow, cast a look of surprise trying to piece together his new surroundings, and the two trespassers who had so unceremoniously entered his domain. Four frightened little eyes looked back with doubt as to whether they should cry, or laugh at the strange man. Then the little girl decided that it was an occasion to win some sympathy from her father who followed closely on their heels. She let loose one of her favourite piercing shrieks, which almost destroyed the visitor's half awake ears. The little boy stood and looked at Simon, as if questioning his intrusion into their morning playground.

"You couple of little monsters," admonished Ahmed with a secret grin on his friendly face, embracing the little girl who had certainly won her point.

Simon, awake at last, laughed heartily, looking at Ahmed with fatherly sympathy, and spreading his hands out in a welcoming gesture to the little five year old miniature of his father.

"This is Kimi," said Ahmed, gently pushing his son towards his friend. "And this little female volcano is Isha. She is three."

Simon, who loved children, lost no time in winning them over with stories of his own children when they were little, and embellishing his tales with his ever active imagination. The children listened intently, as Simon sat and talked to them. Little Isha sat next to him, and Kimi opposite. Both were enthralled in the big man's tale. Presently, a woman entered the room and greeted him. The children ran to her, all three merging in an enthusiastic embrace. Simon now up on his feet towered above this diminutive but well proportioned, attractive woman in her very early fifties. She was immediately introduced by Sicmis, who walked in behind her, as her mother.

Ahmed now joined them. The women disappeared into the kitchen, to finish preparing breakfast. It was presently served in that large room, and eaten amidst much animated conversation.

Breakfast once over, the women left for the market. They took the children with them, giving the men a chance to talk privately.

"Do Sicmis and her mother want to be baptised or is it only you?" asked Simon.

"For now, only me, but when I learn more, then perhaps I can convince them to do so," answered Ahmed hopefully.

Simon then asked his friend to fetch a jug with a little water in it, a basin, and a towel. Ahmed returned with the required objects. The new priest, put the basin on a nearby table, and asked his friend to kneel. He then formally asked if he wanted to be baptised.

After receiving an affirmation he proceeded with the baptismal service.

Simon looked at the Ahmed; water dripping down his face, towel in hand, his large dark eyes ajar, staring into space.

"I felt something!" he whispered. Why? he whispered,... only he knew.

Simon embraced him, took the towel from his hand and put it over his head, stirring him into drying his own hair.

"It's a good thing I only used a little water, or you probably would have drowned," joked Simon with a happy laugh.

After a little while, the young host went off to find his two fishermen friends whom he hoped, would row his esteemed guest to the *Stella*.

* * * * * *

It was early afternoon, on the first day of the week. Jechonias arrived back at his office and began briefing his man on duty with regard to the villainous broad daylight raid, which he had successfully carried out on an assembly of Yeshua's disciples that same morning. They had been caught celebrating a religious service in a private house.

"Go down to the prison, and get all their names and addresses," he ordered. "And make sure that you follow up. Send a man to each address, and ask the neighbours if they know them. Do it stealthily so that they do not suspect who you are, but make very sure of the correct addresses. We cannot afford to go bursting in later, and find it is some innocent person's house."

"When you are finished, you can go home for the day. Tomorrow we will get into the houses and take stock of all their property," he added.

Jechonias sat down quite content with his day's work. He thought of all the interesting discoveries he would make, and the booty he would confiscate the following day. His thoughts were rudely interrupted by a rider from Caesarea, who burst into the room with the news of Simon's arrest and subsequent release.

"Roman soldiers! released by Roman soldiers?" fumed the chief, as he stared incredulously at his subordinate.

"Yes," the man assured him. "And they said we had no right arresting a Roman citizen… Is he a Roman citizen?"

A long silence ensued. Jechonias struggled to compose himself.

"I suppose that technically he i...is," he stammered. "As a Cyrenean coming from a Roman province, would qualify him as such."

It tore at Jechonias' hard heart to admit to this, as he had always in his phobia ignored the fact, having buried it in his subconscious mind, and covered it over by the force of his obsessive hatred for the man.

"Go back," he murmured reluctantly. "Call off your partner. Let the confounded Cyrenean rascal leave on the ship that he awaits."

"I shall live to fight another day," he muttered under his breath, seething with vengeful despair.

* * * * * *

Marius stood on deck on a sunny summer morning, thinking of his friend Simon, and whether he would have the happiness of taking him back to Cyrene on this trip. The *Stella Maris* had now been in port for three days, and had loaded up the new cargo of wine and cork. It was ready to sail the very next day. He had not seen his friend Simon for over three months, having missed him on the last two trips to Caesarea.

'Would he be lucky this time?' he wondered.

He stood on the port side of the ship scanning the quay, and observing the activity which normally bustles around harbours. A man carrying a large sack, headed for his gang plank. The captain stepped back to make room for him, and greeted him with an enquiring smile.

"Good morning!" greeted the man, as he stepped on deck. "Are you Marius?"

The captain nodded in ascent.

"May I speak with you where we will not be observed from the wharf... Please?"

Marius stifled his intended greeting, and led the man into his cabin.

"My name is Ahmed," said the Egyptian. "I am a caravan master, and a friend of Simon of Cyrene. I bring you his baggage in this sack.

A smile spread over the captain's face at the mention of his friend's name.

He has been hiding in my house for the last five days. I am due to leave tomorrow with my caravan on a trip to Jerusalem. He is being persecuted by the Sanhedrin. This ship is most likely being watched in an attempt to apprehend him before he leaves Judea, and we have a plan for getting him on board tonight."

"Please sit down," invited Marius. Ahmed sat on the bed beside the captain.

"As Simon probably told you, my name is Marius, and he is my best friend. I have been most worried about him. I have missed him on two trips already, and had almost given up on him again. Thank the gods, this time I shall take him home to that beautiful wife of his."

"Here is our plan," said the Egyptian, and with a shrewd look in his eyes and much gesticulating of the hands, proceeded to explain the plan to Marius.

"So, I shall leave a rope ladder hanging outside the new passenger cabin so that when he climbs up, he will not be seen from the wharf. He will be able to get into the cabin without being observed as the door faces the starboard side. He will stay there out of sight until we have sailed."

"Perfect," Ahmed assured him. "That will be just great."

"A pleasure to have met you, and may you both have a safe and pleasant voyage."

With these words, the Egyptian left the ship.

Simon awaited the return of his young friend with great anticipation, though the time passed quickly playing with Kimi and Isha. The mischievous little pair had now won his heart.

Ahmed arrived with the very satisfactory news that all was ready, and that Marius was impatient to have him on board again.

Sicmis made an excellent farewell supper, and their last hours together were very pleasantly spent. The children were allowed to stay up late to say good bye to 'Uncle' Simon.

Finally the awaited knock at the door announced the arrival of the two fishermen, and Simon took his leave of all with a sad heart. Once outside, and walking away, he called Kimi over. The boy came for one more hug, and as he did so, he put a small but heavyish bag into his little hand, and said:

"Give this to mummy when I am gone, but wait a little while first before you give it to her."

Off went our hero waving back to them with sadness in his heart.

'Since they refused to take my money, that little bag of coins, will cover the expenses they incurred on my behalf over the last five days. They really could not afford it... I'll never forget their generosity, and they will always be in my prayers. I'll miss those little ones too. Who knows? maybe soon, God willing, our children will give us little ones of our own just like these two.'

So mused Simon as he followed the two men to their boat which sat on the beach adjoining the harbour.

The fishermen pushed the boat into the water with Simon's help. He, sandals in hand, climbed in, and was promptly covered by a large canvas, and camouflaged with nets and baskets.

The rowboat entered the harbour by moonlight, and carefully pulled oars with a minimum of splashing, which the expert oarsmen accomplished with habitual ease. They ran along the starboard side of a number of ships lining the quay before they reached the *Stella Maris*.

Marius, who had been on the lookout for them, watched their stealthy approach. He crossed the deck to port side, and began a conversation with his helmsman Lucius, to distract whoever might be watching, as the rowboat closed in on the ship.

Simon reached for the ladder, climbed on board, pulled up the ladder, and disappeared into the new cabin, closing the door noiselessly behind him.

All this had been accomplished without the rowboat actually stopping. As it cleared the stern, the oars were in full swing making their way to the middle of the harbour. Once there, they dumped the Roman accoutrements, and lighting their lamp, cast a net into the sea pretending to fish. As it turned out they had a fair catch before they made for home.

The spy from Jechonias' Joppa team had, as was expected, been watching every move that was made on and around the *Stella*. He watched with particular interest the antics of the row boat as it emerged from the shadows and made for the middle of the harbour. He was surprised when he saw the men light their wind-shielded lamp, cast their net, and remain there for over an hour before pulling it up. The shimmering movement of the catch by the light of the lamp as they pulled the net back into the boat, seemed to convince the spy of the authenticity of the operation.

Impatiently allowing for some time to pass before going to see his friend, Marius remained on deck and continued his talk with Lucius for another quarter of an hour or so. Then at last, making a round of the deck he disappeared behind his cabin, and went into the passenger cabin to greet him. The helmsman remained on watch.

* * * * * *

The morning of the departure saw the prospective passengers coming on board. Marius and Jason the mate, were busy welcoming and assisting the scheduled fifteen as they arrived, and did not notice a man who had boarded the ship and was making his way to the captain's cabin. Lucius, however, did notice him wandering around, and followed the man who had now opened the cabin door and was entering.

The intruder found a man apparently asleep in a bed covered with a blanket. Simon, who had been relocated to the captain's cabin leaving the new cabin clear for the couple who had booked it, had been watching the passengers through a crack in the window shutter as Marius welcomed the people on board. He spotted a man who was avoiding the captain and sneaking cautiously towards the cabin. He quickly got into the bed fully dressed, covered himself with a blanket, turned to face the wall, waited, and silently prayed.

The sound of the door opening left no doubt in his mind that the spy had finally found him. He tried to breathe normally as if he were asleep, in the hope that the man would go. Then, just as the intruder attempted to uncover his face, the powerful hands of Lucius the helmsman caught the man's arm in a vice grip, and pulling him bodily out of the cabin said.

"Why are you disturbing the crewman? he has been up most of the night. Passengers are not allowed in the cabins."

Marius happened to look over, and having counted the passengers, realised that this must be a spy and hastened across the deck towards him.

"What, may I ask are you doing on board my ship?" asked the captain angrily. "I will not have people prowling around. I have a good mind to hand you over to the harbour security people."

"Did you see him take anything?" questioned Marius with a wink at Lucius, who was at the ready beside the man.

" I… I came to see if you had a pa...passage open," stammered the spy guiltily.

"All my passengers are here now. We are fully booked, and sailing within the hour, so get off my ship before I throw you out."

The man, somewhat shaken, made haste to leave as Lucius who followed on his heels, grabbed the gang plank, and pushed it off onto the quay just missing the spy's retreating ankle by a hair's breadth. The captain went into the cabin to inform Simon that all was now secure, and to remain where he was till they were out of the harbour.

An hour later our hero stood on deck with his good friend Marius, looking back on Joppa, and beginning to relate to him the many adventures he had experienced since they were last together. The large white sail billowing in the morning breeze, and the glorious sunshine of that summer's day, seemed to celebrate with exultant jubilation the return of Simon to his native Cyrene.

CHAPTER FOURTEEN

THE ARRIVAL

The *Stella Maris* glided happily over a lightly undulating blue-green sea, its bow pitching comfortably, leaving intricate frothy patterns spreading at midship with dolphins jumped in and out of it in their aquatic dance. The sail, by its airy fullness provided a welcome shade over the port side of the deck, where around the tenth hour of the day all the passengers were sitting enjoying the sea breeze and having a communal chat.

Ten days had now elapsed since they had left Joppa, and only two days remained before their expected arrival in Apollonia.

Simon stood near the bow, enjoying the view of the coastline which to date had kept them company every day of their very pleasant journey. His thoughts were mixed. The joy of arriving home at last and being able to embrace his family, once again occasioned much impatience in him and made the journey seem longer. On the other hand, he had a great concern regarding Rufus, who as he had learned from a reluctant Marius, had gone off to Rome in search of Letitia, and that could only spell trouble.

'How's he going to get by? thought Simon. "Surely he can't have taken much money with him. I know no one in Rome, and it's such a large city that it's going to be very difficult for him to find Letitia. And then, even if he does find her,' he continued, musing. ' He can't keep her in the way that she is accustomed, and will realise that at the moment he can offer her nothing.'

"There you are!" alone with your thoughts again," boomed the voice of Marius.

"I have much to think about," answered Simon snapping out of his day dream.

"Your head will be covered in grey hairs before long if you worry so, my friend," the captain admonished with a playful smile.

"When you have a family Marius, you spend most of your time worrying about them, and trying to protect them. I should know better by now I suppose, but old habits are hard to change."

"It seems to me that you have changed a fair bit already by all the things you told me and what you plan to do now."

"Yes, I have a big job ahead of me, but God will guide me."

One of the passengers approached the captain with a request for some wine, and Simon was once again left to his thoughts.

The last two days on board had passed painfully slowly for the returning Cyrenean. Now at last, there, up on his beloved hill was Cyrene, and home.

The *Stella Maris* was silently berthed onto the wharf in Apollonia harbour, and Simon took leave of the captain.

"See you soon my good friend," said the carpenter with a happy smile.

"As soon as my cargo is unloaded I shall go up and see the family," promised Marius; in keeping with the invitation that his friend had given him.

Baggage on his back, and a heart full of anticipation, Simon walked up the familiar hill. As he passed some of the shops, people he knew waved to him, and some crossed the road to greet and welcome him back.

On approaching his house, he could hear hammering coming from the shop and knew that Alexander, who was now carrying the weight of the business single handedly, was busy at work.

He crept up to the shop, and stood in front of his son waiting for him to look up and see him. Alexander, seeing a shadow cast over his work raised his head, and with a gasp of joy, shouted, "Father!" Rushing around the work table, he affectionately embraced Simon. They remained locked in each other's arms for a few happy moments. Then, the son ran into the house with the news; the father eagerly following.

The general rush that ensued was breathtaking. Simon, big man as he was, found it hard to keep his balance as the three women jumped on him, smothering him with hugs and kisses, their faces covered with tears of joy.

Utter confusion reigned over the next hour. A hundred questions followed by a hundred answers; laughter and tears, some of joy, some of sadness. They all huddled together in the kitchen whilst Ruth and the girls were preparing lunch, so as to stay close to one another, making up for lost time.

The lunch that followed lasted till supper time. No one wanted to move, as they listened in awe and wonder, to the thrilling story that Simon related.

Baptism registered strongly on their minds as they listened and were gripped with a strong desire to be followers of Yeshua, who had become so crucial in the life of the head of their family, and in whom they suddenly now believed.

The joyous occasion was marred by the absence of Rufus. They all lamented his not being there to share this new enlightened faith, that was to nurture them and give their lives new meaning.

Ruth, who had him very much in mind, sobbed.

"Poor Rufus, God knows where he is and what he is going through. Why could he not be here with us now?"

Simon provided some consolation, assuring her that Yeshua would look after him if the family prayed for him.

"Now," said Simon, "because I would like to 'Break Bread' with you later, I shall, if you are all willing, baptise you, and make you disciples of Yeshua. Our Lord and Saviour."

"Yes!" was the unanimous response, and the necessary preparations were made to carry out the Sacrament.

One by one, the ritual was performed to the delight of all. Ruth and the girls, retired to the kitchen to prepare what would be the most memorable supper of their lives.

Simon's heart was overflowing with love and joy. This had been his dream all the time he had been away from his family. Now it was accomplished. He was back home, his family all having accepted Yeshua; with the exception of his son Rufus, whom he commended to the Lord and asked that soon he may be able to make him a disciple too.

His ministry having now begun with his family, he could hardly wait to spread the good news to everyone.

'I'll start with my friend the rabbi,' he said to himself. 'If he is agreeable to my preaching outside the synagogue. It'll give me a great platform for my work, since both Jews and Gentiles will be able to hear me.'

These thoughts ran nimbly through his mind as he formulated his plan for the 'fishing of men.' Remembering Peter's words that had so shocked him.

"Father!" exclaimed Alexander. "I must tell you all the things that we have done in our work."

"Yes, of course son," answered Simon, coming down to earth again, and realizing that his family's material welfare must also hold a place of importance, as well as their spiritual welfare. Nodding for his son to proceed he sat back and listened.

"Just after you left, we built a cabin on the *Pretoria*. Then before Rufus left, we built three others, all corbitas, and now I am building one myself on board the *Neptune*."

"I'm proud of you both. You've done very well indeed. In fact, I saw the *Pretoria* when it was docked in Joppa, and I had a very pleasant talk with Captain Silas who was most pleased with your work."

Simon related the humorous little episode with Silas, and they both had a good laugh. Lucila who overheard part of the story insisted on them repeating it to the women. They too were much amused.

"I'll join you tomorrow in your work," promised the happy father throwing an arm over his son's shoulders. "I can see that with you working alone it'll take over a week to complete the cabin. It really needs two, so as to cause the ships the minimum delay in their sailing schedules.

Alexander rose from his cushion and walked to the door.

"I am going to close the shop," he announced. "I shall be right back."

Great expectancy filled that large colourful room, as Simon sat with the family around him. Giving thanks to God, he blessed and started the meal.

When the time came for the consecration of the bread, Simon took the time to explain the events of Yeshua's last supper with his disciples and the great importance of the sacrament. The consecration of the wine was similarly explained, and all partook of the sacred meal with great reverence and joy. A touch of benign pride was felt by them at seeing the head of their family so honoured by the apostle Peter on Yeshua's behalf.

"Now my loved ones," he declared. "You are all full disciples of our Divine Lord Yeshua."

As Simon lay in bed with Ruth at his side once more, he had many questions for her regarding Rufus and all that had befallen him: What was the reason for his being forbidden from seeing Letitia? How long had he been gone? What money had he taken with him? What ship did he sail on?

They talked well into the night. She, tearfully explaining all the details to her concerned husband, who was greatly surprised at the main reason for the breaking up of the love affair.

The following morning, the sound of hammers and saws coming from Simon's busy shop announced the start of the work day, as father and son worked diligently to finish the cabin.

"You've done very well my son, all by yourself. Now there are two of us once more, and we should have no trouble in meeting our time schedule."

"Did you know father that all corbitas are not the same size? We have had to pass up six already that allowed no room for a cabin extension; the swan's head took up the space, leaving nothing for the cabin."

"No my son, I wasn't aware of that. Too bad... Too bad."

"At any rate, tomorrow we shall be ready to start assembling on board the 'Ne'... What did you say the name of the ship was?"

"The *Neptune*," asserted Alexander, "and the captain's name is Petronius."

* * * * * *

Rabbi Elias paced slowly up and down the little garden attached to the synagogue, reading a tract from the prophet Isaiah:

"But he was wounded for our iniquities, he was bruised for our sins: the chastisement of our peace was upon him, and by his bruises we are healed."

The venerable old Elias wondered at these words once more, having read them many times before, but never knowing to whom they applied. Simon, who had finished his day's work, now walked into the garden and approached his old friend.

"Greetings to you Rabbi! it's good to see you again."

His words resounded through the garden, and Simon warmly embraced the old man.

"Simon! Simon! my very good friend. How wonderful to have you safely back home."

"What news from Jerusalem?"

"I have much to tell you Rabbi.... Much."

" Sit here," invited the holy man, sliding over a little making room for Simon to sit beside him. " And at least you can make a start".

For the next two hours, Simon sat by the little pond in the garden, on the stone bench beside his old friend, talking to him about his adventures. The rabbi was completely enthralled by what he heard, especially the recounting of Yeshua's passion.

"How very strange," he said, when Simon had stopped to rest. "I have just been reading a passage from Isaiah which I have read many times before, and I could never understand who it was meant to portray. Now, thanks to what you have told me, I believe it referred to Yeshua."

He raised his eyes and hands to heaven in amazement.

"At last I know.... God be praised!"

"You must come and tell me much more about this man that claimed to be the Maschiach. Could it be as you say, that we were expecting the wrong type of Maschiah? I shall give the matter much thought."

And with that, the friends parted. Simon making haste to get home for supper which he had totally forgotten about.

In the weeks that ensued, Simon instructed the rabbi in the new faith with considerable success, and obtained his permission to preach outside the synagogue so that the Gentiles might also hear him.

* * * * * *

Rome had not been too kind to Rufus on his first month in that city. He had found it very busy, the people very impersonal, and even impatient with strangers. He had as yet not begun to make enquiries as to Letitia's whereabouts. After a survey of the city, he became sufficiently acquainted with its good and bad parts, and though a drag on his purse, he opted to find a humble lodging in the better part. He had two reasons for doing so.

'I must find work, and I am more likely to find it in the better side of the city where people will have money to spend on carpentry work. Also, I shall surely be closer to Letitia's residence which will most likely be in a wealthy neighbourhood,' he said to himself. 'I will have to work for someone before I can set myself up, since I have neither tools nor contacts.'

He walked through the neighbourhood searching for carpentry shops. Finding some, he offered his services with his usual friendly smile and enthusiasm. He soon discovered however, that the first question he was asked was, 'had he work to show in the city?' As soon as he answered in the negative they wanted nothing further to do with him.

'My goodness! what am I going to do?... I shall just keep trying that is all. Something has to be there for me somewhere.'

Days went by, and still he had found nothing in his trade. Then he had an idea.

'Why don't I go to the river and find a ship to work on? Maybe I can rent some tools and find a place from which to work. If I have a job, then some local carpenter might, for a share of the profits, allow me to set up shop with him. The river side of the city is on the opposite side of the affluent neighbourhood, but what option do I really have? My money is running out, and it will be cheaper to live in that section of the city. Beggars cannot be choosers.'

He set out one morning with his baggage on his back, and entered the dock area of the River Tiber where he hunted for a lodging which might at least be clean, even if dilapidated, as were most of the buildings there.

It was not until the middle of the day that he found a clean room, and paid the owner a week's rent in advance. The owner, a widow in her mid twenties, presentable in her appearance, and pleasant in her manner, if somewhat crude in her speech, impressed Rufus favourably enough. He left his baggage in his room which was on the upper floor of the house, and immediately went in search of a ship on which he could build a cabin.

Once on the docks he could not see a corbita anywhere. All he saw were much smaller vessels, and many barges that I plied the river. Much surprised, he approached a middle aged sailor who was sitting on a log nearby.

"Good day!" said Rufus with a dubious smile.

"Good day to you young fellow," returned the stranger with a bland look.

"How come I cannot find any ships here, such as corbitas for instance?" asked Rufus.

"Ha! Ha! Ha!" laughed the sailor. "They are miles away downriver. They never get past Ostia; the river is too shallow for them."

Rufus' heart fell. He thanked the sailor, and was about to move on, when the man shouted out to him.

"Hang on there young fellow!" and getting up, went to Rufus and asked why he was upset by the news he had given him.

The young carpenter gave him the reason. He was about to go again, when the sailor took a hold of his arm, and said.

"See that barge over there?" he pointed it out to Rufus. "I need some work done on the interior. If we can make a deal, you can do the work for me whilst we sail back to Ostia for another load of cargo. Then you can get at the corbitas that are berthed there when you are finished."

"I shall pay you of course," said the captain.

"That is very good of you," admitted Rufus with a somewhat perplexed look.

"When do you want me on board?"

"As soon as you come, we shall be off," said the sailor going back to his log.

It was an uncertain Rufus who made his way back to his lodgings fearing he had lost his week's rent.

'Maybe she will give it back to me,' he hoped. But his fears were soon justified.

"You cannot expect your money back," she replied in answer to his appeal. "But when you return," she continued with lustful eyes, and stroking her hair provocatively. You can spend a week rent free.

Rufus went upstairs, took his baggage, and with a disdainful look at her, left. It was late afternoon when the young carpenter boarded the *Mermaid,* as the barge was called. The captain was Lebanese, and went by the name of Bashir.

"Welcome on board," he said, taking him down below deck. There, he was shown a bunk in a small room which he would be sharing with the mate.

The room had a rancid smell of rotted grain and other food remains which made the atmosphere close and revolting.

"It's a bit untidy," remarked Bashir. "The mate is a messy fellow. Perhaps you can straighten him out. He is about your age, maybe slightly older."

Rufus opened the window with some difficulty as it was habitually closed, and asked the captain what he needed done.

He was led through a short narrow passage to a room which took up the full width of the barge, and where there were a number of colourless, dirty looking cushions and a few low tables strewn around the floor. The windows were closed, the wall panelling was rotting and falling apart; the place reeked of humidity and grain. Beyond the room was the galley. It occupied the stern of the barge, and was in no better condition than the rest of the rooms.

The captain looked at Rufus, and the carpenter looked at the captain with an enquiring look.

"What do you want me to do?"

"I want you to suggest what can be done to make this place presentable and livable. Every time I ask my wife to come with me, she refuses and says the place is not fit for pigs."

Rufus laughed aloud at Bashir's admission of slovenliness.

"Ha! Ha! Ha!...you are lucky to have such a discerning wife my friend. I think I know now what I have to do. I shall need to buy materials, so you shall have to postpone your sailing for at least a day."

The trip down to Ostia from Rome took a full day, as the barge was a slow mover and the wind was not always in its favour. The punting was being done by Bashir alone as the younger mate was busy helping Rufus with the cleaning of the barge. By the time they had reached Ostia, Rufus had cleared with the reluctant help from the mate, also Lebanese by the name of Jamil, all the offensive odour-causing material on board, and freshened up the place by keeping the windows open.

All bedding was washed, dried and aired by Jamil on the captain's orders. There were many broken things that required fixing, and these he did first. Whilst at Ostia, the carpenter began to rip out all the rotted panelling around the larger common room. He repaired the floor planks, made the windows good so that they could open easily, and gutted the galley. It took three trips from Ostia to Rome before Rufus declared his work finished.

Bashir was beside himself with pleasure and pride of ownership. Even his two-bed cabin had been cleaned and renovated.

The grand occasion came when the captain convinced his wife Aula to come on board, which she did most reluctantly. Having been introduced to her, Rufus followed closely on her heels to hear her comments.

First she headed for the captain's cabin, and was impressed by its neatness and clean bedding. The mate's room met with similar approval. But when she entered the common or living room, she gasped in awe, beholding the transformation that had taken place: the new and beautifully crafted panelling, the smoothened and stained wood floor; the new colourful cushions; and the open windows which had been freshly painted. Last of all, the tiled and efficient galley, with a hood and a flue to the side of the barge, allowing the removal of cooking odours.

She turned around, smiled at her husband with a look of incredulity in her eyes and hugged Rufus, who blushed profusely. Bashir, greatly amused, laughed heartily at the sight.

"Now! my dear," said the captain to his wife. "Will you come with me on the next trip?"

"Yes!" she replied with a big toothy smile on her round bewildered face.

The captain's wife left the barge in high spirits. Bashir, who had to remain for one more day to load grain for the trip to Rome, paid Rufus handsomely, and allowed him to stay on board whilst he looked for the corbita that would contract him for a cabin.

Rufus was soon walking the long wharves where a number of ships were berthed. He spotted a corbita that needed a cabin but he could not see anyone on board, and the gang plank was lying on the wharf.

'I shall come back to that one on my way back, he told himself,' continuing his walk along the crowded and noisy wharf.

Two warships were next in his path with much activity on board. These were followed by three large galleys. As he continued his walk he came upon two more corbitas. The first one was cabin free. But then....He could not believe his eyes as the *Pretoria* appeared before him with its cabin in full sight. The gang plank being up, he immediately went on the deck.

"Silas!" he called out. "Silas! where are you?"

A small face with a sleepy, puffy look, peered out of the captain's cabin.

"Rufus! my dear boy. What are you doing in Ostia?"

They entertained one another for the next couple of hours. Silas invited Rufus to stay with him in the new cabin until he sailed three days hence. He had yet to load and get passengers signed up for his scheduled trip to Carthage.

This arrangement gave Rufus three more days to find work and a partner carpenter to work with. He lost no time in bidding farewell to Bashir, and baggage on shoulders once again, moved into the cabin on the *Pretoria*.

The next day he tried the corbita which was berthed immediately in front of the *Pretoria*, and to his joy, he got the contract with the proviso that he would have it completed within one week.

He immediately set out around the port area to look for a carpentry shop. The first one he found, refused him on the grounds that they were presently too busy to take on any more work. The second however, showed interest in his proposal, and would allow him to work for half of the profit.

Rufus was excited about the deal though it was a little unfair. He could foresee more work coming his way in the near future, and the other man contributing nothing but the use of his shop and tools for half of the profit. He found lodgings close by and paid a week ahead once again.

The following day he left Silas, who was getting ready to sail next morning, and moved into his room near the harbour. Bashir had paid him enough money to allow him to buy all the materials he needed. He rented a donkey cart, and having obtained all he required, he began the work in his new partner's shop with his habitual dedication; working late into the night for the next three days. He toiled diligently barely communicating with his partner. The latter, did not encourage any conversation and was absent from the shop most of the time. Presumably busy with some project outside the harbour area.

On the fourth day he rented the donkey cart again and delivered the pre-assembled pieces as he and Alexander were wont to do. He worked from dawn till dusk for the next four days going without food for hours. He was determined to finish on time.

The final day arrived. Having completed the cabin, he went looking for the captain to solicit the man's inspection, and hopefully, his subsequent approval. The captain was nowhere in sight. He felt very hungry having eaten very little that day. Leaving the ship, he walked to a shop further down the wharf where he bought some fish, bread, some wine, and sat nearby to eat.

From where he sat he could see the ship which was called the *Dolphin,* and whose captain, named Cratius, had not been as personable as he would have hoped. His comments on the work had been satisfactory, but little enthusiasm had been shown for the project.

'I don't mind his attitude,' thought Rufus, 'as long as he pays me.'

A lamp was burning in the captain's cabin when he returned to the ship at dusk. He went on deck, and knocked at the cabin door.

"Who's there?"

"It's me! Rufus the carpenter."

"Come in!"

Rufus entered and saluted the captain with a smile on his face.

"I tried to find you earlier on but you were not on board. I am finished now, and all is ready for your inspection and approval."

"Very well!" said Cratius, and taking the lamp with him, went around to the new cabin followed by the carpenter.

He looked very carefully at everything. He pulled the table up and it locked nicely in place; he felt the beds, opened and shut the window a number of times, and then closed the door to feel the tightness of the fit. He then returned to his cabin followed by Rufus.

"Your work is well done, I cannot fault it. Here is your money....Please count it."

Rufus took it out of the bag and counted it.

"Yes, thank you, it's exactly right," said Rufus again with a smile, turning to leave.

"Goodnight then," said the captain. "I am sailing in the morning. I need my sleep."

"Goodnight and thank you again," said Rufus. And with the little bag of money in his hand, he walked out of the cabin and closed the door.

"We'll take that," said a raspy voice, as someone pulled the money bag off his hand with a quick jerk before he had taken a step.

"Give back that bag," shouted the dismayed carpenter, as he lunged at the man who had robbed him.

He felt a heavy blow on his cheek. As he reeled back from the force of the blow, the other man punched him hard in the stomach, causing him to double over breathlessly in great pain. Down he crashed onto the deck where he quickly received a kick in the ribs and a few more in the face. One of the two grabbed him by the throat as the other held down his legs, and said.

"Let this be a warning to you carpenter. Don't show your face around here again. Go back to your own town and do your work there. Ostia work is for Ostia carpenters. Do you understand me?" he threatened, as he squeezed his throat once more, the other holding him down.

Rufus, still swooning, suddenly found himself alone on the deck with aching ribs and face, trying to catch his breath. The men had disappeared. He then realised that in all that commotion, Cratius had not come out of his cabin to help.

'He could not possibly have been asleep so soon after I left him,' thought the injured carpenter.

Rufus staggered to his feet, and approached the cabin door. He knocked, but there was no answer. He knocked again. This time Cratius responded.

"Go away! I'm trying to sleep."

"It's me, Rufus, and I have just been attacked and robbed of my money right here on your ship."

"Go report it go the Port Security."

"Very well," said Rufus, now suspecting that the captain was in league with the robbers, and promptly left the ship in search of the Security office.

The office was open all night. Our battered young hero was soon explaining the whole episode to the officer on duty. He was asked if he could recognise or describe his assailants, to which he answered in the negative, other than he thought they were carpenters.

"I am afraid," said the officer, "that there is little we can do then. In cases like this it is imperative that the assailants be at least well described, or else who are we going to look for?"

"Are you very badly hurt?"

"I'll live!" was Rufus' answer, as he painfully walked away to his lodgings and his bed.

Our hero, still felt very sore the next morning and stayed in bed for a considerable while longer than was his habit. The landlady knocked at his door and asked if he would like some breakfast. He answered that he would, but would she kindly bring it in?

"My goodness!" She exclaimed, when she entered the room and saw his face.

"What happened to you?"

"I was beaten up and robbed of all the money I was paid for my week's work."

"Gracious me! did you report it?"

"Yes. But since I could not adequately describe my attackers it being dark out, they could not help me."

"Eat your breakfast, whilst I get some nice warm water to bathe your face," said the kind woman who was about his mother's age and quite attractive; though not nearly as beautiful in Rufus' eyes.

He stayed indoors for the rest of that day and part of the next, but come late afternoon, he started out to meet his partner and explain what had happened. He did not know what to expect from the fellow. They really had not spoken too many words. It was strictly a business deal with very little friendship, if any.

"Now you see what happened," protested Rufus, finishing his story, and showing him his bruised ribs.

"I am sorry you had such a beating, but I am out twenty denarii and that will not do. You must pay me my share right now."

"I cannot afford it at the moment. I will pay you after my next job. It will come in soon enough; merely a matter of days. I expect, there being so many more corbitas in the harbour, that there will be more business coming our way almost immediately."

"I am sorry, but I want my money now, or I shall report you to the Security Office, and then you will be in a lot of trouble."

"So be it," said the frustrated Rufus, and walked away to his lodgings to collect his thoughts.

On his arrival, the landlady whose name was Neta, enquired as to how he was feeling. He explained his problem with his partner carpenter and told her that if he paid the man now he would have no money left to stay with her. To make matters worse he was likely to be arrested soon, he supposed.

"Do they know where you live?" she asked.

"I don't know.... I don't think so."

"You must go as soon as possible. I shall have my daughter guide you out of the harbour area which she knows well, and then you can get away. The security people are active only around the harbour."

Rufus having packed his bag was given supper by Neta. They were waiting for her daughter to arrive, when a hard and insistent knocking at the door was heard. Rufus and Neta, both froze for a moment. But the landlady was quick to react, and told Rufus to go out by the back way. Then, giving him a head start, went to open the front door.

Rufus hesitated only for a moment, he grabbed his bag which was near him and made for the back door. He had to take a chance and hope they were not guarding that exit also. He gingerly stepped out into an empty, narrow alleyway, and with a quick glance back, walked away as quickly as possible. On reaching the main thoroughfare, he quickly lost himself in the crowd..

'Whew! that was a narrow escape!' breathed Rufus. 'That carpenter must have followed me home. Now, what do I do?'

He realised that his time in Ostia had come to an end. He could not set up as a carpenter, which was the only way he could earn a living. Rome was now his only option as it represented the whole purpose of his life.

The eternal city was a full day's walk. His ribs were still aching, and his face needed a bit more time to recover and settle back to its normal look. He decided to put up somewhere for the night and start afresh in the morning. As he left Ostia behind, he regretted having lost contact with ships. It would have kept him in touch with captains he knew, such as Marius and Silas. That, being the only way he could maintain some occasional rapport with home.

'Still,' he thought, 'there is always Bashir. He can find the captains for me if needed on his regular runs from Rome.'

As night fell, he came across a farmhouse, and approaching it he knocked at the door. A dog barked viciously inside the house. A masculine voice told the animal to lie down and keep quiet. Then asked.

"Who is it? what do you want?"

"I am a young traveller caught out, and am looking for refuge for the night. I shall happily pay you for your trouble."

A little window, too narrow for even a child to squeeze through, opened just beside the door, and with a lamp held in the opening, the farmer asked Rufus to show his face and his baggage. Our hero did as he was bid attempting a smile with his stiff and aching face.

"How did you get those bruises on your face?" asked the man sternly.

"I was attacked and robbed of my wages. I have still a little money left with which to pay you for your hospitality."

The man withdrew. A few moments passed. Talking could be heard in low tones inside the house. After what seemed a long time to Rufus, the man appeared again at the window and asked.

"What do you do for a living?"

"I am a carpenter, and my father and brother are also carpenters. I come from Cyrene. My name is Rufus."

The door was finally opened. A big shaggy dog eyed and sniffed him as if performing a final examination before allowing the stranger into the house.

"Is he friendly?" asked Rufus, who liked dogs and was about to stroke the large hairy creature.

"He is fine now, once he knows that we welcome you."

The man was rather short in stature, but squarely built. His face, amply weather worn, had a look of honesty about it. He had a heavy nose, bushy eyebrows, kind eyes, a thin-lipped mouth, and his head was covered by a large crop of grey streaked black hair. The remainder of his face was clean shaven, and displayed a solid square chin with a dimpled centre.

"Sorry about all the questions," he said rubbing his neck. "When one lives in the country, far from neighbourly help, one has to be careful as to whom one opens his door to at night," he asserted apologetically.

"Come in and sit down....Are you hungry?" he asked, all in one breath. Again, rubbing his neck.

"Yes. Very," responded the youth.

"This will cheer you up and warm your stomach."

The statement was followed by a woman who entered the room carrying a bowl between two pieces of cloth, steaming as it came.

"There you are young man," she smiled, and she set the bowl on a low table in front of him. She sat down on some cushions near him. "Don't burn your mouth," she warned handing him a wooden spoon.

She was a cheery countenanced, red cheeked woman, around fifty one or fifty two years of age; a little on the plump side but not fat. Her reddish face was also weather-beaten, and she was missing a front tooth which deterred somewhat from her otherwise congenial aspect. Her large rough hands, which like those of her husband's, attested to their hard outdoors' work, were now restfully crossed over her lap as she peered critically at her young guest.

"You are a good looking boy, but those bruises are ruining your looks," she said in a jovial manner, a twinkle sparkling in her eye. "My Jarius, would have been a little older than you now if he had lived," she remarked, as the twinkle in her eye died, and a sad film gathered over that recent jovial look.

"I am sorry to hear that you lost your son," commented Rufus, as he looked up from the delicious stew that had really found the spot in his hungry stomach.

"This stew is excellent! you are a good cook like my mother, and I thank you."

The man now joined the conversation, and asked the visitor to relate to them some of his story. His wife looked at her young guest with motherly eyes, imagining how his mother would be shocked and hurt if she could see him now in his present predicament.

The couple, who lived a lonely life, listened with great interest and enthusiasm to the story that the young stranger unfolded for their entertainment. He was given a room to sleep in that night, and his hostess went out of her way to make her new boarder comfortable.

Even the dog seemed to take to him. He slept just outside his door and snored his approval of the friendly stranger.

The chirping of the birds, and the rays of the morning sun streaming through the high barred window of his room, brought Rufus to full consciousness as he surveyed the room and became aware of his whereabouts. With all the changing conditions of his new life, it seemed to him that almost every night found him in a different place, and his heart longed for the stability that he had always enjoyed at home with his beloved family.

He lay back again on the cushion that acted as his pillow, and thought of his mother and sisters, and how circumstances had torn him away from them so ruthlessly. At the moment, he had neither the warmth of his family nor of the woman he loved.

He resolved then and there, to work at whatever would make him some honest money. If he could not ply his trade, he would learn another, and use whatever opportunity presented itself for his advancement. Thinking of Marcus, and how he had made his money, he resolved to use the brains that God had given him to progress quickly.

'Time,' he told himself, 'was of the essence.'

Letitia, he felt, might not be able to hold out for long with all the pressure she was under from her family.

"Why did life have to be so tough?" he asked himself (mimicking his father). Getting on his feet, he went in search of the ablutions.

"Good morning!" sang a voice just behind him as he trod down the corridor that connected various rooms, and opened out into the common, or living area of the house.

"My goodness it's late isn't it?" asked Rufus of Tita, his hostess, who followed him into the living area.

"You were over-tired; though at your age you would hardly notice," she said with condescension in her voice. "The ablutions are over there," she continued, pointing to a door immediately off the living room.

Rufus thanked her with a bright smile, and disappeared into the room indicated.

At this point her husband Manius walked into the house followed by Lupus; his big, shaggy, Hispanian dog. Its pristine white colour quite apparent in the morning light.

"I have a meal ready for him as soon as he comes out of the ablutions," answered Tita in response to a question from her husband who had already seen to a good number of things around the farm.

"His bruises are looking a lot better this morning," she commented. "It's amazing how quickly the young ones recover from wounds and such."

"He is a hardy boy, even though his features are so refined," pointed out the farmer with a touch of admiration for his new friend.

Rufus entered the large room once more, and saluted Manius warmly. His host, in turn, pointed to a cushion, and asking him to sit, announced that his meal was forthcoming.

The rural couple did their best to have Rufus stay with them as their guest for a few more days refusing all offers of money or work in lieu.

"Our land gives us all we need," the farmer explained. "And money we have enough to keep us comfortable and look after our few needs. You keep your money, because you will very soon need it. Rome is an expensive place to live in."

"If you ever run into trouble again, remember that you have friends here, and you come back to us....Remember that now. You hear?" assured Tita.

Three days after those assertions of hospitality and quickly formed affection, such as are often engendered in rural folks, Rufus was on his way. Manius followed by Lupus, accompanied him to the farthest hedge of his extensive property.

Soon, Rome in all its glory loomed in front of him once more, and he prepared to face whatever lay in store for him in that proud Imperial city.

CHAPTER FIFTEEN

THE BEGINNING

Simon stood on the steps of the synagogue. A fair crowd surrounded him as he expounded to them with fervent conviction, the parables of Yeshua that he had learnt to repeat with constant and undeviating accuracy. Peter had instructed him never to change the least detail in the delivering of his sermons, and he meant to abide strictly by the apostle's order.

His listeners, though mainly Jewish from that same synagogue, included a good number of Gentiles. This greatly encouraged Simon, who remembered vividly the occurrences in the house of Cornelius the day of his arrest.

The morning service in the synagogue had just finished. Simon had attended and read a tract from the prophet Daniel, and had obtained the rabbi's permission to begin his ministry on the entrance steps. A location which afforded him a good platform for his preaching.

Many were the questions which he had to answer in the course of his sermon. Every now and then, someone would interrupt him in the middle of a parable, appealing for an explanation which he had perforce to address. He did so with aplomb and honesty, secretly praying to the Holy Spirit for guidance.

A good number of requests for baptism followed his sermon, and for that purpose, his friend the old rabbi, had provided a font filled with water that stood in the garden. From it, the birds normally drank, surrounded by the beauty and persistent aroma of the many flowers. A jug of water was also to be found nearby.

"You have made quite a few converts today," commented the holy man as Simon finished his baptisms for the day and joined him on the stone bench where he sat contemplating and praying by the little pool.

"Soon, my friend, you will be baptising me also."

"I pray that that'll be the case," said Simon with a smile. You are already quite knowledgeable with regard to Yeshua's parables. You know that the Hebrew faith and traditions remain. We still follow the Commandments. The only difference is the concept of the Maschiach, and the acceptance of his being truly the Son of our God. When you can accept that, then you'll be in a position to accept Baptism also."

Suddenly the old man began to cough; a hard-sounding continuous cough which made him spit. An alarmed Simon noticed that the spittle was tainted with blood, but said nothing so as not to alarm his friend.

"You must see a physician about that cough," advised Simon.

"Yes, I have been thinking about it. But I suspect it is old age," replied the rabbi.

Simon left his old friend with a sinking heart, for he felt it was a serious matter. As he walked home, his mind was further in turmoil. He contemplated the procuring of a place of assembly for his new congregation.

'I have not solved the question of where to meet in the future, for the 'Breaking of the Bread,' he said to himself with concern, adjusting his slipping blue shawl.

'The numbers will soon be growing and cannot all be accommodated in a house. Peter and James are too far away to be consulted, so I must pray that the Holy Spirit guide me in my decision, whatever it may be. It will also cost money.' He saluted a passerby, with a smile, and walked on.

'If we buy a place, where is the money going to come from?' His mind ran on… 'What if we rent a place for one day every week. Perhaps the first day of the week; the day of the Lord's Resurrection. I think I remember Peter and James talking about that. All who are baptised should contribute to the costs of the assemblies.' He scratched his short beard. 'I must keep a record, of my converts, then I shall know how much money we can afford to pay for the rent.'

Simon began to realise that it was not only a question of preaching, but also the much more complex matter of organizing a community. His tenacity would make him equal to the challenge however, for without being aware of it, leadership qualities were a very definite part of his makeup. Oratory too, was a gift that he had not stopped to consider; until he realised that he was holding people's attention and achieving results. Then, he promptly thanked the Holy Spirit for the gift. He had yet to discover more gifts of the Holy Spirit as his priestly career developed.

One day, as Simon walked back from a meeting with a ship's captain at the quay in Apollonia, accompanied by Alexander, it occurred to him that he had not yet visited Marcus to see if there were any signs of recovery. It was early afternoon. A good time to visit he thought. Alexander had been to the house before, and would guide him there.

They soon reached the house. Tecuno, who was always around the gate area went to enquire of the visitors.

"Good afternoon!" sang the Nubian. "How can I be of service?"

"Recognising Alexander, he greeted him cordially. His big friendly toothy smile exposed a perfect set of teeth, the whiteness of which contrasted vividly with his black skin and were matched only by the whites of his intelligent eyes.

"My father and I have come to visit your master with your mistress' permission. Has there been any improvement in his condition?" asked Alexander.

"No! I am sorry to say. But I shall let her know that you are here," he said, hastening to the house.

Tecuno was back promptly and opened the gate, inviting them to follow him as he led the way to the house.

Julia was at the hallway door leading into the atrium to meet them. She smiled warmly at the pair as they greeted her without resentment in their manner, which perhaps she may have expected; not having seen Simon for many months, and not knowing how the children's tragic love affair might have been judged by him.

"Welcome to you both my friends. It's good to see you. How are Ruth and the girls keeping?" she greeted with a smile and extending her hands to Simon.

"They're well thank you," answered Simon as he took her hands and pressed them.

"I was keen to know how Marcus was faring," he continued. "Your servant informs me that his condition is unchanged."

"Yes, we are absolutely distressed. The physicians have given up on him," she said with a hint of a tear in her eyes and smiling at Alexander, who also pressed her hands, returning her smile.

"May I see him?"

"Yes! of course." And she led the way across the beautiful atrium and into the peristyle where their main bedroom was situate, and where Marcus spent most of his time.

They found him reclining on his couch staring ahead aimlessly as he had done for the last five months.

Simon walked over and took his hand, looked into his eyes, and then, raising his eyes to heaven, prayed to Yeshua for Marcus's recovery. All of a sudden, he felt that wonderful tranquil feeling again and found himself saying.

"Marcus, in the Holy name of Yeshua the Anointed One,... be healed!"

Julia and Alexander, froze in wonder. A few moments of pregnant silence elapsed, then Marcus' eyes fluttered and came to life. He got up from the couch, and looked at them all as if saying: 'Well? what are you staring at me for?'

His wife screamed for joy. She rushed to her husband and hugged him with all her might. He, returned her hug with a look of uncertainty in his eyes as he tried to absorb what was happening. Alexander gave his father a tearful embrace; suddenly realising the magnitude of what they had all witnessed.

Julia left her husband, and threw herself on her knees in front of Simon crying bitterly. The miracle worker stooped, picked her up, and said:

"I am only a man. What you have just witnessed was the act of the Lord Yeshua, the Son of the true and only God, who has worked through me."

Marcus, who had at last pieced together all the occurrences of the last five months, including his terrifying accident, and rescue, embraced Simon with great emotion, ardently thanking him for curing him, and for his son having saved his life.

They all gathered in the atrium, where Silia soon came with a large tray full of enticing morsels and some wine. The whole household sat and listened with great interest to the good news of the Lord, which Simon expounded with inspired eloquence and conviction.

An instant conversion of Marcus, his wife, and servants followed, all being baptised that same day.

Marcus, not being aware of his daughter's unfortunate plight in her love affair with Rufus, and the decision that Julia had made in his mental absence, enquired after Rufus, whom he wished to thank and reward for having saved his life.

Simon looked at Julia with a questioning look, and seeing that she hesitated, merely informed Marcus that his son had gone to Rome in search of his daughter, and that Julia would explain. With that, he and Alexander bid them adieu, and left the new converts to their deliberations regarding the delinquent lovers.

* * * * * *

It was a tired and hungry Rufus, who approached a food shop in the heart of Rome and to purchase his evening meal.

"Here you are!" said the vendor with a cheerful smile on her face. "I got you the juiciest piece of meat I could find on the bone, as most of the meat is fairly dry at this late hour of the day."

She was a young, handsome, dark haired girl, with a bubbly personality, and a little older than him.

"I am very grateful," he said, displaying an appreciative smile which usually won over his victim.

Seeing a certain vivaciousness in her eyes, and remembering Lucila, he remarked.

"You remind me of my younger sister."

"She must be very young, since you cannot be more than eighteen yourself," was the assertive reply.

"I am nineteen and closing on twenty," said he straightening and looking defiantly at the two mischievous eyes that met his.

"So? I am already twenty," she defied.

"Who are you talking to? "A man's voice rang out from a back room, followed by the appearance of the man himself.

Seeing Rufus, and having heard part of the conversation, he made the girl go into the back and faced Rufus with a challenging look on his face.

"Women talk too much," he declared. "Did you get everything you needed?"

He was older than Rufus and obviously did not take kindly to his wife's flirting ways.

"If you would sell me some wine and a few dates, it is all I need thank you," said Rufus politely, not wishing to anger the man further.

The transaction being completed, Rufus, asked the man if there was a clean lodging nearby which might be reasonably priced.

"Try the house down there with the green door and shutters. The owner's name is Drucila. She takes people in at times when her son is away."

The look of anger had now left the man's face, and an aura of resignation took its place as a faint smile developed, which was returned in greater proportion by Rufus, who sympathized with his situation.

"Thank you," said Rufus, and walked away to his prospective lodgings.

He found his room clean and the bed good. After sorting out his meagre belongings, he lay on his bed for a long time musing and planning his next move, which was a total hypothesis. The dreams of the young are the substance of the future. In their eyes it takes only one magical opportunity for wonderful things to develop. It was the desire for that magical happening that kept this particular young and valiant person going. His thoughts soon turned into fantasies, and fantasies into dreams, as he fell asleep to dream once more of his beloved Letitia.

Next morning, on learning that he needed to find work immediately, Drucila, his landlady, who can best be described as matronly, fairly tall, with average though not unpleasant physiognomical attributes, asked if he could read and write. On receiving an affirmative reply, and without much ado; for she was an unusual species of womanhood... 'A woman of few words.' She directed her young boarder to the shop of a merchant who was just down the street.

"Make sure you tell him I sent you... His name is Erasmus."

"Come, tell me what you have done, and I shall see what you can do for me," were the merchant's first words on seeing the young applicant.

Rufus took up the next quarter of an hour of Erasmus' time as he related his work experience. Erasmus, in his mid sixties, was surprised that at such an early age the young man should have such a mature outlook on business, even though his work was mostly manual. In short, he was impressed by Rufus' personality, and the fact that he could both read and write.

"I may employ you young man," said the merchant. "Since above all I like your attitude, and can see that you are not afraid of work. Here! sit down. Take that parchment, and from these other parchments," he pointed to some scrolls that were strewn in a basket nearby. "Take the quantities of the individual items you find there, and write their totals on your new parchment. Think you can do that?"

"I think so," answered Rufus, taking one of them from the basket and beginning to peruse its contents.

"I shall leave you for now," said the merchant, and walked out of the shop leaving the new clerk to carry out his work.

When Erasmus returned in mid afternoon, he was greatly surprised to find Rufus arranging shelves. He looked around with a look of uncertainty in his beady eyes.

"Have you finished your work on the parchment? What have you done with the basket of scrolls?" he asked, with a touch of anxiety in his voice.

"The new scroll is here," replied Rufus, handing it to his prospective employer. "The others are on this shelf and I have taken the liberty of numbering so that we can find them quicker in the future."

Erasmus opened the new scroll, scrutinized the totals, and realising what a neat, well-written parchment he held in his hand, he could hardly conceal his admiration. But being the shrewd businessman that he was, kept it to himself.

'He might ask for more money than I wish to pay at the moment,' he thought.

Erasmus, was a very tall languid sort of man, with a good head of heavily silvered hair which visually added to his age. A long very narrow slightly beaky nose, and large well-formed, slender-lipped mouth tending a little off the horizontal, gave his face a smirky look. His beady light grey eyes crowned by silvery eyebrows showed intelligence and shrewdness. His only deprecating feature was a noticeable stoop which was accentuated by his height.

"Good! Very good!" he said with formality in his voice. "I can see that you are a good scribe. I shall check your totals tonight, and if they are correct, you can count on a good salary if you come to work for me."

"May I leave now? I need to have something to eat. I did not stop for lunch."

"Certainly… Take the rest of the day off. Tomorrow we will come to terms." He gave Rufus half a denarius for his lunch, and sat down to admire the work once again as the prospective clerk left for the nearest food shop.

Arriving at the shop at the third hour the following morning, Rufus was surprised to find two other persons apparently getting ready to begin their days work. Erasmus had not as yet arrived.

One was a boy of about fourteen with blond wavy hair, a very round face, and large light blue eyes, which glared at Rufus with an inquisitive look. The other, a man in his mid thirties of slight build and average height, displaying an authoritative aspect, dryly enquired what was it that Rufus wanted.

The latter was taken a little aback, not having seen anyone there the previous day; though he suddenly remembered seeing an empty desk. Rufus was about to explain, when Erasmus walked in.

"This!" he said looking at the older one, "is your new colleague."

The other, whose name was Publius, nodded his head and produced a sour smile, which was returned by a friendly one from Rufus.

"And this!" continued the merchant, "is 'Servi, our messenger boy."

The boy waved and smiled. Rufus answering in similar fashion.

"Come, let us go for a stroll. I have some things to show you," said Erasmus in a formal tone.

"I want you to see the warehouse where everything is held for distribution. I have to keep it guarded day and night as I have been robbed a couple of times.

During the course of their walk Erasmus explained many things about the business of which the new clerk made careful mental note.

"You have decided to employ me then?" asked Rufus.

"Why yes! I have."

"Then I take it that my powers of addition were not found deficient," said the new clerk, with a jovial smile, which the merchant could not but return.

"Welcome to my business!"

"I shall offer you three denarii a day to start, and if your good work progresses, you shall have more as time goes on," said Erasmus, stretching out his hand, which Rufus was quick to take.

"What hours do you require of me?"

"You can start at the third hour as you did this morning, and you may leave at the eleventh hour, with one hour rest period for lunch. The work week is six days. We are closed on Dies Solis."

"That sounds good to me. I accept!" agreed Rufus, after having made a quick calculation of his prospective expenses.

He greatly regretted having to work on the Sabbath however, but realised there was at the present no alternative. This was pagan Rome, and if he refused this position, he would not be able to survive, let alone progress.

'I shall get back to keeping the Sabbath, at the very first opportunity. I pray God will forgive me,' he said to himself, feeling great guilt.

"Good! then all is settled....Welcome aboard."

Dies Solis arrived after three days of work. Rufus got up early in the morning, and immediately after breakfast took himself to the Forum which he had as yet not visited, and walked around carefully eyeing every woman, in the hope of seeing Letitia.

'Surely, this is where she would take her walks. It is such a fantastic place, that it must attract everyone at one time or another,' he mused.

He was amazed at the architecture of the place.

'No place on earth can rival this. If only Alexander were here, how he would enjoy all this grandeur.'

The Forum was crowded with people from all over the world. The vast majority being well dressed, as if realising that such a place required the visitor to uphold the dignity and elegance which it had been built to express. Those imposing marble facades glistening in the morning sun, produced a magical and ethereal atmosphere that dazzled the eye and seemed unreal. Vendors with carts abounded, some selling a great variety of souvenirs and others enticing the visitor with fresh fruit and a variety of nuts, cheeses, bread, dates, water, wine and other foods. Senators in their immaculate white togas forming small animated groups, endowed this unique space with an aura of learning and judicial severity. The presence of military personnel in full regalia, zealously guarding the many public buildings, lent colour and majesty to this unique architectural wonder, which undoubtedly represented the centre of the world. Rufus spent the whole day there, visiting the public buildings and scrutinizing every suspect face for the likeness of his beloved.

Dusk came at last; casting its grey mantle, robbing those marble facades of their dazzle, and turning them into ghostly creations. Torches, now provided the light required for visitors to find their way into, and around the buildings which remained open until late in the evening. Many visitors were departing with hired torch bearers lighting their way. Rufus took advantage of following other people's torches to find his way home, which posed a few problems for him, as sooner or later, he was left in the dark; the torch bearers having reached their assigned destinations. For safety's sake he kept to the main thoroughfares. It was late in the evening when he finally reached his lodgings.

Drucila opened the door at his knock and smilingly told him that she had left a cold supper for him in his room. For that, he was most thankful, as he had totally mistimed his return.

Tired after a day of vigilance and disappointment, he supped, and sat for a while thinking and musing about his elusive Letitia. Then he went to bed. He dreamt of the evening he told Letitia that he loved her,... by the Venus pool.

"Venus pool! Venus pool!" he woke up exclaiming.

'That's it! That is where she will be. The temple of Venus! Why did I not think of it today?... Oh, stupid, stupid me,' he sighed, and after a while,... he fell asleep again.

Dies Solis could not come soon enough the ensuing week. Though he carried out his duties conscientiously so as to earn the constant approval of Erasmus, he could hardly wait to visit the temple of Venus.

At last, the much awaited day arrived and found him once again at the Forum making his way hurriedly to the temple. It was crowded with people even in the early hours of the morning, as they paraded or grouped around the double colonnaded portico that flanked the temple. Rufus began his watch, walking slowly and observantly among the crowd, peering into any feminine face that he suspected; often meeting with a stern look. He tentatively ventured into the temple. There, the priestesses were burning incense and performing offerings of flowers and herbs, given them by the female devotees.

The statue of Venus herself was huge. He had never seen anything so big in the way of a statue in his life. Lovely women dressed in their finery moved around the temple in an endless tide of colour and fragrance, enchanting the young lover whose impatience clearly showed on his face; his head turning from one side to the other in a frenzy of expectation.

The morning came and went without any success. He became hungry, and leaving the temple with reluctance, went in search of a food shop to ease his hunger pains. He ate as he travelled back to the temple so as not to lose any chance of seeing Letitia.

As he was walking up the temple steps, he felt he recognised some voices just behind him, and turning, came face to face with Zaphira. Her mistress, was busy talking to another older woman who was accompanying them.

He pressed his finger to his lips to warn her to keep quiet, and motioned her to fall behind. The slave reacted quickly and offering some excuse which Rufus did not hear, broke away from the other two, turned, descended the steps and walked away. Rufus allowed a few moments, then followed her until they were out of sight around the side of the building.

"Master Rufus! is it really you? I still cannot believe it. Have you come for her?"

"Yes, but only to talk to her for now. Will you ask her to come with you alone next Dies Solis, and I shall meet her in the temple at this same time, or would she prefer earlier?"

"Yes! perhaps it will be easier for us to come alone early in the morning, since her aunt sleeps in late that day, and will be less inclined to accompany us."

"Zaphira, you are a gem!" said Rufus giving her a kiss on the cheek, which gave her a pleasurable shock.

The amiable slave left in a flustered condition, to join her mistress. The young lover followed her, so as to admire his beloved from a silent distance.

* * * * * *

It was a revitalized, happy Rufus, who walked into Erasmus' shop on 'Dies Lunar' or the second day of the week by the Jewish calendar. He braced himself for a long week however, as he looked forward to the coming weekend with uncommon anticipation.

The routine of his daily work was certainly making the days drag. On 'Dies Joves', he arrived at the shop at the usual time in the morning. Publius was already at his desk and Servi had not got in as yet. At Rufus's morning greeting, Publius looked up, nodded, and resumed his stooped position over his parchment. The former sat down at his desk and checked to see if the owner had left any new work for him.

Seeing as there was no new work required, Rufus got up, and taking an empty wooden box that sat in the corner of the room, used it to reach a high shelf holding a number of scrolls. These were grouped in a haphazard way, and threatened to fall off at the least provocation.

"Leave those alone! they are fine the way they are."

The new clerk, turned to find the old one standing right beside him.

"They are going to fall. And besides, I am going to check through them. There seem to be a few new ones among all those oldies. I have nothing else to do at the moment until Erasmus arrives."

"Here! help me with some of my stuff. I still have around thirty items to enter, so here!" said Publius with a forced smile and handing him a parchment.

"Rufus went back to his desk. He wondered why his colleague had been so forceful in keeping him away from the high shelf. Taking his stylus, he began to write.

Erasmus was late in coming that morning, which was unusual. It was almost lunch time when he arrived, and he was not looking well. He said that he had had a very bad night with pains in his stomach. Having been away longer than he had expected, he looked around to see what his two employees present, and the missing one were up to.

"How come you are working on that?" asked the merchant as he looked over Rufus' shoulder.

"He had nothing to do, and I asked him to help me with my stuff until you arrived," chirped Publius before Rufus could answer.

"Give it back to him," said Erasmus addressing his new clerk. "I have something I need you to do for me."

And with that, he motioned Rufus to follow him into the small stockroom at the back of the shop.

Once out of the other clerk's hearing, Erasmus explained to Rufus, his need of someone reliable to undertake the management of the unloading of a grain cargo which was delayed and causing big problems. One of his best customers was threatening to refuse acceptance unless he had the grain in his possession before the following 'Dies Mercuri.' Considering that on the basis of their efficiency in delivering that order, other orders were dependent, the need for good management was essential. It was something that required Erasmus himself to undertake. He admitted to his new clerk however, that he was feeling very poorly and had not the stamina required for the trip. He therefore wanted Rufus, even though inexperienced, to take his place. He really had no option. Rufus asked where the meeting was to be held, and why Erasmus did not assign Publius who was more experienced than he.

The merchant looked at his new clerk with deep concern in his eyes, and after a few moments, whispered in Rufus' ear, "I do not trust him."

Our hero was taken aback, his eyes staring in disbelief, sighed.

"Oh dear! where is the assignment to be?"

"In Ostia," replied the merchant. "The ship is already berthed. It is having trouble finding a barge to unload it, things being so busy down there. The captain gave us no prior notice of their arrival, so we could not preorder a barge to bring the cargo up river. Let's get out of the shop for a while, and I shall explain the details."

As they left the shop, young Servi showed up with an nasty black eye. Erasmus looked at him, and said. "You probably deserved it," and walked away.

"Let's go and sit with Drucila," suggested Erasmus. "She is an old friend. Being your landlady, she can give you some lunch whilst we talk. She has my full confidence, and does not gossip like other women."

Rufus was beside himself with worry, though he dare not show it. First, the thought of perhaps not being able to get back by Dies Solis for his meeting with Letitia: Then having to run the gauntlet at Ostia where he had been so persecuted, made his stomach twist and turn, so that his appetite lost its edge even before his lunch was served.

Erasmus gave him the details of the arrangements he required to be made regarding future assignments. He gave him the captain's name as Isaac, and the ships name,... the '*Samaritan Star*.'

The scantily eaten meal was over. Erasmus gave Rufus a fair sum of money; more than enough to see to his expenses and left for the shop. Rufus went up to his room and began to pack.

Late evening welcomed Rufus to Ostia as he rode in on his hired horse and dropped it off at the designated stables, which luckily, were not too far from his previous lodgings. However, they were far enough from the port, which he preferred to approach on foot.

He made his way to Neta's house where he felt he would be safe. The treacherous carpenter would have given up on him by now, he supposed. In any event he had plenty of money to pay him off if he needed to.

'Still,' he thought, 'I must keep out of his way. I hope his two thieving friends will not recognise me as it had been so dark that fateful night.'

He reached the house and knocked at the door. It was opened by the landlady herself.

"Good evening Neta! have you got a room for a wayward merchant ?"

"By Jove! is it really you?" she exclaimed with a musical intonation.

"The very one, and I hope this stay will end more peacefully than the last."

"You are most welcome my young friend... So you are not a carpenter any more?"

"If you can find me something to eat, I shall tell you of my recent adventures, and you in turn can tell me how the episode ended that night after I fled."

Rufus' morning visit to the Harbour Registry office resulted in his tracking down Bashir's barge. It was due to arrive in Ostia the following day.

His next visit was to the *Samaritan Star*, which was berthed in the wharf near to the carpentry shop of his old Nemesis. He pulled his shawl well over his head and avoided looking anywhere except out into the water beyond the ships as he went by.

He found the ship amidst a line of others, which included three corbitas.

As he passed the first one, he noted the absence of the cabin, and was disappointed at his discovery, since he was hoping to have someone he knew nearby in case of an emergency. The second corbita he passed had some wood on deck as if preparing for some large repair. He wondered if his dishonest partner was copying Alexander's design and building a cabin.   His first task however, was on board the *Samaritan Star*, and he attended to that immediately.

"This place is bedlam," protested the captain as their meeting began. "I cannot get a boat to take my cargo to your people until the end of next week. I have tried everything including trying to bribe some of the boat owners, but they have so much work that they are not interested. My sailing schedule is totally destroyed. My people are going to give me a rough time when I get back. There is still another cargo to load when I get rid of this one. I had no idea that one had to book ahead for the river conveyance. This route is new to me."

"Well, let me see if I can get you unloaded within the next couple of days. My people are getting very anxious too, as delivery commitments have also been made at our end, and we shall have irate customers on our hands."

They continued discussing other matters related to their transactions. When the meeting ended, the captain was in a more optimistic mood. Rufus had convinced him that he would do his utmost to help him.

Our young emissary left the *Samaritan Star* with some uncertainty. He was banking on Bashir to help him out. Remembering to keep his shawl well over his head, he hastened out of the wharf area. As he approached the second corbita, he heard hammering. He cautiously scanned the ship's deck. His ex-partner was busy assembling a cabin assisted by two other men whom he recognised by their build as having been his attackers.

He hurried past, looking in the opposite direction, and managed to escape unseen.

'What a gang of scheming thieves,' he said to himself. 'They had everything planned, and I got caught in the net like a stupid fish. I shall never trust any stranger again,...certainly not in business.'

He had lunch at Neta's place, and later he went out walking. He kept well away from the harbour area but stayed near the sea, spending a few hours around the more affluent part of town admiring the buildings and villas. On a promontory overlooking the sea, sat many beautiful homes. Their gardens, resplendent with flowers and verdant shrubs, were surrounded by a great variety of trees. Rufus sat contentedly whiling away the time. The sound of the surf striking the rocks below caught his ear. He walked over to the sea wall which was close by, where could see the spray catching the wind and blown far up the cliff; its wet face illuminated by the afternoon sun, glimmering like a huge sparkling jewel.

He stood there for a long time, enraptured and held captive by the hypnotising effect of the waves, which relentlessly assaulted the rocky face of the cliff. Their white crests shattered into a million sunlit pieces and falling back again, reconstituted themselves for renewed assaults. The blue afternoon sky in its gay serenity formed an appropriate background for the spectacle presented. A hundred seagulls, their white plumage iridescent in the sun's rays, glided, dipped, skimmed, and rose time and time again over the mighty maelstrom below them. They kept rhythm it seemed, with the continuous oscillation of that wavy green/blue sea.

* * * * * *

Letitia could think of nothing but her beloved Rufus. The fact that he had kept his promise to find her, filled her heart with inexplicable joy. She envied Zaphira for having received the kiss that was meant for her. She could not wait till Dies Solis to see him.

'The days are going to drag heavily as if made of lead,' she lamented to herself.

Her stay in Rome so far had been pleasant. Her uncle and aunt had made her feel very welcome; giving her every comfort and the run of a beautiful garden which was a great delight to her. She spent much of her time in the company of her new-found cousin Lavinia; the youngest of two cousins, who, being only a year her senior quickly became a good and trustworthy friend.

Her contact so far with Linus, her allotted husband to be, had been sparse. She had only seen him three times in the months that she had been there, and they had behaved very formally with one another which was quite to her satisfaction. The longer she could avoid intimate relations with him, the longer she could hold out; giving Rufus more time to come for her.

She had found her prospective husband rather handsome, very reserved, and somewhat uncomfortable in her presence. He was an avid sportsman and displayed eloquence only in relation to sports. His interest in the opposite sex at that period of his life was but cursory.   He seemed to be in no hurry to show her any serious attention. Perhaps, if she had not had Rufus' love, his inattentiveness would have irked her female vanity, but as things were, they suited her very well. The news of Rufus' presence in Rome had revitalized her hopes and invigorated her whole being once more.

Her cousin Lavinia, a pretty, dark haired, brown eyed girl, who by virtue of her coquettish nature exuded a habitual enthusiasm for life, unconsciously cheered up Letitia; making her stay in Rome more palatable when her grey moods occasionally gripped her. One day, as they walked around the garden, chatting amiably as usual with each other, Letitia suddenly said:

"If I tell you a secret, will you swear not tell anyone?"

"I shall tell everyone," declared her cousin observing Letitia's serious face.

"Lavinia, you exasperate me. Can't you be serious?"

"Serious usually means unhappy," she replied with a dubious smile, "but since you are now my soul mate, I will step into your shoes and become serious for your sake," she confided, as if the matter were some sort of girlish game.

"Will you then… promise?"

"Yes," assured the smiling cousin. "Yes!"

They both walked over to the arbour where they were in the habit of sitting for their private chats. There, on the beautifully sculptured stone bench, enveloped in a mantel of blood red bougainvillea, she began the story of her love affair with Rufus.

Lavinia had heard something from her mother with regard to Letitia's unexpected presence in Rome, but its importance had been greatly understated in her presence. Now, she listened in awe, as her beautiful Cyrenean cousin related her hopes and fears to her.

"Little wonder that you had me promise secrecy," declared the Roman maiden; her lovely mouth forming a well stretched pout, which accompanied by extreme widening of the eyes, gave her an amusing 'monkeyish' look. Letitia burst out in laughter.

"So he is here right now?"

"Yes, and only Zaphira and we, know," said Letitia as she leaned on her cousin's shoulder and whispered. "You must also promise me that you will not uncover Zaphira's knowledge of the matter, as it could go very badly for her."

"Of course I promise. That could be very serious for her, and she is such a lovely person; and so devoted to you."

"May I come with you on 'Dies Solis' to the temple?" asked Lavinia. "I am dying to see him too."

"Oh, I don't know about that," replied her cousin playfully, with a sweet smile and a wink, "you might snatch him away from me."

'Dies Veneris' presented itself as a cloudy day. Rufus was at the Registry office once again, enquiring for Bashir's barge which had been scheduled to arrive that day from Rome.

"It looks as if the arrival of the mermaid is delayed. It will not be in until tomorrow," announced the clerk, as Rufus stood in front of him grimacing visibly at the news.

"Do they say why?"

"No, I am afraid not," answered the man. "In all probability it has not been able to unload its cargo. That happens pretty often as it is just as busy there as it is here."

Rufus thanked him and walked away in a very sulky mood.

'Another day wasted,' he said to himself with annoyance. 'At this rate, I am going to be here all weekend and miss my meeting with Letitia. She is probably just as anxious as I am, and I have no way of sending her word.'

Deep in thought, he almost walked right into his malicious partner who, fortunately was so absorbed in his own thoughts, that he did not pay any attention to him as he walked past.

'Ooh! that was close. I really must stay awake when I am on this wharf.'

Covering his head, he strolled past the corbita where the delinquent carpenters were working, and went off into the market area of the town; where like it or not, he had to wear out the day in suspense.

CHAPTER SIXTEEN

FAREWELL FRIEND

Ruth was up on the terrace with Rachel, gathering a load of washing which the washer woman had hung up a few hours earlier. She spotted Simon and Alexander coming up the hill. As father and son approached the house, she, leaning over the wall, her hair flying in the wind and surrounded by clay pots filled with geraniums, called out to them.

"I suppose you are both starving after your walk. Supper is still a couple of hours away."

"You're the artist," said the father turning to his son. "There's! a picture for you to paint."

"And yet another!" pointed out Simon once more, as a younger version of her mother appeared next, with the same backdrop complementing her striking image.

"Hi, you two. How come you are both so early?" asked Rachel with a happy smile.

"Come down, the pair of you," called Alexander, suddenly finding Lucila's arms around his neck.

Simon walked into the house to get a cup of water, and everyone followed him in.

"Guess where we've been?" announced Alexander. And having captured everyone's attention, proceeded to give them the whole story of the curing of Marcus.

They were all staggered by the news. Ruth went over to Simon and embraced him with tears of joy and wonder at what her husband had done. The girls were also greatly moved, as they tearfully embraced their father with reverence in their eyes.

"Now look here!" bellowed Simon. "That was not my doing."

All eyes were on him with looks of dismay, as Simon continued.

"I want you all to know, and remember in the future, that I am not the man who works miracles. It's the Holy Spirit working through me in the name of our Lord and Master Yeshua, that works the miracles when he wills it. I'm only the vehicle that channels his power. Of my own will, I can do nothing. It is only when he directs me; at which time, I can feel his power running through me. Please! Please, remember that. If anyone asks you, make very certain that they understand."

When supper was over, Simon and Alexander made their way to the synagogue to do their evening preaching. They entered the building in search of the rabbi, but could not find him. There was an assistant there. Simon approached him and asked for the old man.

"He is ill. He did not come in today."

"May I go to his quarters and see him?"

"If you wish," replied the other, who seemed rather unconcerned.

Simon asked Alexander to go out and tell the people in the street that he would be delayed, and to answer any questions that he could with accuracy.

The rabbi's quarters, which adjoined the synagogue were well known to Simon. He had spent many hours there with his old friend. Fearing him to be asleep and not wishing to disturb him, he walked on tip-toes. All of a sudden he heard loud and continuous coughing coming from the rabbi's room, and hurrying in, he found his friend bent over the side of his bed spitting out a good deal of blood. Simon took a hold of him, and held him until the coughing stopped. He then put the frail old man back onto his pillows and propped him up.

"Would you like some water?" he asked with great concern wiping the rabbi's mouth with a nearby towel.

The old man nodded. Simon, poured some into a cup from a jug on the table beside the bed, and gave him to drink.

"Thank you my friend," whispered the rabbi, catching his scanty breath, and drinking a little. "I am so glad you have come."

"Has the physician come to see you?"

"Yes... There is nothing he can do for me."

"I shall stay with you," Simon assured him.

The old man took a hold of Simon's arm.

"I want to be baptised!" he said, his voice failing him.

"Are you sure?"

"Absolutely!" he affirmed with great eagerness in his eyes.

Simon took the jug again, also a basin and towel which were close at hand, and placing the basin on the rabbi's lap, poured a little water over his old white head, simultaneously pronouncing the significant words. He then dried the hair, and putting everything again in its place, propped up his friend once more making him as comfortable as he could.

"I'm overjoyed to have been able to do this for you my very good and holy friend. You can be sure that Yeshua will take you to him when your time comes," assured Simon.

"Now I can rest," whispered the old man with a faint smile, and giving Simon's hand a feeble squeeze, closed his eyes.

At this point a woman who had been taking care of him came in.

"Oh, he has company," she remarked.

"Yes," said Simon. "I'll stay with him for a while," nodding a concerned look at the woman.

She returned the nod, and gently shook her head with a look of hopelessness in her eyes. Old Rabbi Elias breathed his last shortly after, and Simon mourned the loss of a good and dear friend.

* * * * * *

Rufus had taken a turn around the market, idly eyeing the many wares which did not interest him in the least. He realised what a waste of time this was, when he should be trying to do something about the unloading of that ship.

'I shall hire a horse, and ride up the river route all the way back to Rome, and see Bashir. The sooner I see him, the sooner I shall know if he can help me.'

A half an hour later, Rufus was galloping along the river bank on his way back to Rome. He made it under three hours, and rode into the harbour keeping an eye open for the *Mermaid*. He had not passed her on route, so he felt confident that she was there somewhere. At last he found her, tied up to the wharf at the end of a long line of river boats, many of which were unloading amidst much bustle and noise.

He dismounted as he came alongside, and shouted for Bashir. After three attempts, the trap door on the deck opened, and a woman's head appeared. Rufus recognised Aula, Bashir's wife.

"Greetings!" shouted Rufus over all the noise around them.

"Hello, my young wizard," answered the woman remembering the good work that he had done on their boat.

"Where is Bashir?"

"He will be back shortly," she replied, and stepping onto the wharf, approached, and gave him a fleshy hug.

"I better wait for him out here as I have this horse to look after," said Rufus.

"Is your cargo still on board?" he asked.

"Yes!" she said. "We are waiting for the people who are supposed to unload us. They have kept us waiting for over two days and have promised to unload us tonight, no matter the time."

"That is good to know," acknowledged the young merchant, sighing with a touch of skepticism.

"I am working for a merchant now," continued Rufus, "and we are having problems unloading a ship because all the boats have been booked. The captain who is new to the Roman route gave us no notice of his arrival. I am hoping that Bashir can help me out of this jam."

"If he can, I am sure he will. Are you taking your horse in?" she asked.

"No, I don't think so. Once I talk to Bashir, I shall ride back to Ostia, and we will see each other again when you arrive there."

They talked for a while on the wharf until at last Bashir appeared. After listening to the captain's many complaints about the pending unloading, the young merchant managed to talk him into looking after the unloading of his ship as his next task, promising him a bonus for doing so. He then got himself to the Registry Office where he wrote a note and got a young runner who was vouched for by that office, to take it to Erasmus, acquainting him with the problems he was having and giving him a very short progress report.

Having promised to meet Bashir on his arrival in Ostia, he rode back there once again arriving very late for Neta's supper.

"My goodness," scolded Neta with motherly concern. "Have you eaten nothing all day?"

"Just a piece of dried fish and some bread. I had to keep riding to get here before nightfall."

He explained to her the difficult situation he was in, whilst she rustled up something for him to eat. Later he sat talking to her and her daughter Lydia until bed time.

The *Mermaid* finally graced the Ostia harbour well after dusk on 'Dies Saturni.' Rufus had been waiting all day, checking with the Registry Office periodically. Now at last the *Mermaid* was tied to the wharf a good distance away from that Corbita that had posed problems for our young hero. However, it was too late to start the unloading that night and was re-scheduled for the next day, 'Dies Solis.'

Rufus promptly went on board the *Mermaid* and found out what was required of him to rustle up a crew for the following day, as Bashir knew it would be impossible to get any crew to work that night. Immediately following his talk with Bashir, he boarded the *Samaritan Star* to consult with Isaac, and to acquaint himself with the top price that the captain was authorised to pay for unloading. He then got to work negotiating a contract with the people concerned.

It was a very downcast young merchant that went to his bed that night, knowing that he would not see the light of his life the next morning. He had to pay the captain when the unloading was finished, and that would not be until well into the following day.

'Life sure was tough,' as his father would say.

* * * * * *

As 'Dies Solis' dawned, Letitia was at her window overlooking the garden, letting the warm rays of the morning sun caress her breast as she pondered with anticipation the great pleasure that awaited her that day.

'What will he tell me about his adventures in Rome? What plans has he been making to take me away? Where shall we go?'

All these thoughts crowded her mind and jostled with each other as people in a crowd push and jostle to gain an advantageous position.

The head peaking around her door was that of Zaphira; who waited to dress her mistress for the much anticipated meeting with Rufus.

"My lady, you are up already!" she intoned with surprise as she walked into the room.

"I am so excited," confided her mistress," I hardly slept."

"I shall have you ready very quickly. But I doubt he will be there before the third hour. So there is plenty of time for you and the lady Lavinia to get ready."

"Zaphira! I want you to keep Lavinia away until I have had a little time with him."

"Very well my lady, but I feel sure that she realises that," pointed out her devoted slave and teacher. "She has grown very fond of you."

"Yes, and I of her."

The two cousins breakfasted together. Lavinia's mother and father were presumably still fast asleep which suited the girls just fine.

Angeliki, who was the counterpart of Zaphira and also Greek, was to accompany her mistress Lavinia as it would be her parents' wish. This slave, new to our story, was promptly sworn in as a secret supporter of our heroine's romantic cause, which she enthusiastically embraced, despite the dangers involved by virtue of her menial status.

The four women entered the Forum a little after the third hour. The morning was cloudy and threatened rain. As they approached the temple of Venus, four horsemen cut across their path, and stopped immediately in front of them blocking their way.

"Good morning ladies!" greeted one of them, who to Letitia's horror turned out to be no other than Linus.

The girls and slaves returned their greetings none more enthusiastically than Lavinia.

"Are you visiting Venus this early in the morning?" asked one of the men jokingly.

"She may not be awake yet," cut in another of the young horsemen.

"May we join you ladies?" asked Linus looking at Letitia and Lavinia almost simultaneously.

"No, you may not," retorted Lavinia before Letitia who was on the point of acceding had time to reply.

"Why?" asked one of the men.

"It will be a waste of our time," answered Lavinia again. "Venus will not grant any request if the woman is accompanied by a man," she lied.

"Well then," said Linus once again, "we may as well go boys. We cannot have these lovely ladies wasting their time can we?"

"Have a nice day," they chorused, and rode away.

Letitia gave a sigh of relief, and hugged her cousin for her quick wit.

The morning was soon spent. Rufus was nowhere to be seen. Letitia was getting very nervous and upset.

"What could have happened to him?" she asked with tears in her eyes, her hands pressed against her rosy cheeks.

"If I know men," retorted Lavinia, "he probably mistook the day."

"No! no! no!" asserted Letitia, between sniffles.

"No!" agreed Zaphira. "I know him, and he has been detained for some very good reason."

"We had better go. It is almost lunchtime, and your mother will be asking questions if you are late," admonished Angeliki with a knowing nod of her head.

So ended the 'Dies Solis' excursion to the temple of Venus much to the disappointment of Letitia and her accomplices.

"One of us will be there for him every morning of this coming week," Letitia vowed to Zaphira as they were reaching her uncle's house.

Great was their surprise, when on arriving at the house, there were two covered carts with horses already hitched, waiting outside the main entrance. One was being loaded with luggage, and the other was standing by empty, presumably awaiting passengers. Her aunt and uncle were talking in the doorway as the little group approached. Lavinia ran to her mother and enquired as to what was happening.

"Your sister Livia invited us over last week, and I said we would go this week... Today! She is ill with depression. Octavius has been sent off to the wars again, and she badly needs our company to comfort her. Your father is also joining us for a few days of rest before his upcoming trip to Greece. We will leave right after lunch. All is loaded and ready," she continued with a tone of urgency. Her poor niece winced at her bad luck.

Lavinia came over, took her cousin's arm, and said.

"How untimely this sudden trip has come. I am as surprised as you are. I wonder why she did not tell us."

Letitia wondered whether this was not a plot to keep her away from Rufus, who they knew was in Rome. She considered pleading ill, but knew that they would just wait and guard her till she had recovered. She could do nothing but smile, and go wherever it was they were taking her.

"Don't worry," said Lavinia, "we will be back soon. He is going to be in Rome just as long as it takes to find you. Cheer up, my sister's place is beautiful and right by the sea."

"Where is it?" asked Letitia.

"In Antium."

* * * * * *

Rufus got back to the shop the day following the unloading of the *Samaritan Star*. Erasmus was there to greet him.

"Well, you decided to come back and join our ranks again?" he joked as Rufus made for his desk.

"You are looking much better," said the new clerk as he looked at his boss.

"Yes!" he answered. "I feel much better, thanks to your having made this trip for me."

Publius, sitting at his desk did not utter a word, but looked at his colleague with marked dislike in his eyes. When lunchtime came, Erasmus once again asked Rufus to go with him, much to the disgust of Publius, who could see how the boss was taken by the newcomer.

'I wonder if he is beginning to suspect anything. I shall have to watch my step from now on,' he said to himself

Erasmus congratulated Rufus as soon as they were alone.

"You have done a fine job my young friend. I shall repay you and give you more responsibility. I have needed someone I could trust for a long time. I am getting on now. I have worked very hard, and I want to take things a little easier. By the way, how did you manage to get a barge?"

"I have a friend who owns one, and I talked him into skipping one turn from someone else in favour of our cargo."

"Well done! Well done! I will admit that I doubted you could do it, but you are a smart fellow and will go far... Though not too far I hope," he joked. "I need you here."

Erasmus paused, gave Rufus a deliberate look, and continued:

"First of all, because you put in those extra hours, you can take them back as you please this week, anyway you want. Second... On your next pay, you will notice a nice raise in your salary. And I am also giving you a gift of money in appreciation of your good efforts. Now,...I advise you to give me back the gift as payment for a little share of my business. Every time I give you a gift, which I shall do from time to time. I will give you an opportunity to buy into my business, so that in a few years you will own a good piece of it. How does that sound to you?"

"I think you are very generous, and I sincerely thank you."

"And now let us have some lunch," said Erasmus as they walked into a posh inn.

* * * * * *

Marcus and Julia had a long and serious talk after Simon left their house. It was decided that Letitia should come back home immediately. She would, they had agreed, be permitted to marry Rufus if she still wished to, on reaching the age of nineteen.

"I know," concluded Marcus, "that as a mother without my being here to help you, you did your best my dear. But your decision seen from our present perspective was unfortunately the wrong one. We all make mistakes. I know I married a clever and loving girl and I love you now more than ever."

And going over to Julia he took her in his arms, and kissed her warmly as with tearful eyes she kissed him back.

"We owe these fine people my life, not once, but twice. We are now brother disciples of Yeshua. All I want is for Simon to tell me more about the teachings of the Lord, and to have my daughter back here with us."

"Damian!" he bellowed, "are you there?"

"Ye… Yes," came the answer from the other end of the atrium, followed by the prompt appearance of the man himself.

"Find out when Marius will be back in Apollonia. I have another assignment for him."

"R… R… Right away," answered Damian and walked out, bound for the Registry Office.

Simon had just arrived home with Alexander from the rabbi's funeral, at which the rabbi from upper Cyrene had officiated. He sat in the family room sipping some watered wine and feeling very sad indeed. Not only had he lost a good friend, but also the assistance that the venerable old man had given him in the initiating of his ministry. Now, he wondered how the new rabbi would behave towards him.

"I don't see why things should not continue the same," reassured Alexander who liked to see the bright side of things. "It may be quite a while before another rabbi is posted down here, though there are two rabbis up the road and one could come down on a temporary basis."

"We'll see," said the father.

"Rachel! Lucila! Please get things ready for supper," cried Ruth, as she bustled around the kitchen.

Shortly after, they all sat down to supper, preceded by a short prayer of thanksgiving as usual.

"I am going down to Marcus' place after supper," announced Simon. "He wants me to teach him all I can about Yeshua, and he may be able to help us in finding a place where we can meet for our services."

"A place of our own something like a synagogue?" asked Rachel.

"Yes," answered her father, "even though we shall still attend the synagogue. Are we not also Jews?"

"Except for the feasts," ventured Lucila. "Do we not do the same readings as in the synagogue, as well as the new stories about Yeshua?"

"Yes!" answered Simon again. "There are times when I am unsure as to why we need the synagogue, other than as you say, for feast days... I must make a note of these things in case the apostles send someone over here. Then I can get answers to such questions."

"What if we were to write to them in Jerusalem, and ask them whatever we need to know?" enquired Alexander.

"I wonder if it would reach them," said Simon. "I tell you what," he continued. "If we gave Marius or Silas a letter for Simon the tanner or Cornelius in Caesarea, I bet that they could get us answers since the apostles are around there all the time."

"Yes! that's it!" confirmed Ruth who had been trying to think of an answer.

"We can make a list of all our questions. and send it with the first of the two captains that puts into port bound for Judea," she concluded.

The 'Breaking of the Bread' took place next, followed a little later, by the 'Consecration of the Wine' and the supper came to a happy end.

As he got up from the table, Simon said.

"I do not know if we should be 'Breaking Bread' at every meal, or whether it would be more proper to do so with more people around and perhaps even on designated days."

"I shall make a mental note of that, Father," said Alexander as they both made for the door.

* * * * * *

Rufus was a happy man, his earnings having increased to eight denarii a day, and he had a nice promise of two hundred denarii, to keep or give back to Erasmus to start buying into the company.

'My goodness,' he said to himself. 'This puts me in a different class altogether. I could never make this money with my carpentry. I have chosen to do the right thing. I shall give Erasmus my very best, and I am sure before long I shall be in a good position to claim Letitia as my own.'

A laudable characteristic of Rufus, was that he was appreciative of people's efforts on his behalf, and being a hard worker with high moral standards, he would think himself cheating others if he did not give his very best at all times.

His personal charm was an attribute that he was hardly aware of himself. There were no airs about him, he simply was himself. That is the way he was, and that is how he felt. A certain innocence remained with him still. He was the type of person who easily confided in people; assuming the best from them as he himself was wont to give, making him a prime candidate for the knocks of life. Being highly intelligent however, he profited from his mistakes and took quick measures to prevent them in the future. He continued in his work with added zest.

As he sat in the shop over the next few days, he reviewed the transaction pertinent to the cargo of grain which he had been instrumental in unloading, and dividing among the various customers. Every sack of grain was carefully entered on his parchment, and every scroll identified with meticulous care.

Publius watched him with particular interest, as he could see that from now on, a closer tally was going to be kept on things, which did not suit his plans in the least.

Each evening after supper, Rufus made his way to the Forum and to the temple of Venus, where he hoped that one of those times he would find Letitia, or at least Zaphira.

A week and a half passed, and still he had not seen her. Erasmus had another trip planned for him. It would entail going through Gaul to Hispania, and then to Tingis, to establish sources for goods that were needed in Rome and which he wished to import.

Rufus was to leave at the end of the week, and was running out of time to search for Letitia. His coming voyage would keep him away for at least two months, and it worried him to think that she would have to ward off her suitor that much longer with increased anxiety on her part. He would be travelling by land, and would then cross over to Morocco by sea. In Hispania he would source metals such as silver, and perhaps lead, also good quality olive oil, camphor, garum, wine and cork. In Tingis he would order intricately worked leather goods, for which the Moroccans were renowned, and which were becoming very popular in Rome.

The last day before leaving, he went once more to the Forum hoping to be lucky. He reached the steps of the temple of Venus and sat down in the shade of a column facing the main entrance. He had brought his lunch with him so that he would not have to stray too far from the spot.

He would be leaving next morning as soon as he picked up his hired horse from the stables. Erasmus had seen to his needs and had given him enough money to bind him over through the first stage of the journey. Money would be accessed as needed on various stages of his route, as merchants had arrangements between themselves covering all Roman provinces. This minimized loss from robbery which was a common danger to commercial travellers; despite the fact that the main roads were patrolled by the Roman Legions. Such a patrol would be leaving Rome in the morning on his route, and he planned to follow it as far as it would take him. He had also bought a sword (or gladius,) similar to the type used by the Roman army and which he took for protection.

'I haven't trained or exercised for a while,' mused Rufus, thinking of the sword he had bought, as his eyes scrutinised every woman that passed by him in the hope of seeing Letitia.

'I can defend myself well enough, and chances are I shall not have to use it.'

He fell into a reverie, remembering the night Letitia, his mother, and his sisters, had made such a fuss about the little cut on his arm, and smiled happily to himself.

'It doesn't hurt a man to get some loving attention once in a while. Wish I could get some right now.'

Letitia and her family still had a few hours of their return journey left before they arrived at her aunt's house. They had spent two enjoyable weeks in Antium walking on the beach and even bathing in the sea. Lavinia had been constantly by her cousin's side, keeping her spirits up with her contagious optimism and good humour.

Both her uncle and her aunt had treated Letitia like a daughter, and Livia had been a wonderful hostess, and had thankfully recovered considerably by the time the visit came to an end. Again, Lavinia had to be given much of the credit for that.

'Unfortunately we are going to arrive too late to go to the Forum,' mused Letitia as the cart rolled slowly towards Rome.

'Tomorrow morning, I shall go directly with Lavinia and Zaphira. It is just a matter of time until we meet him again,' she thought, picturing her darling Rufus.

* * * * * *

It was now lunch time, and though he had twice been foiled by women with a similar figure and mannerisms, Letitia still shone for her absence. Rufus took out his humble lunch and continued his musings as he ate.

'I have been so lucky to have fallen in with Erasmus. He is a truly wonderful person. I never dreamt that I could make so much money so quickly. And the future appears even better if all continues well. I have now enough money and a large enough salary that I could keep Letitia nicely enough. Not like she is used to, but soon perhaps even that. When I return, I will get a house of my own and a servant. Then, we shall be married whether any one likes it or not. We were made for each other and so it will be. But first, I must find her.'

In this manner Rufus entertained his thoughts as the day wore on. Many were the times he hurriedly got up and followed someone, who on turning her face frustrated the young man's expectations. As dusk arrived, he knew that she would not come that late, and after waiting till dark, he set out for Drucila's with a heavy heart.

'The lady of few words', looked at his downcast face as he walked in, and instinctively knew that something was bothering him. Knowing nothing of Letitia, she asked what had befallen him. Rufus, who was feeling very sorry for himself, sat down at a table where Drucila had placed a cold supper for him, and opened his heart to her. She was a good listener and did not interrupt him except for a nod of encouragement now and then.

"So there it is!" he concluded. "I am away on a long trip. It would have been great for me to have seen her and arranged for her to be ready on my return."

The gracious landlady looked at him with great sympathy in her clever dark brown eyes, and asked.

"Does Erasmus know any of this?"

"No," answered Rufus, "I have told no one but you."

"I really think he should know. He is very fond of you, and with his many acquaintances he might even be able to find her for you."

"My goodness. I never thought of that! But just a moment! I don't know her uncle's name... Yes, I do! If it is her father's brother, it would be Tricius."

"If you give me your permission, I shall tell him. He could be making enquiries whilst you are away. Who knows what he might find?"

This suggestion of Drucila's gave him some hope, and cheered him considerably. Jumping up, he gave her a kiss, and thanked her for her good advice. She, motioning with her hand, for him to eat his supper, turned and made her way to the kitchen with tears in her eyes. She thought of her absent son, who habitually refused her advice, and spent so much time away from home.

* * * * * *

Rufus caught up with the army patrol just as it was leaving Rome. He fell in line behind them as a large group of travellers had already done. The day was cloudy but the early morning sun peeped through, and chances were that a hot day would ensue. He carried a skin full of water and another smaller one of wine. Drucila had packed enough food to last him at least three days.

The first city he would find on his route was Genua, which would take him around six days to reach at the pace that the patrol travelled. Knowing that he could put his horse to a much faster pace, he decided to stay with them until he could make up his mind whether or not to chance it on his own,

As they crept along, Rufus approached a couple of young men also on horseback, who looked a little bored by the pace at which they travelled. After talking amongst themselves they decided to go ahead on their own. Soon they were going at three or four times their previous rate.

The young trio continued together for the next three days, stopping at villages where they found lodgings for themselves and their horses. The fourth day, saw the departure of one of them, having arrived at his village. He invited his two travelling companions to stay the night at his parent's house.

Rufus and the other young man, spent a very pleasant evening with that very amiable family and were back on their way again early the following morning.

The fifth day found Rufus and his remaining companion parting, as they had arrived in Genua; the other's route now differing from his. He took a little time finding the stables where he had to return his horse; Genua being a large city. However, the people were helpful and gave him good directions. Having parted with the horse, he soon found lodgings for himself nearby, so that in the morning he could hire a fresh one with ease.

A day and a half later, he was trotting into Nicea in Gaul all by himself, since he had not met any fellow traveller on the road whom he might wish to accompany, despite the fact that there was a fair amount of traffic on that route. He had passed a couple of army patrols, which told him that that particular stretch of road was popular, and therefore well guarded.

The route which he was following was such that the sea was constantly on his left as he travelled. The landscapes were incredibly beautiful and varied at every turn, so that for anyone who loved the sea as Rufus did, it was a great pleasure.

At Nicea, he obtained some more money from one of the merchants on his list, returned his horse, and found a room at an inn within a reasonable walking distance of the stables.

It was such a beautiful night that he decided to walk along the beach beside his lodgings. He carried his sandals in his hand as he walked along the tranquil shore enjoying the coolness of the water and the slithery sand which sifted through his toes and quickly covered his footsteps.

The sound of low voices coming from some rocks directly in front of him, made him stop, and not knowing the language in which they were conversing, he quickly left the shore and hid among some rocks. The sound increased, and then what appeared to be the prow of a rowboat caught by the light of the moon, mysteriously glided out of the rocks as if by magic. He then perceived four men pushing it towards the shore.

As soon as the boat touched the water, one man stayed with it as the others ran back and forward carrying boxes which they loaded onto the boat. They were almost finished, when suddenly out of the rocks emerged a large group of soldiers, their helmets and armour reflecting the moonlight. They converged on the five, and took them away along with their boxes.

Rufus remained hidden, hoping that the soldiers had not seen him coming down the beach. A voice shouted in Latin from a rock just behind him.

"Did you get them all?"

"Yes, I think so," said one of the others.

Rufus remained where he was for a while, until he felt sure that the patrol had gone. He then crept out and started walking back to the hotel. Suddenly, he felt something flash past him and bury itself in the sand blocking his way. The handle of a spear stood there quivering in front of his eyes.

"Stay!" shouted a harsh voice in Latin. "In the name of Caesar!"

Rufus froze, and waited. Two grey shapes emerged from the rocks to his left and walked towards him; their helmets and bare swords reflecting the beams of the full moon.

"You thought we were gone, eh?" mocked one of them.

"Yes," answered Rufus in Latin as he had been addressed.

"Now we really have the lot of you. Come!" he ordered as the other took Rufus' hands and bound them tightly with a cord.

He winced.

"You think I am one of them?"

"Oh! Listen to this one. Here's a new story. I have not heard that one before."

"I am a merchant and only passing through."

"Ah, I see, a merchant who does not pay for what he purchases," stated the soldier, with a laugh.

"I can prove it if you give me a chance. My luggage is at the inn over there," said the young merchant nodding towards the inn where he was staying.

"We don't have time for that. You will be our guest for the night. Tomorrow you can tell your little story to the centurion when he comes to visit you and your merchant comrades."

The two soldiers took Rufus' sword and marched him up the rocks onto the road where they joined the others. They were sitting in a covered cart with bars all around.

"Say hello to your friends, honourable merchant," joked one of his captors pushing him into the cart; his comrade locking the door behind him.

* * * * * *

Damian returned to the house with news that the *Stella Maris* was due in harbour the coming week, possibly within three days.

"I would like you to have a cargo of barley ready for him when he arrives, so that we can send him off to Rome to bring my daughter back," instructed Marcus.

"Oh! Y... You are bringing the l...lady Letitia home?"

"Yes! she has been away long enough," said the father with sadness in his voice.

"Summer will be gone soon, and the sea will begin to get rough. I want her home before that."

"Shall I s...send w...word to Rome?"

"Yes, please, by the next ship that leaves. I shall write a note to my brother today and you can take it to the Registry Office tomorrow."

Shortly after this talk between Marcus and Damian, a smiling Simon arrived at their house.

"Welcome my friend," greeted Marcus, as Simon appeared with Silia leading him into the peristyle where he and Julia sat awaiting him.

"The peace of Yeshua be with you both," replied Simon pushing back the shawl from   his head.

"Please sit down... Before you begin to instruct us, Julia and I have some good news for you, Ruth, and the family," said Marcus looking at Simon with a look of sympathy in his now very alert eyes.

Simon looked pleasantly surprised as he waited with clasped hands on his lap.

"We have talked, and even prayed, over the unfortunate situation that our children are in because of that arrangement that we made so many years ago. And we have decided to bring Letitia home and permit her to marry your son when she reaches the age of nineteen, if they are still of the same mind."

"The Lord be praised!" uttered Simon. "We have been praying for that since Rufus went off looking for her."

"As far as we know to this day, they have not as yet found each other. But I shall ask my brother to tell me if they have. In any event I shall keep you informed. We are presently awaiting the arrival of Marius, and we are preparing a cargo of barley for him to take to Rome. He will bring back Letitia and our maid Zaphira, who was her tutor, and is now her personal attendant."

"We have little news of Rufus. Only that he was building a cabin for a corbita in Ostia," said Simon. "Ruth is going to be overjoyed at your generous decision."

"Now shall we start?" proposed Simon, taking a sip of pomegranate juice that Silia had brought him.

For the next two hours, Simon related some of what in future times would be called Gospels. Silia, Damian and Tecuno, had joined their masters, and were listening with great attention to what Simon had to tell them.

A prayer which Yeshua had taught the apostles was then said by Simon, and they all attempted to learn it. Following the prayer, Silia and Tecuno returned to their work. Damian remained to talk over the conversion of Marcus' old barn into a meeting place for the faithful, which the latter had generously donated.

Much was discussed, and it was late into the night when Simon rode back up the hill on Pepper, to give the family the good news regarding Rufus and Letitia.

* * * * * *

Rufus could not believe his bad luck, as he sat hands tied behind his back in that mobile prison. The five thieves, ogled him with suspicion. Then, becoming bored, began making fun of him, and creating the impression for the sake of the guards, that he was one of them. Rufus kept quiet, since he could not understand them. He knew that until the centurion appeared next morning, anything he said would avail him nothing.

The prisoners were put into two cells; three men to a cell. The doors were of heavy wood construction with a small grate of iron bars. The floors were of stone, as were the walls. The only thing that offered any consolation, was the barred window which though placed higher than normal offered a view. It allowed the moonlight into the cell, providing a modicum of soft blue light which Rufus in his present distress found soothing.

With only two thieves in the room, he felt rather more relieved since they left him alone and talked to each other in muted voices. He was concerned however about the money he had just obtained in Nicea which was in his belt, and he dared not fall asleep. After a while, he made his way to the window, as his inmates it seemed had fallen asleep. The smell of the ocean, and the sound of the waves crashing against the rocks below, gave him some solace. He tested the bars in the window, and found them firmly entrenched. A guard came a little later and peered into the room through the grate. Rufus whispered a request for water as he had not had a drop to drink for hours. The guard returned with a small water skin, and squeezed it through the bars. The thirsty prisoner drank his fill, and with a grateful smile, thanked the man who nodded back.

Morning finally arrived. A solitary piece of bread was given each of the prisoners through the grate. Again the skin of water was passed through, from which they drank in turns. All three sat expectantly on the stone floor. The morning sun had been shining for a few hours when the centurion was finally announced. The door was thrown open, and in came a tall thin man dressed in full regalia, with a proud imperial look in his stern eyes. He literally looked down his long Roman nose at the prisoners. Rufus was the only one to rise, which created a good impression, and made the jailor scream at the other two to get up. They reluctantly complied with a look of defiance on their faces.

"You will remain here till the Chief Justice arrives two days from now and you can then plead your case. The goods you carried have all been identified by their owners. You are going to have a tough time getting out of this one. You can start thinking of a future in the galleys," threatened the centurion as he pointed his finger accusingly at all three.

"You will be fed adequately and not chained till you have been convicted. That is all."

As the centurion turned to go, Rufus, who had not understood a word that had been said, spoke:

"May I have a few moments of your time privately please?" he requested in Latin.

The centurion spun around again to confront the speaker, and met Rufus' appealing eyes.

"What could you possibly have to say?" he asked in the same language.

"I may surprise you," responded Rufus politely.

The officer looked at him for a moment, considering his request.

'Well, we learn all the time. Perhaps this is a new approach, and besides, what else have I got to occupy my morning?' he said to himself.

"Very well. Tie him up, and bring him along," he said, addressing the jailor. And with a stern look on his face led the way out of the cell.

Rufus heard the clonking of the cell door behind him, as they walked down the passage accompanied by the jailor. They entered a room furnished with a desk, some chairs, and a long shelf with many parchment scrolls sitting on top of each other in multiple rows. The morning light filled the room through a large window that opened into a small garden surrounded by very high walls.

"Now man. What wonderful story are you going to tell me?" growled the centurion, removing his helmet and placing it on the table before him with an air of authority.

"May I sit?"

Somewhat surprised by this unusual and bold request, the centurion acceded to Rufus' plea. He pointed to a chair in front of his desk, and with a wave of his hand directed the prisoner to proceed.

Rufus, his hands still tied behind his back, then explained his little adventure on the beach.

"But my men caught you with them."

"Well not really. Though I must confess it was easy for them to connect me with the robbers it being dark and I was definitely among the rocks very close to them. But I assure you, that as I told your men at the time, I am a merchant. I carry a sum of money with me, which kept me awake last night for fear that I might be robbed of it."

He asked the centurion to take the money out of his belt, which the latter, getting up and going around the desk, proceeded to do.

"That money, you can trace back to the merchant who was authorised by my employer to give me as a partial route payment, so that when I travel I do not carry an excess of it. You are welcome to check. Also, if you enquire at the inn on the beach where I was apprehended, they will confirm my being a guest, as my baggage is still there."

The centurion's manner gradually changed as he realised that there was truth and conviction in what his prisoner was saying, and putting back the money, he said.

"I tend to believe what you are telling me, young man. It is very possible that my soldiers mistook your purpose that night, but unfortunately once an arrest has been made I have no power to release you."

Rufus had another thought which he promptly presented to his captor.

"One last thing that comes to mind which may help further establish my innocence. I passed two patrols on the way here from Genua. Both times I saluted the sergeants in charge as I passed. I am sure they will remember me if they saw me again."

"By Jupiter," lamented the centurion, "it looks as if my men really made a mistake...I tell you what. I shall put you in a separate cell tonight so that you can get some sleep."

Addressing the jailor, he instructed him to unbind the prisoner.

"Prepare a cell for him with fresh straw for his bedding and provide him with proper meals," he further ordered.

"It is the most I can do for you," he told Rufus," till the Chief Justice hears your case hopefully two days from now.... In the meantime," continued the embarrassed but now sympathetic centurion, 'I shall have a man follow up your claims, so that when the trial comes, the evidence will be strong in your favour."

Rufus thanked him and they parted. The centurion, ready to enjoy his day, and our hero off to the new cell that had been assigned to him.

* * * * * *

Letitia and Zaphira were on their way to the Venus temple by the third hour, hoping against hope that this would be the day when they would meet Rufus. Leaving her slave outside, our beautiful heroine surveyed the inner temple with great alacrity but to no avail, and she soon rejoined her in the peristyle. Zaphira reported having seen Linus and his habitual friends ride by, but no sign of Rufus; bringing a tear of frustration to Letitia's eyes.

"I have a strong presentiment," said the mistress, "that we are barely missing each other all the time. Venus is not coming through for me at all," she said with great sadness in her voice.

They waited the morning out, until lunch time had come and gone, and then with much regret they had to take leave of the Forum for the day, hoping that he did not show up after they had gone. Her aunt met them at the door when they arrived, with a look of concern on her face.

"Where have you been? I have been so worried about you."

"We were browsing around the bazaars and forgot how late it was. Please forgive me," pleaded Letitia as she lied to her aunt, much to the amusement of Lavinia who was standing behind her mother making funny faces; making it difficult for her cousin to maintain a serious and repentant expression.

"We have just had news from your father," she said, "which you will want to hear."

"From my father, or... my mother?" asked the niece with a strange expression on her pretty face.

"Your father," she repeated. "Yes! He is well again."

Letitia jumped for joy.

"He is well again," she sang, dancing around happily, as Zaphira, opening her arms, looked up to heaven with a thankful gesture.

"A man called Simon cured him rather miraculously it seems," continued her aunt. "Is this Simon a physician?"

"No!" said Letitia emphatically. "If it is the same Simon I know, he is a carpenter; the father of Rufus."

"The famous Rufus," said her aunt sarcastically.

"Why do you say that?" asked her annoyed and flustered niece.

"Never mind! Your father wants you home right away, and he is sending for you within the next two weeks or so. You will leave on the same ship you came on, the *Stella Maris*."

This was bittersweet news to Letitia. She wanted to go home, but not with Rufus trying to find her in Rome. Lavinia stayed up almost all night talking to her, and pacifying her fears.

"Sooner or later, he is going to learn that you are back home, and then he will certainly go to you. Besides, you will be away and out of the reach of Linus' parents. What more could you want?"

"You really like Linus don't you?" asked Letitia

"Yes, I care a lot for him," owned her cousin.

"I have noticed that though he is distracted with his men friends and sports right now, he looks at you in a special way; which means he cares for you but does not want to show it for now. Some men are like that," assured Letitia. "Soon, after I am gone, he will come to you and all will be well. You will see."

* * * * * *

The trial of the robbers was well under way. The Chief Justice had asked the prisoners to speak in their own defence, which they all had, and then it was Rufus' turn to speak. He gave the explanations that he had given the centurion, and waited for the latter to corroborate his story. The centurion asserted all of Rufus' claims and the judge was disposed to accept them also. He felt that the evidence, plus the personality and deportment of the accused all amounted to innocence.

He was about to acquit our hero, when of sudden, all five thieves shouted in their own language that he was their leader, but being a clever rascal, he was trying to get away with it. The judge on hearing this, wondered why the five ruffians were accusing the young man.

"Young man, do you hear these people accusing you of being the ring leader in these robberies. What do you say to that?"

"I say they lie! They are maliciously maligning me for no good reason, just out of mischief to a stranger who does not even know their language."

The judge took his head in his hands and with downcast eyes, remained thoughtful for a few moments. Presently, he looked up, and directing all present to wait, asked the centurion to join him in his chamber. The two dignitaries conferred together for a while, and re-entered the courtroom.

The proceedings continued. All of a sudden the judge whom Rufus was facing, and was being addressed by,...shouted.

"Watch out!" in the language of the Gauls, as the centurion who was behind Rufus threw a scroll at his head.

Rufus did not move, but when the scroll hit him, he turned around rubbing his head, looking to see who had thrown the scroll.

"You are acquitted, " said the judge in Latin with a satisfied smile on his face; impressed by his own wisdom.

"I find you innocent of the accusations. You are free to go."

Turning to the robbers he said:

"I was about to sentence each of you, to three years of hard labour in the mines. However, since you tried to ruin this honest man's life with your malice, you are all hereby sentenced to six years each. Guards! take them away!"

The centurion apologized to Rufus for having thrown the scroll at him. He explained how the judge had devised the little charade to ascertain that he did not speak the language of the Gauls, and therefore it was not credible that he be their leader.

"If you had tried to get out of the way when the judge warned you in their language, you would have been guilty of lying, and all the evidence in your favour would have had to be re-examined, making your trial drag on," explained the centurion.

"How clever of the Chief Justice. And I thank you for your help."

"I wish you a safe and uneventful journey from now on," said the centurion, with a smile. "Judging by the itinerary of your journey to Tingis and back, you will be a much wiser man when you have completed it."

And taking Rufus' arm, he said.
"Look me up on your return trip. I shall look forward to hearing about your adventures."

CHAPTER SEVENTEEN

A CHANGE OF HEART

Simon's news that Rufus could now marry Letitia on her reaching the age of nineteen, was joyfully received by his family. Especially Ruth, who instantly thanked Yeshua for answering her prayers

"If only Rufus knew," said Rachel stroking her shiny black hair.

"We must inform all the captains we know. Especially, those whose routes include Rome, such as Silas, in case he tries to contact them for news of home," said Simon hopefully.

Alexander, who had been contemplating a journey to Judea, suddenly presented the idea to the family in his direct open way, casting an apologetic look at his mother.

"Father!" he began, "If I find you a temporary assistant, could you do without me for couple of months or so?"

Everyone was aghast at the question. Where was Alexander thinking of going and why all of a sudden? Ruth could see the nest being abandoned at an alarming rate.

'Who would be the next to fly off? I cannot even count on my girls. They too, could be enticed away any day now, and then what?' she said to herself.

She was so preoccupied with her musings that the words just rolled off her tongue.

"Where are you going my son?" she asked.

"I want to visit Judea and talk to the apostles just as father did. I, too, have many questions to which I need answers, and I wish for the 'Laying of Hands.'"

Simon stared at the ceiling for a few moments, his hand scratching his beard as he tried to piece his thoughts together. Alexander waited with apparent concern, as he realised that this might not be the best time to go.

'But the summer is almost over, and the sea will be getting rough again,' he thought, 'I shall be giving the family much anxiety if I travel in winter.'

"For once, I am at a loss for words."

Those words from Simon captured the attention of the whole family.

"I do not want to deprive you of what would certainly be a most rewarding adventure my son, and it's one that I'll see that you have," said Simon, looking at Alexander and nodding his head. " But at the moment you are my right hand in everything I do whether it be work or ministry. You are going to be more involved than I in the renovation of the barn that Marcus has given us. This is a time for ideas and good management, and I have to lean on you for many things. Could you not wait until spring?"

Alexander, who had been intently listening to what his father had been saying, became aware of Rachel snuggling up to him. He was struck by the beauty of her eyes as she looked at him brimming with tears. She remained silent. But he knew that for now he must stay.

"Very well Father. I'm sorry. I suppose I was thinking rather selfishly... Another time will do just as well," he admitted, though not without a great deal of regret.

Lucila kissed her brother with some relief, Rachel did the same. Ruth clapped her hands in joy, and sitting down beside him gave him a long, tight, motherly hug. A major planning session then started with regard to the work on the barn which would now become the communal meeting place.

"We now have a record of all our disciples," began Simon.

"So we have to begin collecting money from all, including ourselves, and have someone accountable for its safe keeping and dispersal as needed."

"Any ideas as to who that person will be?" asked Alexander.

Simon thought for a few moments, and answered.

"Only one person is properly fit for that job and that is Marcus. He has the ability, and he has Damian, who is highly experienced in the keeping of accounts and can assist him. He has money, which he will I'm sure continue to share generously with us to promote our ministry, and he has the love of the Lord, which will inspire him in his efforts. Also, Julia is a very clever, and well-educated woman, who can direct many of the women disciples in their much needed and useful endeavours. Not to mention Letitia, once she accepts Yeshua," concluded Simon.

"We have a few carpenters and masons in the congregation also, and we can all work together in our spare time and donate work instead of money," pointed out Alexander, who, getting up invited his sisters to take a walk with him before supper..

"We will visit the barn and see just where we can start," he called out as he went out the door, leaving his parents to go over all the things that had been discussed that day.

* * * * * *

Arelate which took two days and two nights to get to, was reached and passed without incident. Rufus was now approaching his final Gaulian destination, before entering Hispania. One day and one night remained before he would reach Narbo. He continued to follow the coastal route, the beauty of which he had grown accustomed to, as each town and village whether urban or rural, could still boast of a maritime scenery comparable to the very best in the world. He preferred to spend his nights in villages rather than towns, for he found the country people much more amiable, the food better, and the fare cheaper. On occasion, they were congenial enough to accompany him for a while as he departed, to ensure that he took the right road.

The biggest problem he faced was one of communication. He had picked up very little of the Gaulian language, and neither Latin or Greek was spoken by the average farmer and country folk he encountered on his route; an interpreter being constantly needed. Three others were now travelling with him, two of whom spoke fluent Latin, whilst the other spoke that language very badly.

The weather was turning raw as a powerful and humid wind blew in from the sea. The sun had disappeared behind heavy cumulus clouds, the sky was a deep metallic grey, and rain was imminent. They could see a village about half an hour ahead, and they broke into a gallop to try and gain some time. A quarter of an hour later, however, the thunder and lightning began, and the rain came down in merciless torrents. Visibility decreased considerably, the horses became very nervous and they desperately looked for cover. They could just make out a hill nearby, which had been sliced by some erosion, and formed an indenture, something akin to a very shallow cave. It was surrounded by trees which promised some shelter for all, including their horses.

The four dismounted, took shelter and waited for the storm to subside enough to allow them to resume their journey. They tried to light a fire, but everything was far too wet to allow that commodity. An hour passed and still the rain continued, though it had at last slackened a little in intensity. Rufus, who had grown somewhat restless for no particular reason, got up and ventured out of the hollow trying to decide whether it was worth sitting there, or continuing, since he was soaked through, and things could hardly get any more uncomfortable.

"I'm going!" he shouted to the others as he climbed on his horse, and started off.

Two of the other men waved back indicating that they were staying. The remaining one got up, and made ready to join Rufus. Just as he was about to mount his horse however, the cave suddenly collapsed; sliding down at him and Rufus. The man and the horse were carried down towards the road. Rufus who was at the edge of the landslide managed to get his horse clear just in time as the hill collapsed, burying the two who stayed behind. He watched in horror as both man and horse were swept down past him. He dismounted, tied his horse to a tree and followed the slide on foot until at last it stopped. The man's head and arms were visible, as he waved them around, trying to free himself from the muddy soil. The horse also struggled to its feet, but found it hard to move. Our hero got as near as he could to the man, but could not reach him. The horse was tiring itself out, trying in vain to extricate himself.

"Help me!" shouted the man in perfect Roman,... and in perfect panic.

"Wait! calm down! I shall get you out as soon as I can."

'At last, my sword is going to come in handy,' thought Rufus. He broke off and trimmed a long narrow branch, and ran to the man's aid.

"Grab on to this and I will pull you out," shouted Rufus.

His travelling companion grabbed the end of the branch, and Rufus began to pull. The man moved a little, aiding himself by pushing with his legs, but made little headway. Half of his body had been extricated, but presently he fell back again to his original position in almost neck-high mud.

Rufus, having greatly underestimated the situation tried to think of some new method of rescue. The only thing that came to mind was his horse, who could pull many times more than he. But how was he to tie a branch to the horse securely enough to take the strain.

After a few tries, he gave up. That, was something that went against every fibre of his being. Rufus was a fighter, and that upset him terribly.

'His only chance is a rope tied to the horse. If I cannot do that, then I am of no use to him whatsoever.... I must get a rope,' he told himself.

"I have to get a rope, and I shall soon be back," he shouted to the man. "Stay calm, and conserve your energy. Follow your horse's example." He noticed that the horse, now worn out, was just standing there belly high in mud.

Rufus galloped off as fast as he could towards the village to which they were headed. The blacksmith shop was the first thing he encountered. Dismounting, he ran in, and articulating with his hands, quickly explained to the man what had happened and asked for a good length of rope. The blacksmith looked at him with a disoriented look in his eyes.

"Can't you understand me?" pleaded Rufus in Latin, and repeating it in Greek.

The man replied something, and disappeared into the back of the shop. Rufus who was beside himself with worry waited impatiently. At last a young woman about Lucila's age came out and asked in an odd and broken Latin, what was it he wanted. On hearing what had happened and the request for the rope, she ran to the back of the house once more, and explained it to the smithy with great trepidation in her voice.

The man returned with a coil of rope and left the shop in search of his horse. Rufus followed him, and once the horse was saddled they rode off together. The unhappy fellow traveller was still where they had left him and expressed much relief at their arrival.

The blacksmith had brought without Rufus having noticed, a special harness, which he immediately attached to his horse, tying the rope to the iron ring that was part of the harness. He then made a large loop on the rope. Rufus quickly ensnared it on the end of the branch he had cut, and passed it on to the entrapped man; directing him to put his arms through the loop. The man, then lying on his back, was easily pulled out by the horse.

The arrival a little later of a group of villagers who had been alerted by the blacksmith's girl, gave impetus to the rescue, as they considered the plight of the horse next. Rufus got the shaken man onto his horse and walked beside him as they made for the village. They left the villagers on the scene to rescue the horse, and consider the tragedy that befell the other two unfortunate travellers.

The people of the village received them with great warmth and sympathy; lending them dry clothes and feeding them royally. In the course of the evening they learnt that one of the men who had been buried in the landslide belonged to that village, which caused much sadness to all its inhabitants.

The digging to reclaim the dead men's bodies began the next morning, the weather having cleared, and the soil being considerably drier. There was a great desire among the villagers to retrieve the bodies, especially the one of their own.

Knowing the exact spot where the bodies were to be found, Rufus and the rescued man remained to help with the digging the following morning. By midday, however, they had to give up, as the soil was still not dry enough and posed a hazard for the rescuers. It was decided later by the village council, that the retrieval of the bodies should wait until the soil was totally dry, since there was no hope of survival for those two unfortunate men.

Rufus and his travelling companion whose name was Cassius, a New Carthaginian, also on his way to Tarraco, his home town, were advised by the villagers to continue on their journey. It would probably be a week or more they said, before they could extricate the two bodies.

Our fortunate Cyrenean thanked God for his good fortune as he and Cassius rode out of the village on the next lap of their journey.

* * * * * *

The *Stella Maris* arrived in Apollonia on a beautiful summer's day. Marius awaited Damian's arrival to schedule the unloading of the cargo, before setting off to visit Simon and family. Marcus' man arrived in the early afternoon having received the captain's message. He soon related with much excitement, the amazing news of his master's cure at the hands of Simon.

"Surely, that is incredible," blurted out Marius at hearing the news. "I am so very pleased to hear it. He is a good man that master of yours. But how did Simon cure him? Did he give him some rare herbs?"

"No, no, nothing like that. It was a real miracle performed by our God Yeshua through Simon," Damian assured him without a single stutter.

"By Jove! that, is more than just extraordinary."

"Yes, it certainly is, and now he wants you to bring his daughter back. He is giving her to young Rufus you know!"

"By Jupiter! Ruth and Simon must be so happy," celebrated Marius, his arms reaching for the sky.

" We are all happy. Everyone likes Rufus. If only he can be found."

"My friend Silas, who does the Rome route, enquires for him every time he touches at Ostia. We shall find him yet. I hear that he is occasionally involved with shipping."

"May God will it," responded Damian.

"You will have a cargo of barley to load as soon as we can unload the wine and cork," were Damian's parting words, as he left the captain to his thoughts and walked down the gang plank.

Marius was as usual, most warmly received at Simon's house. Soon, he was at supper relating the latest news of Judea, and his latest adventures. On finishing, his eyes swept the room and rested on Simon, his hand on his friends shoulder. "I never cease to be amazed at you my friend," he said with a big smile.

"Now I hear that you are a miracle worker. What am I going to hear next?"

Simon soon set Marius straight on the subject of miracles. The captain responded and said, with honest conviction:

"This Yeshua is truly a powerful God."

"That's because he's the Son of God," explained Simon.

"As you know, I am not a religious man, but if I were, Yeshua would be my God," asserted the captain with conviction.

Simon and the family spent the rest of the evening trying to make Marius believe in Yeshua but to no avail, though he did promise to think it over.

"It has to be Yeshua himself who makes him believe," said Simon after his friend had left, "I can do nothing for him, but pray.....as can we all."

The *Stella Maris* was in port for a whole week. The captain spent a good many happy hours with Simon and family. He visited Marcus, and was surprised to learn that they had all accepted Yeshua and his teachings, which impressed him even more. It was a very pensive and confused Marius who sailed off for Rome to bring back Letitia.

* * * * * *

Dusk was settling, as Rufus and Cassius rode into the city of Narbo. The last city that they would pass through in Gaul. The journey had been uneventful, and Cassius had now fully recovered from the traumatic effects of the landslide.

"Soon we will be in my country, my friend," said Cassius with a joyful intonation in his voice." If all continues well I shall be home in Tarraco in two more days. I can hardly wait to see my beautiful wife and the rest of my family. I have been away for almost a month."

Rufus smiled, thinking of the welcome this young man would receive. Cassius was twenty four years old and from a good family. He was of average height, had very dark brown hair, and regular features, except for his ears which though of average size stuck out of his head more than usual, and gave his profile an odd look.

"What do you do for a living?"asked Rufus.

"I work at the family business. We own a silver mine near Tarraco."

"I work for a merchant in Rome, and would you believe that silver is one of the things I am travelling to buy."

"I shall be pleased to help you. My family has owned the mine for over a hundred years."

"I am very impressed," commented Rufus with a slight bow of the head.

"You will stay with us I trust whilst you are in my town, and meet my family."

Though they had travelled many miles together these two young men had not talked much to one another. It was only since the landslide that they were getting to know each other.

"I believe you told me you were from Cyrene."

"Yes," confirmed Rufus.

"What made you go to Rome?"

Rufus related some of his story with some reticence since he was just beginning to get acquainted with Cassius. The other however, being of a romantic disposition politely urged Rufus to tell him more, and so the rest of the way was pleasantly spent as the pair became better acquainted with one another.

The Hispanic coastline resembled the Gaulian, though there were more beaches and less cliffs. The Mediterranean had been their constant companion, its blue waters providing the backdrop for all the wonders that they had enjoyed in the way of landscapes. Most of the villages made their living from the sea. There were fishing boats everywhere; their white sails floating merrily on the shining sea. The white washed houses punctuated the landscape with their sharp contrast against the vivid greens of the surrounding foliage and the purple mountains beyond. The sun was hotter than it had been to date, and they had to stop more often to sit in the shade and rest their horses, which seemed to tire quicker than before.

There was greater traffic on the Hispanic roads, and they met with more military patrols than on the Gaulian roads. The last two nights, were passed in villages as was their habit. Their suppers made memorable to Rufus in particular, by the freshness of the fish which he loved and the cordiality of the people. They finally arrived in Tarraco, much to the joy of the Hispanian, who singing his native songs with a good tenor voice, had kept Rufus entertained for the last hour of the journey.

The city was alive with activity. The midday sun animated the scene they encountered as they rode cheerfully towards the district where Cassius' house was located. They approached a large iron gate flanked by two high walls, presumably surrounding a house which could not be seen from the gate. The wide path beyond, bent to the right and disappeared from view behind the many trees and shrubs in the garden, which was akin to a park by virtue of its size.

A bell about the size of a man's head hung on an ornamental iron post outside the gate; a thin rope dropping from it. Beyond, inside the property, stood a little white-washed building where apparently the gardener lived. Cassius jumped down and approaching the gate took hold of the rope, and rung the bell over, and over, with a big smile on his thin sallow face.

Nothing occurred for a while, and then the sound of many footsteps was heard on the gravel path. The pair of travellers waited for the coming avalanche of people that soon materialised. The first to arrive was the gardener, who immediately began to remove the bars that locked the gate. A pretty young girl perhaps thirteen years old and wearing a very colourful dress came next, screaming:

"It's Cassius! It's Cassius!"

Then came Petrina, Cassius' wife and then last of all, his mother.

"No one rings the bell like that," sang his mother as she arrived, joy written all over her face, as she, Petrina and little Lucia overwhelmed him with their hugs and kisses amidst fluent tears of joy.

Rufus shuddered, remembering the landslide and their lucky escape.

When the storm of love had subsided, and Cassius emerged once more from the midst of all those arms, hands, hair, happy faces, tears and dresses, he approached Rufus and throwing an arm over his shoulder in a friendly embrace, introduced him to his family as having been his saviour.

Rufus was warmly welcomed by all, and they immediately wanted to know how he had saved Cassius' life. The latter promised to tell their story after the 'cena' when his father would be home. The party then walked back to the house, the path taking a long turn and straightening into an avenue lined with poplar trees, at the end of which the house appeared in all its stately glory.

It was the most beautiful house the young Cyrenean had ever seen. The marble facade and the entrance portico with its marble columns, sculptured frieze and tympanum, though in much smaller proportion, reminded him of the temple of Venus. The portico, elevated on three steps, made a powerful statement, giving it an imposing aspect in perspective. The door of the main entrance was double-leaved, of gilded wood with copious mouldings, and protected by ornamental wrought iron panels.

The front, a single story facade; featured three windows on each side of the portico, surrounded by individual stone frames with sculptural details, and protected by wrought iron grills. It was capped by a continuous red tiled roof extending the full length of the frontal facade, and lining up with the apex of the cornice which enclosed a sculptured tympanum featuring the grape harvest. Well tended shrubbery extending through the entire length of the front and was shaped to fill and complement the space between the windows.

'What would Alexander have given to see this?' thought Rufus to himself as he beheld that remarkable house.

The first thing Cassius did, was to send a servant to return the hired horses.

"Later, I shall show you our stables, and tomorrow we shall ride excellent horses, when we visit the mine," promised Cassius as they entered the house.

The opulence heralded by the striking exterior was again reflected in the treatment of the interior. Every element had been expertly and tastefully designed towards that end, but by no means sparing comfort.

The house followed the general plan of the standard Roman residence in as much as it had an atrium, and an unusual peristyle, which feature, was generally subject to a great variety of treatments. The design of this particular one had therefore its own uniqueness and was a feast for the eyes. It was composed of two strong elements; one, being the usual colonnaded lower area, and the other being the double storey at the rear end.

This upper structure presented a colonnaded arched front with ornamental wrought iron railings, and overlooked the similarly colonnaded lower area which was virtually a large indoor garden. It was interspersed with carved stone benches arranged in groups, and replete with exquisitely carved and well placed statuary. At its centre, and rising out of the impluvium, a life-size statue of the sea God Pluto holding his trident in one hand and a large fish in the other, contributed much to the opulence of the peristyle. The impluvium was surrounded by potted flowers; mostly carnations of varied colours. At one of the corners of the peristyle and built into the wall of the house, was a well embellished with colourful glazed tiles and crowned by an ornamental iron superstructure supporting a whimsical water bucket.

Rufus, who expressed great admiration for the house, was given a quick tour engendering in him a sense of envy, which had hitherto been alien to his nature. Being young and certainly ambitious, he realised how much was left to be accomplished even to come close to Marcus' standards, regardless of the standard that Cassius' family was used to.

'But it has taken them four or five generations to accomplish this most affluent state, so I cannot expect to equal this, and really I do not need to. It is Marcus that I have to match, or even who knows.... Surpass.' He told himself.

They all sat in the peristyle having refreshments and awaiting Cassius' father and younger brother. Rufus had to go through the usual well meant interrogation, as they all wanted to learn more about him.

"We are an old New Carthaginian family," began Cassius, in his turn. "It has taken over one hundred and fifty years to build up what you see; each generation adding to what was inherited by them. Our family is quite large, but we are the closest in line to the original family, though the silver mine is owned by a number of us from different branches. My father is presently the chief officer of the group that operates them. We also have extensive olive orchards, and a camphor operation," he explained in a 'matter of fact' manner, much as expected of people born into a luxurious standard of living.

"My goodness!" exclaimed the young merchant, "I can almost do all my purchasing here with you. The only thing I need now is wine."

"That we do not have, but I have a very close friend who does, and he is on your route in Carthago Nova," said Cassius as he reached for an olive and invited Rufus to try one too.

"These are our own olives; we cure them. Some we stuff with pimentos, and some with anchovies. Perhaps you can import them to Rome. They are quite popular there and the market can only increase as the demand grows."

"They are not on my list, but it is a good idea. I shall think about it," said Rufus, putting one in his mouth and smiling approvingly at his friend.

"You will taste our olive oil tomorrow. We have a number of grades. You can choose which ever suits you best. We ship them in amphorae a little smaller than those used for wine," explained Cassius with enthusiasm.

At this juncture the expected father and brother arrived, and great was their surprise and joy at seeing Cassius. After another bout of physical welcoming, the visitor was introduced for the last time. All retired into a large and sumptuous dining room where an excellent supper or 'cena' awaited them.

Cassius' father whose name was Appius, confirmed all that his son had stated in the way of products that they could offer, and suggested his son take their guest on a visit to the mine and also show him their olive groves, oil presses, and camphor operation.

After supper the adventure involving the mud slide was colourfully narrated by Cassius as promised, to the utter horror of the family. Our hero, became their hero also as the story unfolded.

Rufus spent a truly enjoyable week with that congenial family. He made excellent arrangements, and received most satisfactory promises regarding his future business requirements. He left that extraordinary Hispanian family with the assurance of a return visit on his way back. He subsequently rode out of Tarraco again on a hired horse which a servant had brought him. Cassius gave him a beautifully crafted dagger from his collection as a parting gift, and for added protection. Rufus now made for Carthago Nova, by way of Sagantum, a journey of an estimated four to five days.

After three hours on his journey, he caught up with some people who were headed in his direction, and tagged along for company. Again, there was a fair amount of traffic on the roads. Many donkey carts were passed carrying all kinds of vegetables and fruit to the various country markets. Roman patrols were also encountered every now and then which gave the travellers some reassurance.

The weather was sunny and getting hotter as they travelled south. Every now and then, he would leave the road, and go down to the beaches to walk his horse in the water along the shore, refreshing both man and beast alike.

Sagantum was bypassed after four days of travel. The town was a little further inland and Rufus having no business there, remained on the shoreline roads. He continued to stay at villages overnight and bought his daytime food at little local markets as he passed.

Most of the group he had been travelling with had stayed behind in the Sagantum area. For the next day, he travelled with only two others who were bound for a large village near Carthago Nova. They were brothers who owned and worked a large cattle farm, and having been at a fair near Sagantum, were now returning home. Rufus learnt something of the raising of cattle during the course of the day, which ended rather quickly as by the tenth hour a storm was brewing, and they decided to put into a nearby village until it had passed. It took all night for the storm to abate.

Early the next morning they were on the road again, the storm having refreshed the air considerably making their ride more comfortable for a while. Further down the road Rufus' horse dropped a shoe. He broke off with the brothers, and walked his horse to the next village. As he reached the village, he could hear the sound of many voices, and soon discovered that a Roman patrol was making a house to house search looking for something or someone. He ignored them, and concentrated on finding a smithy.

He was half way past the place where all the commotion was taking place, when one of the patrol soldiers called for him to approach.

"Where are you going?" asked the man his hand resting on his sword, seeing that Rufus was also armed.

"I have just arrived, and I need a blacksmith to shoe my horse," replied Rufus.

"Where were you going?"

"I am a merchant on my way to Carthago Nova."

"Did a man riding a light brown horse cross your path?"

"No, I'm sorry."

"That horse of yours is on the light brown side," observed the soldier.

"Yes, it is a hired horse. I got it in Tarraco, and I am to return it at Carthago Nova. I hope you are not thinking that I am the man you're after?"

"Well, if the sergeant has any doubt about you, we shall accompany you to the horse exchange and verify what you are telling me."

"You are welcome to do that as soon as I get the horse shod."

At this point the sergeant approached and asked the soldier what he was about. The soldier explained his suspicions and the sergeant, looking at Rufus asked how much money he was carrying.

"Why would you want to know that?" asked Rufus. "That is a personal matter, and I have committed no crime. Is this not rather unusual procedure? I am a Roman citizen you know."

"You are riding a horse that meets the description of a bandit's who has stolen money, and stabbed a traveller. That gives me the right of interrogation," said the sergeant angrily.

"Very well, since you are so insistent, but I shall expect an apology from you momentarily when I can account for the money I carry. Go ahead search me."

The sergeant hesitated as he realised that the young man he was accusing was bold enough to challenge him on his violation of rights, and might make trouble for him.

"Well?" said Rufus, seeing that the man was uncertain.

"You may go, but if you come across a man on a light brown horse you are to report it in the first village you come to."

"There are lots of men on light brown horses. What other identification can you give me besides that?"

His accuser scratched his face and looking back at the soldier, asked if he knew of any other feature which might provide further identification. The soldier shook his head and raised his shoulders.

"You have wasted enough of my time," said Rufus, "would you kindly tell me where I can find the village blacksmith?"

"Take the first left down that street," replied the sergeant and with an exasperated look on his face he turned and walked away.

An hour later, Rufus was galloping off to make up for lost time. Having gained a few miles and his horse beginning to tire, he slowed down to a trot and was enjoying the sea view once again. Unexpectedly, another rider caught up with him and asked where he was going. The newcomer addressed him in Greek.

"I am headed for Carthago Nova," replied Rufus.

"That is a nice sword you have there," said the man with a smirk on his face.

Rufus looked at the man and the horse, which was actually very light brown; a lighter brown than his horse, and quickly realised who he was dealing with.

"Yes, it looks as if it has a nice weight to it," continued the man getting his horse closer.

"Can I see it?" he asked, as he made a grab for the gladius, thinking to take the young fool by surprise.

Rufus reacted quickly, and catching hold of the man's wrist, gave it a hard wrench, throwing him off his horse. The man glared at him with menacing eyes and getting up pulled out a long bladed knife and lunged at Rufus, who, as the man came forward, slipped his foot off the stirrup and struck the man with his heel sending him down a second time. Drawing his sword, he jumped off his horse and got ready for the next lunge that he knew would come.

"You are the bandit that the patrol are looking for, aren't you?"

"Those fools will never catch me. Neither will you stop me."

As he said this he scooped up a handful of dirt and threw it at the young man's eyes. Some sand got into Rufus' left eye, however, his right eye was sand free. But he had momentarily turned his head, and his assailant took the opportunity to strike.

The bandit's dagger cut into Rufus' arm. The pain made him drop his sword. But with his other hand, he managed to catch the man's wrist, that held the knife, and forcing his arm up, gave him a powerful punch on the chin with his bloodied right hand, simultaneously sticking his foot out behind the man. The bandit tripped, and fell in a twisting motion, ending up face down on the ground, his knife still in his hand.

Rufus found himself very favourably positioned on top of him, his knees pressing on the thief's shoulder blades, allowing him to reach into his tunic, with his bleeding right hand, and reach the dagger that Cassius had given him. Quickly pulling it out, he pressed the blade menacingly across the bandit's throat.

"Drop your knife, and put both your hands together," commanded Rufus. The man reluctantly obeyed, and it was instantly swept away out of his reach. He then tried to raise himself. But as he did so, Rufus quickly removing the dagger from the man's throat, gave him a heavy blow in the back of the head with its hilt knocking him out.

When the bandit came to, he found himself half naked, lying over his unsaddled horse, with his hands tied to his feet underneath the belly of the horse with strips of his own shirt.

Rufus rode beside him, his arm roughly bandaged, and headed back to the village where he had left the patrol earlier that day. He was wondering where he could find a physician to treat his sore and bleeding arm, when he spotted the patrol coming his way.

"You see how wrong you were," said Rufus with a serious look on his face, as he drew alongside the sergeant.

The latter, looked at the prisoner with a sinking heart, which was apparent in his face.

"How about finding me a physician to take care of my wound?" asked Rufus.

"There is one in the village," said the sergeant. "Can you make it by yourself? We have to take this fellow back to Sagantum."

Rufus assured him that he could, and off he went.

"Thank you!" shouted back the departing sergeant from a distance, as if ashamed to have thanked him to his face at closer range.

* * * * * *

Marius stood on deck, reviewing the chaos that reigned in the wharf at Ostia. It was utter madness. People were rushing here and there, fights were common and belligerence reigned, as ships unloaded their cargo onto the river boats and barges that were tied alongside.

Damian with his wide experience of cargo management, had booked a barge well ahead of time to be present at Ostia for the unloading of the barley cargo on board the *Stella Maris* as soon as possible on her arrival. He had also arranged for another barge, to be ready to load a cargo of marble tiles for the home bound passage.

'It will be days before I can get out of this mess,' thought Marius. 'I will send word of my arrival to Letitia's uncle, Claudius Tricius, so that he can start preparing her for the voyage.'

A courier bonded by the Registry Office was dispatched with the news of the arrival of the *Stella Maris* and all that Marius could do was wait. Letitia's aunt Lucia was home when the courier arrived, and immediately called her niece. Letitia, appeared, with Lavinia in tow, to find out what her aunt wanted.

"The *Stella Maris* is in Ostia, and we are to get you ready for your departure within three days or so," said her aunt with a combination of regret and relief.

To Letitia the news was bittersweet, but to Lavinia it was devastating, and she burst into tears which was most uncharacteristic of her. She had come to love her cousin, and now that the actual time of departure had arrived, the reality of it all suddenly hit her. On this occasion it was Letitia who did the consoling as the two girls walked away into the garden arm in arm.

"We will see each other again," assured Letitia, giving her cousin's arm a loving squeeze. "Soon, you will come to Cyrene on your honeymoon with Linus, and I bet it will not be far in the future."

"It will still be a couple of years away at least," was the protesting reply.

"Who knows if I too shall have to wait that long for Rufus to find me," consoled her Cyrenean cousin, hoping that would not be the case.

Four days later, Letitia, uncle and family, were at the wharf taking leave of one another on a warm cloudy day, as Marius watched from the deck.

"I have a big surprise for you Letitia," said her aunt. "I left it until now so that your journey home would be more pleasant."

The parting niece was most surprised at these words which seemed to make her aunt and uncle very pleased. Lavinia looked at her parents with an enquiring look as the two girls waited to hear the rest of the news.

"Your father has told us that he will let you marry that boy Rufus when you reach the age of nineteen, if you still want him."

Letitia was ecstatic, tears streamed down her lovely face and she embraced her aunt; Lavinia embracing the pair at the same time.

"I shall start hunting for your young man," assured her uncle warmly embracing his niece, "as soon as I break the news to Linus and his father. Your mother will doubtlessly be writing to his mother."

"All aboard!" chanted the captain with his strong bass voice, as Letitia and Zaphira hurried up the gang plank.

Moments later the *Stella Maris* put out to sea once more with a pair of very happy passengers on board.

* * * * * *

His wound properly sutured, and the prescribed two days of rest completed, Rufus was back on the road headed once more for Carthago Nova; his sword back in its scabbard and the dagger strategically concealed within his tunic. One day and night remained till his arrival there.

The weather remained sunny and hot, but a strong breeze from the sea did much to make his day more comfortable. There was still a fair bit of pain from the swelling around the wound in his arm. He mused as he went, thinking of home once again, and what a fuss would be made of his wound this time if the women of the family were there with him.

Around midday he stopped a donkey cart that was carrying fruit, and bought some figs and custard pears from the farmer. The latter was on his way to market accompanied by a young boy with an impish face and a large straw hat. Rufus ate as he rode, enjoying the fruit and the panorama simultaneously. He hoped the day would be kind to him and bring no further troublesome incidents his way.

Shortly before dusk, he rode into a very picturesque village situated on a promontory which in the twilight and with a light fog coming in from the sea, gave it the appearance of being suspended in mid air.

Some fishing boats were coming into the beach below him, as still some others were going out for a night of fishing on that relatively calm sea.

'Those boats now coming in will doubtlessly bring that fresh fish that I hope to have for my supper… Mmm…' thought the hungry merchant, whose stomach shared the same feeling of anticipation as his head.

Supper being over, and his craving for the fresh fish happily satisfied, he sat on the porch of the inn watching the continuous breathing motion of the heaving sea, and trying to guess what tomorrow would bring on his arrival at Carthago Nova. He turned in early, and despite the throbbing of his wound, which kept him awake for a good while, he eventually fell asleep.

It was not quite noon as he entered the city the following day and began to enquire for the street Cassius had directed him to. Carthago Nova was a large rambling sort of town, buzzing with activity, with people scrambling for the shade as the midday sun beat down mercilessly with stifling effect. Eventually, with the help of a number of locals, Rufus located the building he sought. He quickly entered a shady courtyard where a number of horses were tied up.

A wicket on one side of the yard captured his attention, and approaching it, he asked the man who sat there fanning away insistent flies, where he could find Decimus.

"You will find him upstairs… The fourth door," answered the man curiously eyeing Rufus and pointing in the general direction of the upper floor.

Having tied up his horse and given the man a coin to keep an eye on it, he climbed the stairs and soon found the fourth door.

Decimus turned out to be a young man, possibly twenty eight years of age, rather small in size but with a slight squint in one of his otherwise good looking blue eyes. He looked up inquisitively as our merchant entered the room. Rufus introduced himself, and presented a small parchment that Cassius had given him by way of introduction. The wine merchant read it, smiled, got up, welcomed Rufus, and enquired as to his friend Cassius and family.

"What happened to your arm?" enquired Decimus, noticing the visitor's bandaged arm.

"I was assaulted by a bandit near Sagantum," explained our hero, and he had the advantage of me for a few moments, and dealt me a deep cut. I managed to subdue him however and bundled him off to the Roman patrol."

"You got it sutured though?" Asked Decimus with a concerned look.

"Yes there was a physician at the village close to where the incident happened," explained Rufus, with a smile.

The pair chatted for a while, and then left to pay a visit to the warehouse, that the wine merchant wanted his prospective client to see, and which was within walking distance. Rufus was most favourably impressed by the size of the place, and the variety of wine that was stored there.

"You must come and see our vineyards," said Decimus, noticing that his new companion was greatly impressed by the warehouse. "If you meet me tomorrow morning we shall ride over, have lunch there, and you can taste our wines. I think you will enjoy them."

"Yes, that would be wonderful. I shall keep my hired horse one more day then, and return him tomorrow."

"Do you have a place to stay?"

"Not as yet. If you would be kind enough to direct me to a decent inn near here, I would appreciate it."

"No! No! You shall stay at my house. Bring your horse with you, we shall see that it is groomed and fed, and you can take it back and pick up a fresh one as you leave town, whenever you decide to go. You are welcome to stay as long as you wish."

"That is very good of you, but a day will do," assured Rufus. "I must continue my journey as soon as possible. This arm has already lost me a couple of days, and I have still to visit Malaga and Tingis, via the pillars of Hercules, where I shall be looking for ornamental leather goods. I have no idea how long that will take."

During the next two days Decimus entertained Rufus with great cordiality, having introduced him to his family who were most attentive to his needs. The vineyards presented a truly magnificent sight, and the quality of the various wines excellent. Some very favourable prices were agreed on, and Rufus rode off with a fresh horse after having placed his first order with Decimus, who accompanied him to the outskirts of the town, and made him promise to visit him again on his return trip.

Once more Rufus, with his arm recovering well, presented a solitary figure on the road to Malaga, where he hoped to negotiate for garum and cork.

Though the sea continued to hold his attention on his left flank, the right flank was accentuated by awe inspiring purple mountains. Fertile plains greeted him on the third day of his journey from Carthago Nova. All types of orchards proliferated on this scenic route which grew hotter as he got closer to Malaga, now only one day ahead. Many rivers criss-crossed those fertile plains, presenting a striking tableaux with the surrounding verdure reflecting on their surfaces as in a mirror. Little stone bridges here and there enabled farmers to convey their products to the various markets, including Malaga which boasted of a grand market where every commodity could be found.

Rufus enjoyed the oranges, which being everywhere, he would often find lying in his path. Donkey carts abounded, but what really caught his eye were the carts that were loaded up to three or four times their height with cork, giving the impression that they would topple over at any moment.

That night he stopped at a village surrounded by cork woods. In the morning after a hearty breakfast at the little inn where he stayed for the night, he was introduced by his host to one of the village elders. The latter took him into the woods to show him how the cork, which grew on the tree trunks, was harvested. Rufus was most impressed and asked if he could negotiate with the owners of that land as he wanted to place an order once he had ensured their integrity.

He interviewed his prospective supplier, and convinced himself of the honesty and reliability of that person, whom he was assured was highly respected in the village. Rufus then followed Marius' advice regarding the protection of the wine amphorae with the cork, and ordered an immediate shipment. He left explicit instructions, that the cork was to be delivered to the port in

Malaga, and was to be surrendered to Decimus' agent who would designate the ship, and coordinate the loading of the wine cargo. The captain of the vessel was to be instructed by the agent on loading the cork, to stuff every nook and cranny around the amphorae, to avoid it shifting in rough seas.

Having now dealt with the cork. The last thing needed from Hispania was to establish a source for high quality mackerel garum, and this was to be accomplished in Malaga, during the next couple of days. The village elder he had met, insisted he stay another night with them gratis in the village, where they entertained him most enjoyably with wine and song. It was not until the following day that he got on the road to Malaga in high spirits and a slight headache.

Rufus, riding into Malaga, was appreciative of the city's impressive architecture. The day was very hot, and he was most relieved to find a suitable inn reasonably soon. His Innkeeper was kind enough to have his horse returned to the stables which gave him a chance to rest in their cool shaded courtyard and enjoy some excellent wine as he awaited his meal. Once again he supped most enjoyably on fresh fish, as Malaga had a reputation for its sea food.

The following day following the directions of his host. Rufus acquainted himself with the the main attractions of the town during the day, and in the evening, he met with a garum merchant who visited him at the Inn where he was staying. In Malaga, to his surprise much business was conducted in the cool of the evening out in the open. There were many shops which served wine and juices and it was the custom for traders to meet there and conduct their business.

It took him a few days to settle with a reputable merchant, as he had no experience with regard to that commodity. From his meeting with the merchant he met with at the Inn, he discovered, much to his amazement, that there were there were many grades to be investigated. He was most fortunate to meet quite by accident, a merchant from Rome who by sheer luck happened to know Erasmus, and whose advice he followed. He settled on a superior quality product, as was advised him, and placed a modest order accordingly.

The garum contract once secured, and having hired a fresh horse, Rufus continued on the coastal route. He stopped over at a roadside inn for the night, after a very tiring day on the saddle owing to the oppressive heat. He would reach his final Hispanian destination, in the morning. Next morning having rested and hoping to beat the inevitable heat of the day as much as possible, he set out earlier than was his custom. He could just make out in the far distance one of the renowned Pillars of Hercules. It appeared ghostlike in the morning haze; aloof, purple and majestic, marking as it were with proud independence the end or the beginning of an illustrious continent.

As he later approached, looking up as he rode, at the close to perpendicular limestone escarpment, its pointed summit seemingly piercing the heavens, he was overwhelmed by a sense of awe at its height. On observing the clouds skimming past that pointed summit overhead, he felt a giddying effect which made him tighten his hold on the reins as he passed.

He went directly to the harbour, where without much difficulty he secured a passage on one of the boats which transported travellers from one continent to the other on an almost daily basis. The voyage to the African continent he learnt, took anywhere from five to seven hours, depending on weather conditions, which often made it a hazardous undertaking.

Once again, as he browsed around the wharves, he was cognisant of the fact that the reliable corbita, was also, not surprisingly, the workhorse of this southern route.

The town, bearing the name of Calpe, small in size, and wrapped around the harbour, was a hub of activity and commerce. Shops and bazaars, were loaded with goods from all over the world. Groups of traders negotiating with each other on the streets were a common sight, as many trading posts had been established on that rock which was the gateway to Hispania and the continent beyond.

His designated ship, the *Mons Calpe* was due to sail on the following morning, allowing Rufus time to acquaint himself with the town and its immediate surroundings, which he did on foot having returned his hired horse.

As he sat on a hill, surrounded by trees, contemplating the calmness of the sea in the large bay before him, and watching the many sails and seagulls, his thoughts went back to his beloved Cyrene: the same limestone rock on which he sat; the same hill down to a harbour, that was just as busy as Apollonia; and the familiar and beloved Mediterranean.

Thoughts of his family had once again been occupying his mind, when he suddenly became aware of company. Turning his head he beheld three apes looking enviously but with determination, at a package of fruit and nuts that lay open on his lap, as snacking had been accompanying his thoughts. They were strange creatures, without tails, different from other apes that Rufus had seen. Since he was alone and not wishing to excite them since they appeared to be wild, he sacrificed most of his meal to them, and walked away down the hill in the direction of the town, where he soon found lodgings suited to his taste.

He supped well once again on fresh fish beautifully fried in olive oil and other local specialties, after which he took a late evening walk through the town, which was still animated at that hour. The light of the many torches and oil lamps which constantly burnt in the shops and bazaars, provided cheerful lighting for the main street of the town where his lodgings were located. It was a noisy place. People sat in the bazaars drinking wine and herbal teas, eating crayfish and mussels, whilst chatting in diverse languages. Drunken sailors arm in arm, singing loudly and discordantly, swayed uncertainly in their inebriated walk, often bumping into people and causing fights to erupt; keeping the patrolling Roman soldiers busy as they tried to keep peace on the streets.

It seemed strange to Rufus that women were absent at that time of the evening; only those who were tending bazaars or shops being visible. Except of course for those who plied their nightly trade and were much in demand by the constant flood of sailors. He returned to his lodgings after a while, and sat talking to the owners of the little inn for the rest of the evening, during which time, his curiosity with regard to the absence of women in the streets was duly satiated.

"We keep our women indoors in the evenings mostly because of the drunken sailors," declared his host, as he leant forward stressing his words.

"They present a constant problem for us. Fights flare up at a moment's notice and we cannot risk them being caught in the middle. There are too many nationalities here, and one can never be sure of their behaviour. We have had abductions and lost some women as a result, so we take no chances now," he concluded, glancing at his wife as if for validation of his statement. She asserted with a nod, adding nothing further.

The young traveller bid his host and hostess good night, and retired to his upstairs room. From the window he beheld the many ships that crowded the harbour, their dark shapes silhouetted in the moonlight. Hundreds of lights emanated from their decks, reflecting on the calm blue/black sea, and creating a scene of quiet serenity. Rufus nostalgically contemplated this tableau, as his thoughts ran once more to Letitia. With that scene vividly imprinted on his mind, he tumbled into bed and promptly fell asleep.

It was a fair wind that propelled the *Mons Calpe* across the straits to Tingis, on a reasonably calm sea, with Rufus on board. The five hour passage marked the end of the young merchant's long journey.

Tingis offered many varieties of merchandise. Rufus, had to choose and order, in the three days he spent there, the exact type and quantity of items that he felt would be attractive to the Roman taste. This he accomplished after enjoying many mint teas, amidst the noise and frenzied activity of that world famous and cosmopolitan trading town.

On his return to Calpe, he sat in his room at the same inn in which he had previously stayed, contemplating whether to begin his return journey back to Rome, by land again, or by sea.

Favourable enquiries at the harbour, the following day, led to his securing a sea passage to Tarraco as first leg of his return journey, and by morning of the following day, he was on his way, having decided after much deliberation on the sea trip. The rock gave the impression of a crouching lion, as his ship floated out of the bay driven by a moderate wind.

An uneventful passage brought him into harbour in Tarraco a few days later, where having disembarked, he found his way to Cassius' house.

His friend was delighted to see him and invited him to stay for a few days, during which time they rode around the surrounding countryside enjoying the varied vistas, bathing in the sea, and feasting to their heart's content.

"Your first cargo of silver, is waiting in our warehouse ready for the first available ship." announced Cassius with an air of satisfaction as he observed the look of pleasure in his friend's eyes. "Let me know how much olive oil you will require, and I shall send it down to Malaga where your cork supplier can arrange to ship his cork at the same time. Decimus' agent will look after the coordinating and supervising the packing of the oil amphorae with the cork, as he does with his wine,"

In the morning of the fourth day, Cassius accompanied Rufus to the harbour where he boarded a ship bound for Rome.

"I bid you farewell for now," said his Hispanic friend, "until we meet again in Rome, as I plan to be there a couple of months from now."

"Farewell my good friend," said Rufus, in turn embracing Cassius, "and thank you for your wonderful hospitality. Give my warmest regards to your family. I shall look forward to seeing you again soon."

A corbita, devoid of the celebrated passenger cabin, welcomed our hero. He climbed the gang plank, and stood by the rail, bidding adieu, to his Hispanian friend, and his memorable odyssey.

His thoughts were now with Letitia, and Rome, as the little ship sailed out of the Tarraco harbour and into the blue Mediterranean.

* * * * * *

Simon and Alexander looked at the empty barn. Even though it was in great need of repair, it had a certain ethereal quality which by virtue of its high roof and impressive size, created a sensation of spirituality even before its conversion had begun.

"This'll make a wonderful meeting place," said Simon, walking around feeling the space, and assessing its potential.

Alexander too, could feel the ambience of the old building and grew progressively more excited. He went back and forth examining its condition and trying to visualize it performing its new function. Simon stopped, and addressed his son with a determined look in his eye.

"If you come up with what needs to be done, I'll look after finding the funds to pay for it and organize the work force."

Alexander looked at his father with earnestness in his eyes.

"I am beginning to get some ideas already," he said, in the grip of inspiration.

Father and son left the barn feeling very optimistic, and rejoicing at Marcus' generosity in having donated it.

The renovation of the barn now became a priority in the life of Simon and his flock. The preaching, which had been so unencumbered during the life of the old rabbi, had now become a problem. The new temporary rabbi pressured by some members of his congregation, objected to the gatherings outside the synagogue, and as a result, they were obliged to perform the 'fishing for men' in a garden near but independent of, the synagogue. There, both Gentile and Jew heard the words of Yeshua in the course of their daily thoroughfare.

* * * * * *

The beginning of autumn, saw the completion of all construction, and ushered in the establishment of the first Cyrenean church or meeting place of the followers of Yeshua the Nazarene. The decorations were however still a work in progress, as Alexander single handedly continued to invest many hours in the execution of colourful and instructive murals, which would bring to life for all future congregations, the wonderful and exemplary life of Jesus. These stories had been dictated by Simon with his usual care not to deviate in the slightest from them as instructed by the apostles. There remained however, a number of spaces awaiting further depictions which would in time be filled with colourful descriptions of other stories as they became known to father and son. To this end, Alexander was eagerly looking forward to his prospective visit to Judea.

The question of whether to continue attendance at the local synagogue where there had been threats of expulsion from the new rabbi, or to ignore its services altogether, became a problem worthy of the utmost consideration to all the previously Jewish followers of Yeshua. Simon prayed and spent much time in thought regarding these things and was therefore finally receptive to Alexander's proposed journey to Jerusalem where he might consult with the apostles, and learn their wishes as to procedure with regard to their services and liturgy.

Since there were no directives for him to follow, Simon had to make certain decisions after much prayer, as to the frequency of the 'Breaking of the Bread' ceremony in the new church. He, being the only one who had received the 'Laying of Hands' from the apostles was in fact the only authorised person to perform the service. He pondered as to how, and how often he was to do this with so many believers attending

The new converts, had been very generous in donating their time and money to the church project, and now wished to attend and receive the ' Body and Blood of Yeshua.' A service procedure or liturgy had to be determined, and was tentatively established after a number of meetings between Simon, Alexander and those who had been designated by Simon to bear some responsibility for the group, and assist him in the performance of the liturgy. The 'Breaking of the Bread', however, and the receiving of the 'Body and Blood', was restricted to Simon only, until such time, as a practical solution in procedure was established. Alexander's forthcoming trip to Judea, would, everyone hoped, solve their problem.

The *Stella Maris* was due in harbour within the next two or three weeks, and Alexander was looking forward to sailing with her.

David, who showed great interest in learning the carpenter's trade when proposed to him by Alexander, was to assist Simon in the latter's absence, and make a start as an apprentice. It would also give the young neighbour a chance to see Lucila more often, and that would be a great boon in his life as he had been growing fonder of her as she matured into womanhood, and growing lovelier by the day.

Alexander's day of departure finally arrived, and the whole family saw him off at the wharf in Apollonia. Ruth was much saddened at the thought of not having her two boys around her any longer, and it would take a good number of days for her to accept her lot. 'It is the cross I have to bear,' she finally said to herself, reconciling to the reality. She stood beside Simon and the girls on the wharf, bravely but regretfully, waving her son God Speed, as the *Stella Maris* left the harbour. Its white sail billowing in the morning breeze, its blue pennant flying high.

Letitia had been back home for over a month, and though great had been her joy at seeing her father back to normal, she was much grieved at her lack of knowledge regarding Rufus' whereabouts. Her uncle had promised to look for him after his return from Greece, but she had had no news from her aunt, or Lavinia, and so she knew nothing of him. The more frequent visits from Lucila and Rachel, made life more bearable for her. She learnt much from them with respect to the teachings of Yeshua, and soon came to believe that this God was much more powerful and real than her Venus.

The curing of her father at the hands of Simon had made a great impression on her, and she too, spent many hours sitting in the peristyle with her parents, listening to the carpenter's preaching. Her seventeenth birthday was near at hand, and she pondered with a hopeful but impatient heart at the two years which would have to elapse before she could become her beloved Rufus' wife.

* * * * * *

It was a clear autumn day at Ostia as Rufus walked down the ship's gang plank, bag over his shoulder and made for Neta's house. The sea voyage had been long and uneventful, but the nights had been chilly and uncomfortable. He longed for a good night's rest in a proper bed after a hot home-cooked supper. Neta, who opened the door herself, delighted in seeing him once more.

"Where have you been my dear boy?" she asked, hugging him with genuine fondness. "I have missed you. Come, tell me of your adventures."

Rufus spent a very pleasant evening at Neta's. Her daughter Lydia had dropped in as usual to form a very cordial trio.

Next morning, the returning merchant set out for Rome on horseback, where another fond welcome awaited him in the person of Drucila, who quickly prepared a lunch for him as she too, demanded with great enthusiasm to learn of his adventures.

"My goodness! what dangers you faced on your journey. It is so good to have you back safe and sound," she said with a look of relief. She filled his cup once more with watered wine, and sitting next to him again, inspected the wound on his arm, and shuddered.

"Ooh! Quite a gash," she said. "But it has healed nicely."

"How is Erasmus?" enquired Rufus.

"He has been having trouble with his stomach, and is anxiously awaiting your return. He seems not to have much confidence in his clerk Publius."

"It's good to be back. It has been a long arduous journey, and I hope I can stay put for a while and see if I can find my Letitia... Incidentally, did Erasmus do anything about finding her do you think?"

"I did mention it to him, but I have not heard anything as yet," replied Drucila, shaking her head.

Erasmus was elated to have his favourite clerk back once more. He rewarded him handsomely, and invited him to his home for the first time, where his wife and only daughter received him with great cordiality.

Rufus was disappointed to learn that his boss had not been able to trace Letitia and determined to redouble his own efforts in finding her.

His visits to the Temple of Venus became less frequent as he continued to have no success there. Instead, he began to enquire among the merchants of Rome as to the residence of the Tricius family, which he felt sure would be known, as he may perhaps be a merchant also as was his brother, Letitia's father.

Three months had now expired since his return to Rome. A number of cargoes originating as orders from his travels had now arrived and sold, and his position in the firm of Erasmus continued to solidify. He was now earning a very good salary and had also been allowed to buy another small share in the business. Rufus had been to Ostia a number of times during those three months, but as yet made no contact with Silas or Marius. Both captains, it seemed, were temporarily engaged elsewhere, and so he had to bide his time. Bashir, his friend from the *Mermaid* had promised to alert him as soon as either the *Pretoria*, or the *Stella Maris* made it to port, so for the moment he felt there was nothing he could do but wait.

In the meantime, he made a discovery which disturbed him considerably. Erasmus, seemed to be creating circumstances where his daughter would find herself more and more in his company. Invitations to his home were frequently given to the new junior partner, and it became obvious to Rufus, that Vibia, for that was her name, was showing much interest where he was concerned.

"You are quite a favourite of Papa," she smiled as she met him at the door on one of his work related visits.

"I do my best, and he appreciates it, that is all," he answered, in as a matter-of-fact way as he could manage, trying to avoid her beguiling look.

"Do you have the parchments that we have to review at hand?"

"Yes, I have them here," she replied, as she walked over to a table in the atrium and sat on a stone bench in front of it.

"I cannot make up my mind," she began, "as to which of these leather cushions to choose. You must help me since you are the one who bought them in Tingis."

Her voice was soft and flattering. She looked at him with admiring eyes.

The twenty three year old Vibia knew how to charm. She was attractive, though not beautiful; tall, slim of figure, and graceful in her movements which she practiced with regularity, particularly in Rufus' presence. She was prone to temper tantrums, but only in the young man's absence however. Being a very spoilt woman she was used to having her way. As our young hero soon witnessed, she was quite talented musically, as was evident in her dexterity at playing the harp when the occasion arose; though she did not sing.

Rufus sat beside her, perusing one of the parchments that she held in her slender and bejewelled hand. The cushions, illustrated in the parchment varied in design, which attested to the skills of the leather craftsmen of Tingis, and also gave her an excuse for entertaining the young man.

"I cannot make up my mind as to which of these three designs would suit me best."

Her light brown eyes searched her companion's face as she said this, her large well formed mouth spreading in an amiable smile.

"It is difficult to make a choice since all three designs are very pretty," remarked Rufus in a non committal way. Unlike his older brother there was a certain deficiency in his sense of aesthetics. To him, one would have served just as well as the other, as long as it made her happy.

Gaia, Vibia's mother, who was puttering around with the plants in the atrium not far from the pair, approached them wishing to see the designs that were being considered by her daughter. The duo, became a trio, much to Vibia's annoyance who would have preferred to have Rufus all to herself.

Our hero, greatly relieved however at the mother's intrusion, extracted with political acumen, a quick decision from his admirer, and promptly left; with the excuse that work was waiting for him at the shop.

'She's a nice enough girl,' thought Rufus as he walked down the road to her father's shop. 'She is of course old for me... A full three years at least. Not nearly as beautiful as Letitia, though one cannot say that she is ugly. I have to watch myself though, or I can end up in trouble with her father, and that would present a huge problem. I really must try harder to find Letitia.'

Six months later, Rufus was still telling himself that he had to try harder, but had not had any luck at all in his investigations with regard to his beloved Letitia.

The merchants he had approached had not been helpful, and the few times that he seemed to be getting closer, his investigations had evaporated into thin air. He occasionally visited the Temple of Venus and more often the Forum, but to no avail. He had missed the *Pretoria* on two occasions through being involved in his work, and similarly the *Stella Maris*, but he still hoped that the next time either ship got into port he would be able to make contact. To this end he set out one morning for Ostia, with the explicit purpose of paying someone at the Harbour Registry office to send him word the moment that either of the two expected ships entered the harbour.

'I should have thought of this before... It makes a difference when their palms are greased,' he told himself as he trotted down the road past Neta's place, and on to the wharf where the Registry Office was located.

He noticed as he rode down the wharf that there were two corbitas with cabin extensions, which made it clear that the rascal carpenter who had tricked him, had profited well from stealing his family's design. He felt much resentment for the man. 'A lesson learnt the hard way,' he reminded himself.

Having settled his business with the man at the Registry Office, from whom he had also enquired for the *Mermaid*, only to have her absence confirmed. He dropped in to visit Neta; enjoyed a meal in her company as usual, and then rode back to Rome.

It was late in the afternoon when he got back to the shop. He found Erasmus sitting at his desk all by himself. A worried look on his face.

"Thank goodness you are here!" he exclaimed as he waved a parchment around his ear,   "I smell a rat... Something is going on in the stores and I cannot put my finger on it."

"You mean someone is stealing from you?" asked Rufus in wonderment.

"I want you to look over these orders and deliveries, and see what you make of them."

His junior partner assured him that he would, and promptly sat down at his desk with all the pertinent scrolls around him.

"You'd best be off to supper. You look quite done in. I shall get started," said Rufus as he began to unroll a scroll. "I would appreciate your bringing me back anything at all to eat when you return. We may be here for quite a while tonight."

Erasmus had been gone for some time before Rufus found something disturbing in the distribution of the cargo of silver from Cassius. It was evident that quantities of silver delivered, were not tallying with the amounts seemingly remaining in stock.

On Erasmus' return, the matter was thrashed out between them, and it was decided that the very next morning they would pay a surprise visit to the warehouse and find out just what quantities of silver remained. Other discrepancies were also found, which would have to be checked. Publius was to be left in the office, and uninformed.

There were two men employed at the warehouse; one had been there for a few years and the other, the assistant, only one. The silver stock was kept in a cellar under the floor. It had a large heavy box sitting on the trapdoor covering the entrance to the underground vault. A special locking bar and iron lock secured the trapdoors and the warehouse superintendent kept the key himself.

The silver was carefully counted and examined, but was found to be in good order; indicating a clerical error without further implications. However, Rufus had a couple of further points to investigate with regard to two barley shipments and one of wheat.

The superintendent grew very nervous and tried to distract their attention, but the clever Cyrenean insisted that he let them count the remaining bags of those commodities, and were subsequently found deficient. The man deemed the deficiency to be a clerical error in an attempt to free himself from suspicion. Erasmus however was dissatisfied with the excuse and immediately took all the keys from him, and made him leave the warehouse. He then locked the door, and directed the pair to follow him and Rufus back to the shop. When they arrived at the shop, Publius was sitting at his desk ignorant of all that had occurred at the warehouse.

In the course of events Publius accused the warehouse superintendent, and the latter accused the clerk. One incriminated the other, until it became clear that the two had been conspiring together; the assistant being innocent of any wrongdoing.

Both clerk and warehouseman were immediately dismissed and threatened with legal action if they showed their noses near warehouse or shop again. So ended the episode. The assistant was placed in charge of the warehouse, with two new positions requiring to be filled.

It seemed to Rufus, that Erasmus should have discovered this loss of stock well before now.

Rufus, who was now in the middle of his twentieth year had matured considerably as a result of his voyage, and seeing how much Erasmus depended on his efforts, resolved to set up a system which would keep track of all transactions and a closer watch on the warehouse personnel in the future.

"Papa looks at you almost like a son," said Vibia on their next encounter.

Rufus noted with some trepidation, a look of love in her alluring eyes.

"He has been very good to me and I have much regard for him," he explained with an appreciative nod, fidgeting somewhat uneasily with his hands.

"He tells us that you are now a partner and that you have a very bright future with the business. He treats you as family."

A tear appeared in her eye, which registered strongly on our hero's defensive mechanism. Fortunately for him, Gaia made an unexpected appearance once again, which instantly provided a means of retreat, for he now felt up to his neck in trouble.

'What am I to do?' he asked himself as soon as he was alone again. 'Things are coming to a head here. If I am honest with her, and tell her about my love and commitment to Letitia, it is going to hurt her badly as I am pretty certain that she is in love with me. Her father knows all about my commitment to Letitia, but he chooses to let his daughter run the risk of having her heart broken in the hope that she may still win me. Also, I could be making the wrong decision in regards to Letitia as she may be married already, and here I am about to throw away an excellent opportunity to make a very good life for myself. They are an excellent family, the business is very strong, and even now I own a sixth share which is considerable seeing that I have only been with them for a little more than a year and a half.'

At Rufus' suggestion, Erasmus had a special cellar built in his house where the silver could be stored. Away from prying eyes, and delivered straight from there to prospective clients. Employees would not know what they were transporting, as the silver would be deceptively packaged, and the partners would always be in attendance. The record of all transactions would then be kept separately and in the house.

"Silver is too precious a commodity to be warehoused," asserted the junior partner.

"Yes, indeed," agreed Erasmus, "only family can be trusted in matters like this."

Rufus, on hearing this statement spoken in such an emphatic way, looked at Erasmus with a quizzical expression on his face.

The older partner walked over to the younger, and putting his arm around him, said.

"Rufus! It's time we talked."

Our hero felt trapped. Not only was he being fondly held physically, but emotionally also. Though he had hoped not to find himself in this situation, he had had a growing feeling that it was inevitable. It seemed the moment had arrived. His only recourse now was to play for time, since a decision, the honourable thing to do, was now imminent.

"I and the family, have grown very fond of you," began Erasmus. "Not only because of what you have contributed to the business, and considering how young you are, it far exceeded my expectations. But your personal manners and honest ways have endeared you to us in a way we had not expected. The fact that my daughter has very strong feelings for you, raises you even further in our esteem."

Rufus raised his arms as if to speak, but Erasmus with a quick motion of the hands stopped him, and clearing his throat, continued:

"I am well aware of your commitment to your young woman; though many young men at your age are fickle about their love affairs. I erroneously thought you would forget her after a while. But now that I know you, and how honourably you hold to your convictions, I respect your commitment until you find out whether she has married."

He had been looking out the window as he spoke, and now he turned to face his young partner once again, and with a quirky look in his eyes said:

"If I am to be honest with you, I hope she has married. You are everything that I would desire a son-in-law to be, and eventually the whole business would be yours. My daughter and my wife would be well taken care of I am sure, when I am no longer here."

Rufus, greatly moved by his partner's sincerity, gave him a fond hug, assuring him that he was very fond of his lovely daughter, and promising him to make a decision in the near future, having already made further enquiries concerning Letitia's whereabouts.

* * * * * *

"I have a message for Rufus," came the voice of a young man, as he burst into the shop one day, and found the junior partner sitting at his desk perusing some parchments.

"I am Rufus!" he affirmed, as the man approached him and gave him a scroll he was carrying.

Rufus quickly tore its seal and read that the *Pretoria* had just arrived in Ostia.

"Here you are my friend," he said, handing the messenger a denarius, which produced a big smile on the man's face.

"Thank you sir!" sang the man with enthusiasm and left the shop, thoroughly pleased with himself.

Rufus, leaving the new clerk in charge of the office, and instructing him to tell Erasmus that he had gone to Ostia, made haste to hire a horse and gallop off to meet with Silas.

He found the *Pretoria* moored almost exactly where he had seen it the last time, and he hastened up the gang plank shouting for his friend to appear.

"How is my favourite carpenter?" bellowed out Silas, greeting him aboard.

"Silas you old sea dog," exclaimed Rufus in a jovial tone, putting his arm over the big bulk of the captain who was thrilled to see him.

"I cannot believe I found you at last," said Silas with a face splitting smile.

"I have great news for you, my young friend," he continued enthusiastically, as one who had a mission to accomplish and wanted no interruptions until he had done it.

Rufus made no effort to interrupt him. He guessed that whatever the news was, would be positive, judging by the bright light in Silas' merry beady eyes.

"Your young lady is in Cyrene, and waiting for you."

Rufus felt his legs weaken at the knees, and supporting himself on Silas' arm looked up at that small head with unprecedented admiration.

"Ha! Ha! Ha!" laughed Silas contemplating our young hero's startled face.

All of a sudden, Rufus, was a new man.

"Come! tell me all you know," he cordially demanded. "Tell me all!"

Our young merchant took Silas to Neta's place, where over a good supper, the story of Letitia's return, the extraordinary curing of Marcus by his father, and many other interesting happenings were brought to his attention.

Neta insisted that Rufus stay the night. The party having finished quite late with much unwatered wine having been drunk. She had never seen her beloved lodger so happy, and it moved her considerably. She fussed over him until he was safely in his bed.

The *Pretoria* would remain at Ostia for the next five days, and then leave for Caesarea with a stop at Cyrene to allow our hero to disembark. Erasmus, much disheartened by the news of Letitia's return home, agreed to keep Vibia ignorant of the matter and explain his young partner's departure as a business trip to Judea. Gaia however, would be told. Erasmus was still hopeful that Rufus would be refused by the girl's father again, not knowing the full story of Simon's miracle

CHAPTER EIGHTEEN

ALEXANDER

The *Stella Maris* was approaching Joppa as the day dawned. Marius walked across the deck to awaken Alexander who was fast asleep. He was covered with a heavy cloak, which had kept the night chill at bay throughout the voyage.

"Good morning young man!" Marius' voice was loud and clear, shaking Alexander out of his world of dreams as he propped himself up on an elbow and scanned the soft grey-blue sky above him.

"And to you," he replied cordially, smiling sleepily at the captain.

"We are almost there. If you stand, you can see the town of Joppa very clearly."

Alexander stood up. He was very pleasantly surprised at the proximity and beauty of the little town, reflecting the soft morning sunlight through a thin evaporating haze. The harbour bore evidence to the busy nature of the town with many ships at berth and anchor. The *Stella* glided past a few, heading for its berth in front of another corbita. The latter ship, much to Alexander's disappointment, lacked the cabin extension which had become so important to Simon's family.

Alexander soon forgot the corbita, as he excitedly prepared to leave the ship and begin his adventure in Judea.

"Marius!" he said, "I thank you for your enjoyable company during the voyage, and I trust we will see each other again in the not too distant future."

He stretched out his hand to the captain.

"Remember what I told you," said Marius squeezing Alexander's hand, followed by a warm embrace.... "Leave me messages as you need at the Registry Office on that wharf over there." He pointed to the place.

"Thank you, I shan't forget," replied the young adventurer, and walked down the gang plank headed for Simon the Tanner's house with all the eagerness of youth.

Marius stayed on deck watching him until he disappeared around a warehouse.

"The God of your father go with you," he muttered under his breath, as he walked cross deck to talk to Lucius the helmsman.

* * * * * *

Hannah stood at the wall of the renowned terrace of Simon the Tanner's house, saying her morning prayers in that now holy place. Her heart was at peace and full of hope for the future, now that her life was governed by Yeshua's plan, in which she devoutly believed.

Her mind wandered as she dreamily contemplated the calm early morning sea, shimmering and mildly oscillating in the warm rising sun. She reminisced over her solitary life with her father as her only companion. He had been a truly devoted father to her, doting on her every wish, but teaching her with loving care all the virtues that a woman should possess. She had missed the presence of her dead mother many times during her life, particularly at those times when a young woman really needs female company and advice. Her much older neighbour and very close friend Sarah, had very amiably and lovingly come to her young friend's aid on many occasions. Hannah loved her as one of the family, but she believed that a mother's love would have been incomparably better. Her young imagination, greatly influenced by her father's description of his adored wife, made her idolize her mother's memory whose absence had been the cause of much sadness in her life.

Her father, Simon the tanner, had given her a good education. She had been taught to read, write, and speak Greek and Latin from an early age. Her mother tongue being Aramaic. A tutor had been hired to teach her to play the harp, another had taught her the feminine graces. She, being highly intelligent and of a very sensitive nature, responded admirably to all those disciplines, as well as the moral and religious instruction zealously and continually given her by her father.

In her younger days, Simon had made up stories of how she would meet a young man and fall in love with him, and how he would love her for being so beautiful, marry her, and make her forever happy. He was a good storyteller, but now she was almost twenty one years old, and because of her venturing out but little in the social sense, she was beginning to think that the young hero of her childhood dreams would never materialise. It had been her habit since Peter's visit, to go up to the terrace very early in the morning to pray to Yeshua. Now as she stood there on this particular morning she addressed him with the usual hope in her heart

"Lord!" she prayed. "Every day I come up here... Right here where I know you hear me, to ask you for a good husband... For how can I go out and find one? Is it Thy will that I go through life alone, without little ones who I would teach to love you?"

She was suddenly conscious of someone passing by on the street below, and presently there was a knock at the door. She hastened downstairs to find out who would be calling at such an early hour of the morning, especially since her father was still asleep.

* * * * * *

The house of Simon the Tanner was easy to find, as it had become famous by the vision that Peter had witnessed up on its terrace. Alexander was thrilled as he stood in front of the heavy wooden door enclosed by an unusual arched stone entrance. He knocked, and waited for a few moments. Then, it slowly, but partially opened. There, in front of him appeared a face of exceptional beauty. An apparition as it were in the soft morning light, sending his senses reeling and generating an involuntary smile on his handsome face.

The apparition opened the door completely, incarnating into the person of Hannah, who was equally affected at the sight of

Alexander. Her face lit up with pleasure at his winning friendly smile.

"You must be Hannah!"

The words felt unreal to him, as if someone else had uttered them.

"My father told me about you," said enchanted visitor.

"Who is your father?" she asked, though she could guess from the resemblance that it was Simon.

"Simon of Cyrene!"

"I might have known!" was her response, as she felt her hair band to make sure that it was correctly placed across her brow.

"Who's there?" came a voice from somewhere in the house, followed closely by Simon the tanner in all his hairy glory.

"Can you guess?" she asked, as her father tried unsuccessfully to tidy up his uncombed hair and beard which were all entangled from sleep.

He peered at Alexander, but lacking his daughter's keen female perception, could not guess.

"This is Alexander, the son of our very good friend, Simon of Cyrene."

"My! Oh, my! there is a resemblance right enough," he declared, and proceeded to give his young visitor a tight hug, and ushered him into the living room with much joy in his heart.

Hannah was beside herself with excitement, realising that she had made a favourable impression on Alexander who was finding it difficult to keep his admiring eyes off her. He was sure that she was every bit as beautiful as his beloved sister Rachel; even the hair was similar. She, in turn, was truly thrilled with him.

Hannah soon had breakfast ready, and the three sat and chatted like old friends for a good while until Simon got up to go to work in the shop. He invited Alexander to join him just as he had asked his father before him. The young man, after having been shown the workings of the shop, committed himself to helping Simon in his work for as long as he stayed in the house, once again, exactly as his father had done.

The young carpenter had passed a few weeks in the tanner's house, helping the father in the shop and getting to know the daughter better each day, whilst learning Aramaic which she enjoyed teaching him. The more he got to know her the more he liked her ways, and soon she had so endeared herself to him, that he could not imagine a life without her. She in turn expressed her admiration for his talents and quiet manner in such a way that a strong but undeclared love burned in their hearts, which inevitably, soon found its expression in words.

"I have informed your father that I shall be leaving for Antioch in a few days time. I need to find answers to many questions which my father and I have with regard to the manner of conducting services, and the ' Breaking of the Bread' during those services."

As he talked, he tentatively took her hand which was in the act of folding a small table cloth, lunch being over and Simon having returned to the shop.

"I shall miss you terribly," she confessed with a sad pout, and placing her other hand over his gave it a gentle squeeze, which bespoke much.

"It is something I really have to do," he assured her. "That was the reason for my coming. Now however, I have a good reason to hurry back," he said as he drew her to him.

She came willingly but nervously, unaccustomed to a man's touch; her body stiffening slightly as their eyes met in an enraptured gaze, bonding together in oblivion as if by enchantment. Their lips involuntarily pressed together ardently, discharging the fire that had been burning in their hearts since the moment of their first meeting at the door that fateful morning.

"I love you!" he whispered lost in the softness of her eyes.

"And I you!" was her answer as she tenderly caressed his cheek.

"I shall ask your father for your hand right away," he said, as he started to walk towards the shop, but then turning quickly he asked, "Will you be my wife?"

"Ha, Ha! Ha!" she laughed. "You almost forgot to ask me first."

"You bewitched me," he said, with a look of astonishment at his own forgetfulness, and they both had a good laugh.

"What is so amusing?" came that well known voice from the shop.

The humorous little episode was explained by Alexander after having asked Simon formerly for the hand of his beautiful daughter. He contracted as was the Judean custom, to continue working gratis for Simon for two years after his return from Cyrene, since money in lieu, he had none to offer.

Simon was greatly surprised at the rapidity with which their commitment had been made, but felt very happy for them both. He quickly set a date two days hence for a betrothal celebration prior to Alexander's departure for Antioch.

The question then arose as to how they would be married. The apostles were all away on their missions, and in any event, no particular liturgy or rites, to their knowledge, had yet been established by the apostles. The customary Judean commitment, might no longer be approved.

"I shall ask when I see John Mark in Antioch... Perhaps he will know what the apostles think we should do," suggested the young Cyrenean with his usual candour.

The betrothal was celebrated as planned, with a few friends of Simon and Hannah attending. Sarah and her family were there, and a few other neighbours. It was a modest affair, but all managed to enjoy themselves and were sincerely happy to see Hannah settled. All looked forward to the wedding.

Now that their betrothal had taken place, the two lovers were permitted to take walks together unaccompanied in the evenings, which had hitherto not been permitted.

Their evenings had been spent up on their unique terrace with Simon in attendance, as may well be expected from a zealous father; there being no woman in that house to perform the task of one who in later days would be known as a *chaperone*.

A garden near at hand in full view of the house with a crude but charming little wooden bridge was now the place of their evening stroll. Torches were lit every evening by the local authorities as other young couples were in the habit of walking there also, and because it was in close proximity to the now renowned 'Tanner's house,' which had acquired a certain popularity with some of the townspeople.

Alexander and Hannah, stood at the little bridge hand in hand. The moonstruck stream below them reflected their shimmering images as it flowed past. It bubbled quietly into the dark blue sea beyond, like a soul's passage into the unknown vastness of eternity. The perfume of the surrounding trees and flowers mixed with the briny smell of the sea, gave the evening breeze a delicious aroma as they talked of their plans for the future.

Hannah gave Alexander to understand in her own sweet way, that she could not abandon her father and go to Cyrene to live.

"My father," she told him, "cannot do anything for himself, and when he gets wrapped up in his work he often forgets to eat. Besides, he cannot cook."

"I would never ask you to leave your father, my love," said Alexander sympathetically. "I will set up here and make a start. I shall need to rent a small shop, and I shall—"

He continued to explain all his needs and ambitions, to be put into practice once they were married, after the marriage contract had expired. She listened to his plans which would entail his remaining in Cyrene for perhaps as much as two years, since his father needed help in setting up the church there and was depending heavily on him. She contributed some suggestions, but for the most part, she listened and considered his proposals. They walked and talked on their evening strolls in the little park, bewailing the time it would take before they could marry.

At last the evening prior to his departure arrived, and was spent in making ready for his trip to Antioch. Hannah fussed over every little item that he was to take, which reminded him of his mother, and how she behaved in a similar manner when he or his brother travelled anywhere.

"You would love my mother," he said, as Hannah was busy folding some of his clothes.

"I often think of her, and wonder what she would think of me. Would she approve of me?"

"You resemble her in so many ways," he said with perfect candour, "that she could not help but like you. When I get back from this trip, I shall paint your portrait, so that I can show her and the family what a beautiful wife I shall have."

She smiled contentedly and gave him a quick kiss on the cheek as at that moment her father was not looking. He was however, sitting nearby keeping the two young people company.

"I can hardly wait for you to get back," she confessed with a sad countenance.

"And don't you go looking at any other women," she said with firmness; her eyes widening in half joking reproach.

Alexander, catching Simon's attention assumed a look of incredulity and replied:

"How can you expect me to do that, with all the beautiful women that I shall meet in Antioch?"

"I think that is asking too much of you," joked back Simon in mock sympathy with his future son-in-law.

Two pieces of clothes went flying through the air wrapping themselves around the two faces that were nearest and dearest to her heart, as her beautiful eyes glared at the pair in seeming disgust.

Early the following morning, having hired a horse, Alexander set out with his well organised baggage and carrying enough food for a good part of the trip. He trotted off to Antioch in the hope of finding John Mark whom his father had suggested he contact.

'I wonder if this John Mark is empowered to perform the "Laying of Hands" on me? Will he think me fit to carry out a ministry?'

These and many other thoughts concerning his new religion kept Alexander's mind occupied as he travelled the coastal route north. It was not too long before he ran into a Roman patrol. That being a main route, was well guarded. He was advised by them to put in for the night at the nearest village, and await there till at least four or five other horsemen would join him to form a group the following morning. It is far safer to travel in the company of others, and during the day, they told him. They also advised him to carry a weapon when travelling.

As dusk fell, Alexander stopped at a quiet little village by the sea and found himself lodgings for the night and enjoyed a tolerably good supper at reasonable cost. Unlike his brother who travelled with all expenses paid, Alexander had to penny pinch, since his funds were limited and he had yet to find work in Judea.

The following morning he joined a few horsemen who were leaving the village in a northerly direction. There were also people travelling on foot forming another larger group.

Alexander had much time to think of his future as he travelled along, keeping mostly to himself as the others were doing. They had grouped mainly for safety on the road with little fraternising.

As he rode along, he thought of his commitment to Hannah and her father, with whom he would have to work for two years prior to his marriage. Also the length of time that he would have to stay in Cyrene to help his father build the church to which they were both so committed. His heart fell as he realised the years involved before he could claim Hannah.

Regardless of what Alexander thought, one thing was for certain; his life had now changed, and circumstances would dictate his future which was as always, in God's hands.

It took him five days and nights to get to Antioch. On his arrival, he found reasonable lodgings close to a synagogue, where he thought he would find some disciple who in turn could take him to John Mark, or any of the apostles who might perchance be there at the time.

'If any preaching is being done, and I feel sure there is much, it will probably be outside the synagogue as my father has done in Apollonia,' he mused, as he turned in for the night.

The next morning, soon after breakfast, he visited a synagogue and found a small gathering of people waiting outside for someone to appear. Not knowing much Aramaic, only what Hannah and her father had as yet taught him, he waited around in the hope of hearing some Roman or Greek spoken. To his utter surprise two men in front of him were having an animated discussion in Cyrenean.

"It's a man called Paul," one was saying with apparent conviction, as the other nodded in acceptance of the statement that his friend had made.

"Pardon me," broke in Alexander, "but I overheard you speaking in my language, and I would like to know if either of you could tell me who this Paul is?"

"Everyone has heard of Paul of Tarsus."

"Yes, of course I have. My father has told me much about him… So it is that, Paul," confirmed Alexander.

'I must see him when he has finished his preaching,' he said to himself.

The assembly grew bigger. Half an hour passed and still no sign of Paul. Then from behind one of the columns emerged a man of medium height, with a large dark beard, his head covered with a shawl, and walking confidently, stopped at the edge of the top step.

He looked at the crowd below him, smiled, and with outstretched arms greeted them all in the name of Yeshua the Christ.

He held the crowd spellbound for the next hour, and then blest them. Having finished, he invited all those who wished to be baptised, to go up. There, a table had been placed with a large bowl and jug of water on it for that very purpose. Alexander waited until all the baptisms had been performed. He then climbed the steps and addressed Paul in Latin.

"I am the son of Simon of Cyrene, and I am honoured to meet you," he said with a certain reverence in his voice.

"I have heard of your father, and I am very happy to make your acquaintance," replied Paul, embracing our hero. "And what brings you here to Antioch?"

"My father and I are in need of answers to many questions, particularly with the way in which to celebrate and share the 'Body and Blood' of Yeshua. Also, I have a question on the performing of a marriage ceremony. Do we perform it in some new rite, or do we Jews continue in our own ancient way.

Paul listened intently to what Alexander had asked him before he replied.

"I am too busy winning souls for Yeshua to pay too much attention to the actual performing of services," he said, "which is also extremely important. But if you talk to some of our disciples here, they will share with you what they do, and you will know more."

"There is an attempt being made at formulating some ritual, that can be shared by Gentiles and Judeans alike as there should be no difference between them," continued Saul.

"So then we no longer need the synagogue?" asked the young man.

"I am Judean, and I have a choice, but the Gentile has no choice other than our new ways. If you come with me, I shall introduce you to a few disciples who will acquaint you with procedures which are now common to all, Judean or Gentile."

Alexander accompanied him to a large house where many people were gathered. Paul was received with much acclamation and love. The young Cyrenean was introduced to John Mark, a countryman of his as my faithful reader may recall, and a few other men who presumably would be able to help him with the liturgy, the new and correct term for the new ritual.

The two Cyreneans soon found themselves deep in discussion regarding the questions that Alexander had asked.

"I am about to leave with Paul on a tour of the Churches, but when I return, I would like to visit Cyrene and see your father. Perhaps we can go together," he suggested.

"That would be excellent," replied Alexander with a grateful smile, and taking a hold of John Mark's arm, added, "I would be greatly honoured, if you or Paul would perform the 'Laying of Hands' on me as Peter did for my father. Then I could help him with the services as he is getting very busy."

John Mark in turn took Alexander's arm and they approached Paul. After hearing that Simon had a working church in Cyrene, and that they had won over many new disciples there, he asked Alexander a number of questions regarding the life and miracles of Yeshua and other articles of faith. Being convinced that the young man would make a competent minister, he acceded to his request. Calling together those present to witness the ceremony, he performed the 'Laying of Hands', ordaining him to the ministry and empowering him to forgive sins in the name of the Father, Son and Holy Spirit.

Alexander was ecstatic with joy, as the whole assembly sang a hymn of thanksgiving on his behalf.

He took a fond farewell of Paul and John Mark a few days later, having discussed many things, and promising to keep in touch in the future as more assistance would be required with the church constantly evolving.

Having now established a base in Antioch, and having had himself ordained, Alexander set out for Joppa with another ordained disciple who was on his way to Jerusalem. The man had been asked by Paul to accompany Alexander back to Joppa, as it was on his route.

As they rode together with other horsemen who formed the travelling group, they had some very interesting discussions regarding the new liturgy.

Alexander's companion was a young man five years older than himself, whose name was Judas surnamed Barsabas. He was a tall man of medium build, swarthy complexion, and formal bearing. He addressed Alexander in a sober tone, his large dark brown eyes depicting a character deep in commitment and sincerity.

"At the present moment," he explained, in answer to a question his new friend had asked, "there is no set Christian liturgy."

"Christian?" interrupted Alexander.

"Why… Yes! That is what we are now being called in Antioch, and it suits us well so we have not objected," said Judas with a satisfied smile.

"So we now have a name. That's wonderful. Whether we were Gentile or Jew, it makes no difference now. We are all Christians. My father will be thrilled to hear that."

"Now, getting back to the liturgy," continued Judas "At the moment, as I pointed out, there is no set form. From what we learned at Antioch through disciples who met there recently, each congregation is doing things as seems right to them, based on what they have been informed concerning Yeshua's teachings. The reverential performance of the consecrating of the 'bread and wine' which is the whole purpose of the liturgy, is the most important thing," concluded Judas, raising his thick dark eyebrows and gesticulating with his hands.

"But what do they do when it comes time to distributing the bread and wine, especially to a large crowd?" asked Alexander with a perplexed look.

"Again there is no set procedure, and we are presently trying to standardize one for that also. But as yet, every church does it as they find most practical."

There was much discussion between the two 'Christians' as they travelled towards Joppa, though nothing conclusive was achieved as may well be supposed, considering the infantile state of the new Christian church.

* * * * * *

Hannah, not having the least idea when Alexander would return, kept a prayerful vigil for him up in the terrace. There she loved to pass her leisure hours contemplating the sea and enjoying all the sounds and smells which animated the harbour and its surroundings. She loved living by the sea and could not imagine herself living anywhere away from it.

'Alexander told me that from his terrace one can see the sea,' she said to herself, 'so even if eventually I end up living in Cyrene, I shall be looking at this same sea.'

She found solace in that pleasant thought.

'He will not take me away against my will, I feel sure of that, but what right do I have to hold him here. His father needs him just as my father needs me? Oh dear Lord, what are we going to do?' she asked. It was her habit to talk to God as if he were standing there beside her.

'You have answered my prayer. You have sent me a husband, and what a wonderful and handsome husband. You took your time, as You usually do, but You always answer my prayers and I now trust You to solve this problem for me.'

Carrying these thoughts with her, she went downstairs to prepare supper.

Simon the tanner and his daughter were in the middle of supper, when an impatient knocking at the door was heard. Hannah got up, opened the door, and found herself in Alexander's arms even before she could announce him to her father.

On seeing Judas, she quickly released herself from her lover's embrace and with a somewhat embarrassed look and flushed cheeks, smiled sheepishly at the amused visitor, and announced their presence to Simon, who was soon at the door to greet the two men.

"Welcome back Alexander!.. and, who have we here?" he asked giving Judas a big smile, and extending his hand in friendship which the other clasped warmly.

Judas was then introduced and heartily welcomed. Hannah was soon back in the kitchen forgetting about her unfinished supper and happily cooking another supper for the newcomers.

After they had eaten, they all went up to the terrace taking some refreshments with them. Judas was keen to see where Peter had witnessed the well known vision. They sat enjoying the cool evening sea breeze, exchanging stories, and becoming acquainted with their new friend who was Jerusalem bound within the next day or so.

Alexander expressed a wish to see Peter, and wondered whether he, too, should visit Jerusalem. But he decided it would be too soon at the moment seeing that he wished to spend time with Hannah, and his Aramaic was still rather weak.

Judas informed him that since Peter often travelled around that area on route to Caesarea, Antioch, and other towns to the north of Judea, there was a good chance that he might drop in on Simon in the not too distant future. In any event he would tell him of his meeting with Alexander and Hannah, and how Simon too would love to have him visit again.

Judas shared the Cyrenean's room just as the latter's father had shared with Peter, it always contained two beds to accommodate visitors. Alexander asked Judas to tell Peter of the miracle that Yeshua had worked through Simon, explaining to him the full story of what Marcus went through, and his condition during the six months or so that he was afflicted.

Very early the following morning, Judas took leave of the family with many thanks. With him went a provision of food that Hannah had prepared for him. He would be travelling with one of the caravans that made the Joppa to Jerusalem run.

Chances were he was to travel with Ahmed, but there was no certainty on that score. As yet, Alexander had not visited the caravan master; something that he had to do before returning home as his father had asked of him.

Alexander was now a part of the 'Simon the tanner' household. He continued to work and learn Aramaic which had now become mandatory in that house, so that he would be forced to practice it. He also spent a good portion of his free time writing down all the important information that he had obtained from the disciples in Antioch. That would be invaluable to his father in his formulating of a practical liturgy which even if temporary, would serve the needs of the congregation in Cyrene until a standardized, approved, one was established.

Hannah and Alexander got to know one another so well over the next month that barring the conjugal union of the pair, they might just as well have been husband and wife. The unusual circumstances which dictated their lives gave them that opportunity.

Alexander, having enquired at the Harbour Registry Office, now expected the *Stella Maris* to come into port the following week. He had been in Judea for three months and he knew that his father would be expecting him soon.

Seeing that time was running out, he made his way to Ahmed's house following some directions that his father had given him. He ended up getting lost and found himself on the beach. He recollected being told that the caravan master's house was near the beach, but quite a distance from that of the tanner's. Feeling rather stupid at having got his directions wrong, he approached a couple of fishermen who were sitting around a boat talking.

"Good day!" said Alexander with his usual bright smile.

"Good day to you!" answered one of the men whilst the other one merely smiled.

"I am afraid I have lost my way. I am looking for Ahmed the caravan master."

"You are not too far lost. He is a friend of ours and his house is only a street away," said the fisherman who had not returned his greeting.

"It is the house with the blue door and shutters," and he pointed in the general direction of the house.

Alexander thanked them, continued on his mission, and soon found the house. The door was opened by no other than Sicmis who asked him what he wanted.

"I am Simon's son, and you must be Sicmis," he said, with a big smile.

"Simon's son! My goodness, what a lovely surprise," she cried as little Isha peered inquisitively behind her mother's stolla at the mysterious young man.

"Come in! Come in!" she sang.

Alexander followed her in and sat on a cushion as she motioned him to do.

"I am delighted to meet you," she said, as Kimi made his appearance; but rather shyly, keeping to the other side of the room.

"Uncle Simon, asked me to give you both a big hug," he said smiling happily and reached for Isha who was quite near him and not at all awed by his presence.

She hugged him, pulled his ear and laughed, as her mother scolded her for her boldness which greatly amused the visitor.

Kimi, seeing that the ice had been broken, came forward and allowed Alexander to hug him.

Sicmis' voice broke in.

"Ahmed should be here shortly. He got back in from his latest trip only yesterday and he went to see some friends of his. He has been away for quite a while now so I expect him shortly.... Please tell me about your visit to Judea."

Alexander began to relate his adventure, but before he had gotten too far into the narrative, the door suddenly opened and Ahmed appeared. He was immediately tackled by the pair of little ones, wanting to know if he had brought them the sweets that he had promised. Seeing Alexander, he approached with a quizzical look on his dark face, the whites of his eyes like two torches in a tunnel, his eye brows arching high over them.

"I am Alexander, Simon's son," said the Cyrenean, extending his hand for Ahmed to take.

"Simon of Cyrene?" quizzed the caravan master, taking Alexander's hand and embracing him at the same time.

"What a wonderful surprise... Who would have thought?" he sang.

"Does he not look like his father?" chirped Sicmis.

"My goodness! Yes," responded her husband as the children looked on happily eating their sweets.

Alexander told them how keen his father had been for him to visit them, and his indebtedness to them for their hospitality during his adventurous visit and escape. He was also thrilled to learn that they had all embraced Christianity, and he made them very happy when during the lunch that they insisted he share, he 'Broke Bread' with them, as he was now ordained to do.

It took all Alexander's resources to get away from that most amiable family before supper time, and only on the promise that he would visit them again before his departure for Cyrene.

The following day, he went on board the *Stella Maris* that had pulled into harbour, and brought Marius to meet Hannah, her father, and Sarah and have supper with them. Marius was quite astonished when he met Hannah.

"By Jupiter, another beauty in the family!" he declared with much excitement, and addressing Simon, he continued. "Not only has this young fellow a beautiful mother, and two lovely sisters, but now he is to have a beautiful wife as well... What a family."

A certain envy gripped his good natured soul.

"That's what you get for spending so much time at sea," joked Alexander. "You miss out on all those beautiful women out there."

They all laughed at the captain as he jokingly assumed a look of utter dejection.

"I shall be ready for you my young friend," said Marius presently, looking at Alexander.

"In three days I shall be loaded up with wine for Marcus, and cork again. Make sure that you have enough warm clothes. It's still chilly on deck at night."

Marius took his leave soon after supper, as he had to make preparations for the next morning. The foursome were left to their own devices as night fell.

Hannah was very sad the night before Alexander's departure. She spent a good part of the night with him up on the terrace, talking of his sea journey and how lonely she would feel without him. She promised to call on Sicmis soon after he had gone and give them his apologies for not returning to bid them farewell. They stood at the terrace wall for a long time in each other's arms. She, with tears in her eyes, he, with saddened countenance; both regretting with anticipation and pained hearts the forthcoming months or years, during which they would be separated.

"I have your portrait in my bag... I am so pleased that I finished it on time. I must not let it get wet, or it will just disappear."

"You have painted me too favourably. If your family ever see me in person they will be disappointed," she protested.

"Nonsense, you are even more beautiful than I have painted you."

"I wonder if I shall ever get to meet your family," she sighed as she wiped tears from her lovely eyes.

"Please God you will... I shall pray for that too," he asserted, squeezing her slim waist and pulling her to him once more as she laid her head on his shoulder.

"I hope I have put enough food for you in your smaller bag. There is a cup in there as well, and a knife... I don't think I have forgotten anything. Your clothes are all in your large bag. Be sure to keep warm," she advised.

"The worst part of it all will be not knowing if you have arrived safely," she continued. "That really torments me. But I shall trust in the Lord, and every morning as I stand here I shall be praying for him to keep you safe," she concluded, as he, lifting up her chin, kissed her lips tenderly.

It was close to morning when they both went down to prepare for breakfast and give everything a final check.

"Good morning to the pair of you," Simon's voice boomed out. "I can see that neither of you have had a wink of sleep. You must have been up on the terrace all night."

"Yes, father," replied Hannah, who like her future husband was loath to lie.

"I cannot blame you my daughter. It's a cruel thing particularly at your ages to have to part from someone you love. But take hope in God. Time passes, and soon you shall be together again for good."

The *Stella Maris* once again played an active part in the life of Simon of Cyrene and his family. Marius, that trusted and beloved friend, seemed fated to be involved in every move they made. Being now considered one of the family, he took their welfare to heart.

"Be of good cheer," he told Hannah as she gave Alexander a final hug on the deck of the *Stella*, "I shall look after him as if he were my son."

Hannah gave him a hug as well, and with tearful eyes she took her father's arm and walked down the gang plank. Alexander stood by the rail looking at her and waving till they were out of sight. The *Stella Maris* committed itself to the blue Mediterranean once again, this time bound for Apollonia.

CHAPTER NINETEEN

CHRISTIANS

After a rather chilly but otherwise reasonably calm passage, Alexander stood by the rail looking at Cyrene high up on that familiar hill, as they sailed into the harbour at Apollonia. His thoughts were running as his eyes feasted on the beauty of the landscape that lay before him.

'Here I am! home again… Or is it home?' he pondered.

'I suppose I shall never be truly happy again; for now half my happiness lies in each port. Until the day that we can all be together here in Cyrene, my life will not be complete. How will such a thing happen?...Only the Lord knows. If it is meant to be, it will be. I shall pray for that, and let Yeshua sort it out for me. My trust is in Him.' so mused our returning hero as the Stella finally berthed at the quay.

The gang plank had hardly touched the wharf, when to both Alexander and the captain's surprise, there stood Simon with David beside him. Both with great big smiles on their faces. Simon embraced his son first, and then his sea faring friend.

"How did you know we were coming?" asked Alexander.

"David and I are working on that corbita," he said pointing to the ship, "and we saw you slipping in."

"He, having better eyes than me, read the name much sooner, and here I am,... and there he is," said Simon turning to David, who promptly gave Alexander a big hug.

"We had a good run," volunteered Marius, anticipating Simon's next question with a smile of satisfaction at having brought Alexander home safe and sound.

"Come and have supper with us Marius," said Simon, "we will all be happy to see you."

"No, thanks, not tonight, but perhaps tomorrow or the next day, I shall be there."

"You disappoint me my friend. You are one of the family and we will miss you if you do not come."

"No, really, you go ahead. There are things I must do so that the cargo can start unloading tomorrow, including checking in with Marcus. Give everyone my love."

Simon and party now made for the corbita that they were working on, and loading their tools, and Alexander's baggage, into the cart made their way up the hill, with Simon in the cart, and the two young men walking beside it.

* * * * * *

"Tonight will be a night of surprises," announced Simon, as Pepper, pulled the cart up the hill.

"Your mother and the girls are going to go crazy when they see you, and there is also a big surprise for you," finished the father, as he smiled at his son.

"And I have a big surprise for all of you, too," smirked the son with an uncharacteristic mischievous look that would have better suited Lucila.

I shall leave you, my esteemed reader, to imagine the pandemonium that ensued on the arrival of our friends at the house; since it defies description. The story continues, after the initial emotional upheaval has passed and a more sober intercourse takes over, making the festivities more comprehensible to the normal mind.

"Rufus, it's great to have you back," were words that escaped Alexander as he hugged his brother for the fifth time. The family were at last beginning to recover from the shock of the impromptu reunion.

"I am keen to hear Rufus tell me his exploits," stated Alexander, but first I have a surprise for you all."…Instant silence prevailed.

"Well do you want to know?" he asked, with a quizzical look on his face, "or shall I keep it to myself?... Actually, I have two surprises."

His sisters rushed over and sat down beside him, staring at him with a demanding look on their pretty faces as the others looked on eagerly awaiting the promised surprises.

"I am betrothed!"

Silence,...and then an explosion. The girls were all over him with hugs and kisses, Ruth rushed over and took an active part in the melee; Rufus, Simon and David all making a grab for his hands, to congratulate him.

Again,... another storm passed leaving smiles and tears of joy in its wake as order restored itself once more, at least temporarily.

"Tell us about her," pleaded Lucila who was shaking with emotion.

Alexander looked at his father with a meaningful look, a smile spread his lips and the word, "Hannah!" exploded from his handsome mouth. Simon jumped up like a big ape, his hands in the air and shouted.

"The Lord be praised!"

Everyone was stunned, as the name 'Hannah' did not immediately register; until Ruth remembered that she was Simon the tanner's daughter, and she, too, was ecstatic.

"Simon the tanner's daughter," yelled Simon above the noise for all to hear.

Alexander got up, found his bag, and taking out the portrait, passed it around for all to see.

"She's beautiful," they all chorused, as Simon confirmed their assessment with great conviction.

"I told her father when I first saw her, that she reminded me of you Rachel," he said glancing at his daughter.

"Yes," agreed Alexander, "I saw a similarity too."

Ruth could not stop crying for joy. This had to be one of the greatest days of her life. She had both her sons back, both betrothed, and her girls and husband with her. Barring some unforeseen circumstance, David, she hoped, would be joining the family soon.

'I am the happiest woman in the world,' she affirmed to herself as the tears rolled down her lovely but overheated cheeks.

Alexander then announced that he was now officially a minister or priest, like his father, which again sent a wave of joy and congratulations around the room.

"Now, Rufus, let us hear from you," said Alexander, as they all sat down to listen once again, as he had already narrated his exciting story to all the family before.

Supper was late in coming, but they were all so excited that eating was not a priority on that particular evening of evenings.

The following day there was still much left to be said, but it would have to wait until the evening when Simon and David were back from their work on the ship. Alexander and Rufus took the day off as they both had so much to tell each other, and Rufus wanted Alexander to go with him to see Letitia. She was now allowed to be courted openly, in the presence of Zaphira of course.

Ruth was still in a daze from all the excitement of the previous evening. They had all stayed up late, except David, who had gone home at midnight as he had to get up early the next morning.

'Oh, how I would love to meet Hannah,' mused Ruth. 'Yes, she is beautiful, but it is her other qualities that will make her a good wife for my son. Simon makes her out to be formal in her manner and wise beyond her years. She has run her house since she was a young girl. That says a lot to me. Of her love for him, I have no doubt. She is a good follower of Yeshua, which further endears her to us.'

These thoughts ran through Ruth's mind as she prepared breakfast for the family, whilst the girls were at their toilette.

'I feel sorry for her though, having to part with Alexander just as they were getting really close,' she rambled on to herself. 'Though I want him to be here forever, I shall have to press him to go to her as soon as Simon can make do without him. But then he is such a clever boy,...so wise for his age, and Simon confides and depends on him so much. It will be a huge loss for him, particularly in his ministry... And to think that he too is a priest of Yeshua. I am so prou— No! I must not be proud, but I am the happiest woman in the world... Thank you Yeshua! You have given me far in excess of my prayers. What more could I want? blessed be thy Name for ever."

So continued Ruth's thoughts as the girls still bubbling over Alexander's adventures, joined her in the kitchen. Breakfast became a continuation of the previous day's celebrations, absorbing the remainder of the morning in its joyful exuberance long after Simon and David had left.

"Well Lucila?" asked Alexander with a teasing tone to his voice, "What's happening with you and David? You seemed to be looking at him a lot last night, and he kept very near you as he listened to my adventure."

Lucila did not expect such an affront from her older brother who was normally so quiet and considerate. Her cheeks turned red as apples, as she stammered:

"N— Nothing!"

The others burst out with laughter at her response.

"He is just learning the trade from father, that is all," she stated, her vivacious eyes betraying the lie that she wanted the others to swallow.

"I wonder if that was his only reason for coming to work for father," teased Rufus, getting back at her for the times that she teased him regarding Letitia.

"Enough!" broke in Ruth. "Leave the child alone."

Lucila, quickly got up and went into the kitchen where the women of the house always felt safe from the men's barbs.

"I am pretty sure that David is serious about her now that she is seventeen and quite a woman," whispered Rufus in his brother's ear.

"That's wonderful," replied Alexander, "and how is he making out with the carpentry?"

"Father says he will be make a good carpenter a couple of years down the road, as he learns easily and seems to enjoy his work."

"I cannot believe the adventures you have gone through," said Alexander throwing his arm over his brother's shoulder and giving him a big smile. "And all that you have achieved in such a short time. God has been good to you, even though he made you go through a difficult time at first during the time that Marcus was ill. But then! That is the way the Lord works. He does things for one's betterment, but always in his own good time and in his own way. After all, what do 'we' know?"

"I suppose you are right. I had not stopped to think of that. I was too busy trying to make a life for myself and finding Letitia who led me a 'merry chase' as they say."

"You heard of father's adventure in Judea no doubt, said Alexander.

"Was that not extraordinary? And what about the miracle that Yeshua performed on Marcus through father? That is what changed the climate of *your* life and allowed you to have Letitia, even if you do have to wait another couple of years."

"Yes," replied Rufus a little perturbed at his brother's words. "I am afraid my enthusiasm for Yeshua is not as ardent as the rest of the family's, though I do not doubt that what you and Father are telling me is true. I just do not experience all those wonderful feelings that you all seem to share... Even the girls."

"Faith is a gift from God," assured Alexander, "you cannot get it by your own efforts. We will be praying for you. Though he has given you much, he has yet to give you that gift. Why? We are unable to understand. His ways are above our ways."

After lunch, Rufus walked with his brother and the girls to Marcus' house. Alexander wished to see them again, especially Letitia who had been away for so long and was now virtually espoused to his brother.

Letitia, who had not been present when her father was cured, had not as yet embraced the "new faith; " though she, like Rufus, had no doubt as to the authenticity of the miracle. Her belief in Venus still lingered on; though waning, and awaiting further confirmation from the new faith, which at the moment had not fully absorbed her.

The visit, which lasted a couple of hours was, as expected, a very pleasant one, with Alexander having to tell of his adventure once again to the joy of everyone in the Marcus household who held him in high esteem. Letitia was particularly warm with him as she already considered him her brother-in-law, and was thrilled to hear about Hannah and admired her beauty in the little portrait that Alexander proudly passed around for all to see.

* * * * * *

Simon's mind was hardly on his work the next morning. His hands mechanically worked of their own accord leaving his brain to muse at will. He had so much on his mind that it seemed he could not entertain one more thought.

'Alexander, now an ordained minister just like me. My goodness! And all the things that he said he had written down and has still to show me. Answers I hope, to many of my questions and some of his. Fancy meeting Paul! Yes, and he was surprised to hear that we had a building of our own... A church they called it in Antioch... Christians. We are Christians. What a wonderful name,...celebrating the anointed one of God. We have so much to do, so very much.' He slowed down his sawing.

'You Yeshua, are going to be very busy leading us, inspiring us, and making sure we make no mistakes in the way we perform our duties. But I am so happy, so very happy Lord,' he prayed. A tear glistening in his eye.

"Simon!"

A young eager voice tore into the fabric of his thoughts, making him suddenly conscious of the rasping sound of his own saw, and turning his head, he met David's deep green eyes with an enquiring look about them.

"Yes, David?" he asked stopping his saw, and giving his assistant a blank look.

David, who after last night's celebrations, felt more a part of the Simon family than he had ever felt, had spent most of the morning trying to work up the courage to confront Simon with a matter that was vital to him. Without allowing himself to hesitate, he took a deep breath and blurted out.

"Would you permit me to court Lucila?"

Simon had suddenly to make room for one more thought in his crowded head which he now did. He displayed a warm paternal smile, feeling justified in his suspicions that there was an ulterior motive in David's wish to become a carpenter.

"Of course, my dear boy, as long as Lucila desires it."

David's face beamed with satisfaction as he thanked Simon, and turning nervously back to his work proceeded to drop a board on his foot.

In the days that followed, Simon's evenings were spent with Alexander, as they worked to design a meaningful and practical liturgy for their services. Alexander had heard that the first day of the week was being favoured by many as the new Sabbath, being the day of Yeshua's resurrection and also the coming of the Holy Spirit; especially where the Gentile Christians were concerned.

"Then we shall never go back to the synagogue," pointed out Simon.

"No! I suppose not," agreed Alexander. "Paul was thrown out of a synagogue I forget where. And besides, how do we reach the Gentiles by preaching in a synagogue?"

"We cannot have half of us doing one thing and the other half something else," ventured Simon with a feeling of satisfaction. "However, since the converted Gentile Christians can't go to the synagogue, then all should come to the same church; which we fortunately have, thank the Lord...and Marcus too," he asserted.

"So,... then," summed up Simon, who was quite tied and yearning for his bed, "we are agreed that as from this coming first day of the week, we shall have them all come to church every week on our new Sabbath Day; in the morning at the fourth hour."

"We can perform the 'Breaking of the Bread' at the service, and we shall receive, but cannot distribute the 'Body and Blood', until we have a proper procedure worked out," observed Alexander as they made their way to bed.

Seeing, that as Alexander had said, there was no standard for celebrating the 'Breaking of the Bread', they would have to set up their own ritual or liturgy as it was being called. This topic led to much thinking and was to keep father and son very busy during many meetings. Finally, a procedure was decided on by both of them which seemed practical and most reverential, since it dealt with the 'Divine Presence'; the Body and Blood of Yeshua. Everything had to be meticulously handled. Only those ordained, such as they, were empowered by the Apostles to consecrate the bread and wine.

Because there were now close to one hundred and twenty baptised Christians in the assembly, the distribution, would have to be done in such a way that there would be no accidents, such as dropping crumbs or spilling wine. After much deliberation, they decided that the bread would be broken by them into small pieces such as would fit easily into the mouth. This would be done prior to the service, on a large silver tray and placed on the table of worship (which in later times, as my dear reader knows, would be known as an altar).

After the consecration, each person approaching would receive a piece of consecrated bread presented to him or her on a small silver platter from which they would take it; the minister would hold the dish under the chin of the person receiving until the bread was actually in the mouth. That way, should any crumb fall, it would fall into the platter, and returned to the tray. Simultaneously with the person receiving the bread, the minister would say, "This is the Body of Yeshua." Once everyone had received the body, then either Simon or Alexander would carefully eat all the crumbs that had been collected and whatever pieces were left over, carefully wiping the tray with a special moist cloth, which would later be burnt.

After a prayer of thanksgiving, the people would come back up to the table, again one at a time, to receive the wine.

For this second phase of the liturgy, the priest would consecrate some wine in a silver chalice and a larger supply in a small jug with a narrow spout. Each person receiving would bring their own tiny silver cup which would have been given them as a gift by the church when they were baptised. The celebrant, taking their cup, and holding it over the chalice, would pour a very small quantity of wine from the jug into the cup and hand it to the owner, who, having drank the contents, would hand it back to an assistant for cleaning.

The assistant, using a special cloth would wipe the cup clean and return it to the owner. This would be done every time someone received the wine. The cloth would be changed every seven cups or so, and then put into a small basket. As the service ended, the basket with all the cloths would be burnt as part of the service, and the ashes taken later to a special place in the church grounds where they would be reverentially buried.

Again, the priest would say "This is the Blood of Yeshua," as each person was handed the cup of wine.

The service was to start with a dedication prayer to the Blessed Trinity, followed by the Lord's Prayer, which everyone had now learned, prayers of repentance for sins committed, and petitions. This was to be followed by the recital of a parable from the life of Yeshua, with, if necessary an explanation, and some preaching. Then would come the 'Breaking of the Bread', which included the consecration of the wine, followed by the congregation receiving the sacred Body and Blood. Prayers of thanksgiving would then be said and a   final blessing given. The service would end with a hymn which would be sung.

That was to be the service that Simon and Alexander had formulated for their congregation in Cyrene.

"We have as yet to collect enough money to buy all those little silver cups for a start," said Simon, "not to mention all the other things that we're going to need to carry out this service every week. We better meet with Marcus and Damian and see what ideas they can come up with for collecting money," suggested Alexander.

"Though," he continued, "in Judea all the disciples shared everything they had, and many of the richer people even sold some of their land and brought the money to the apostles," he concluded, with a hopeful look in his eyes.

Marcus, who had taken the lion's share so far of the expenses of setting up the church, received Simon and Alexander with his usual warmth and graciousness.

"Damian and I have been giving the matter much thought," he said, and calling for Silia they all sat in Marcus' favourite corner of the atrium..

"Bring us some refreshments, please," he ordered, as Silia bowed, smiled, crossed the atrium, and went into the kitchen.

"We have devised a liturgy, which will aptly deal with the 'Breaking of the Bread' ceremony, but entails a certain expenditure which we would like to cover by donations from every soul in the community, each contributing as per their means. Everyone must be involved, including my family," pointed out Simon, "especially, as we are no longer Jews and will not be paying tithes to the synagogue. We are done with them as it would hurt those who like yourselves, were not Jews prior to their conversion. We are all Christians now and will develop our own ways with God's help," explained Simon, as the others listened intently to his words.

"Let us address the congregation at the next service, and get a commitment from them, with contributions coming in the following Dies Solis," suggested Marcus, with Damian nodding his approval, and giving one of those long smiles of his.

"I will f...find a silversmith up in Cyrene who will undertake to m...make as many little cups as we need, for a g...good price... I shall let you know more within a few days," promised Damian.

"We shall also need a chalice and a particular type of jug, both also made of silver. I shall give you a sketch for each, so that you can get the silversmith to price them all at the same time," said Alexander.

Silia arrived with some wine, water, bread, oil, olives, and other delicacies, and laid the tray on a table beside them. They ate as they talked and managed to settle a number of problems; mostly monetary, before the evening wore off. Father and son departed feeling much more at ease.

* * * * * *

The house of Simon the Tanner was at peace as its two occupants slumbered. A violent knocking at the door jarred both Simon and Hannah out of their peaceful sleep with a rude awakening.

Father and daughter looked inquiringly at each other, as they both went to the door; Hannah adjusting her stolla which she had hurriedly donned; Simon trying in vain to put his hair in some sort of order.

The knocking continued with unabashed ferocity, until Simon, placing his head close to the door, enquired as to who it was, and what did he want at that hour of night.

"Open the door, in the name of the Sanhedrin," said a course, loud voice.

Simon, who had no reason to suspect any wrong doing on his or Hannah's part, slipped the bolts, and opened the door; which flew at his face, knocking him down, and bruising his cheek. Hannah, who attempted to aid her father, was pushed rudely back, as four men entered the house.

"Get something on, both of you and make it fast," growled one of the men.

"Please tell us what's going on," asked Simon, his hand on his aching cheek.

"You are a couple of Christians, are you not?"

"Yes," came the answers simultaneously and fearlessly.

"Let's get going then," ordered the same man as he pushed Hannah into her room, closed the door, and then followed Simon into his room instructing him to dress.

The exodus from the house followed shortly after, with two men boarding up the door after locking it with Simon's key.

"This is my property. Why are you boarding my house up?"

"We are confiscating your property," replied the man in charge in answer to Simon's question.

"Who gives you the authority to do that?" again asked Simon, as Hannah still in a state of shock remained silent.

"The Sanhedrin," barked back the man.

Both father and daughter knew from all the stories they had heard, and remembering the other Simon's adventures in Judea earlier, that they were living under suspicion of the Sanhedrin. People knew that Peter had visited there a few times, and of his miraculous vision which had captivated the imagination of many in Joppa. Also, all those visitors to and from Judea, many of them well known Christians had given the house a certain reputation which inspired both admiration and hatred depending on the viewpoint taken.

Being slightly past midnight, their abduction went totally unnoticed by the neighbours. The group walked to the local synagogue which was not far from the tanner's house. As with the other Simon from Cyrene, a similar partially underground room, recently converted into a makeshift prison, received them unceremoniously as they joined a few other people who had been apprehended earlier that day. The door to the room was locked behind them, and the jailers took the oil lamp back with them, leaving everyone in complete darkness.

There was but one window in the room. An iron grill had recently been installed, so as to turn it into a prison cell. All the prisoners were evidently sitting on the stone floor. Both father and daughter had to be careful not to trip over someone's legs, as they tentatively tried to find a space that would accommodate them, aided solely by the light of the moon that filtered in through the window.

Once having settled down, both sitting together, their backs to the wall, Simon's voice broke the silence which had settled over the room following their entrance.

"Are we all Christians here?"

A moment or two of silence followed,...and then a "yes" repeated a few times was heard.

"Have you been praying?" was his next question.

"Yes, a little earlier," came the timid reply.

"We must be strong in prayer to our beloved Yeshua, if we expect his help," continued Simon, as he tried to count in that scanty light, the number of people present.

With that said, Simon kept his peace; but Hannah began to pray the prayer that Yeshua had taught his apostles. Soon, they were all accompanying her, as she repeated the prayer a number of times, in the hope that it might register well with God, on whom they were all hoping for their delivery.

* * * * * *

The morning sun had been shining for a while, as Sarah made her way to the tanner's house to call on Hannah as she often did. She was stunned to find the door of the house boarded up. The oddness of the scene, caused her head to experience a lightness verging on vertigo, as she beheld it.

'What has happened here?' she asked herself, totally disoriented.

There was no point in knocking, so collecting her scattered thoughts, and went back to her house to think. She sat there alone for a long time. Her brother had gone to work, and her sister-in-law was at the market. A knock at the door gave her edgy condition a start and she arose to answer it.

"Good morning Sarah!"

The greeting came from a tall man with the familiar face of Marius, who beheld her with a look of concern in his weathered face.

"Not a good morning, I am afraid," she replied, as she motioned her sea faring friend to enter.

"I am as shocked as you seem to be. I take it you have been to the house?" asked Sarah.

"Yes, I have this scroll for Hannah from Alexander."

"Where on earth can they be?" she cried, "what could possibly have occurred?"

"Oh my, I am absolutely distraught. I cannot think! I just cannot think!" she continued bursting into tears.

Marius whose heart was moved, felt sorry for her and drawing near embraced her. She found some solace as she cried on his shoulder.

"Come! Come!" he said sitting her down on some cushions, and following suit himself.

"Let us calm down and think this thing through. We can be sure that the authorities have done the boarding up. So if we are dealing with the authorities, it is either the Roman or the Jewish. The Romans would not normally interfere on any matter dealing with religious beliefs. Now, judging from what my very close friend Simon of Cyrene tells me, the Sanhedrin in Jerusalem has been persecuting every Christian it can find. I myself saw this when I rescued him from here as they were trying to apprehend him."

Marius, putting two and two together, was convinced that enquiries had to be made at the the local synagogue or local Sanhedrin headquarters, and advised Sarah accordingly.

"I shall go to the synagogue right now and find out. Will you come with me?" she asked with some hope in her eyes.

As they walked, Marius asked Sarah if she knew Ahmed. She said she had heard of him, but that she did not know where he lived. Simon promised to find him, as a caravan master would not be difficult to find.

On arrival at the synagogue, Sarah entered by herself, as the Roman, knowing that he would not be permitted inside, took temporary leave and went in search of Ahmed whom he strongly suspected would soon be needed.

The local rabbi whom Sarah knew well was sympathetic, and admitted that the Sanhedrin had been involved in the arrest of her friends and lamented the fact. He also had known them for many years and was quite fond of them.

"I am so sorry Sarah, but unfortunately the matter is out of my hands. It is the local Sanhedrin that is carrying on the persecution of Christians under direction from Jerusalem."

"May I see them?"

"I shall try to find out. I know that they are locked up in the storeroom downstairs," said the rabbi as he headed towards the back of the building.

He returned shortly, and reported that his request on her behalf had been denied. He did not tell her that Simon was their most wanted man and that he would be subjected to "interrogation," as soon as Jechonias, their boss, who had been sent for, arrived from Jerusalem. This news left the rabbi much concerned. Sarah made her way home with a very heavy heart feeling useless in the circumstances.

Hannah was praying near the window as the stench in the room was getting unbearable. It was afternoon, the jailers had brought them some water, bread and dried fish and had left an hour ago. Simon and his daughter were two of seven people who occupied the cell, which was small for that many people.

The unfortunate group consisted of one family of four and one other man who was well advanced in age, and was rather ill.

A young couple in their mid thirties with their two children, a boy of six and a little girl of about four, made up the little family. The couple were trying to keep the children occupied with stories and a single toy each that they had been allowed to bring. The extreme sadness in their young eyes told of their huge concern for their children, who could become the property of the state with a horrific future ahead of them; regardless of what would happen to them, the parents.

A cautious rap on the window grille attracted Hannah's attention as she recognised Marius's face which wore an encouraging smile. He told her to get ready, as they were about to pry the grille off the window. Hannah's heart raced as she heard those words and quickly informed her father and everyone else to get ready to make a run for it once the grating was removed.

Marius, who had been busy all morning arranging the rescue, was now in the most critical part of the operation. He chose to do it in the middle of the day, when the noise from the street would muffle the noise from the grate as it got pried off.

Earlier, he had found Ahmed's house, but the caravan master was away on a trip to Jerusalem, and was not expected back for over a week and a half. In his absence, Sicmis, his wife, had promised to contact the two fishermen friends of theirs and make plans for Simon and Hannah's escape. They were all to go to her house once they had gotten away from the synagogue prison, and remain there until Marius and the fishermen devised a plan.

The iron grille had been installed recently on the outside of the synagogue building, and Marius having earlier that morning surveyed its garden, following the information given him by Sarah, found the cell easily since it was the only window that had a grate. He and Lucius, using muffled chisels, chipped at the mortar in the joints and with the aid of a long handled pry bar, wrenched the bolts out of the wall and removed the iron grille.

Soon, all the occupants of that stench-filled prison were outside, with the exception of the old man, who insisted on staying.

"I have lived long enough," he said, "I shall hopefully be with our Lord soon. So all you young people go with God's blessing and mine."

Marius threw the pry bar into some bushes nearby, and all four made their way to Ahmed's house, walking at a normal pace so as not to attract attention. The young couple with their children, took off in a different direction; no doubt to some other members of their family, who would aid them further.

* * * * * *

A Sanhedrin official, one of the men who had arrested Simon the tanner and his daughter, arrived in Jerusalem after three days of hard riding from Joppa. He staggered into the presence of his boss, Jechonias, reported his accomplishments and sank into the nearest chair utterly exhausted. Jechonias congratulated him, told him to take a couple of days off as a bonus, and then to follow him to Joppa.

"Are you off again Jechonius?" enquired his sister, as he burst into the house, went up to his room and began to pack with great urgency.
"I am off to Joppa, there is very pressing business for me there."
"When will you be back?"
"I have no idea... Probably two weeks or so at most."
"I shall pack some food for your journey," she volunteered giving him a suspicious look.
"Do eat something before you go.
"I have no time to lose. I shall eat on my first overnight stop."
Soon, Jechonias was galloping off on his way to Joppa relishing the prospect of torturing Simon the tanner so as to loosen his tongue, and have him implicate others.

* * * * * *

Ahmed, leading his caravan to Jerusalem, was now in the second day of the journey and on the ascent. For some strange reason which he could not explain even to himself, he was not at ease. He looked at all his passengers, expecting to see something untoward, but all seemed normal.
He said a prayer to Yeshua, as was now his habit, and tried to distract himself with the beauty of the scenery as he glanced back at the fertile valley they had left earlier, and which had made such an impression on Simon the carpenter that other time.
All continued well for the next day; nothing of any importance marring the habitual normality of the trip. However on the fourth day, as the descent on the Jerusalem side of the mountains was in progress, a lone rider crossed their path at the point where the little wooden bridge connected one escarpment to the other, and where, my dear reader, as you may recall those wonderful little fountains of water were located.

"Get out of my way," yelled the rider who steered his horse towards the bridge as Ahmed's camel entered it.

"What's your hurry?" asked the camel master, stopping his camel in the middle of bridge and looking at the man with disdain.

"I'm in a hurry."

"So? can't you wait a moment till my people cross over?"

"No! just back up and let me through."

"And why should I do that?"

"Because I am an official, and am on Sanhedrin business."

"Pardon me," replied Ahmed, beginning to get annoyed with the boisterous stranger, but not budging at all.

"What is your name, camel driver?"

"My name is Ahmed. What is yours?"

"You will have reason to remember mine," said the stranger. "My name is Jechonias."

Ahmed's quick mind turned over this name many times in one moment, until he remembered that Simon had told him that this man was persecuting him and all Christians.

The members of the caravan were getting impatient at this standstill, and began also to enter the bridge making it more difficult for Jechonias to get through or for Ahmed to back up. However, obstinate as usual, the spy tried to push his way through, but the caravan master realising that his charges could now be at risk, directed his camel straight at Jechonias with the intention of forcing him to back out of the bridge. Unfortunately, his horse reared up, causing him to topple off and over the railing into the ravine.

All dismounted and rushed to the railing to look. The body of Jechonias lay lifeless on a ledge far below.

"Served him right," shouted one of the travellers.

"Obstinate idiot," said another.

The caravan continued without much more ado, the guards taking the loose horse with them, as instructed by Ahmed, who inwardly rejoiced at the extinction of the vicious enemy of the Christians.

"The Lord knows what crimes he was racing to," he said to himself.

Then all of a sudden it hit him.

"I am a Christian now.... Did not Yeshua say, love thine enemies?"

Remorse and repentance came like a black cloud stifling him. He looked around guiltily. Everyone had resumed their chatter as if nothing special had happened.

"Do they not have a soul?" he asked himself.

"I have committed a grave sin. I can feel it, just as I felt something strange at the beginning of this trip. I must find Peter or any of the apostles as soon as I reach Jerusalem. They have the power to forgive sin, just as Simon and Alexander have."

Thus ended the infamous career of Jechonias who had sworn to wipe out Yeshua's followers whichever way he could. Others like him, and far worse would come, but that would be in the future and would only make the church of Yeshua stronger as the years and centuries passed.

On arrival at Jerusalem, Ahmed, left his camels in the care of a friend, and made straight for the Sanhedrin, taking with him three witnesses of the bridge incident, and leading Jechonias' horse. Though he felt very guilty from a moral and religious standpoint, he had not intended to throw his opponent over the bridge; merely to force him back out of it.

The accident, was duly reported, the three required witnesses, were questioned, identified, instructed not to leave Jerusalem, and temporarily dismissed. Ahmed, however, was not so lucky, and was unceremoniously held for further questioning and possible trial.

'A real pickle I've got myself into now,' said Ahmed to himself as he sat on the cold, hard floor of his cell, 'God alone knows how long they are going to keep me here.'

He badly needed to confess to Peter or some other apostle, as his hate for the Sanhedrin spy, had caused him to deal with the situation more harshly than he would normally have.

'Had he not been so cocky, and if I had not known who he was, I would have let him pass, but he really got to me. I suppose it was meant to be, and probably for the good, only Yeshua knows.'

He continued to muse and worry about the consequences, until he resorted to praying to Yeshua for assistance, and finally left everything in His good hands.

The hours passed, and no one came near his cell, it had grown dark and he was hungry, thirsty and cold. He decided to create a rumpus, hoping that someone would hear.

"Is there anyone down here with me?" he shouted, hoping that there would be some occupants in the other cells, who might at least inform him as to the gaoler's habit with regard to the prisoners' sustenance.

"You can shout all you want, someone called back. No one will come till tomorrow morning." The voice seemed to come from a great distance.

"Where are you?" shouted back Ahmed, "You sound so far away."

There was a momentary pause. Then another stronger voice answered.

"We are in the dungeons below you. There are a number of us here. They arrested us because we are Christians."

Ahmed was dumbfounded at the frightening news. He kept silent for the next few moments, and then the inevitable question followed.

"Are you also a Christian?"

Again silence from Ahmed, as he pondered his reply. This was a precarious situation indeed. Was he going to deny Christ? Was he truly a believer? Or was he just a hypocrite?

There comes a time in a man's life, when his beliefs are challenged. When any existing complacency, is unceremoniously shattered. When he must face himself, and find out at what worth he rates his beliefs. He felt like praying to Yeshua for help, as he often did. But this was one time, when he knew that his decision was his own, regardless of the consequences. He would appeal for Yeshua's help later, if the consequences were dyre.

With one big leap of faith and abandoning his many reasons to the contrary, he shouted.

"Yes!"

There was another pause. The same voice shouted back.

"If they don't know, don't tell them, and pray for us."

"I shall," shouted back Ahmed, and prayed that no jailor had heard the conversation.

The night wore on. Ahmed sat on the floor in the corner of his cell unable to sleep, afraid the rats which he could hear around him, would attack him. The weak rays of dawn filtering in through the small, barred, window of his cell, gave him some mental comfort, but his body was stiff and weak, his mouth was exceedingly dry, and he suffered badly from hunger pains.

He forced himself to his feet, and once again began to bang on the cell door, and to shout for a gaoler to no avail. Ahmed, continued with his prayers for the next hour or so. The sound of a heavy bolt sliding, and the creaking of an old door, brought him back to reality. Heavy footsteps were heard on the stairs, and two men soon appeared at the iron grate of the cell door.

"Did you have a comfortable night?" asked one of the men in a mocking tone.

"You left me with nothing to eat or drink all night," responded the prisoner.

"Oh! That was a terrible oversight on our part….But here, we brought you something today," said the jeering gaoler, as he handed Ahmed a bag with some things in it.

The caravan master, opened the bag and seeing a small skin of water, took it, and proceeded to drink his fill. There were also two pieces of dry fish and a small loaf of bread.   Having examined the contents of the bag, he put it aside until the gaolers had gone and he could eat in peace and quiet.

"When am I going to get a hearing?" asked Ahmed tentatively.

The other man, who had as yet not spoken a word, informed the prisoner that he would go before the Sanhedrin that very afternoon. Both men then left, and the unfortunate camel driver was left on his own to eat his meal which had been so long overdue.

"The fact is, you killed a member of the Sanhedrin staff," asserted one of the individuals who sat behind a table in the Chamber of Justice. Ahmed had just stated his case, and assured them that the death of Jechonias had been an accident.

The safety of the people of his caravan had been compromised, and his action had been in their best interest, he told them.

"You have the testament of three witnesses which should exonerate me from any charges," further appealed the prisoner, and continued saying: "your men arrested me, put me in prison, without food, and kept me in the dark, for a whole night, despite the fact that I came to you of my own free will and even brought back his horse. If I were a murderer, I would have had ample time to get out of your reach."

"You may leave us now," said another of the judges, motioning to one of the guards to accompany him outside.

Ahmed awaited the result of his trial sitting in silent prayer, his hands tied behind his back. Ironically, he sat on the same stone bench that Jechonias had sat on when he awaited the results of his proposal to the Sanhedrin regarding his career.

At length, the hopeful caravan master was summoned back into the Chamber of Justice. Ahmed's eyes scanned every face behind the table as his heart pleaded with Yeshua for His divine help.

"It is the decision of this assembly," stated one of the judges, "that the death of Jechonias, an agent of this Sanhedrin, was the result of an accident... You are free to go."

Ahmed, gave fervent thanks to Yeshua and on being released, made his way directly back to his friend's house where his camels were. His mind was on Peter and how was he going to find him? His friend not being a Christian he thought, made it impossible for him to elicit his help. On mentioning Peter's name however, Ahmed was greatly surprised to see his friend's eyes light up and asked what could he want with the man.

"I need to see him, I have a message to give him from a friend in Joppa," lied Ahmed, not wishing to expose himself as a Christian.

"I can arrange for you to see him." was the surprising answer from Jacob, as his friend was called.

"You know Peter?"

"Yes, I met him once, but I have a friend who can take you to him."

"Are you a Christian then?" asked Ahmed, his eyes glaring in surprise.

"Yes!"

"The Lord be praised!" exclaimed the caravan master, his eyes and hands raised to heaven.

"I was baptised a month ago," explained Jacob with some pride.

The friends embraced each other, and Ahmed related all his adventures with Simon of Cyrene, the Jechonias incident which now troubled him so much, and the detention of the Christians in the temple's dungeons.

The following evening, Ahmed found himself kneeling in front of James confessing his sin, as Peter was away on a mission.

"By the power vested in me, and in the name of the Father, Son, and Holy Spirit, I absolve you of the sin you have confessed and all your sins. See that you never do that again; no matter the provocation. You are a Christian now, and therefore a man of peace."

* * * * * *

Marius had loaded his cargo, arranged for his passengers to board the following morning, and was ready to sail. He sat in Sarah's house after supper waiting for nightfall to climb the wall to the terrace of Simon the tanner's house, with Lucius' help. Simon had disclosed to him where his money was kept, and had also asked him, if he could, to bring back some of their clothes.

Lucius was to meet him at the house just after dark and take a small wine skin with him as a prop in case he had to distract any one that came by, with a favourite act of his, whilst the captain was in the house.

Hannah and Simon were at Ahmed's awaiting the arrival of the two fishermen friends of the camel master, who would be rendezvousing with Marius as had been arranged, at a secluded little bay early next morning. Hannah entertained by the children, who took to her very easily. Sicmis prepared a nice supper for them, as they talked about Alexander and how impressed they had been with him.

The hour arrived for his attempt at getting into the tanner's house. Marius took a reluctant but fond leave of Sarah, with a meaningful embrace, as the two were beginning to feel something special for one another.

"You be careful now!" admonished Sarah. "God keep you. I shall look forward to seeing you on your next trip,... and thanks again for your wonderful help."

Marius smiled back at her and melted into the night.

Lucius was at the house when Marius arrived. They lost no time, as the latter jumped up on Lucius' broad shoulders, and gaining a good hand grip, pulled himself over the terrace wall. He found his way around the house by the scanty light of a small wax taper a mariner friend had given him from one his voyages to India and that he had brought with him; finding it much less cumbersome and more practical than an oil lamp.

His first task, was finding the hidden money. He went into the shop where he found the money very cleverly hidden in a dummy part of the mechanism used for squeezing out the water from the pelts, and following Simon's directions, extricated it without much trouble and without the need of tools. The bag containing the money was quite heavy. He took it up to the roof, dropped it in a corner, and went back down into the house. He had just finished putting some of Hannah's clothes into a bag he had brought, when he heard Lucius' voice singing a sailor's drinking song, which required the singer to sound inebriated.

He quickly extinguished his taper, and creeping quietly into Simon's room began to feel around for some clothes. He collected a few things feeling at random, and putting them also in the bag, made his way very gingerly up the stairs which creaked at almost every footstep. On reaching the terrace, he crawled over to where the money bag was, and sat there waiting He could now hear Lucius talking to some people with a drawl and enticing them to join him in his drinking.

"Are you fellows too proud to sit and zzrink with a shailor?" asked Lucius as he took a swig of wine from the skin.

"No, no," said one man, with some hesitation, wondering whether they should humour the drunk or send him on his way. "We are not supposed to drink when we are on duty."

"Dootsy…" asked Lucius, "What dootsy?"

"We are watching this house in case somebody tries to enter," said the other.

"Whoosh going to enter, itsaaal boarded hup," he said with a feigned hiccup.

"We have to keep it that way," said the other.

The captain waited impatiently for something to happen that might steer them away from the house, but Lucius was having trouble getting them away to where they could not observe the terrace.

"I shink I'm going to sit in the park ooooover there," drawled Lucius rather loudly, so that Marius could hear him and take advantage of their giving their backs to the terrace for a few moments, as they walked towards the park.

"Come and sit with me. You can shee the house better from over there."

The two men from the Sanhedrin, seeing some benches in the park, followed Lucius at last. He held their attention by tripping and falling, making the men pick him up and help him to a bench. Once on it he pretended to fall asleep, and wait for Marius to come and get him later, if indeed he had escaped.

As for Marius? No sooner had he heard footsteps departing, than he crossed the terrace to the side away from the park and threw down the two bags. The money bag landed noiselessly on top of the one with the clothes. Lowering himself down he jumped the last remaining man-high distance, picked up the bags and hurried back to the ship.

The captain sent Jason to bring back Lucius. He briefed him as to his mate's drunken act so that he would continue the charade. In the meantime, he hid the money, and lay down to get some sleep, as he would be sailing at first light.

* * * * * *

Early morning saw Marius welcome sixteen passengers on board. He then pulled out of the harbour making for the rendezvous point where the rowboat carrying Simon and Hannah would meet with them. After a half an hour's wait, the rowboat came alongside on the starboard, away from prying eyes on shore, and delivered their precious cargo of father and daughter, who had the passenger cabin at their disposal. The *Stella Maris* took to the blue Mediterranean once more, with the familiar seaport of Apollonia as its destination.

CHAPTER TWENTY

UNCERTAINTIES

The arrival of the *Stella Maris* in Apollonia was behind schedule, having been delayed for over two days, due to bad weather which had caused damage to the upper supparum mast, and some of the rigging. There had been no loss of life, though a few of the passengers had sustained minor injuries and everyone's food supplies had run out two days before arrival.

Marius berthed the ship in the early morning, and once the hungry passengers had been dismissed, he made his way to where Simon and Hannah were standing, contemplating Cyrene with mixed feelings.

"I shall go and bring back some breakfast for us," said the captain with enthusiasm, as the discomfort in their stomachs could no longer be ignored.

"Since no one as yet knows we are here, I shall have someone run up to Simon's house and let them know that you have arrived and to come down in their cart to get you."

Marius made for the Registry Office.

"Where is that little fellow that hangs around here in the hope of running errands?" he asked the clerk who was at his usual place behind his desk.

"He is around here somewhere," replied the man, as he pulled out a bell from under the counter. He went to the door gave it a number of rings, turned around, and got back behind his desk again.

"You are Marius, of the *Stella Maris*, are you not?"

"Yes!"

"I shall enter your arrival. Any reports to give me?"

"Yes, I have some damage to my supparum mast and rigging, and some passengers with minor injuries only, thank goodness," as he secretly thought... 'Thank Yeshua.'

"You will be making insurance claims no doubt?"

"Yes!"

At this point the young messenger ran in eagerly.

"Who wants me?" he asked in a confident tone.

The captain explained to the little fellow his mission, and giving him half a denarius sent him on his way. Soon Marius reappeared on the ship with breakfast for all five as Jason and Lucius joined them.

Half an hour later Simon and Alexander arrived, with the cart drawn by their two horses. Although very elated, both were trying to unravel the cause of the surprise visit. The reception of father and daughter was bittersweet, as the circumstances became clear to our heroes. Though Alexander and Hannah were overjoyed to see each other, the horror of the reality which led to their losing their home and everything they owned, was engraved very deeply in their minds at present. Tears tears of joy mixed with tears of sorrows filled Hannah's eyes as the displaced pair sat in the cart; her father at the reigns, and Alexander and Simon walking alongside.

The welcoming committee was at the door as father and daughter arrived, and the usual bedlam prevailed for some time, before any one even thought of entering the house. Eventually, they all found their way into that large room where so many wonderful things were celebrated.

Hannah was received with great love and enthusiasm by the ladies of the house and she soon felt the warmth and sincerity of the family. The men formed another party around the new Simon, who had now gained control of his hair enough to make himself presentable, and enthralled them with many tales of Joppa.

Everyone was aghast at the rough treatment that the two refugees had received at the hands of Jechonias' people, and Simon the carpenter hugged his good friend warmly as he realised what horrible things could have happened to him, if that wonderful Marius had not been there at the time; for he was a marked man.

The captain joined them later for supper to a rousing welcome and much applause, for the way that he had carried out the rescue.

"I did what anyone would have done for a member of his family," said Marius as his eyes showed the love that he had for all these excellent people who filled his life and brought out the very best in him.

Simon and Hannah spent the next few days integrating into the Cyrenean family who accommodated them as best they could until some permanent solution could be found. Hannah shared Alexander's room with her father since there were two beds there, and a curtain was installed by Alexander which gave them both some privacy. He himself moved to David's house where he shared his friend's room.

* * * * * *

Marius who was due to sail to Caesarea after spending six days with the Simon family, sat having a final supper with them, and offered to take messages bound for Judea.

Alexander gave him a scroll for Cornelius, which the centurion was to pass on to one of the apostles when the opportunity presented itself. Hannah asked him to visit Sarah, telling her how warmly she and her father had been received by Alexander's family, and sending her love.

"You can fill Sarah in on our voyage and arrival, when you see her," said Hannah with a mischievous look, as with feminine intuition she suspected that something was in the air between the pair.

"What would this family do without you dear, Marius," she continued and getting up she went over and gave the gallant sailor a loving hug.

"This family," said the captain with some emotion in his voice, "is the only family I have, and I too thank Yeshua for that."

"What was that I heard?"

The voice of the big carpenter boomed across the room.

"I had no idea that Yeshua would be interested in taking an old sea dog under his wing."

Everyone laughed, as Marius answered with a twinkle in his eye.

"You would be surprised at what Yeshua can do."

The evening came to a happy end, as they all wished the well loved sailor a safe trip.

* * * * * *

Simon riding Topo, and the captain on Pepper, set out for the harbour, and the *Stella*.

"Here!" said Simon, " take this with you. Alexander carved it especially for you."

There in Marius' hand was a beautiful wall plaque of the *Stella Maris* battling its way through a tempestuous sea, with a hand hovering over it.

"It is the hand of Yeshua, that is protecting the *Stella*. He and I have both blessed it. May Yeshua sail with you, keep you safe, and bring you back to us soon."

After a final embrace, the friends parted, Simon riding back up the hill on Pepper, with Topo in tow.

* * * * * *

The augmented family of Simon got on very well together. Hannah became a very useful member of the household, and an able assistant to Alexander in his work. He was very busy with mural painting and decorating.

Through the auspices of Julia, the young priest/artist, had obtained some well paid commissions, which he was executing with enthusiasm and dexterity. Simon and David continued to work in the shop, temporarily assisted by 'Simon T'. (For so I shall describe our good friend the tanner from now on to avoid confusion.)

Simon T, seriously weighed the possibility of establishing his trade in Cyrene, and was taking steps towards that end. Through Marcus, who knew so many people, he had been introduced to another tanner who would consider taking a partner or selling the business altogether as he was beginning to age, and found the work too tiring.

After supper every day, Simon and Alexander went about the business of the church. On the first day of the week, they would have the new Sabbath service in their church with attendance growing at a very good pace, which was a thorn in the side of the local synagogue, who were constantly losing members. As a result, a certain antagonism was beginning to be felt between the Christians and the Jews of the town.

Both Simon and Alexander were out preaching in the garden near the synagogue at least twice during the week, usually late in the evening. It was the only way to win new souls, which could not be done from the church unless the people came of their own accord.

Among the news that Hannah and her father had brought, there was an astounding piece that was to absorb Simon and family, and indeed all the congregation of Christians in Cyrene. The extraordinary occurrence had taken place shortly after Simon had left Jerusalem for Joppa, but neither he or Alexander, had heard of it. Consequently, it came as a great surprise to every Christian in Cyrene.

Mary, the mother of Yeshua had disappeared. She had not been seen by any one of the apostles or disciples to date. The last they knew of her, was that John had taken her back to Galilee to his house, shortly after Pentecost, accompanied by a few disciples and the other women who were with her in Jerusalem. He had then returned to Jerusalem, as expected, to accompany Peter on a visit to Samaria.

Mary Magdalene had subsequently returned to Jerusalem with the disturbing news, that Mary, Yeshua's mother, had simply disappeared in the middle of the day, whilst she was alone picking flowers in the Zebedee's little garden at the back of the house. The basket she carried with her and her slippers were found there, but she was nowhere to be seen.

This extraordinary incident led to much speculation and investigation by the apostles who suspected the Sanhedrin of having abducted her. However, the suspicion was proved false following an investigation by both Nicodemus and Joseph of

Arimathea, who with their usual tact and thoroughness, did not leave a stone unturned.

"Could Yeshua have taken her to him alive?" suggested Simon, as he and Alexander were contemplating this mystery which Hannah had talked about.

The son looked at his father, his mind reaching back into the Torah.

"Was not Elijah taken up in a burning chariot?"

"Indeed," agreed Simon, "that opens up quite a possibility!"

As was often the case with both father and son, their minds shot back to Judea, and wondered what Peter and the apostles must be thinking in that regard.

"We shall know all, in God's own time," said Simon, looking up to heaven, arms out-stretched. "After all, she was the mother of God, and had suffered enough on this earth of ours."

"And to think that I actually met her, and she thanked me... Oh my!"

* * * * * *

Rufus had been back in Rome for over two months, maintaining a good working relationship with Erasmus who reconciled himself to the fact his young partner would never be his son-in-law. Such was not the case with Vibia, whose love for him had turned into hate. Being the spoilt creature that she was, she made her mother's life very unpleasant; constantly complaining and trying Gaia's endless patience, as she tried her best to pacify her daughter with little success.

As a result, Rufus had not been invited back to Erasmus' house, much to his regret. He was very fond of the family, but could not accept their daughter other than as a good friend.

He had now met Marcus' brother Claudius and family, and became great friends with Lavinia, who entertained him with her quick wit and gay mood. He had as yet not met Linus his would-be rival, whom as Letitia had told him was the object of Lavinia's love.

Marcus had been very impressed with Rufus' progress in the mercantile trade, and seeing how he had achieved so much in such a short time, had offered him a part in his business on marrying Letitia. He had recanted from his original condition that she wait till she was nineteen, and now left it to the young couple to set their own date for the wedding.

Rufus sat with Drucila one day, (as he still lived in her house, her son continuing to be conspicuous by his absence) discussing all these matters that were influencing his life and demanding decisions. She listened without interruption as usual till Rufus halted his audible musings.

"You have so many coins in your pouch that it is difficult for you to find the one you want," she said with a knowing grin on her face.

"If I take Marcus' offer, I shall have to stay in Cyrene, which is great, as my whole family and hers are all there. That seems like the obvious thing to do. On the other hand, I could marry her and bring her to Rome. Erasmus has been so good to me, that I owe him a debt of gratitude. He, too, is like family to me, and in time Vibia may perhaps come to treat me like a brother, and all would be well in that regard.

"I feel that what I have earned in Rome I have achieved by my own efforts, and that, always registers better with one's self-esteem than taking something that is handed to one on a platter. Besides, Marcus is still fairly young, whereas Erasmus is not, and he really does not need my help. He has an excellent man that manages his business beautifully. Letitia has her favourite cousin Lavinia here in Rome, together with her aunt and uncle where she would feel very much at home as she has already spent time with them."

Rufus stopped, and looked pleadingly at his wise friend.

"Ah! my dear boy."

The words came out slowly from Drucila's lips as she got up and squeezed his cheeks with both her hands.

"Drucila dare not help you. It is a hugely personal matter… Your whole life hangs on your decision."

So saying she ran off to the kitchen to get him his supper.

'She is absolutely right, and I shall have to make that decision soon, especially as Letitia also refuses to help me. It is, I'm afraid, a man's decision,' he told himself.

* * * * * *

Simon was having a very busy week; not only had he been out preaching, but he had been called out two nights in a row to pray over two parishioners who were very sick. One had actually died, being well advanced in age.

The funeral took place the following day, and both he and Alexander had officiated, as they were trying to come up with a standard burial service that would be totally Christian in liturgy. This and other visits to various homes to cool down some minor domestic crisis, had cut very sharply into their working days. The congregation had already proposed that Simon should leave his trade and dedicate himself totally to church affairs.

As each day passed it became more obvious to Simon that even with Alexander's help, he could not cope with his religious responsibilities on a part time basis.

The family was gathered together after supper on their new Sabbath....The first day of the week as per the Jewish calendar. The room was unusually quiet. All seemed to be absorbed in their own thoughts.. Ruth watched her husband, who sat in a corner of the room on his own looking quite preoccupied with something or other.

"What's pto happen?" queried a concerned Simon all of a sudden, addressing no one in particular, and jolting everyone out of their reveries. "I have been praying to Yeshua for a better solution, but it seems to be his divine will that no other is possible. I shall have to bow to the wishes of the people and dedicate myself fully to his work. The congregation promises to collect money for our needs, which at the moment are still many.

"We will make out," said Ruth, reacting quickly to what her husband had just said. "Yeshua shall see to that. Besides, Alexander is making very good money now, and David is well on his way with the carpentry, needing only your direction."

"If the business gets really busy," cut in Lucila now that David came into the picture, "we can always hire some help."

"Too bad I am not a man," commented Rachel. "I am the odd one out and have no special role to play."

"Yeshua has a special role for you too, my love," said Simon with a consoling smile. "I can feel it. You are altogether too good and beautiful to be overlooked by him."

* * * * * *

Alexander, standing on a scaffold, was painting a morning sky on the ceiling, which would finalise the mural in the breakfast room; the last of three rooms in that spectacular house which he had decorated. The owners, being great bird lovers, had asked him to include many birds in his mural, and the sky in that particular room served as background for a varied species of birds which the artist would profusely but skillfully portray to please his clients.

As he mechanically went about his work, his mind was absorbed with Hannah. She was assisting him by preparing his colours and other little chores that would save him time as he painted. Since Rufus had been given permission to marry Letitia any time they chose, it occurred to him that perhaps he could marry Hannah at the same time.

'Would that not be fantastic?'

'As well as fantastic, it would be most unusual. But then, why must we always be governed by old customs? The only thing that would keep that from happening, would be that both Rufus and Letitia were unbaptised, and Simon could not perform the Christian ceremony for them. Always problems,' he said to himself.

'I too, must talk to Hannah's father. Now that circumstances have changed, perhaps he will break with tradition, and allow the wedding without expecting the contract honoured. I must pray for that, and also for Rufus and Letitia's conversion.'

* * * * * *

Letitia was now impatiently awaiting Rufus' return from Rome so that the much awaited wedding could take place. She, too, wondered how they would be married. Her parents, as well as their whole household had adopted the new faith, as had Simon's. She fully believed that her father had been cured by the God of Simon... Yeshua. Much as she had asked Venus to cure her father, nothing had happened. Was she just in love with that beautifully carved statue in her pool simply as a piece of sculpture? When pitted against all the marvellous stories that Simon and Alexander had recounted as they sat in the atrium on so many evenings, her Venus really amounted to nothing.

'Simon said that if I prayed to Yeshua for the gift of faith in him, I would be given it. Perhaps I should do that now that I am convinced that Venus is nothing but a beautiful statue. Later, when I am alone in my room, in the quiet of the night, I shall pray to Yeshua.'

* * * * * *

Rufus had spent the night tossing and turning in his bed, trying to decide what to do about his life with Letitia. The morning sun's rays reaching his bed, were playing on his tired eyes, as if tormenting him, and forcing him to find a solution to his dilemma. He turned once again, and taking hold of his pillow, covered his face with it.

'This is the most difficult decision of my life. Who can help me?' he inquired of himself, with disgust at his own mental impotence.

Turning over yet again, he took the easiest way out of his situation... Procrastination.

'I don't have to solve this right now. I shall wait till I get back to Cyrene. Then I shall make my decision.'

The *Pretoria* was due in harbour at Ostia within the next three days. Rufus decided to take it, cabin and all, and sail back to Cyrene. He broke the news to Erasmus the following day, committing to nothing, but informing him of his purpose.

"As yet, I do not know what I shall be doing once I get married, but whichever course I take, please be sure that it will not hurt our business. You must trust me in this, my very good friend."

"I have no fear on that account," answered his partner with a confident look.

"I have heavy decisions to make," said Rufus, and giving Erasmus a loving hug they parted.

Silas, who had been waiting at Ostia for Rufus to set sail, stood at the port side railing wondering how much longer his friend and chief passenger was going to be. His cabin was all clean and ready for him now that he could well afford that luxury. The passengers, all fourteen of them, were on board and strolling around the deck watching the activity on the wharf.

Rufus, who had been delayed owing to his having stopped at Neta's to bring her up to date with his activities, finally arrived, baggage on shoulders and full of apologies for his good friend the captain.

"I was a little concerned about you as you are usually punctual, but happily now that you are here, we can set sail this very moment."

"Cast away!" shouted Silas as he quickly climbed up the ladder to the roof of his cabin and took charge of the helm, his two man crew making for the rigging.

The main sail opened like a beautiful red fan, catching the morning breeze, and away pulled the *Pretoria* on her way to Joppa via Cyrene.

The ship had been at sea for three days and nights, the weather was good and all on board seemed in good spirits. Rufus lying on his bed was looking at the moon out his cabin window, still trying to decide what to do after his marriage.

For some unknown reason, he began to think of Yeshua. His family was all wrapped up in this new God, and all were living a totally new life which he knew little about. Even Alexander, whom he had always looked up to since they were children had changed. He knew his older brother to be a level headed intelligent and gifted person given to much thought. He believed the miracle his father had performed by the power of this Yeshua, whom he had assisted in carrying his cross that day in Jerusalem.

'Why was he not feeling the same enthusiasm for this living God? Yahweh was a living God also, as he had proved so many times to the Jewish people through his prophets. The difference was that this Yeshua who claimed to be his son, had become human, and had worked all those miracles that his brother had related to him. He had lived among his people and evidently given his life for all men.

'He totally changed my father's life,' he said to himself. 'I must pray to him. Perhaps he can help me too, since no one, including myself, can.'

With these thoughts Rufus fell asleep, and dreamt. He felt himself floating around Rome, around the Colosseum, and then towards what looked like a tall needle-like structure made of stone with many engravings on it. There, not far from it, was an inverted cross with a grey haired man tied to it hanging upside down, and he inevitably drifted over to him.

He woke up with a start as the window shutter banged against the side of the cabin. The dream was gone.

'It was Rome for sure, and who may that man have been? It was all so clear, so very real.'

Even with his eyes upside down and no sound emerging from his mouth, Rufus could sense that he was asking for his help. He got up and walked around the deck, saying to himself that it was a nightmare.

"What are you doing on deck at this time of night?"

Rufus looked up to find Silas at the helm.

"A nightmare woke me up and now I cannot sleep."

"Go have a cup of wine and you will fall asleep again," advised the captain with sincerity.

"I shall just stay here with you for a while if you don't mind, it's such a lovely night."

Rufus made his way up the hill in the middle of the day, shouldering his baggage. The *Pretoria* had berthed briefly to let him off, rehire the cabin, and would soon be off again on the run to Joppa. He had no idea that Hannah and her father were in town and staying in his old room. On arriving at home he was taken aback. To his great surprise, it was she, whom he came across first as he opened the door and shouted.

"I'm home."

They were both staring at each other, when Ruth and the girls made the usual charge at him as he stepped into the room. By the time the welcome frenzy died down, Hannah, had become aware of who he was. She went over and gave him a hug.

"I am Hannah!" she said before Ruth had time to introduce her.

"Goodness me! What a surprise to find you here," he said and with a big smile returned her embrace.

He then complimented her on her good looks, and promised to love her like another sister, which greatly impressed her. Ruth quickly explained to him the reason for her coming, and he gave her another hug and said how sorry he was for her and her father, whom he was looking forward to meeting.

They all sat down to lunch, and Rufus brought them up to date on his visit to Rome. They then talked about the prospective wedding, and many other things. Simon arrived late,...shortly after lunch; having been delayed with some parochial business.

"Well! the prodigal son is back," boomed the father as he went over and embraced his son.

"Great to see you again, Father," said Rufus with a big smile.

"We've given away your old room to this beautiful creature here and her father," said Simon with a wink at Hannah. "You're going to have to stay at Marcus' place, and I am sure you're going to hate that.... By the way, where's your father?" he asked turning to Hannah; his eyes wandering around the room.

"He walked down to Apollonia to talk to a tanner that Marcus knows," she answered.

Shortly after, Rufus mounted old Topo, as Alexander had taken Pepper, and rode down the hill to Letitia's house where he was heartily welcomed. His future wife was overjoyed at learning that he was to stay with them until the wedding day.

"How is the family? Did you see Lavinia? Did you meet Linus?"

All these questions were thrown at him one after another by his espoused as she sat with Julia and Marcus in the atrium. The questions were duly answered, and the family became engrossed with other topics, including the impending wedding.

Later in the evening Simon arrived at Marcus' house as he often did, to discuss church affairs with him and Julia who was also involved in a charity program. Letitia and Rufus joined them as they were not nearly as well acquainted with the parables of Yeshua as the others. The priest finished the parable of the day from a list of headings that Hannah had written from the many parables that he knew; permitting him to choose whichever he desired each day of the week. He looked at Letitia, and with a paternal smile on his face, he asked.

"Have you decided on being baptised yet?"

Letitia looked first at Rufus, and then at Simon, and answered.

"Yes, I have."

"Good girl!"

"Now Rufus, has Yeshua reached you yet?"

"I don't know. I had a very vivid dream, or nightmare, during my voyage, and I do not know what to make of it. Perhaps Father, you can help me with its meaning."

"I shall try," assured Simon, slowly rubbing his hands as he waited for his son to start.

Rufus explained his dream in detail and awaited his father's interpretation.

"The fact that it involved a cross relates to Yeshua. However, an upside down cross with a grey haired man crucified upside down, that is quite baffling. No son, I am afraid that I cannot make sense of your dream."

"I have a strong feeling that it is a message with intent," surmised Rufus. "But what am I expected to do if anything at all? As far as receiving baptism, I would like a little more time. I believe all the things that you are all committed to, but I do not feel anything."

"I do not know that one has to actually feel anything. Though it is necessary that one believe, which is more a matter of acceptance than a feeling that may or may not be there," said Simon as he looked around, expecting concurrence.

"That is true," agreed Marcus, "I did not actually feel anything when I was cured. I merely accepted your father's explanation, as I was not conscious of what had happened until I was told. If you believe that Yeshua is the Son of Yahweh and the Messiah, then that is all you need; feeling does not come into it."

"Yes, from what you have told me, the miracles that he constantly performed and continues to perform and that he came to save everyone whether Gentile or Jew through love of mankind. And, recognizing that he rose from the dead, even ate with the apostles whom you met Father... I do believe all those things."

"Then that is all you need for baptism. Who knows? Later you may even get to feeling something. Yeshua may want you to do something for him yet, at some future time. Perhaps the dream is prophetic in some way or other. Only he knows," said Simon, as he got up to take his leave.

"I can only marry you if you are baptised and become Christians."

"Good night to you all! May Yeshua's blessings remain with you."

And away went Simon leaving the young ones to their thoughts.

CHAPTER TWENTY-ONE

WEDDINGS

The matter of his wedding greatly occupied Alexander's mind as he met with Hannah up in the terrace of the house. She stood there looking at the sea and thinking of her other renowned terrace far away. On seeing her lover her face lit up and going to him, kissed him.

"You are a little early today my love," she said, her look pleading an explanation.

"I am much troubled with regard to the two year contract that I made with your father for your hand," he replied with a look of grave concern. "I am hopeful that due to the change of circumstances, and the fact that we are now Christians and no longer subject to our traditional Judean law, he might choose to break with custom and allow us to marry at the same time as my brother and Letitia, as we all four have been dreaming."

She looked at him with hope in her eyes, and said.

"A woman is powerless in these matters, but I shall try to coax my father into dispensing with your commitment, as he, in any event, has no shop for you to slave in for me," a smile spreading her luscious lips, which she presented him for another kiss.

He was encouraged by her good humour, and promised himself to put the question to her father as soon as the opportunity presented itself. Hannah, with true feminine adroitness, proposed to strengthen her position prior to her requesting her father by recruiting all the women of the household to champion her cause.

One mild evening after supper, Alexander and Hannah with their own nuptial problem still unsolved, walked down the hill hand in hand shortly after their *tête-à-tête* on the terrace. Their topic of discussion was that which had the two families praying for Rufus' and Letitia's conversion. The impending weddings of both brothers at the same time, were in danger of becoming merely conjecture.

"It is so unfortunate that neither one of them were here at the time of Marcus' cure; it would have made all the difference as far as feeling Yeshua's love goes."

Hannah listened to her future husband's words as he made the statement, and agreed that the immediacy of the miracle would certainly have influenced the pair emotionally.

"I think you are right dear," said Hannah. "However, I feel that she is more ready to accept our Lord than he. The cure of her father struck closer to home in her case."

"I agree, and that makes my brother the stumbling block. I must try harder to win him for Yeshua. But, in the end, it is His divine grace that will be needed to solve the problem."

"He must also understand that being a Christian brings commitment and obedience to our new laws, as well as adhering to many of the old ones," pointed out Hannah as she slowed her pace and looked at her espoused.

Alexander came to a stop. Hand clasping his chin and looking down, he said with much concern.

"There is no marriage for them other than a Christian one. I have no doubt as to his fulfilling all the commitments. He is a very dedicated person once he undertakes something. The problem is in getting him to accept. However, if he does not accept our faith, he will be forced into a civil arrangement, as he cannot marry in the Jewish faith, she being a Gentile. What a horrible thought, living in sin and their little ones all lost to the Lord."

As they began their walk again, she pointed out that his father had said he would never accept Rufus into the faith unless he genuinely wanted to. This also brought up another rather nasty problem.

"This could create a big rift in both the families. I know my father would not recognise a civil arrangement. I have no idea how Marcus' family will react… And even us. I would not attend the wedding either," said Alexander with intense sadness in his heart which clearly reflected on his face, loving his brother as he did.

Hannah, at seeing his sorrow, embraced and kissed him, and they continued their walk in utter confusion, silence, and fervent prayer.

* * * * * *

Simon was going through great mental turmoil. He spent more time than usual in church where in the silence and solitude, he tried to get closer to his beloved Yeshua. He had resorted lately to keeping a few pieces of consecrated bread which had been left over from their last service and a small cup of similarly consecrated wine in a very pretty wooden box made of cedar wood, as was the Ark of the Covenant. It was fitted with a secret locking device, that he had made from Alexander's design and which sat on, and was secured to the altar, as he was now calling the table of celebration, following Simon T's news from Judea.

He knelt in front of the box and prayed.

"Yeshua, here I am kneeling in your presence, begging you to solve the huge problem facing our families. Give me the power to win Rufus and Letitia for you. I know you do things in your own time Lord, but this uncertainty is killing me. I shall try again tonight. Please be with me and guide my tongue to say the right things."

Having once more appealed to Yeshua for assistance, he walked out, bestowing a blessing as he passed on the volunteer who was keeping watch over the church at the time.

That evening Simon rode down to Marcus' house and leaving Pepper with Tecuno, he asked Rufus to take a walk with him.

"Son!" began Simon as he silently prayed once more for guidance.

"This reluctance of yours to accept Yeshua as the Son of God, is giving us all much concern. Our families are praying very hard for your conversion to our new faith as Christians. You are a Jew, and as such, you have always believed in a living God. Yeshua, is also a living God in as much as he is Yahweh's son. Once again, the world being so lost in sin, God's just anger was once again aroused, only this time he did not want to destroy the world. Instead, because of his love for the world, he sent down his son to be sacrificed and redeem us from our sins. I had the great honour of assisting his divine son, at the only time apart from his birth and childhood, when he required human help,...little as it was in my case. As I once told you, his look captivated my very soul and gave me this marvelous feeling of tranquility that I now experience when he wishes... On my own, I cannot experience it."

Rufus remained silent as his father talked, listening intently to every word, as he knew the importance of the walk that they were sharing. Simon continued as he looked at his son's attentive face, and explained something new to Rufus that he had only ever shared with Ruth, as you my faithful reader will recall.

"Take your mind back to the storm we went through on the *Stella*, the day you saved Marcus. The waves were coming at us from the bow and crashing into us as at the stern, with such great force, that they took our breath away in their relentlessness. Do you remember how quickly they stopped accosting us?"

Rufus looked at Simon for a few moments, and answered:

"Yes! I remember it well."

"It was Yeshua who calmed the storm, just as he had done on the Sea of Galilee once before, as you heard your uncle say when we were in Jerusalem. I had in my tunic, the parchment that I showed you, which had been nailed to the cross. Well, I put my hand over it, and yelled for Yeshua to calm the storm and save us all."

"I heard you scream something, but could not make it out," burst in Rufus, with sudden enthusiasm, triggering a prayer of thanks from Simon, who now felt that Yeshua had taken over.

"Do you remember how suddenly the waves stopped coming?"

"Yes! Yes! I do... They just sort of lost their strength very quickly, the sun burst through the clouds, and the sea became calm. Did Yeshua really do that?"

"Now do you believe?"

Rufus stopped. Simon stopped. The son embraced the father with great repentance as he realised what a terrible time he had given him with his incredulity. Simon's eyes were moist as he drew back and looked at his son. His heart filled with gratitude to the divine ruler of his life.

"Father," said Rufus with marked anxiety in his eyes. "Since this is a day of repentance for me, I shall confess something to you which has been troubling me greatly for almost two years."

"What is that, my son?"

"I have not kept the Sabbath, since I became a merchant and agreed to the terms of my employer, Erasmus. I accepted the commercial work hours of Rome and made the Dies Solis, the first day of our week, the day of rest. If I had turned down that position I would have been destitute, as I was down to my last farthing and my prospects as a carpenter were nonexistent at that time. Perhaps I should have trusted more in God, but I was alone and afraid."

Simon looked at the repentant face of his son and felt great compassion for him. However he could not excuse his breaking the law of God.

"Yes my son, you are indeed guilty of a grievous sin. Indeed many times over. Though you will now be a Christian, the Lord Yahweh is still our God, he being Yeshua's father,...so your sins remain. However, God be praised, the wondrous thing is that I by the grace of God and the authority of the apostles, am empowered to forgive sin in the name of the Father, the Son, and the Holy Spirit. Provided you are sorry, which obviously you are."

Rufus' eyes widened in surprise as he listened to his father's words, but now with hope in his heart. He remained silent and allowed Simon to continue.

"So, since you are truly repentant, once you are baptised, I shall absolve you from your sins. That is why Yeshua died, to atone for our sins. He became the sacrificial lamb as he offered up his life to his Father for our salvation. Seeing that as Christians we celebrate our new Sabbath on Dies Solis, it being the day of our Lord's resurrection, as well as the day of Pentecost, when the Holy Spirit came, you are no longer bound to the Jewish Sabbath."

"You can forgive sins?" exclaimed Rufus in wonder.

"Yes, it is my humble and awesome privilege,... your brother is also empowered."

Rufus hugged his father again, and turning together, they walked back to Marcus' house with solemn but joyful thoughts in their hearts.

The baptisms of Letitia and Rufus were celebrated in Marcus' house, with both families in attendance. Great was everyone's joy as they saw their way clear for the double wedding which they had all been praying for so fervently since Hannah's arrival.

One would be remiss not to mention the fact that Alexander had finally found the opportunity to approach his future father-in-law and to his great relief, had had him waive the contract. Simon T acceded with great joy, admitting that he himself had already decided to do so of his own accord, since this was a new life for him, and new measures were the thing of the day.

* * * * * *

Simon and Alexander were just putting their finishing touches to the wedding liturgy that had taken them weeks to formulate. Alexander had written everything down and the scroll was lying open on top of the altar as they both went through the prescribed motions of the brides, grooms, and others.

They had received no directive from any one, other than what Alexander had heard in Antioch which was very sketchy and inconclusive.. Father and son were ready to submit their format for their approval to any apostle, who happened to visit Cyrene.

John Mark had expressed a willingness to visit, and Simon was hopeful that he would come. Alexander and Hannah, had been doing a lot of scribing. They committed some parables to parchment so as to prevent future inaccuracies in the Gospels as parables and stories of Yeshua were now called. All these thoughts and practices would be submitted for John Mark's approval, if and when he came.

The day of the weddings finally arrived. All were dressed in their best. Both brides looked as beautiful as they could possibly be, while the grooms looked very handsome indeed.

The day had been set to coincide with the arrival of the *Stella Maris*, so that Rufus and Letitia, could sail off to Rome, and Marius could attend the wedding. The two couples would spend two days at an inn that a friend of Marcus owned by the beach about half an hour down the coast. On their return, Rufus and Letitia would leave for Rome, and Alexander and Hannah would move into a little house that they had rented down the hill from Simon's house with a view of the sea from their terrace. Simon T would remain in his room at Simon's house for the time being until the newlyweds had spent some time together and made preparations for his permanent accommodation with them.

The service, which had been designed by Simon and Alexander, began with some prayers of invocation to the Holy Spirit, and the welcoming of the brides and grooms; who were received at the entrance of the church, by the celebrant. He would then lead the two couples, and their attendants, in procession to the altar. This was followed by the exchange of marriage vows, and pronouncing of the union in the name of the Blessed Trinity. The relating of one of Yeshua's parables, 'The marriage feast at Cana,' was next, and finally, the receiving of the 'Body and Blood,' followed by a jubilant hymn being sung as the service came to an end.

As it was an ordinary day of the week, they had the church almost to themselves. Simon wore a plain white robe with a white waist band and had a small wooden cross on a piece of leather cord hanging on his breast, which he felt would mark his position as celebrant. He wore his usual sandals, and his head was bare.

It had been decided, following a rumour that Paul had advised it, that the men should have bare heads in church, and the women should wear pallas or veils on their heads, as the beauty of their hair would tend to distract the men from their prayers and concentration.

Being a small group, they all gathered close to the altar.. Lucila assisted Letitia, and Rachel helped Hannah. David, who had been recently baptised, was the keeper of the rings, handing them out to the four participants as Simon called for them.

The marriage vows were taken with love and deep sincerity, the husbands promising to love and cherish their wives; the wives promising to love and obey their husbands; 'all until death do them part.' Simon choked a little on his words now and then, as this was a particularly emotional occasion for him. Ruth and Julia could not keep their eyes dry. Marcus thanked God that he was there to witness and enjoy the happy day. Simon T, with his hair much shorter, now well under control, and feeling as proud as a peacock, pressed Marius' arm meaningfully as he stood beside him; knowing that without his help and Yeshua's, he would not be there now admiring his beautiful daughter. Damian, Zaphira and Silia were thrilled to be in attendance. Marius felt very proud to be there but also felt very left out when the others partook of the consecrated bread and wine. Simon slowly shaking his head and smiling kindly at him, heartily regretted that he could not include his beloved friend in the reception of the sacrament.

It was a joyous group that climbed on the colourfully decorated carts, bound for the reception banquet which was to take place in Marcus' house. Tecuno, much to his disappointment, had been left behind to direct and supervise the caterers in their preparations. Other guests who had been invited to the banquet were waiting in the garden for their arrival; not being Christians, they had not attended the church service.

The group arrived to a rousing welcome. The brides and grooms were made much of by all their friends, The festivities lasted till well after the honoured foursome had left for the inn by the beach.

Marcus was quite distressed at the thought of losing his daughter again so soon, but because he understood Rufus' position, as it related to his well earned efforts in Erasmus' business, he reconciled himself to his new son-in-law's decision. Perhaps also, on reconsidering, the fact that he acted in similar fashion in his youth made his decision easier.

The wharf at, Apollonia was once again the scene of animated farewells, as both families were in attendance to see the newly-weds off.

"Your father and I will visit you in the summer," promised Julia as she kissed Letitia for the last time before she boarded ship.

"We shall be looking forward to that," said Rufus, as he, too, got a hug and a kiss from Julia, who had changed much since she became a Christian.

Rufus had some special words for his mother which made her cry once again, but they were tears of hope. Rachel and Lucila were sad at losing their brother. Both thought a Roman holiday far in the future for them, possibly never, and wondered whether he would ever return to Cyrene.

"All aboard!" sang Marius, with his deep bass voice bringing an end to the farewells.

The newlyweds stayed on deck waving to their loved ones on shore. The morning wind caught the *Stella's* sails, and in that wind, coming from the direction of the helm, another strong bass voice could be heard.

"We are a honeymoon ship! …la, la, la… We are a honeymoon ship!" sang Lucius as he steered for the open sea.

* * * * * *

Hannah was busily tidying up the living room in her little house, and thinking how messy men were. Alexander left things lying about just like her father did. Now she had two to clean after. But she was happy, as her father who had now moved in with them seemed content enough with his new life as he called it, as he waited and hoped for a shop of his own again soon. He was now working with the tanner that Marcus had put him on to, and he waited to see if he would be allowed to purchase the business outright.

It was two months since their wedding, and Hannah loved her new role as a wife. The family was just a short walk up the hill, and she had a visitor from there almost every day. Some days however, she would accompany Alexander to grind and mix his colours which she enjoyed doing. She was happiest when she was near him. He was working on a new project which would bring in a good bit of money, allowing them to buy a few pieces of much needed furniture.

A light knock at the door announced Rachel, who had her own particular way of knocking. Hannah greeted her with a hug at the door.

"How is everyone up the road today?" she asked.

"All are well thank you. I wondered whether you had accompanied Alexander this morning, but I see you are busy with your house work," said Rachel, spotting a broom lying on the floor and the cushions stacked in one corner of the room.

"Come let's sit and have a nice cup of mint tea. I have a lot of mint in my garden back there; it grows like a weed," said Hannah.

"Yes, it grows very quickly, and I love the smell of it," smiled Rachel.

As the women sat and chatted for a while, the inevitable subject of men crept into the conversation, and Hannah remarked:

"You have never mentioned having any boy friend. A girl with your looks must be accosted by boys all the time. But you are so quiet, just like Alexander, you have never said anything about them."

"No! I do not have any. I do not go out much, and I have not met any man that I would like to marry as yet."

"There will be more opportunity now that we are all Christians. You will be able to meet more men whether they are Jew before or Gentile. I think Julia is organizing groups of young people to help with some of the church work, so you will get to know more men of your age."

"Yes, I suppose you are right," replied Rachel taking a sip of her tea. "It will be fun working on things for the church. There will be flowers to arrange, cleaning has to be done, also learning of hymns,...and singing them. I will play my lyre and sing with Lucila, and you must play your harp and sing with us. Mother sings very well too."

They sipped their tea and enjoyed each other's company for a while, then Rachel left and Hannah resumed her chores, contentedly chanting to herself.

* * * * * *

It was now summer, the church had continued to grow during the winter months and Simon ever busy looking after his flock, wondered if anyone from Judea would ever come to visit. He had received a couple of scrolls from Cornelius, giving him some news of the progress of the church in Caesarea, and of Paul's travels, but no specifics with regard to liturgy and other things that he was interested in having confirmed.

The *Stella Maris* was in port once again, and he wondered whether the captain had brought him news from Judea. He saddled up Topo and rode down to the harbour to meet his dear friend.

"No! said Marius, "I have no scrolls for you this time, but a man by the name of John Mark has come to see you, and left about a quarter of an hour ago. I gave him directions to your house. Did you not pass him on the way?"

"I may have, I was so wrapped up in thought… I must hurry back and catch up with him. See you tonight?"

"Yes, but I must get back early, as I start unloading for Marcus tomorrow morning and Damian is always so punctual,"explained the captain.

Simon coaxed Topo into a trot which was as fast as the old horse would ever go. The trot soon became a walk as the hill began to take its toll on the poor animal.

'I'm am going to have to put this old thing out to pasture, for good,' thought Simon, as he rode impatiently with half a mind to get off and walk Topo back.

He was just about to alight, when he drew up beside a man who was making his way up the hill with a large bag on his shoulder. As the man turned, hearing the sound of the horse's hooves, Simon recognised the face of John Mark, and dismounting, he heartily embraced his old friend, who was equally glad to see him.

"Give me that bag," said Simon taking the heavy bag and putting it on Topo's saddle.

"There, that's better. Yes?"

"Thank you, it's the hill that makes it seem heavier than it is."

"It's wonderful to see you again. I've been praying for the Lord to send you. There's much I wish to show you and hope for your approval since I have had such little guidance."

"It will give me much pleasure to help you any way I can. Peter, James and the other apostles all send you their love."

"I often think and pray for you all."

"Here we are," said Simon as he got the bag down from Topo's saddle and took the horse to his stable, followed by John Mark.

"My sons used to take care of the horses, but now I'm left with this old fellow, and I have to look after him myself. We can talk whilst I rub him down and feed him, then we shall have a good lunch, and Ruth, my wife, will see that you're well looked after whilst you're here with us."

The two friends talked until Simon had finished his chore, and leaving Topo comfortably in his stable, they went into the house. Simon introduced John Mark to the family who were much impressed and warmly welcomed the long-awaited visitor.

After lunch, Simon took his guest to see the church.

"The Lord be praised," exploded John Mark on entering the church. He looked around in awe. "This is wonderful, just beautiful. Those murals depicting the parables of our beloved Yeshua; they are so alive, it fills the church with colour. I can feel the holiness of the place."

"My son Alexander whom you have met, is an artist, as well as a priest. He painted all of these things," said Simon with unavoidable pride in his son.

"And what is this?" asked the visitor, as he approached the altar, and touched the box.

Simon went over, and genuflected in front of the box, got up and explained what it contained, whereupon John Mark fell on his knees and bowed. As the pair backed away from the altar, the visitor congratulated Simon on his idea of the sacred contents of the box.

"But what if someone steals it or opens it?" asked John Mark, with a concerned look.

"Little chance of that, as it is secured to the altar and has a hidden locking device which I challenge anyone to open. Also, that man over there is member of the congregation," said Simon, pointing to the man on watch. "They take it in turn to watch the church."

"Really?"

"Yes! The Jewish community accuses us of stealing their members, and could get nasty as they did in Jerusalem when I was there. Remember? Tomorrow, we shall have the weekly service since it is Dies Solis, which being the day of our Saviour's Resurrection, is our Sabbath day. I believe you're all in agreement with that, or so I have been given to understand."

"Yes, that has now been agreed upon. I am eagerly looking forward to tomorrow so that I can witness your service."

"I won't tell you anything about it, unless you wish otherwise, until you have attended. There are other services also which we have had to come up with such as weddings, burials, and prayers at death beds. We have much to talk about."

"Indeed, my friend. Tell me, how many people attend your service here?"

"The last count was three hundred and twenty."

"That is quite a sizeable congregation. They must keep you very busy."

"I had to abandon my trade. The congregation insisted that I dedicate myself to looking after their spiritual welfare exclusively. Now they look after my needs and those of my family, though my sons contribute also."

"Excellent!" Remarked John Mark, walking around once more admiring the murals.

The following morning the visitor from Judea accompanied the whole of Simon's family to church, including Alexander, whom he had met in Antioch. John Mark did not officiate as he did not know the service. He was astounded at the way that Simon and his son had designed the liturgy and was particularly impressed at the reverential manner that the bread and wine in their consecrated state were distributed and consumed by the congregation.

When the service was over he embraced Simon and Alexander and congratulated them on their beautiful and well organized service.

"They will be most impressed as I have been, when I relate all of this to Peter and the apostles. They may well adopt much of your service as there are no two services that are exactly the same as yet."

Simon was very happy, as was his talented son, at the compliments that John Mark had paid their work. Happier still, when John Mark showed his surprise and endorsement of all the parchments that Alexander and Hannah had written of the parables and also liturgy with regard to burials, and tentatively marriages.

In short, John Mark's much awaited visit, dispelled all the doubts that Simon and Alexander had had regarding the liturgy and celebration of their faith in general. During the weeks that followed, John Mark and Simon toured the area around Cyrene preaching and baptising, and got to know one another very well.

Alexander stayed behind to look after the church, as he was engaged on his latest mural commission, and also had to direct David in the wood shop.

"I shall go back to Alexandria from here," announced John Mark, having returned from their evangelical tour, and discussed with Simon as how best to proceed.

It was a journey of around five hundred miles, and he wondered whether it would be better to proceed by sea.

"The sea trip will get you there quicker," suggested Simon, "but if you want to preach along the way and time matters not, then the land route is obviously the better way. However, the route will be very barren and the villages far apart. Dangerous for someone travelling alone."

"I shall pray on that; I still have three days before the ship sails."

As he talked, John Mark suoerficially browsed through the scrolls that Alexander and Hannah had written.

"Soon, I shall be dedicating my life to this," he said, holding up a scroll, firmly pouting his thick red lips, and looking up at Simon. "Alexander has covered some of Yeshua's parables, but I shall write about his whole life, and as many parables and miracles as I can learn of from the apostles. I pray that the Holy Spirit who has been prompting me, continue to enlighten me, and guide my hand."

"When it comes to his journey to Calvary, I shall get Alexander to write it out, and I shall send it to you care of Cornelius in Caesarea," promised Simon. "He will get it to you somehow."

John Mark was much younger than Simon, perhaps only five years older than Alexander, but already his hair had almost gone completely white, which gave his sallow thin face a look of maturity though there was not a wrinkle on it.

"You still have many years in which to accomplish that, God willing," remarked Simon.

At this point, Ruth came into the room announcing supper, as she smiled happily at the men, glad to have them back safely from their tour.

"Alexander, Hannah, and her father will be here shortly," called out Rachel who had just arrived, and was taking off her palla and hanging it up by the door.

"That will be nice," remarked John Mark. "Poor people. Imagine having their house and belongings confiscated and then imprisoned. He is badly missed in Joppa, his house being the magnet for all the disciples who happened to be passing along the coastal route."

"A big loss for many in that town," remarked Simon. "That celebrated terrace is just sitting there abandoned and waiting to be desecrated, who knows. In that adventure I have been the winner since I have them here with me, and in the family. God be praised for that," he concluded, and kissed Rachel who had come over to greet him.

One more satisfying day was coming to an end in the lives of those gathered for supper that night, as David and Lucila, followed by Hannah, Alexander and Simon T, made their appearances. They were followed closely by Marcus and Julia, both of whom had greatly impressed John Mark, with their sincerity and generosity towards the development of the church in Cyrene. Supper got under way, with much talk and animation.

The 'Breaking of the Bread', was performed by John Mark, as supper came to a glorious conclusion, much to the delight of all.

A beautiful hymn that Hannah and Rachel had secretly composed and rehearsed along with Lucila and Ruth, was sung in honour of their guest.

Resounding applause followed as the hymn ended, which pleased the women greatly. John Mark was so touched by the excellence of the performance in his honour, that getting up he looked into their happy faces and said:

"I was aware that the men in this family had been blessed with great gifts from God, but now I find that the women, having already received the gift of beauty, have also been blest with such musical talent; indeed I have never witnessed a better performance. Thank you so much, I shall always treasure the memory of this wonderful evening."

The following day, which would be the final day of John Mark's stay in Cyrene, was the Christian Sabbath day… Dies Solis. Both families attended the service which was usually celebrated in the morning at the fourth hour. Marcus, Julia, Zaphira, and Damian, greeted the Simon family as they entered the church, which was resplendent with the morning sun pouring in through the windows. The altar, surrounded by colourful flowers and accentuated by the lighted lamps which rested on it, imparted an aura of spiritual significance, as if confirming the Divine Presence that reposed in that beautiful now 'gold gilt' wooden box at its centre.

Once again the apostolic representative sat by the altar but did not assist in the celebration which was performed by Simon, with Alexander assisting. A hymn was sung by Hannah, Rachel, and Lucila in concert, as they accompanied themselves on their instruments.

Some introductory prayers were said by Simon, and then stepping to one side of the altar, he stood, and recounted a parable from Yeshua's life. This he followed with a quarter of an hour of preaching. This particular week, he chose to explain the necessity of keeping the new Christian Sabbath day, with the same sense of commitment that some of them who had been Jews, had celebrated their Sabbath in keeping with the Commandments given to Moses.

"The day of rest from servile works," he told the congregation, "has to be upheld. "However," he continued, raising his hands as if to convey his message with greater significance, "the attendance at the Sabbath service is paramount, and on no account other than that of sickness or other unavoidable reason such as travel, can it be excused."

The next stage of the service was the consecration of the bread and wine, and the distribution thereof to John Mark and the congregation, following the procedure that you, my good and patient reader, have been made aware of, thus ending the 'Breaking of the Bread' part of the service.

Simon was about to start on some final prayers, when suddenly, John Mark who had been following the service with great attention, got up, and going to the altar stood beside Simon, who looked at him in wonderment, not knowing the reason for the interruption.

"My dear brothers and sisters in Yeshua the Anointed One, or Iesu Christi as he is known in the Latin," began John Mark addressing the congregation. "I am an emissary of the apostles in Judea, and today I shall be performing a service of a different kind to what we have just witnessed."

"Simon, please kneel." Simon, completely baffled, did as he was bid.

"Simon of Cyrene," called out John Mark, looking up to heaven, hands stretched out together over Simon's head. "By the power vested in me by the apostles in the Blessed Name of Yeshua, I consecrate you Bishop of Cyrene. In the name of the Father, the Son, and the Holy Spirit."

Taking some oil that he carried in a tiny crucible, he anointed Simon's forehead making a cross, again repeating the same words.

Simon was petrified. He could not believe his ears, but suddenly the tranquil feeling came over him once more, the nervousness disappeared and was replaced by tears of joy and thanksgiving as he realised the great privilege that the apostles had accorded him through John Mark.

It was a while before Simon managed to leave the church as every single member of the congregation went to congratulate him.

"When eventually I get back to Judea," said the emissary. "I shall have a proper parchment written confirming the appointment, and sanctioned by one or more of the apostles. However, you can take it for certain that you are empowered just as I was by them."

"I am at a loss for words," admitted an emotional Simon as they finally reached his house.

John Mark left by sea the following day, promising to stay in touch through Cornelius, with Marius acting as the courier.

* * * * * *

For the following two years the church in Cyrene, continued to grow. Alexander preached in the upper town. There he could reach many more people. Most of his commissions had come from upper Cyrene, and as a result he had met a good number of influential people who could and would support another church there when the need arose. Both father and son preached in the more distanced villages when they found an opportunity, these things all contributing to the growth of the church.

The latest news was that Rufus and Letitia were now parents to a lovely baby girl, and the grandparents on both sides of the family wondered how and when they could get to Rome to see her. Alexander and Hannah's baby boy, had arrived only six months earlier, and was now the pet of both Simons' families. Lucilla had been espoused to David for over a year, with the wedding coming up within the next month or so. As a consequence, Ruth had to refuse an invitation from Julia to go to Rome to see the new baby, much to her disappointment. It was then decided that Zaphira would accompany her instead, and remain there to serve Letitia... Marcus having done with the sea for the time being; if not for good.

"Don't be sad. Rufus will bring her for you to see you just as soon as she is old enough to travel," whispered Simon to Ruth as they lay talking in bed one night.

"I hope The Lord will permit me to see her," she sighed, as she closed her tired eyes and fell asleep.

David was now experienced enough that Simon could rest easy that the business would continue to thrive. A number of corbitas had been outfitted with the cabin, with the assistance of a hired young carpenter, and there had been a good number of other projects completed, with more coming in.

Lucila grew more and more excited as her wedding day drew nearer, and the whole family was involved in making it a memorable occasion for her and her espoused.

Rachel, as yet, had not settled on any one man, even though she was greatly admired and popular among the young people of the church, and had broken a few well meaning and sincere hearts in the bargain. She was dedicated to the needs of the church and very active in the work of the congregation, including the singing of the hymns at the services.

Finally, the day of Lucila's wedding arrived. Julia was in Rome, but Marcus attended. Again, it had been arranged so that Marius would be in port and could attend. He had just come back from Rome after leaving Julia and Zaphira, and he had seen the baby, whom he described in great detail for Ruth and Simon's benefits.

The service, which once again took place in the middle of the week, was carried out by Simon, now the first Bishop of Cyrene with Alexander assisting. David was a Christian, but his family were still Jewish. They attended nonetheless, and Simon tried his best to make them feel at ease. The reception was held at Simon's house which had undergone some changes, and now looked quite inviting. The terrace was also placed at the disposal of the guests, who whilst enjoying the view, sang and danced in the light of many lamps on a balmy summer's evening after all the eating had been done.

Simon and Ruth spent most of the time with their in-laws trying to make them feel at home. Tobias and Esther were their closest friends; a friendship that went back to their children's childhood as they had always been near neighbours.

Finally, the festivities came to an end. The newlyweds having departed on their honeymoon earlier in the day for the same inn that Alexander and Rufus had stayed at two years earlier.

Tobias pulled Simon aside, as he and his wife were leaving.

"Simon, keep a good watch on your church I have heard rumblings and mischief might be afoot. I have tried to dissuade them, but I don't know if I have succeeded. Keep it to yourselves."

"Thank you Tobias, my good friend," said Simon, "I'll see to it right away."

Simon called Alexander over and gave him the grim news.

"I shall go right away and get a couple of sturdy men from the congregation to go and keep watch with me tonight. I shall be there to open the altar box and consume the sacred contents if it is threatened in any way by vandalism."

"Be careful," advised Simon, as his son went to the stable to harness Pepper.

Simon was much perturbed. He had a feeling that the Jews would try some act of vandalism; if not that night, then at some future time. He would have to organize a watch for day and night, if that were possible. He could not go to the authorities because nothing had happened yet, but Tobias had been very sure, and he was not a man given to idle talk.

Alexander managed to find two volunteers who would spend the night at the church with him. It was not easy to get volunteers as most of the younger people had to work during the day and at night they could only contribute a couple of hours, and not too late at that.

Having arrived at the church, the three men, along with the man already there, went in and locked the two doors. They sat down and waited for events to unfold. They had been conversing together for a while wondering whether their precautions had been unnecessary, when they heard loud voices outside followed by the sound of a horse galloping away.

'O dear! That's Pepper,' thought Alexander. 'They have probably whipped him and sent him scurrying off. I should have dropped him off at the house as we passed.'

"We know that there are some of you in there!" came an angry voice from outside.

"You better come out now, or we will burn you up along with your filthy church."

The three men looked at Alexander, their eyes enquiring what to do next.

"I am going to speak to them," said Alexander.

"No! Don't go out, they will burn the place down."

"I don't think they will torch it knowing that we are in here. They are angry people, but I do not think they are murderers," said the other.

"Who is out there?" yelled Alexander. "Is that you Moshe?" Suspecting the trouble maker, who with regularity stirred up the Jewish community against the Christians.

"Yea," came the answer.

"We are not coming out. You will have to burn us too. We have done you no harm. We share the same God. We would not harm the synagogue. Why do you want to destroy our church?" yelled again Alexander.

"You are poisoning our people, telling them that Yahweh has a son. The Torah does not support that."

"That is debatable... But this is all so silly. Surely every man has a right to worship as he sees fit. Why are you so angry because some people accept a different kind of Messiah than you do? There is no reason why our God cannot have a Son."

A shower of stones made themselves heard as they crashed against the side of the wooden church, a few coming in through one of the open windows high on the wall. One of the men found a ladder and quickly moved to close the window shutters as another shower of stones crashed against the wall once more, barely missing his head as he closed them.

Silence prevailed for a few minutes, and then something crashed into the door resounding through the building. The door held, as the iron bars behind it reinforced the heavy wooden panels from which it was made. A second blow was struck and this time the door gave way a little, but still held.

"Let's wedge it with some wood planks if we can find any," said Alexander with urgency.

The four dispersed as they searched for some suitable pieces of wood.

"Here are a couple," said Alexander, as he hastened to fit one under the door to serve as a wedge, and the other he propped up against the door as a strut.

BANG! A third strike on the door was delivered, but thanks to the effect of the planks, it took the blow once more without damage.

"Will you stop this nonsense, and go home to your wives?" shouted Alexander.

"Not till we do what we came to do," was the reply.

Simon was most uneasy. Pepper had come home and was neighing as he went into the stable by himself.

'Alexander is in trouble, and I need help Lord. I have no option but to assume there is trouble at the church. I better get to the authorities in a hurry.'

He got Pepper out of the stable, and telling Ruth to keep all doors locked, he galloped off down to the Roman military barracks in Apollonia.

"There is trouble at my church up the hill, and I need your help please," he blurted out to the sergeant on duty.

"Octavius!" shouted the sergeant. "Saddle up six horses, and find five soldiers to ride with me right away."

The five men presently showed up, one of them protesting.

"Something always happens when I am winning."

Moments later, the riders were on their way up the hill to the church. On approaching, Simon could see a few torches. As they got closer, he beheld six men running with a log and crashing it into the door like a battering ram.

The soldiers quickly dismounted swords in hand.

"What's going on here?" shouted the sergeant.

"This has nothing to do with you," said one of the men holding the log.

"Oh really? And who told you that?" asked the sergeant.

"This church is attended by many Roman citizens who are not Jews, so it *is* your responsibility," said Simon addressing the sergeant in a low voice.

"Who speaks for these people?"

"I do!" came the bold, unrepentant voice of Moshe.

"Take him!" ordered the sergeant. "If you are not all out of here before I count to twenty, I shall take you all in."

They all dispersed, leaving their ring leader in the hands of the soldiers.

"Let him go. We are not going to press charges," said Simon to the soldier, making sure that Moshe heard him.

The sergeant, looked at Simon with an enquiring look, and turning to Moshe, said.

"You can thank this man for getting you off, but if you give him any more trouble in the future, we know you now and it will probably be the galleys then."

As Moshe walked away, Simon shouted to Alexander to come out. He thanked the soldiers for their help, and the sergeant some money for their trouble. The patrol rode away, leaving Simon, Alexander and the men all to themselves.

The bishop looked at the besieged men with relief in his eyes.

"That will keep them off our backs for good I hope," he said with a sigh of relief.

"That Pepper is an incredibly intelligent horse," continued Simon, "you have him to thank for coming home without you, which told me very clearly that you were in trouble. You go home to Hannah. I am staying here tonight. Tell your mother as you go by the house, or she will worry all night."

The bishop then thanked the men who had assisted Alexander, and sent them home. He then entered the church, locked the door, and made himself as comfortable as he could for the night.

* * * * * *

It was the second day of the week. Rachel was tidying up in the church, Alexander had just gone, and soon the man on watch would be arriving... Then she would leave. A strange noise, as of air rushing around like a wind seemed to come from the vicinity of the altar, specifically from the Holy box.

Reaching it, she knelt down in front of it to listen further.

"My daughter," said a manly voice very softly and lovingly, "I desire that you dedicate your life to Me."

Rachel was stunned. She felt as if in a dream. The voice had come from the box, of that, she was certain. The Lord had spoken to her. He wanted her to live for him alone. No wonder she could not take men seriously; it was he who had planned her life for her.

"I shall do your bidding Lord," she whispered, and getting up just as the watchman appeared, made for home with a heart brimming with joy.

"I have something wonderful to tell you all," she cried as she rushed into the house.

This was so unusual an entrance for Rachel, that Ruth and Lucila followed closely by Simon, came out of the kitchen where they had been chatting, and gathered around in wonderment.

"Tell us! Tell us!" repeated Lucila with great excitement in her voice.

"The Lord has spoken to me!"

"And?" blurted out Lucila again impatiently.

"He has asked me to dedicate my life to him."

Utter silence reigned. No one dare ask what that meant, though it was awesome in every sense and even Simon was dumbfounded.

"Are you sure my dear?" asked the bishop tentatively, recovering his composure.

"Yes Father...I know it is hard to believe, but I heard a rustling noise, as if it were a gust of wind. It came from the Holy box. I approached it, knelt down in front of it, and then the voice of a man spoke."

"My daughter, I desire you to dedicate your life to Me," she repeated.

Simon embraced his daughter and said:

"It is the Lord... What a wonderful privilege. Did I not tell you that he had something special planned for you?"

The women suddenly jumped out of their stupor and embraced Rachel lovingly, but deep in their hearts there was disappointment as they had both hoped for a happy married life for the most beautiful one of the family. But then, Ruth thought.

'God gave her her beauty, does he not have the right to claim her for himself? especially when she is such a noble soul.'

Lucila brooded all night long.

'It will be a lonely life for my sister, as she will never marry and have children. Oh! such beautiful children she would have had. Why could not God have given her a happy married life?'

It is difficult for many people to see things in their supernatural context. Their evaluation of things are assessed with reference to what they consider an actual, palpable realism, not being able to project their thinking beyond the restrictions of their human nature which confines their thoughts to that realism. That elusive phantom, the metaphysical, defying logical understanding, inhabits the precincts of the infinite, the antithesis of finite thought, which is governed only by the palpability of the five senses.

Lucila was worldly in every sense of the word. Though she had accepted Yeshua, and all he stood for. She had however, without realising it, accepted her new religion more as a crutch; something that would come in useful when life became difficult or unpleasant. She shunned the idea of having anything interfere with what she would call the joy of life. Joy, in the sense that life would fulfill one's desires, devoid of any unpleasantness which could not be quickly remedied.

Rachel in turn lay in bed thinking over the extraordinary happenings of that day; thrilled at having been addressed by Yeshua, whom she truly adored and had been getting closer to as the days passed. She felt uniquely privileged and humble. Her concern now was, how was she to serve him. She knew that marriage was not to be considered, but that posed no problem for her.

'But how else can I be of service to Yeshua? I shall begin a daily ritual of prayer to Him, asking him to show me the way. If he has gone to the trouble of choosing me, then I am sure he is going to direct me. But I must show him that I am yearning to serve him. My goodness, the Son of God chose to talk to me… He himself… I still cannot understand it… Oh my!'

Her head was giddy with excitement of the soul. Not that, unrestrained, physical, effervescent type of excitement, but a deep joyous sense of expectation which promises fulfillment.

'Tomorrow morning, I shall have a heart to heart talk with my father, who may perhaps be the one through whom Yeshua will instruct me,' she promised herself.

Sleep covered her like a mantle gently falling over her…

'Yes! it was all true.'

Rachel's talk with her father was still in abeyance, as he was called away early the following morning to perform a service for a sick member of the congregation who was on the point of death. She then decided to visit Hannah and Alexander who as yet had heard nothing of her extraordinary encounter with Yeshua. After breakfast, she made her way down the hill to Alexander's house, arriving just as the pair were saying their goodbyes in the doorway.

"Good morning to you both," greeted Rachel, as she embraced her brother and sister-in-law.

"What are you doing here so early?" asked Alexander, perceiving at the same time that his sister's visit must herald something important, or she would have called later in the morning as was her custom.

"I have something truly wonderful to tell you," cried Rachel with uncharacteristic bubbling enthusiasm. All three rushed back into the house, where with great joy, she related her experience with Yeshua.

Both brother and wife were dumbfounded on hearing the story, but were quick to rejoice, as she stood there with grateful tears in her eyes, and humility in her heart.

"How, am I going to serve him?" she asked, her voice breaking.

Hannah was the first to speak.

"Little wonder, my dear sister that you felt no interest in men. Now I understand why. Our Lord had you all singled out for himself."

Alexander, deep in thought, pressed his sister to him and said as he met her beautiful eyes:

"You obviously have been destined not to marry, but to serve him as you are already doing. In his own good time, he will guide you. You will instinctively know what his wishes are by the very pattern of your holy life. Prayer will be the most important way for you to serve him at the moment. His infant church needs prayers from humble hearts like yours."

Rachel's eyes bonded with those of her brother as he spoke. She had always respected and admired him for his quiet wisdom. He continued, as he looked into her beautiful and eager green eyes.

"Doing works of charity and giving your life selflessly for his sake would be yet another way, as well as continuing with what you are already doing. He wants you by your example of his ways and your prayers, to win souls for him."

"I was going to ask father," said Rachel getting up on tiptoes and kissing her brothers cheek fondly, "but you have answered my question so beautifully that now I know the way. Thank you my dear brother, and may the Lord continue to bless all in this house."

Alexander went off to his work, and both women made for the baby's room to fuss over little Simon who was loudly summoning their presence.

CHAPTER TWENTY-TWO

FOR THY GREATER GLORY

Young Simon ran into his grandmother's kitchen with great excitement to see if he could coax her into telling him what present grandfather was going to give him for his coming tenth birthday. Ruth smiled and gave her grandson a hug.

"If I tell you, it will spoil your surprise."

"Mother won't tell me either, and I have to wait another five days for it," said Hannah's boy with an impatient sigh. Running his fingers through his mop of dark brown curly hair he eyed with longing, the cakes that Ruth had taken out of the oven and placed on the window sill to cool.

"Is your mother bringing your brother and sister later?" asked Ruth, as Lucila joined them in the kitchen followed by her little six year old daughter, who had her pretty eyes on the cakes as well.

"I am going down to see Hannah as soon as the cakes cool," said Lucila, "I am sure that Barth and Judy will want one too." She threw a mischievous look at little Simon who enjoyed tantalising his excitable aunt. "And I shall take this little rascall with me too."

Simon's family had grown considerably over the last ten years, as had his Christian community in lower Cyrene. So much so, that another Church had recently been built in upper Cyrene itself, with Alexander as pastor. He had become well known as an artist there and had also won many people for the Lord.

He and Hanna had three children, two boys and a girl, and would soon be moving to the upper town. They had found a comfortable house near the church with a terrace overlooking the sea, which was Hannah's priority. The house was on a good sized property where they could keep some animals and grow a few crops to meet their family's needs if necessary.

Simon T was living with them and making a good living from the tannery shop which he had finally bought almost nine years before down in Apollonia. He rode to work every day, allowing him to visit Simon often.

With Hannah and Alexander moving to Upper Cyrene, he was contemplating, retirement though he was only in his mid fifties and still very fit.

Lucila and David having added a couple of rooms to the house, were living with Ruth and Simon, as was Rachel, who remained single as per her vow to Yeshua. She had been instrumental in winning many souls for the Lord, and was greatly respected for her virtuous life.

Rufus was now a major partner in Erasmus' business, since the latter had died recently, leaving his family's welfare in his good hands. He and Letitia lived their good Christian lives in a beautiful house in Rome near their cousins Lavinia and Linus and were the proud parents of two girls. They had visited Cyrene only twice in the past ten years, and both the Simon, and Marcus families were hoping they would be coming again in the near future.

The first Christian church that Simon presided over in Lower Cyrene was named "The Christian Church of Yeshua of Nazareth," as you my good reader will recall. It had a congregation of over eleven hundred souls, which filled the church to overflowing on Feast Days.

Simon had ordained one priest. A young man by the name of Saul, to assist him. His bishopric covered a large area around Cyrene. He travelled around constantly supervising his flock and ministering to their needs, and having performed a number of miraculous cures, he had become well known for many miles around and much respected by his people.

Ruth, had not been well of late, and was the object of growing concern in the family. She was accosted by a pain which had begun in her lower back, and was now being felt in her abdominal area, causing her much grief and interfering badly with her household duties. Lucila and Rachel took over much of their mother's heavier duties, and tried to give her as much rest as possible.

Simon was very concerned and spent many of his praying hours asking the Lord for her recovery,... but to no avail. To his utter dismay, Ruth's condition worsened.

The physician who had looked after the family for years was at a loss to diagnose the complaint, and Simon, who witnessed her constant suffering was much grieved and disturbed.

'I had better send for Rufus,' he said to himself. 'She is always expecting him, but he keeps postponing his visit. Marius will be arriving before the end of the week. If Marcus would send a cargo of grain to Rome, perhaps Marius can bring him back on his return trip.'

Thus thought Simon, as he realised the gravity of Ruth's ailment, and hoped that she might experience some improvement at seeing her son, whose visit she was constantly praying for. Marcus was as usual keen to help. He had the *Stella* loaded with yet another cargo of grain and authorized Marius to bring back Rufus if possible.

The two months that followed brought further distress to the family as Ruth's pain intensified, confining her to her bed. Simon was constantly at her bedside. The whole congregation prayed for her recovery with great love and fervour, but no positive results were forthcoming.

The time not spent with his wife, Simon spent on his knees in front of the Holy box. (Which would in future times be known as a tabernacle).

'Lord, you are not responding. How many times have you empowered me to cure a sick member of my flock, but now, that the most important person in my life needs your help, you're ignoring me. What do you want of me? Name it, and I'll do it, but please Lord empower me to cure her; she is my life. After you, she is my reason for living, Lord, do not abandon me.'

Ruth's pain worsened as the days passed. Many medicinal herbs and roots were given to her to ease her pain, but she could not keep anything down. Simon could not bear seeing his darling wife in so much distress, and kept urging the physician to find something; anything, that would ease her constant pain. Finally, the physician administered a mixture of herbs containing some ingredient which numbed the pain. He warned however, that it would have mental repercussions, as it would keep her in a state of delirium. She could no longer eat, and was losing weight at an alarming rate. Her legs and arms were beginning to swell as her condition worsened.

Rachel and Simon took turns being with her day and night. The weight of the church duties was carried by Alexander who with the help of the new priest, had to look to the affairs of two parishes.

The family was anxiously expecting the arrival of Rufus, whom Ruth was insistent on seeing during those occasional conscious moments when free of her delirium; between medication.

Simon sat beside his beloved Ruth in the middle of the night; her life slowly fading, her mind deteriorating, and he wondered why God was punishing him in such a hard way. He examined his conscience over and over with little success; trying to find some forgotten sin of his which would merit the mental anguish he was experiencing.

He was a simple man by nature. He had never been ambitious other than for that which would give his family a comfortable life, and meet their modest needs. His only ambition had been to have his sons learn to read and write, which he, though having learnt to read, had never mastered writing. He had excelled at his trade, and his business dealings he had always carried out with complete honesty and integrity. Now by God's grace, he was a man chosen by God, and in his service.

'Why, Lord? Why?'

As his thoughts ran on, and his tired and weary eyes beheld his once beautiful wife, with her peace loving nature, and zest for life, he realised that she had been God's gift, having allowed him all those years of happiness.

But now, would he really take her away from him?

A thought which he had often contemplated, but never entered his troubled mind as poignantly before, now took root in a powerful way. His mind went back to the crucifixion. He remembered how terribly Yeshua had suffered. What unspeakable suffering. What more could a human body endure? And what of his mother? What anguish had she not felt through all those horrible hours?

'What real sufferings have I had in my life?' he asked himself.

He could find but very few indeed, which were of any significance. This brought him to the realization that if Yeshua had undergone so much for him and for mankind, and his mother, to whom he now appealed for help and understanding, had borne such great mental anguish. Surely, this suffering which was so towering in his life should not only be accepted, but borne with courage and resignation.

'By thy grace, give me strength Lord,' he prayed there and then, 'to accept what you have destined for me. Please take her as soon as possible that she may suffer no more... I shall bear it for Your sake.'

The soft morning light filtered through the cracks on the wooden shutters. Simon shook himself from his dosing as he heard Ruth's moan. Approaching the bed, he blessed and kissed her tenderly, as her tired eyes appealed to him for another dose of the tranquilizing medicine. He was about to reach for the cup, when there was a knocking at the door, and he made haste to answer it. Hoping!... Hoping!

There in answer to his prayers, stood Rufus. Sorrow was written all over his face. In his arms, was a lovely fair haired little five year old girl. Father and son locked in a long, silent embrace, and then Simon, giving Marius who had accompanied Rufus, a faint smile, took and hugged his little granddaughter. He was meeting her for the first time, as this was the only one of Rufus' two girls who had not visited Cyrene. She had not been born on her parent's last visit when they had brought her elder sister with them.

Not a word was spoken as Rufus went straight to his parents' bedroom followed by Simon carrying little Letitia, and a very down hearted Marius.

"Mother!" called Rufus, as he leant over her; his sad, concerned eyes brimming with tears.

Ruth, who was looking at the rays of morning light coming through the crack in the window shutters, slowly turned her head. Her eyes were suddenly alive again; she smiled one of her beautiful smiles, and tried to raise her swollen arms to hug her much awaited son. Instead, he, with tears in his eyes, took her head gently in his hands and kissed her tenderly. Simon came forward with little Letitia.

"Here's Letitia, my love! is she not beautiful?" he tried to smile, as he showed his wife her new granddaughter.

Ruth bravely fought back the tears that were choking her as the child was held over her for her to kiss. She gave her a weak, loving smile, no longer being able to move or talk.

They all stood around the bed, joined by Rachel, Lucila and David, who had all been awakened by the knocking. They greeted their brother and new niece, with much sorrow in their hearts.

Ruth groaned. Simon made haste to give her a sip of the narcotic, which thankfully was the only thing that she could keep down. She closed her eyes, and was soon absorbed into the stupor that engulfed her.

Rufus looked at his frail and wasted mother and left the room, bursting through the back door and up to the terrace, his heart in shreds.

Alexander, Hannah and her father arrived a little later. David had gone to fetch them and inform them of Rufus' arrival. They brought the children with them to see their uncle and meet their little cousin.

The family was all there, as Ruth's soul took flight to her beloved Yeshua, leaving a devastated family around her deathbed.

* * * * * *

Ruth's funeral service at the church, was attended by most of the congregation. All who had known her came to pay their last respects. The service was conducted by Simon, and assisted by Alexander, but the eulogy was read by Marcus. He related to the congregation the virtuous life that his beloved friend Ruth had lived; how badly she would be missed; and how much she had contributed in the development of the church by her dedicated assistance to her husband, their beloved bishop.

"How privileged we are to be Christians," said Marcus, finalising his address to the congregation. "We can all find solace in the knowledge that our beloved sister is now resting safely and happily in the arms of our Lord and Saviour, Yeshua. Blessed be His Holy Name."

Simon was once again kneeling in prayer as was his habit, in front of the tabernacle. A week had passed since Ruth's funeral.

"Now you have her with you Yeshua, what do I do now?"

There was no reply, but the tranquil feeling once again engulfed him and comforted his grieving heart.

'Yes, Lord! now I'll live only for you, giving up all earthly things and trying to win you as many more souls as I am able; whatever the future of your church will be. I shall preach further afield, 'fish more men' for you, and build as many churches as the span of my life will permit... All for Thy Greater Glory O' Lord.'

Joseph L. Cavilla is a writer and visual artist.
He lives and works in Hanover, Ontario.

CPSIA information can be obtained
at www.ICGtesting.com
Printed in the USA
BVHW031308311219
568253BV00001B/4/P